SECRET INHERITANCE

SECRET INHERITANCE
HOUSE OF THE SPIDERKING™
BOOK ONE

MICHAEL ANDERLE

DISRUPTIVE IMAGINATION

DON'T MISS OUR NEW RELEASES

Join the LMBPN email list to be notified of new releases and special promotions (which happen often) by following this link:

http://lmbpn.com/email/

This book is a work of fiction. All of the characters, organizations, and events portrayed in this novel are either products of the author's imagination or are used fictitiously. Sometimes both.

Copyright © 2024 LMBPN Publishing
Cover Art by https://fantasybookdesign.com
Cover copyright © LMBPN Publishing
A Michael Anderle Production

LMBPN Publishing supports the right to free expression and the value of copyright. The purpose of copyright is to encourage writers and artists to produce the creative works that enrich our culture.

The distribution of this book without permission is a theft of the author's intellectual property. If you would like permission to use material from the book (other than for review purposes), please contact support@lmbpn.com. Thank you for your support of the author's rights.

LMBPN Publishing
2375 E. Tropicana Avenue, Suite 8-305
Las Vegas, Nevada 89119 USA

Version 1.00, September 2024
eBook ISBN: 979-8-89354-263-9
Print ISBN: 979-8-89354-264-6

THE SECRET INHERITANCE TEAM

Thanks to the Beta Readers
Rachel Beckford, Kelly O'Donnell, Mary Morris, John Ashmore

Thanks to the JIT Readers

Christopher Gilliard
Veronica Stephan-Miller
Jackey Hankard-Brodie
Sean Kesterson
Dave Hicks
Diane L. Smith
Jeff Goode
Peter Manis
Paul Westman
Jan Hunnicutt

Editor
SkyFyre Editing Team

CHAPTER ONE

Elana Bishop wiped the sweat from her brow, her arms tingling from the exertion. Another day, another load hauled. She felt the eyes of the burly men on her as she effortlessly hoisted the final piece of heavy furniture into the truck. She knew her ability to outpace them in strength despite her relatively small stature and lean muscles impressed and irked them.

Some days she liked the attention. Others, she didn't. Today, she felt sassy.

"Damn, Elana, you some kind of fang-banger or something?" one of the guys teased with a smirk as he watched her secure the straps.

She shot him a playful glare, a wink, and laughed, tossing her ebony hair that had come out from under her hat over her shoulder with a confidence that said she'd heard it all before. "In your dreams, Zac," she retorted with a grin as she flexed her bicep. "That's all human, bitch!"

He chuckled and shook his head. "Hey, you wanna grab a drink later? Unwind a bit?"

Just like that, the moment was gone.

Elana sighed and slammed the truck's back doors with a definitive *clang*. "Sorry, I'm unhappily married to the business at the moment." The weight of recent loss tinged her voice. "You know my dad passed."

Zac's expression softened. "Yeah, we know. Jeremiah was a good man. Just thought you might like some company, is all."

Well, maybe the guy wasn't completely thick-headed. That sentiment, she could appreciate. Nevertheless, she shook her head again. "Another time, maybe. Thanks, though."

"Any time, Elana. You have a good one."

"You too, Zac."

The sun had already dipped below the horizon as Elana climbed into her truck's cab, the day's last light fading fast. She started down the Outside Haven Loop, the long highway that skirted the imposing wall of Haven. It was a familiar route and had always filled her with curiosity and longing as she gazed at the shadowy perimeter that enclosed the vampire society.

Tonight was hardly the first time she'd yearned to explore what lay beyond the wall. Her daily digest of Haven news awaited her on her phone. She would devour it when she got home. If she were lucky, there would be an update on the latest drama. Archon Du Pont had shuffled his cabinet of sentinels, and gossip ran *rampant* that he was angling to tempt several promising guardians away from Archon Bayard's council.

Elana drummed her fingers on her steering wheel. She couldn't wait to discuss the figurative chess moves with her friends online. MysteryVixen91 always had the best and *hottest* takes.

The darkened stretch of road lined with nothing but dense forest was the least of her concerns until a sudden blur of movement caught her eye. Instinctively, she slammed on the brakes. The tires screeched in protest. The *thud* that followed sent a jolt through her heart, and she realized she'd hit something—or someone.

Elana cursed under her breath as she jumped out to inspect the damage, only to see a dazed figure sprawled in front of her smashed truck. She recognized the disoriented, pale young man as one of the level one vampires who'd risked it all to escape Haven's walls.

"A *Runner*," she murmured. She was wary. She'd read too many fantastic accounts of Runners escaping Haven and sweeping a human off their feet to live happily ever after to believe any of them. Elana Bishop was too smart for that.

As she approached to help, the vampire's eyes flickered with a desperate cunning. "You will help me into your truck. Then you will help me feel...*better*," he whispered, eyeing her body up and down, his tongue caressing the top of his lip.

Her mouth dropped open. "Well, that's a fine *fuck you* for caring enough to check on your useless ass!" To his shock, Elana's response to his supernatural suggestion was a fierce right hook that sent him reeling to the ground and his eyes rolling back in his head. "Nice try, asshole," she spat, standing over his comatose form. She also considered spitting on him for good measure but decided he wasn't worth it.

She pulled out her phone and accessed Haven Security, an app designed for such encounters. While she might have felt bad if he had been a nice guy, she didn't care about self-absorbed people who probably cheated their way into getting pulled into the vampire hierarchy. Depending on which family had given him the Rights, they would probably do something pretty ugly to him. Based on how he'd treated her, the idea didn't bother her much.

A warm, rich male voice came across the line and sent tingles down her spine. "Haven Security, how can I help?"

Dammit. Even their support people sound sexy as hell on the phone. She blew out a breath to keep it together.

She sat on the Runner's chest. She needed a chair, right? He was about as useful as a log anyway. "Yeah, I'm sitting on one of your Runners. Come get him." While she was mostly irritated, a current of satisfaction painted her tone. She knew full well the reward for such a call could be substantial. Haven didn't appreciate those who thumbed their nose at the SpiderKing's hospitality.

"One moment," he replied. The phone line crackled. Elana assumed he was turning to speak to someone else.

She cast her gaze around the darkened trees. The only light in the area came from her old, trustworthy truck's halogen beams.

She squinted and noticed that the lights hadn't been cracked when she hit the asshole. She grinned. "Nice!"

While she waited for the honey-voiced dispatcher to get back to her, she watched as the app confirmed her location for Haven Security, and she settled in. Although her headlights weren't visibly damaged, she couldn't confirm the collision had resulted in no damage without a visit to the autobody shop. The money from the reward would be necessary to pay those fees, at the very least, and to repair her truck if there *was* damage.

She glared at her unconscious ottoman, whose sudden appearance had thrown her one hell of a curveball. "Damn you," she muttered.

Now her stomach told her she was hungry, too. The job had run late, and she hadn't had time for supper. She sighed. "Fuck my life…"

Mr. Wonderful's voice came back on the line and startled her. "Guardians will be there in ten minutes at the latest. Do you believe the Runner will waken?"

She poked the vampire, then craned her head back to peer into her windshield. She couldn't see into her back seat from this angle, but she knew what she had in her truck. "He's out. I hit him with my truck. I have a wrench that can help him *stay* asleep if he gets any bright ideas."

The answering chuckle sent warm waves through her core. "*Try* not to kill him before the consort gets there. It will be less paperwork for everyone."

Inside the Haven Security dispatch center, Matt Richelieu waited several seconds in silence before inquiring, "Ma'am? Are you still there?"

The woman on the other end hastily replied. "I'm sorry, did you say the consort's guardians are coming?"

"No," he clarified. "The consort was in the action room next door and heard our conversation. She opted to retrieve this Runner herself. She and a pair of guardians are on their way now."

His gaze lingered on the door that had closed behind the white-clad consort. She might have been bored, or perhaps something in the report had piqued her interest. This was hardly a routine occurrence, but one did not question the decisions of a consort if one valued one's life, which Matt most certainly did.

The woman had not yet responded. Matt cleared his throat. "Are you okay, ma'am? Has there been an issue with the Runner?"

"Oh, no." He heard the faint rustling of fabric on the other end of the line before the woman stammered, "It's just, uh… I'm underdressed."

Matt chuckled. Based on the woman's initial reaction, he had suspected she was more familiar than most with Haven's hierarchy. This confirmed it.

He attempted to reassure her. "Ma'am, I have on a two-piece suit, starched shirt, and gold cufflinks. The consort could be wearing three-day-old clothes and I'd still be underdressed."

He glanced at the clock on his desk. Eight minutes, give or take, until the consort and her guardians arrived. He needed to ensure the woman remained on the line in case the Runner woke. Usually that was a chore—he fielded far too many calls from humans who were either in the throes of hysterical panic or seized by repulsive greed—but talking to this woman was quite pleasant. "Tell you what. If you ever come to the Citadel, I'll treat you to coffee."

Elana gaped. "Uh." She stared at the Runner. He was her ticket inside Haven! If the bastard hadn't intended to use her in the worst way, she could almost have forgiven him. "How do I get a ticket?"

"Oh, you mean permission?" Another one of those chuckles that made warmth pool between her legs. "Hm. We can make that part of the reparations. You said you hit him with your truck?"

"Yes. Which surprises me, since, you know, the whole superhuman speed thing. Maybe he was drunk. Do vampires get drunk?" Elana looked back at the vehicle. It was no more possible to tell the extent of the damage with the halogen lights glaring than it had been five minutes ago. *Five minutes until a consort would arrive.* She swallowed to moisten her dry mouth.

"They can," the dispatcher assured her. "We'll sort all that out, don't worry. Is your vehicle damaged?"

"Probably just body damage, but it's my work truck... my only truck, actually. But hey, 'built Ford tough' has to stand for something!" She nervously chuckled. "I doubt the frame is damaged, but I'll still need to get it looked at. I know enough to make trucks run, but I can't make 'em pretty."

He laughed. She decided she liked making him laugh. "All right. I'm Matt Richelieu. Obviously, I work for Haven Security. Your name is Elana Bishop, according to the app. Is that correct?"

"Yes," she managed. She pulled her phone away from her face, stared at the app screen for a split second, then returned it to her ear. He was a *Richelieu*?

The Richelieus were...a *powerful* family. Part of the

House of Cardinals and one of the few Houses over eight hundred years old. The House of Cardinals was not as powerful in the United States as in Europe, but connections were connections! A *Richelieu* was going to take her, Elana Bishop, for *coffee!*

And he has a sexy voice... She winced and reminded herself that the sexy voice had a name. She needed to get her shit together.

Matt's uber-sexy voice spoke in her ear again. "The consort is about a minute away. When she arrives, I'll hang up, but I'll reach out through the app to provide you with information regarding the reparations as well as a pass to get into the Citadel for our business meeting."

"Business meeting?" she parroted. She still wasn't thinking straight between the consort's imminent arrival and the continued adventures of Mr. Sexy Voice Richelieu, who was going to *take her for coffee.*

She eyed Mr. Asshole Definitely-Not-Richelieu. He was still out cold. Should she chance ducking into the truck for the wrench so she could give him a whack for good measure before the consort arrived? With every minute that passed, her anger at his revolting behavior subsided in favor of begrudging gratitude at his getting her into Haven. She was having a hard time mustering the anger to want to hit him again.

If he stirred, however, she would swing for the fences, gratitude be damned.

Matt interrupted her mild homicidal musings. "You must sign the reparation agreement," he reminded her. "If you don't do it through the app, you'll have to sign it here at the Citadel. It's your call."

"Oh." Elana shook her head in an attempt to clear it. The tingles in problematic places intensified every time he spoke, but she soldiered on.

He wasn't so much giving her a pass into Citadel, otherwise known as the Neutral Zone, as he was reminding her of the rules governing business between vampires and humans. Vampires *always* wanted a signature in person for anything important.

As an outsider, someone living outside the walls, she was permitted the option of doing it via the app for "reasons." That usually translated to "religious reasons," which basically amounted to "I don't want to get my human hands spoiled by touching you diseased, infested monsters."

Elana didn't think that way, although she knew plenty of people who did.

She hadn't realized that reparations were considered important enough to merit a pass into the Citadel. Lucky her. Maybe Mr. Asshole was Mr. Good Luck Charm.

"One option includes coffee," Matt purred—no, *professionally informed her*.

She cleared her throat. Strobe lights flashed on the foliage at the next bend down the road. They were red and white, unlike human cops, whose lights were red and blue. "I'll meet you there, Matt. I see the lights."

"Excellent. In that case, I will bid you good night. I look forward to meeting you, Ms. Bishop. And…"

"Yeah?" Elana's gaze was glued on the approaching, flickering lights. The breathless anticipation of meeting a consort was rapidly overtaking the mesmerizing effect of Matt's voice.

"Good job. Not just anyone can take out a Runner."

The compliment sent a wave of warmth below her Mason-Dixon line. She bit her lip and rolled her eyes at herself. *Damn him and his sexy voice!* She would need to change her undergarments if this kept up. "Thanks. That's sweet of you to say."

"Most welcome. Have a good night, Miss Bishop." A *click,* and the line closed at the same moment as the consort's small motorcade rounded the bend.

Oh, thank God for small favors! She wouldn't have to deal with Matt's dulcet tones distracting her from giving the consort the respect she deserved. Nonetheless, she felt a certain pang of regret at the loss.

She glanced at the app and grinned when she discovered the call had been recorded for reference. She smirked. She would *definitely* listen to it again later.

Two large, blacked-out SUVs and one sleek white AMG Mercedes glided to a halt not twenty feet away. Elana's heart dropped into her gut. Not two days before, she'd stayed up into the wee hours of the night on a deep dive into the consorts' vehicle preferences. Some opted for elegant imports, others for impeccably kept vintage models, but only one consort had adopted the AMG Mercedes as her signature ride.

"Oh, shit," Elana whispered.

She was about to talk to the Arbiter of Shadows.

The passenger door of one SUV opened first. A tall, broad-shouldered Black man in a black suit, shirt, tie, and shoes stepped out. Elana spotted the faint outline of a blacked-out sidearm on his belt as the clean-shaven bodyguard crossed to the driver's side door of the Mercedes and opened it.

He stepped back to allow the consort out, and Elana reflexively swallowed.

The snow-white figure that emerged was among the most imposing of Haven's elite. Her white-clad foot preceded her white-clad leg, then the rest of her followed in pristine, snow-white perfection. One of her famous white pantsuits with matching shoes—nothing like Hillary Clinton's. Valeria Draven exuded power and authority without any hint of ostentatious self-importance.

The razor-sharp line of Valeria's silver hair cut her cheek in two as she unfolded from the vehicle. She wasn't overly tall—a few inches shy of six feet—but she effortlessly towered over them all.

Her ice-blue gaze held Elana in place like a butterfly pinned to a table. Elana had instinctively moved to stand, but the emergence of the Arbiter of Shadows had arrested her movement as surely as though *she* had been the Runner.

"Ma'am." Elana bobbed her head in deference. She'd dreamed of making a good impression if she ever got the chance to meet an arbiter. So much for that. Her mouth was drier than the Gobi Desert.

"Miss Bishop." Draven's voice was velvet over marble and poured from her perfectly shaped lips like chilled white wine. Her skin was so pale she could have been a statue. Elana would have admired her with equal breathlessness in the Louvre.

And she knows my name. If Matt Richelieu had taken

Elana's breath away, Valeria Draven had stolen her soul with two words.

Elana was terrified and smitten in equal measure. Not in the way of romance, although she couldn't have refused anything of Valeria at that moment, but in the way of *belonging*.

"Arbiter Draven," Elana breathlessly replied.

Valeria's lips curved into a delicate smirk. "Always an honor to be recognized. Especially by an outsider."

Elana didn't get a chance to stammer a denial about her vampiric obsession because Valeria motioned to the Runner beneath her and added, "Please accept my thanks for so neatly…*taking care of*…this misbegotten fugitive. You've made my job easy. Did he happen to speak with you before he fell unconscious? I can't help but notice the bruise forming on his cheek, and if you hit him in the head with your truck, I'd expect a *touch* more damage."

Elana swallowed again. Lying to Valeria Draven was among the stupidest things you could do, and besides, Elana wanted to do everything the woman asked. "Uh…just a bit," she admitted. "He, um, asked me to…help him."

Valeria's eyes narrowed a degree.

The sudden shifting of the body beneath her prohibited Elana from asking why that was interesting. Mr. Asshole was waking up just in time to face the music.

CHAPTER TWO

The Runner blearily opened his eyes and leered at Elana after a couple of beats. "*Hey*, sweetheart—changed your mind, did you? Decided to stick around and see what all the fuss is about?"

Elana scowled, got up, and shoved the man into the pavement as she stood. "Not on your life, asshole. I called the guardians on you. You're going back where you belong."

The man grunted as Elana pushed him, then scrambled to his feet. Elana was between him and the arbiter. His lascivious demeanor rapidly turned to belligerence as color rose in his face and his hands curled into fists.

"*Fuck* you," he spat. "You have *no* idea what it's like inside those walls. They'll *kill* me when they get here, you *bitch*. Can you handle my death on your conscience?"

Elana shrugged. "That's up to the consort."

The vampire blanched. "Wh—" he stammered. "Th—the *consort*? But you said—you said the *guardians*—"

Elana could tell the precise moment when his gaze

traveled beyond her and lit on Valeria. His words died on his lips, his mouth hung faintly agape, and his eyes widened.

She kept herself from smirking. *Serves you right. You knew what you'd get.*

Elana stepped aside and pivoted to allow the arbiter an uninterrupted view of the miscreant who had, as she could see now that she was no longer sitting in front of her blinding headlights, oh-so-kindly dented her Ford's front bumper.

Valeria's hand rested on top of her blazer, white on white with delicate half-moons of French-manicured nails adorning the hem of the jacket with a scalloped edge. Based on the hand shape, Elana suspected the consort was carrying. It would not have surprised her.

The arbiter did not speak. She stared the Runner down with a gaze colder than the single winter trip Elana had made to North Dakota in January.

To tell the truth, that trip seemed like as big of a mistake as the one the Runner had made.

The man squared his shoulders and lifted his chin. Elana spied the rapid bob of his Adam's apple that turned the shaking of his fists into trembling. If she didn't know better, she would have said she could smell his fear.

Who would be so shortsighted, so *stupid*, that they'd risk throwing the life of a vampire away?

"Your name." The pair of words made Elana flinch. Valeria had delivered them with the gravitas of a double-tap execution.

A muscle twitched in the Runner's jaw. He sneered. "I won't tell you anything."

The consort did not blink. She stared the Runner down. Not a hint of anger or disappointment showed on her face. She was perfectly cool and composed, waiting for the man to crack.

The seconds ticked by. Elana's gaze flicked between Valeria and the unnamed Runner. She swallowed the nervous saliva slicking the back of her throat. At this rate, *Elana* would break down and confess, and she wasn't the one facing a literal firing squad.

"I always meant to leave." The Runner spoke with the wavering aggression of one who knew resistance was futile. These would likely be his last words—Valeria Draven was not known for mercy—and he was determined to speak his mind before he died.

Indeed, he clenched his fists, took half a step forward, and renewed his indignant glare in the arbiter's direction. "I never wanted to be part of your stupid secret society. It's *bullshit* that you keep all the power for yourselves. So yeah, I talked my way in, got the Rights, and beat feet as soon as I could. And I don't fucking regret it!"

Valeria remained impassive through the Runner's tirade. When he finished, she repeated herself with the slightest touch of insistence. "Your *name*."

"Acari." The man bit the word off as though it were unpleasant and left a sour taste in his mouth.

Smooth as silk, the consort flicked the panel of her jacket back, unholstered a slim pistol, raised it, and fired.

Elana jumped, and the Runner collapsed to the asphalt with a perfect hole in his forehead.

Valeria slid the pistol back into its holster and strode past the body. "Bag him," she told the guardian behind her.

Elana swallowed hard. Her gaze remained glued to the intimidating, black-clad figure as he calmly retrieved a body bag from the trunk of the SUV and approached the cooling corpse. Thanks to her many nights of obsessive reading, she knew enough about vampire law to know this decree meant the Runner would be subjected to a formalized death punishment. Vampire law was ruthless in the extreme.

Something briefly broke the beam of Elana's truck's headlights, making the scene in front of her flicker, and Elana looked up to discover the consort examining her truck.

Elana cleared her throat. "Can I help you, Arbiter?"

"I am curious." The woman's tone was deceptively casual, as it had been since she stepped out of her Mercedes. Neither crime, death, murder, nor cleanup would cause the Arbiter of Shadows to be swayed from her purpose.

The only thing was, Elana couldn't divine what that purpose might be. Why would Valeria Draven be curious about *her*?

"Anything I can do to help, I will," Elana offered.

The consort hummed. She examined Elana's truck for several more seconds, eyeing the front bumper and the hood thoroughly before turning her piercing gaze on Elana. Again, Elana felt pinned under a magnifying glass, and she worked hard to maintain her calm under Valeria's intense scrutiny.

"I believe you," the arbiter declared.

Elana exhaled a breath she didn't know she'd been holding.

Valeria stepped closer to Elana. She was not yet within arm's reach, but Elana was near enough to smell the consort's perfume. Elana couldn't place the scent—perfume was not something she often wore unless it was *eau de* coveralls—but it had a sharp tang of something like pine.

"When I arrived, you told me the Runner asked you for help."

"Yes." Elana's upper lip curled with the memory. "He wanted a little more than *help.*"

A low chuckle rose from the consort's alabaster throat. The laugh had little amusement in it.

"Many initiates like to test the limits of their powers," Valeria explained. "This does not surprise me. What *does* surprise me is that you were able to subdue him."

"Oh, that." Elana shrugged. "I've got a wicked right hook."

The arbiter's eyebrow rose in a subtle arch. "Most humans would be hard-pressed to render even an initiate unconscious with a lengthy assault with a weapon, much less a single blow."

Elana glanced at her truck. "Well, I mean, I'd already hit him with Jessie, and I was going at least fifty... He was dazed. He got one sentence out and I wasn't interested, so *pop!* to the jaw, and he was out like a light. The truck probably did most of the work."

Valeria remained silent long enough that Elana looked at her. The consort regarded her with the same look Elana got when faced with a particularly interesting gadget to fix. Heat rose on the back of her neck. She sincerely hoped it didn't spread to her cheeks.

Maybe this was how the Arbiter of Shadows regarded everything. It stood to reason that you didn't skyrocket through the ranks of the Sanguine Nexus in twenty-five years without singular focus and determination.

Elana was undoubtedly making a fool of herself by spinning something out of nothing. Time to tone down the fangirling a few notches. *Be cool. Be real. Be you.* She had nothing to hide.

Elana drew a deep breath, let it out, then shrugged again. "I've always been strong," she lightly admitted. "Ever since I was a kid. Nobody ever beat me in tug-of-war, and everybody wanted me to push them on the swings. Nowadays, it comes in handy for my job."

"What is it that you do?" the consort casually inquired.

"Hauling sh—stuff." Elana rapidly course-corrected. She wasn't sure swearing in front of an arbiter was wise. The last guy who'd done it had disappeared into a body bag in an unmarked SUV.

"Hauling stuff and fixing electronics. I took over my dad's business after he died."

"My condolences."

"Uh—thanks." The familiar lump grew in her throat, and Elana resolutely swallowed it. "I appreciate that. Is there anything else I can help you with, Arbiter?"

Valeria held her gaze a moment longer, then broke it by glancing at the SUVs. "One more thing, yes. I require a drop of your blood."

Elana blinked. In all her reading, she'd never heard of this procedure. Evidently, there were depths of vampire lore she had yet to plumb. A drop of blood wouldn't hurt. "Of course."

The arbiter gestured, and a guardian approached with a small black bag. Moments later, Elana sucked on her fingertip as the snow-white woman sealed the tiny crimson vial and tucked it into the bag.

"You will be contacted in due course by the guardians according to your stated communication preferences in the app," Valeria informed her. "The SpiderKing recognizes your assistance in the apprehension of this Runner, and you will be properly compensated for your time and inconvenience. A good evening to you, Miss Bishop."

The consort's heels tapped on the pavement as she strode away. Her bodyguard opened the door of her Mercedes. She entered in one smooth motion. The car's lights flicked on and the engine purred to life the moment the guardian shut the door behind her.

The motorcade's taillights receded into the night. A single raindrop landed on Elana's forehead, and she numbly climbed into her Ford before the heavens could get more ideas. She had no way of knowing if the Runner had done more than cosmetic damage to the truck, and the last thing she wanted was an electrical short.

Between the trepidation and excitement of her impending trip to the Citadel, she barely registered the road home. She would have to research that blood draw before bed.

Haven never disappointed when it came to secrets.

CHAPTER THREE

Elana's phone buzzed as she turned into her driveway. She waited until the garage door had closed behind her and she'd shifted the truck into Park before retrieving it from her cupholder.

It was a notification from the Haven Security app.

Your meeting will take place the day after tomorrow. I'll be in touch with a specific time for the reparations meeting and our coffee.

Her heart jittered, perhaps in anticipation of the coffee...but more likely in anticipation of *going into Haven*.

Elana drew a deep breath and let it out slowly before exiting her truck. She methodically picked up the tools and gear she brought in every night—some could be left in the truck bed, others could not. Then she shouldered her well-worn backpack that carried her lunch and whatever files she needed for the day's jobs.

Her feet floated over the concrete garage floor and the

wooden decking between the garage and the house. She unlocked the back door as though she were moving in slow motion. Everything felt surreal.

In two days, she would be in *Haven*.

Elana set her bag down at the door and toed off her boots. She put her lunch containers in the dishwasher and rinsed her coffee mug. She replaced the job files in the filing cabinet in her office, which was still set up the way her dad had liked it.

Then she stared at herself in the bathroom mirror. She'd intended to immediately hop onto the online forums to screech about getting into Haven and *meeting Valeria Draven*, but now that she was home, it didn't seem as important.

Everything had changed. Everything *would* change. Hitting that Runner with her truck had set off a chain of events that would alter her life forever.

Now was not the time for fangirling on the Internet. Now was the time to make a clean break. Before and after. The Elana Bishop of today and the Elana Bishop of two days from now.

She drew another deep breath while gazing into her own eyes. Then she took the most luxurious shower she'd had in years.

Normally, when Elana got home from work, she scrubbed herself down as fast as she could. No thought, no consideration, certainly no lingering. In and out, get the grime off, toss on a pair of sweatpants and an old T-shirt, then sprawl on the couch.

Tonight, she washed as methodically as she had put away her tools and files. She massaged shampoo into her scalp and through her thick hair, slowly rinsed it out, then worked argan oil conditioner in. The conditioner's rich aroma mixed with the steam and brought to mind luxury and romance.

While letting the conditioner sit, Elana picked the scented body wash she only used before going on dates instead of her typical, all-purpose bar of Ivory soap. The creamy liquid smelled of honey and shea butter and made a thick white lather on her skin.

Elana took her time. Watching the gray water and white bubbles swirl around the drain, she felt as though her old life was swirling away with them. She was shedding her old life in preparation to step into a new one.

She rinsed the conditioner out with cold water, then scrubbed her hard-earned calluses with a loofah and a pumice stone. She shut the water off and shaved, using a cream that added subtle floral tones of jasmine and ylang-ylang to the pleasant steam.

At last, Elana turned the water on as hot as she could bear and stood under the cascade. She closed her eyes and allowed the water to stream over her head, face, and shoulders, rinsing away the day's end.

She stepped out of the shower onto the spartan bath mat, wiped away the condensation on the mirror, and looked at herself again. She didn't *look* different, but she certainly *felt* different.

Underneath the weighty certainty of entering a new chapter in her life, discomfort curled its tendrils in Elana's gut. Entering Haven would fulfill a lifelong dream, but her father's disapproval lingered in the back of her mind.

Jeremiah Bishop had *hated* vampires. He had disliked

what he perceived as a casual disregard for humans born of an "unfounded belief" in their superiority. Elana couldn't see how the belief was unfounded. Vampire technology was the next best thing to *magic*, for crying out loud. Didn't that automatically make them greater than humans? Sure, there were cruel vampires who abused their resources, but plenty of humans did the same.

Elana drew a deliberate breath and spread her fingers on the damp counter, consciously letting go of the twin spikes of grief and resentment that pierced her whenever she thought of her father and vampires at the same time. She had to prepare for her entry into Haven, and that would only be more difficult with malcontent in her soul.

"I love you, Dad, but I have to do this," she told the bathroom sink. Her father's face floated in her mind's eye, and she wished—not for the first time, nor the last—that she could hug him one more time. "I have to do this for me. I'm sorry."

The next morning dawned bright and early. As usual, Elana hit the ground running, hauling on work clothes and pulling her hair into a tight braid before shoving a bagel with cream cheese into her mouth on the way out the door.

She bought coffee on the way and made several phone calls while stuck in the construction between Elm and Seventeenth. There was no other route to this job site, which she'd known when she'd booked it the week before—hence the need for the early start. It was handy that she was stuck in traffic, honestly. Normally, she'd listen to the radio while waiting for the other drivers to learn how to zipper merge, but today she had appointments to make.

Before falling asleep the night before, Elana had done some Internet sleuthing to find the highest-reviewed nail and hair salons in town. She had learned many things in her study of vampire culture, and among the most salient lessons was the importance of appearance. In line with Matt Richelieu's comment about being underdressed in a two-piece suit, Elana *needed* to show up looking her best.

That meant for the first time in her life, she was getting her nails done…and for the first time since high school prom, she was having her hair done. After those appointments, she planned to browse the high-end boutiques to find an appropriate outfit and accessories.

All in all, Elana fully expected to drop up to a thousand dollars on herself by the end of the day, and not a penny of it would be wasted. She'd never had this excuse to spend money on herself. Part of her felt deeply uncomfortable about it, but mostly, she was excited.

She ended her last call as she pulled into the work site. The sight of her colleagues' familiar cars made her smile. She could always count on Jerry and the boys.

Elana jumped out of the truck and waved at Jerry. The burly man was reliable and level-headed, an ideal foreman for most of Elana's jobs. He'd worked for her dad for many years. In truth, he could easily handle this contract on his own. It was a quick turnaround job, hauling old office furniture to a storage facility so the management company could start renovations.

Jerry didn't need Elana here, and they all knew it, but she'd been working with the crew for so long that it would have felt wrong if she didn't show up. It wasn't about supervising—it was about family.

"Morning!" Jerry hollered over the rumbling diesel engine of the moving truck he was directing to the office building's loading dock. "How's things?"

"Same old, same old," she replied. "Hit a Runner on my way home last night."

Jerry's eyebrows shot up. "You did what? Hit a *runner*? Everybody okay?"

The truck grumbled to a stop and hissed as its driver shut it off. Elana coughed on the whiff of diesel exhaust, then clarified. "A *vampire* Runner. I'm fine, he's fine—or, well, he's not fine anymore. But my truck sure didn't hurt him."

Jerry grimaced. "I've heard the fangs don't take too kindly to their recruits jumping ship."

"That's putting it lightly."

Jerry's discomfited face darkened. "Are the stories true? Do they…"

Elana raised an eyebrow. "No one's really sure. No one outside Haven, anyway. Vampire law is notoriously ruthless, but sentencing details are kept secret."

Jerry shivered. "No wonder the human governments don't like 'em. Nobody likes anyone *else* havin' a black site…and nobody has any jurisdiction over these guys. Creeps me out."

"I hear you."

A healthy dose of wariness tempered Elana's fascination with vampires. It didn't make her any less keen on getting into Haven, but it kept her from losing her mind like some of the "bloodwives" on the forums, who were all but *rabid* about vampire culture. Vampires were dangerous, no two ways about it. You needed to be smart about how you interacted with them, or you could easily get yourself in trouble.

"I'll be heading out early today," she casually told Jerry, as much a change of subject as it was necessary information for her foreman. "Appointments this afternoon."

The thoughtful look in his eyes instantly shifted to concern. "You okay?"

She smiled. "Yeah, I'm fine. Not doctor's appointments. You don't have to worry about me, Jer. I'm not following in my dad's footsteps *that* closely."

The big man heaved a sigh of relief. "Thank God for that. What're you up to, then? If you don't mind my asking? Anything interesting?"

Her smile twitched toward a smirk. "I'm getting my hair and nails done."

"No kidding!" Jerry's eyebrows shot toward his receding hairline, and the exclamation was loud enough that two of the guys hauling pallets nearby paused.

"You're doing *girl stuff?*" Luke commented, equally astonished.

"Who are you and what've you done with our boss?" Zac teased.

"Yeah, do you even know *how* to style your hair?" Luke added with an ear-to-ear grin. "You gonna haul couches with gel nails? My girlfriend gets those. She does data entry, and I have no clue how the hell she can type with those things."

Elana rolled her eyes, but the smirk stayed firmly on her face. This was exactly the reaction she'd anticipated, and she was happy to play along. "Bet you fifty I can still haul more than you afterward, Luke."

Luke laughed. "You're on!"

Zac punched Luke in the bicep. "Idiot! You've just lost fifty bucks!"

Luke scoffed. "No way she wins that! Have you *seen* gel nails?"

"Have you seen our *boss?*"

Jerry chortled and shook his head. "It's a good thing she only bet you fifty, son. Better tell your girlfriend you're not buying lunch this month."

Luke raised his hands in mock surrender. "All right, I give!"

"You're not getting off the hook *that* easily," Elana retorted. "You'll still owe me fifty bucks, and I intend to collect!"

CHAPTER FOUR

Elana contentedly lost herself in the rhythm of moving furniture and the accompanying playful banter. Her phone chimed in the middle of their coffee break, and she slid it from its protective case to find a message from Haven Security.

> **Further important information regarding your upcoming reparations meeting has been submitted by Richelieu, Matt. The Arbiter of Shadows will be in attendance. Prepare accordingly.**

The blood must have drained from her face because Jerry nudged her with a hand still holding half a donut. "Everything ten-four?"

Elana swallowed and gave herself a light shake. "Yeah. Yeah, I'm fine. Just got news about this meeting I have tomorrow. Someone really important is gonna be there."

Jerry's eyebrows drew together. "You *sure* you're okay? This to do with the guy you hit last night?"

Elana stared at her phone screen for ten more seconds before returning it to the case holstered to her belt. She scrubbed a dusty hand over her face. "Yeah, it is. That's why I'm getting my hair and nails done. I have to go to Haven tomorrow for a meeting about how much they're gonna pay for damages and...stuff."

Sitting on a tool chest a few feet away, Zac sucked a breath in through his teeth. "Oh, shit. You have to go *in* there? Beyond the wall?"

"That I do."

"*Shit*, son. That's a big deal."

"Yup. And I just found out the Arbiter of Shadows is coming to the meeting."

Zac's eyes got big. "Oh, *shit*." Elana was rapidly coming to suspect he didn't know any other words. "I don't know shit about vampires, but even I know who *she* is. She's the terrifying one who always wears white, right?"

"Except when she wears black. And when she wears black..."

Zac swallowed hard and blinked at the jelly donut in his hand as though the jam had turned to blood. "You better hope she doesn't turn up wearing black to this meeting."

"I damn well *do* hope that," Elana affirmed.

Jerry clapped her on the shoulder. "You'll be fine, Elana. You kick more ass than any lady or man I've ever known. Maybe the vamps figured that out and wanna offer you a job or somethin'. Who knows, maybe Bishop's Electronics and Hauling is gonna be the first local company with a Haven contract."

His reassuring smile was authentic and earnest. It

warmed Elana's heart and eased the anxiety that had blossomed in her gut.

"Maybe," she echoed.

"That'd be cool," Luke put in. "But I call dibs on hauling stuff that isn't coffins."

Elana snorted. "They don't sleep in coffins. That's a myth."

She checked her watch, then wiped her sticky fingers on her jeans. "I gotta go."

Jerry grinned. "You go get yourself all gussied up, my girl. Knock 'em dead…but maybe try to avoid hitting any more of 'em on the road?"

Elana elbowed him as she poured herself another cup of coffee from the carafe. "Better keep your distance, Jer, or I might run over your foot next."

The men's guffaws serenaded her all the way back to the truck. They truly did make her feel better, although the good humor and well-wishes did not fully assuage the butterflies that were taking up insistent residence.

Why *would* Valeria Draven attend a simple reparations meeting? Had Elana offended her somehow by inadvertently contravening a vampire social more? Or maybe the Runner had been more important than she'd thought… Elana hadn't recognized the House he'd named as his lineage, but there were wealthy and powerful Houses that weren't as well-known as most. Maybe the House insisted on negotiating.

Elana blew out a breath as she turned the key in the ignition and the big truck rumbled to life. The reason for the consort's presence could be as simple as needing her signature on the paperwork. She'd been the answering guardian, and she'd personally killed the Runner. Elana would have thought a consort would be able to sign paperwork without attending a reparations meeting, but maybe vampire law was as strict for vampires as it was for humans.

A display of prom dresses in a shop window caught her eye. Poofy skirts were in this year. Elana snickered. In her senior year, slinky microskirts had been all the rage. She'd insisted on something that went at least *halfway* down her thighs, and she'd spent the entire night sniggering at the girls who were constantly yanking their skirts down.

She'd bought precisely *one* dress since then, a standard-issue little black dress. Form-fitting, stretchy fabric forgiving to minor weight fluctuations, a hem that hit just above the knee, and a neckline that promised more. Simple, straightforward, and eminently reusable.

Elana had no idea what she wanted to wear tomorrow. She couldn't afford the designer brands people in Haven wore, but she needed to up her fashion game regardless. Pantsuit? Cocktail dress? Was it better to downplay her physique or accentuate it? She didn't want to show off, but she didn't want to hide.

She pulled into the parking lot of the strip mall containing the hair and nail salon, uncomfortably aware of the size differential between her diesel behemoth and the compact cars and shiny SUVs crowding the pavement.

This was *not* her world, but today she would brave it. Elana had told herself many times that she would do anything within reason to get into Haven. A manicure was hardly a death sentence.

She turned on her trademark smile—warm, friendly,

disarming, the kind of smile that twirled subcontractors around your finger and soothed any anxious client—and pushed open the door. The butterflies in her stomach fluttered at the bell's ring, but her smile did not flicker.

"Hi! I'm Elana, booked for eleven AM?"

A short, stout woman bustled over from one of the chairs, leaving behind another woman with enough twisted foils in her hair that she looked like an alien. "Yes, yes, come on in. Molly will be with you in just a second."

The woman was effusive, and her short black hair was cut in a bob that perfectly accentuated her jawline. When she came close enough, Elana made out the hand-stitched name on her apron. Barbara.

"Thanks. I haven't been in a salon since high school. Anything I need to know?"

Barbara beamed at her. "Sit back and relax, doll, and let us take care of you. What's the occasion?"

"Business meeting in Haven."

The woman's hands, busily tapping something into the ancient computer behind the desk, paused mid-stroke. She straightened and looked Elana over.

"You're not wearing that, are you?"

"Oh, *God*, no."

Barbara nodded in satisfaction. "Good. D'you know what you're wearing?"

"Honestly, no. I'm going shopping after this."

Another nod. "You ask my Molly what she'd recommend. Her fashion sense is impeccable, and she gets bargains I'd never dream of."

"I'll do that."

Two hours later, Elana emerged from the salon feeling

like she was in the first stage of emerging from a cocoon. Her hair settled pleasantly around her shoulders, falling in gentle waves that framed her face and highlighted her collarbone. Or it would, once she was wearing something with a neckline that *showed* her collarbone. Her nails were a perfectly manageable length but glossy and a deep blue.

The experience felt like the second act of a play, where her shower last night had been Act One. Act Three was clothes shopping, and Elana had never felt so *excited* about the prospect.

True to Barbara's promise, Molly had showered Elana with savvy advice on what to buy and where to get it without emptying her wallet. First, she'd plied Elana with questions about her preferences and dislikes in between snipping off inches of her hair, washing it with products that smelled heavenly, then blow-drying and styling it. The fashion recommendations had followed, occupying the manicure portion of the morning.

As a result, Elana was headed for a boutique called Pax Vesta on the west side of town. The shop was sandwiched between two others on a street that had seen better days, but Elana stepped over the litter blowing in the gutter and mounted the dusty steps. Molly had looked like a million bucks, so she couldn't have been *too* crazy.

The sight that met her upon entry couldn't have been further from the outside. Behind the grimy windows, hidden from view by thick velvet blackout curtains, a technicolor kaleidoscope of elegance awaited. Mannequins garbed in sophisticated dresses and pantsuits lined the walls, showcasing the exacting care and attention to detail in each outfit. The center of the small shop was empty save for a platform big enough to stand on, which sat in a semi-circle of mirrors. A folding screen stood at the back with an empty clothing rack beside it.

The bell that rang when Elana opened the door was a pleasant, single-chime affair and sent a silvery echo through the shop. In response, a slight man emerged from behind a curtain in the opposite corner of the folding screen. Upon seeing him, Elana had no doubt that this was Zizi, the flashy owner of Pax Vesta whose praises Molly had liberally sung.

Zizi was shorter than Elana by about four inches—five if you removed the sequined silver pumps. He wore his platinum-blond hair in a stylish pixie cut, the tips of which were tinted lavender. His thin, rectangular glasses were rimless, but the arms were a gold polished so bright it hurt Elana's eyes. These matched the long necklace draped over his flowing white blouse and the row of tiny hoop earrings lining his right ear.

Zizi's eyes were a piercing light blue, and his skin was the brown of a well-roasted coffee bean. He wore dark gray slacks that brushed the tops of his silver pumps, and his long fingers ended in perfectly manicured cream-painted nails.

"Welcome, welcome!" he gushed. He seized Elana's hands and drew her further into the shop. His voice reminded Elana of birdsong—light and melodic, yet incisive. "Who sent you?"

"Molly. Molly, from—"

"From Pearl Beach!" Zizi dropped Elana's hands and applauded. "Oh, Molly, you never fail to send me customers. And who are *you*, my dear? What's the occasion?"

Zizi ushered Elana onto the platform and produced a seamstress' tape measure from a hidden pocket in the blouse. He began measuring Elana before she could respond.

"Elana Bishop...and I have a business meeting in Haven tomorrow."

Zizi was the first person Elana had encountered who did not hesitate when presented with this news. He made a small noise of acknowledgment and kept measuring.

"You've come to the right place. Dress or pantsuit? Haute couture? What's your budget?"

"Uh..." Elana ran some calculations in her head. "I can go up to a thousand, but I'd be more comfortable with something in the five hundred range."

Again, Zizi acknowledged with a slight grunt. He rolled up the tape measure and shoved it back in his pocket, then turned to the mannequins and thoughtfully bit his lip. "What kind of business meeting?"

"Reparations, mainly. I hit a Runner with my truck, and they're telling me how much they can pay me for the damage. But..."

Zizi cocked an eyebrow. "But?"

Elana nervously fingered the seam of her jeans. "The Arbiter of Shadows will be there. She came to, um, *handle* the Runner. I don't know why she's coming. And...I think I'm having coffee with the dispatcher who took my call afterward."

Zizi did not blink at the mention of Valeria Draven, but his mocha-colored lips curved into an enigmatic smile at the mention of *coffee*. "Sounds like your outfit needs to check several boxes."

Elana nodded.

Zizi crossed his arms and tapped a finger on his bicep. "Draven wears white and black, so let's avoid those. You've got warmth in your skin tone, and your hair's dark. Thick eyebrows, full lips. You're in good shape. Do you shave?"

Elana started. "What?"

"Your legs," Zizi clarified. "You obviously work a physical job, judging by the calluses on your hands and your current clothing. Some women who do physical labor don't bother and aren't comfortable in dresses. I'm narrowing down our options."

"Oh. Uh, yes. I do. And dresses are fine with me. I just don't wear them much."

Zizi nodded. "What time is the meeting?"

Elana grimaced. "I haven't been told yet, sorry."

Zizi dismissed the apology with a wave. "No matter. We'll manage."

He flitted toward the mannequins. The sequins on his shoes flashed under the overhead lights, and he muttered under his breath as he walked among the models, occasionally poking one and shaking his head.

At length, Zizi clicked his tongue and grinned. "I have just the thing." He promptly disappeared behind the curtain he'd entered from when Elana arrived.

Elana was left alone, surrounded by the faceless mannequins, feeling like she'd wandered onto a *Doctor Who* set and unsure what would happen next. Presumably Zizi would reenter with something for Elana to try on, but she couldn't begin to guess what it would be.

A lime green pantsuit with bright red Converses? A cocktail dress covered in ruffles and ribbons, like the monstrosity in the corner that resembled a wedding cake? Zizi's designs spanned the spectrum from avant-garde to Baroque. Elana might walk out looking like a runway model from any decade in the past five centuries.

A rustling of fabric heralded the fashionista's return. Elana turned to look, and a wave of relief washed over her when she spied the dress over Zizi's shoulder. Elana would not be wearing a mess of layered taffeta today, thank God.

Zizi held the dress out to Elana as he approached. "I think this will do nicely. Try it on while I find the matching shoes."

Elana delicately accepted the dark red dress and stepped off the platform. She examined it as she headed for the folding screen. Below the knee length, with a wide neckline that would show off her collarbones. Sleeveless to accentuate her well-defined arms. A leather belt in a mahogany color to emphasize her waist.

Behind the screen, she hung the dress on the provided hook, then stripped off her dusty jeans and T-shirt. Her bra was the wrong style for the dress, but she didn't have another one here, and Zizi didn't appear to sell them. She'd have to stop at a boutique and pick up some underthings to match.

She folded her shirt and jeans, placed them on the chair, then slipped the dress on. It zipped at the side, and a fold of fabric cleverly hid the zipper. The fabric was smooth and lightweight but stiff enough not to be flowy. A swirl of something shinier, maybe satin, sketched the silhouette of a flame over her right knee. Apart from the three-inch leather belt, the accent was the only decoration on the dress.

A pair of leather stilettos the same color as the dress appeared at the corner of the screen, deposited by Zizi's deft hands.

"I have jewelry that goes nicely if you're looking," he volunteered. "Come out when you're ready."

Elana warily regarded the stilettos, then strapped them on. High heels weren't her forte, but she'd manage. She'd have to practice at home tonight. The last thing she wanted was to do a faceplant in front of Valeria Draven…or Matt Richelieu.

She drew a deep breath and stepped out from behind the screen. Zizi's face lit up, and he excitedly applauded as Elana approached the platform.

"You look *marvelous*," Zizi assured her.

"You're just saying that," Elana scoffed. Then she stepped onto the small dais and turned to look in the mirror, and her jaw dropped.

Elana knew she was attractive. Regular physical activity and a healthy diet did that to a girl—not to mention, her father had always told her she'd inherited her mother's looks. Her hair was glossy, her skin stayed clear, and her eyes were big and dark.

Still, she'd never seen herself like *this*.

The heels made the curves of her calves pop. The hem of the dress fell just above them, and the flame accent shimmered in the light and pointed the eye up the skirt to the belt. The extra-defined waistline matched the boat neck and her collarbones, which stood out under the warm waves of her hair. She looked like a million dollars.

Zizi quietly advised, "If this is a day meeting, you'll want a thin eyeliner and a smattering of something shiny on your eyelids. Go with a light brown or a pink lip and a touch of blush. Mascara to match. If it's an evening meeting, switch to a smoky eye, a slightly thicker eyeliner, and a darker brown lip. Don't match the dress too closely."

Elana nodded. She couldn't take her gaze off herself. "You mentioned jewelry?"

She caught Zizi's grin out of the corner of her eye. "Look on the stool beside you."

Elana hadn't noticed the small footstool. She looked down and discovered a fire opal pendant on a thin leather strap. The pendant was teardrop-shaped and as large as her thumb. The matching stud earrings next to it held round opals the size of her pinky fingernail set in polished brass.

She picked up the pendant and turned it in the light. Its inclusions flashed gold and green and shifted within the gemstone's depths.

"It's *beautiful*," she whispered.

"I don't sell anything that isn't. Put it on."

Elana did. First the pendant, then the earrings. The pendant sat above her sternum and the earrings sparkled behind her hair.

Elana beheld herself in the mirror. She looked like a queen. She couldn't imagine a better outfit to show up to Haven in.

"How much?" She was afraid to ask.

"Six hundred for the lot, but you have to drop my name."

"Deal."

Elana kept glancing at the garment bag hanging in the back of her cab. The pendant and earrings were safe in a box in her backpack, and the shoes were wrapped in a shoebox. Three new bras, plus matching underwear, were tucked in a black bag beside the shoebox.

She'd come in under budget thanks to Zizi's generosity—but only just—and Elana decided she might as well finish the day with a bang. She treated herself by ordering takeout from her favorite Italian restaurant, which she picked up on the way.

As she pulled into her driveway with the scent of chicken cacciatore filling the truck, her phone went off with the unmistakable sound of the Haven Security app. She put the vehicle in Park and eagerly read the message.

Business meeting at ten. Brunch at eleven. See you tomorrow. M

The butterflies surged anew but with excitement instead of anxiety. Her new life would begin tomorrow, and she was ready for it.

CHAPTER FIVE

Elana tugged the hem of her dress farther down over her knee as she approached the gate into Haven. She hadn't thought about how ill-fitting her mode of transportation would seem when contrasted with her appearance until she'd left home, and she regretted the oversight. She'd left enough time to be early but didn't have enough time to rent a nicer car.

She exhaled a breath that puffed her lips out. It would be fine. The meeting was about reparations for damage to her truck anyway, so surely she would be *expected* to bring the vehicle with her. Unless they expected her to, what, have it towed to Haven? No. Matt would have told her.

The gate loomed ahead of her on her left. She slowed, signaled, and turned in. The wall's shadow engulfed her truck, plunging her into twilight. The stone and steel structure was only twelve feet thick but easily two hundred feet tall. As far as Elana knew, there were no gaps in the wall other than the official entrances, and high-tech security features protected the top of the wall. Had the Runner scaled it and jumped?

Her truck's diesel rumble hid her shiver. The security checkpoint was immediately beyond the wall. The enclosed tunnel meant she saw nothing of the legendary city...yet.

That would change in a few short minutes.

She stopped beside the checkpoint window, which looked like any other customs stop. *If it ain't broke, don't fix it,* she figured. Vampires were flashy but not insensible.

The attendant slid the window open and leaned out a touch. His three-piece navy suit was flawless, his cravat had a slight ruffle that matched the wave in his glossy black hair, and his cufflinks were pearls. Despite the elegance, Elana had no doubt he could put her on her ass in two seconds or less if she caused trouble. The set of his jaw and the coolness in his eyes spoke volumes more than the spit-and-polish of his wardrobe.

"Good morning, miss. What brings you to Haven today?" His voice was smooth like good peanut butter. Rich and warm, but not oily.

Elana had to swallow against the dryness in her mouth before she could reply. "I have a reparations meeting at ten o'clock at the Citadel. I hit a Runner with my truck."

No flash of emotion crossed his face, but he glanced at the truck's bumper. "Do you have a confirmation number from the Haven Security app?"

She grabbed her phone from her purse and opened the app. "Uh, yeah. Hold on. Just...here."

Elana swiveled to show him the screen where she'd found the confirmation number and fumbled her phone.

She caught it before it tumbled to the asphalt, but her heart skipped several beats, and she clamped down on the reflexive blue streak rising in her throat.

He raised an eyebrow by a fraction. "You can just read me the number, miss."

She swallowed and did so, ignoring the warmth rising in her cheeks. He tapped it into his workstation as she recited, and a pleasant *beep* emanated from within when she finished. Her app made the same sound, and she almost dropped her phone again.

"The app will provide you directions to the Citadel," the attendant informed her. "Please drive ahead. Enjoy the beauty of Haven, Miss Bishop."

Elana managed to mutter, "Thanks," before easing her foot off the brake and onto the gas. While the heels weren't easy to drive in, that wasn't the distraction. The distraction was the pair of doors sliding aside two feet in front of her truck, revealing the city beyond the wall.

The tunnel's dim illumination brightened, although not to the sun's full intensity. More powerful vampires were less susceptible to the sun's rays, but ultraviolet light was quite painful to initiates. As a result, Haven's canopy dimmed the light by a few degrees—enough that an Ashford resident would notice on a bright, sunny day but not so much that it seemed cloudy.

The mood lighting was not why Elana's jaw dropped as she rolled through the checkpoint.

Vampire society had progressed, technologically and scientifically, to such a degree that the incredibly advanced technology appeared magical to the unsuspecting eye.

Therefore, Haven's architecture was unmistakably *beyond human*.

Spindles of skyscrapers stretched toward the clouds at heights and angles unimaginable to human engineering, and many sprouted what Elana could only describe as umbrellas that covered the sky in layers like leaves. It looked like a synthetic forest canopy.

Elana could not tell from ground level whether the "leaves" were entirely intangible or if they had physical components. The overlapping layers created soft, dancing shadows. It was a good thing Elana wasn't going more than fifteen miles per hour, or else she would have been a danger to everyone else on the street. The effect was mesmerizing.

The skyscrapers were not the only buildings, although they were the most noticeable. The street Elana was on—the Kingsroad—was lined with edifices much closer in style to those Elana was familiar with. The signs of advanced technology were still clear if you knew where to look. Elana saw no exposed power lines nor obvious lights, and the floating road signs were a dead giveaway. Maglev, maybe. She couldn't begin to guess.

The app *beeped*. Elana glanced at it and chuckled when she saw it was telling her to drive straight ahead. The attendant at the gate couldn't have known she already knew the way to the Citadel, but Elana certainly did.

The Citadel of Accord, occasionally called the Neutral Zone, sat in Haven's center, which was built on a wheel-and-spoke plan with eight sections. To get to the Citadel, you drove through one of Haven's eight gates and kept going. Elana had entered via the main gate, the King's Gate.

To her left and right were two of Haven's trade districts. Premier was on her left, and Octava was on her right.

As one might guess from the name, Premier was the district for trade in luxury goods. In a neat row of carved stone façades and dignified pillars sat high-end boutiques with window displays of physics-defying couture, enchanting jewelry, and *enchanted* accessories. Elana had heard tales of bags that could hold infinite amounts of items. She hadn't decided if she believed them.

Across the street, Octava boasted the finest arts and music venues. Museums, concert halls, and art galleries with avant-garde architecture sat nestled among daring sculptures and magnificent natural arrangements. Elana caught a glimpse of a stunning fountain down a side street and almost wished she didn't have an appointment. Would she have time to sight-see afterward? She hoped so.

Elana turned her gaze to the marvel at the city's center, the collection of structures that marked her destination and stood as an ever-present reminder of Haven's history. At the end of the road, the Citadel rose above the cityscape in a mélange of architectural styles that went beyond Haven's deliberate combination of human and vampire.

The Citadel had been built with the remnants of those buildings that had survived the ill-fated rebellion over a century ago. Now, those remnants illustrated the poignant history and the unflagging hope and determination that formed Haven's foundation as a place of refuge from conflict, its peace meticulously maintained through order, respect, and memory.

Although humans were welcome to live in Haven, it was a vampire city. This was not up for debate. Humans who chose to live under the SpiderKing's protection enjoyed a diverse and vibrant community that celebrated differences. All its inhabitants found common ground in their desire for peace and stability, but the SpiderKing's authority was unquestionably law.

Twenty thousand people lived and worked in the complex of governmental and administrative buildings that formed the Citadel of Accord. None were human, but humans were welcome to enter the Citadel to interact, share ideas, and engage in cultural exchange under the watchful eyes of the consorts.

The SpiderKing had built Haven as a refuge from the drama of the Old World, a place where vampires could live freely. The delicate balance between engaging with the wider world and keeping vampirekind safe was a constant struggle, and every piece of the Citadel's structure highlighted the potential cost. If that balance tipped, there was no telling what would happen.

Elana shivered again. Anxiety lingered In the back of her mind. Once upon a time, she would have considered any entry into Haven auspicious—a dream come true—but under the circumstances, she didn't know what to expect.

She followed a Parking sign at the edge of the Citadel's wall and paused to allow half a dozen pedestrians to cross before proceeding into the indicated entrance. Foot traffic was heavier in Haven than in Ashford and car traffic was lighter. The cars she'd seen on her way in were far pricier than her Ford F150 by several orders of magnitude.

No one drove inside the Citadel of Accord. You walked, and if you couldn't walk, they provided means of personal transportation. Nothing motorized. It was considered an equalizing measure. As she stepped out of her truck and noted the stall number on the concrete wall, Elana privately thought the sheer "wow" factor was an added benefit. She suspected her sense of awe would multiply tenfold when she walked into the plaza's courtyard.

She was not wrong. She stopped dead in her tracks after a single step and stared, mouth faintly agape, at the majestic pieces of history towering over her. She'd never felt so out of place yet so much like she *belonged* as she did at that moment. Something about Haven resonated with her soul.

"Miss Bishop?"

Sexy voice strikes again. "Y—yes?" Elana stammered, then wrenched her gaze away from the skyscrapers to see Matt Richelieu standing in front of her, looking every bit as sexy as he sounded on the phone.

Smooth brown hair fell to his ears in thick waves. A neatly trimmed beard and mustache. Eyes that looked like the sea and eyelashes you could haul yourself to shore with. Impeccably tailored suit and polished shoes that could have walked off any runway in Italy. A quirk of his full lips hinted at a roguish smile behind the sophisticated demeanor.

He was tall, but not overly so—maybe six feet, six-one at the most—yet Elana felt he towered over her like everything else in this city.

Matt smiled at her and closed the distance between them. "Matt Richelieu."

He extended a hand, and Elana automatically and firmly shook it. She thanked her lucky stars that her business acumen took over and saved her from more awkward stuttering. "Elana Bishop. Thanks for meeting me. I'm not late, am I?"

"No, not at all." He smoothly shifted from shaking her hand to tucking her arm in his and leading her forward. "We make it a point to escort our guests to their meetings. Courtesy isn't merely a suggestion in Haven. It's a matter of pride and principle."

Elana fought to keep the pleased surprise in her chest from spreading into a full-blown blush. "That's very kind of you. Which way?"

"Just through here."

Matt led her to the most imposing of the buildings on the edge of the central plaza. Twin Doric columns framed a stark black and white façade and a set of wooden double doors at least twenty feet tall and banded with polished iron. The columns appeared to have been shattered and deliberately rebuilt to highlight the line where they had broken with a gleaming gold line. Similarly, the façade showed gold-filled cracks, and as Elana approached the doors, speckles of gold dotted the doors like buckshot.

"The consulate," Matt informed her in a low tone as he swung open the door, as though Elana didn't already know…which she did, and the knowledge made her breath catch in her throat.

The consulate was the legislative home of the arbiters. This was where the consorts lived and worked, fulfilling their duties to the SpiderKing day in and day out.

The entrance hall was huge. The interior was entirely white marble shot through with black and gold. Their footsteps echoed on the floor as they walked over the inlaid mosaic of the SpiderKing's insignia, an eight-pointed spiderweb with a phase of the moon in each point surrounding an hourglass. Staircases rose from the atrium to each arbiter's wing of the building, all passing under arches that bore the consorts' symbols in the same style.

Elana and Matt ascended the staircase marked with a single circle made of shards of black glass. The new moon —the shadows. The mosaic's facets shimmered and glittered in the light thrown from the wall sconces, and each flash made the butterflies nesting in Elana's stomach rustle.

They climbed long enough that Elana was grateful for her physical job and resentful of her high heels. Her calves burned by the time they arrived at the landing that granted access to the offices of the Arbiter of Shadows, and she breathed slowly to hide the fact that she was slightly out of breath.

The décor in this wing was minimalist, even spartan. The dominant colors were white, black, and gray, but the marble had been swapped for flecked granite. The wall sconces were stainless steel instead of the atrium's wrought iron, and their light was cool and steady.

Matt waved a hand over a panel beside the last of the innumerable white doors, and the lock *clicked*. He swung it open to reveal a luxuriously appointed study—luxurious, that is, to the discerning eye.

Elana had hauled enough furniture in her day to recognize a designer's touch in the curve of the chairs' arms and the cut of the large desk's legs. Scandinavian, she guessed. Not a piece in this room could have cost less than a few thousand dollars. Chump change for the SpiderKing.

Matt motioned for Elana to take a seat, and he sat across from her in a second chair. The steel gray chairs were surprisingly comfy for designer furniture, contouring pleasantly to the spine and naturally supporting the arms. Elana didn't often feel powerful sitting in a chair, but she did in this one.

Matt flashed her a warm smile. "You look lovely. That dress suits you."

"Thank you. I didn't want to be underdressed this time." Elana smiled, but the instincts cultivated from years as a contractor flashed a warning in the back of her head. Opening a business conversation with a personal compliment was a standard way to get someone in a good mood, especially if you didn't have previous job experience to comment on.

Matt chuckled. "I completely understand. When I received the message that Arbiter Draven would be joining us, I dug out my best suit."

"Always good to put your best foot forward."

"Certainly. Or best bumper, as the case may be."

Matt winked, and Elana resolutely ignored the answering swoop in her stomach. That was a textbook segue into business, and he'd performed it admirably.

He continued, "We'd like to offer you forty thousand. That ought to cover any repairs and all inconveniences. What do you say?"

Elana narrowed her eyes. "I'd say that's very generous."

Matt shrugged. "The SpiderKing pays his debts and then some."

"I'll say." Her street smarts were kicking in on the heels of her professional experience. Sexy voice or no, Matt had to have an ulterior motive. Nobody dropped five figures on a *dent*. "Are there conditions attached to the compensation?"

Matt's gaze flickered to the right. Elana couldn't tell if it was a nervous tic or if he was glancing at the door, which was over her shoulder in that direction. She did not follow his gaze but kept it trained on him.

"I'm not at liberty to disclose the particulars of an arbitration, but suffice it to say that there are no conditions as to your use of the funds. Should you accept it, what you do with the money is up to you."

Elana was not fooled. No conditions on using the funds didn't mean no conditions on her *acceptance* of the funds. She might be able to spend the money however she wanted, but they might expect something else in return.

The impending presence of Valeria Draven weighed on her. The unspoken conditions had to be related to her reasons for attending. If that were the case, why wouldn't Matt say? Was he not *allowed* to say, or did he not *want* to?

A single knock on the door brought Matt's head up. "Come in, Lady Valeria."

CHAPTER SIX

All the stability Elana thought she'd gained by leaning on her professional persona evaporated. The Arbiter of Shadows was at the door for reasons Elana didn't yet know, and Elana hadn't decided whether she would take the forty grand.

Way to throw off a girl's negotiation game, she silently grumbled...until the clacking of the consort's heels brought the monochrome woman into view.

Today's pantsuit struck Elana as having an Oriental bent. The silhouette was angular, with a leg that tapered to the knee and flared slightly to the ankle. The jacket's shape was similarly hourglass-esque. It had no lapels, a sharp and deep V-neck, and a wrap-style closure with a single clasp of silver filigree above the waist. The sleeves featured birds flying above stylized waves embroidered in shimmering mother-of-pearl and silver thread. Earrings matching the birds glimmered in the consort's hair.

Matt stood and bowed. Elana hurried to mirror him and ignored the trembling in her protesting legs.

"My lady," she murmured.

"Your time is appreciated, Arbiter," Matt added. "Please sit if you'd be so kind."

Valeria swept around the desk and sat in the high-backed white leather chair, which seemed to be the cue for Matt and Elana to sit. Elana followed Matt's lead again, then kept quiet and desperately hoped he'd make the next move.

"I had just made our offer to Miss Bishop," Matt informed the consort.

"Has she accepted it?"

The corner of Matt's lips quirked up in a smile. "Not yet. Unlike so many to whom the Citadel offers reparations, Miss Bishop is bold enough to ask questions."

The arbiter's eyebrow rose a fraction of an inch, and she shifted her gaze to Elana. "Do tell."

Elana swallowed. "I asked if there were any conditions attached to the reparations, ma'am."

Valeria's lips flattened into a thin smile. "A wise inquiry. And, Mister Richelieu? What did you tell her?"

"That I could not comment on the details of an arbitration, but that there were no restrictions on Miss Bishop's use of the money, should she accept it."

"Which doesn't mean there aren't conditions," Elana blurted. Then she clenched her jaw and cursed how she felt every time she encountered Valeria. Her aura of authority and dominance pervaded every inch of the space, and Elana wanted *so badly* to prove herself worthy of the attention the arbiter was bestowing upon her. Badly enough that she would make a fool of herself.

Valeria said nothing for a spell, only regarded Elana

calmly. The scrutiny made Elana long to squirm in her seat, but she kept a tight hold on her discomfort and held the arbiter's gaze. The Arbiter of Shadows did nothing without cause, and she did nothing without the SpiderKing's implicit approval. Therefore, it stood to reason that whatever Valeria was here for, it was significant—which meant *Elana* was significant.

"There are no conditions on your acceptance," Valeria began, then paused. It was not a pause that invited comment, and Elana held her tongue.

"The reason I am here is not related to the affair with the Runner. That is settled. The reparations are yours should you accept them. I am here because of the blood test."

Elana blinked. She'd almost forgotten the tiny drop of blood the consort had taken two nights ago. She'd been so hopped up on adrenaline that it had slipped her mind.

The butterflies in her stomach surged to life. She gripped the arm of her chair. "What…did it say?"

"That you are a vampire."

The words fell like claps of thunder on Elana's ears. Her vision blurred for a split second, and her breath first caught in her throat, then refused to move at all. The thunder turned to deafening ocean surf as her blood pounded behind her eardrums. Her hands twitched as she white-knuckled the arms of the chair.

"I'm…a *what?*" Her response was barely audible. She wasn't even sure she'd spoken aloud.

"A vampire," Valeria repeated, proving that she had. "You have vampiric blood."

Elana's heart beat an unsettling, panicked tattoo against her ribs, and her breath came back shallow and rapid.

"I can't be," she numbly replied. "That's impossible. My dad was human, and so was my mom. They're both dead. She died when I was born. I *can't* be a vampire."

"Your heritage is not in question." The Arbiter of Shadows' tone was calm and collected, as though she were discussing nothing of more import than the weather, but the feeling of being pinned under a magnifying glass returned to Elana in full force. She longed to wither under the scrutiny.

"Then how can this be true?"

"The how is not yet known, but it is eminently clear that vampire forces have influenced your life for a very long time."

Elana exhaled a shaky breath, then whispered, "Holy shit."

Matt watched Elana closely. Among his tasks as a Haven Security dispatcher was getting a handle on callers' personalities and gauging their likely reactions. He'd pegged Elana from the get-go as a no-nonsense woman with a head on her shoulders, and he'd quickly figured out that she knew plenty about vampires. He'd been pleasantly surprised to discover she wasn't the type who salivated after the fantasy versions of vampires but instead had a solid understanding of *actual* vampire society.

Even more surprising had been the note in the file, made by Lady Draven, that she had obtained a blood sample from Miss Bishop. While it wasn't unheard of for a guardian to take a blood sample from a *Runner*, in case they lied about their house before they were disposed of, it wasn't standard practice to take one from the *caller*.

When he'd seen the terse explanatory note that Elana had knocked the Runner out with a single right hook, he'd understood why the consort had done so, and a pit of dread had opened in his mind. If Valeria Draven suspected Elana Bishop of being a vampire, that meant someone had gone to extreme lengths to hide her existence from the SpiderKing. Who that was and why they'd done it were mysteries, and Valeria Draven loved nothing more than a good mystery.

The question was whether this would be an *interesting* or a boring mystery.

Boring mysteries were typically born of disgust and resentment. Someone had a bone to pick with someone else, so they decided to take revenge in the form of a long con that amounted to thumbing their nose at the offending party. If it turned out that Elana Bishop *knew* she was a vampire, and she'd been hiding from Haven for God knew how long, there were a host of other questions that needed asking and none of them had happy answers.

Why would a vampire in hiding allow a blood sample to be taken?

Valeria had explicitly requested that Matt watch Elana's reaction to the news. He was excellent at his job, and she trusted him to provide an objective second opinion on whether Miss Bishop was terrified that she'd been found out, scared for someone else, or frightened for herself at the sudden news that she was a vampire.

Matt hadn't argued that there might be other options for emotional reactions than "terrified." He'd witnessed the results of several unsanctioned turnings, and to a one, the newly turned were, well, *terrified*. Discovering you'd been transformed into an extra-human creature without your consent was enough to knock even the most level-headed person for a loop.

The Arbiter of Shadows was trained to be suspicious. Her job was to maintain order within vampire society and ensure the stability and supremacy of the House of the Arachnid. She could execute any task she wished with impunity and with skill beyond that of nearly any vampire.

Valeria had intuited that something was not normal about Elana Bishop. She had *expected* to find a sordid, boring mystery, with at least one person to kill once the dénouement had settled. She had requested that Matt be her second set of eyes to keep her well-honed paranoia from blinding her to the remote possibilities.

Therefore, Matt Richelieu turned every one of his highly trained observational skills on one Elana Bishop.

She had gone out of her way to present herself appropriately for the occasion. Her dress was gorgeous, and her style matched. She owned the look, but Matt could tell the outfit was unfamiliar. He hadn't only suggested the highest study for Lady Draven's convenience. Elana hid her fatigue well, but her feet would be *killing* her when she got home. If she'd known she was a vampire, she would have experience in eradicating physical pain. She did not.

Elana had been unfailingly courteous in her communication, but her responses were unpolished and lacked the practiced cadence and turns of phrase that were standard in vampire society. Matt could tell that Elana had done her research—probably a *lot* of research, judging by her obvious familiarity with the general trappings of Haven life. Still, she did not have the well-rehearsed tones of someone who had gone through even the first level of initiate training. Unless she was an Oscar-winning actress and nobody had told him, she wasn't faking it.

That, beyond all else, clinched Matt's conviction. Elana was genuinely stunned by Valeria's point-blank revelation. She would have tried to bolt or beg if she had been scared for her life or someone else's. Neither would have saved her, but they were the normal responses. The third option was bluster, which Matt had nixed out of hand. "Overbearing" was so far out of Elana's range that it wasn't worth considering.

That left one possibility. Prior to today, Elana Bishop had not known she was a vampire. She had accepted her uncommon physical strength as a quirk of genetics, the way some people are born with above-average eyesight or excellent hearing, and she'd thought nothing more of it.

He kept his gaze on Elana for several more seconds, paying close attention to where she was looking and how she held herself. Her eyes were unfocused, her breath was shallow, and her hands were alternately grasping and releasing the arms of the chair, but her legs were still. She was making no movements to run, only the twitchy indications of a brain overwhelmed with sudden information. The impact would pass, and they would see her process.

The frantic movements faded, and her breath calmed. She blinked a few times, and her gaze dropped to her knees.

"I'm a vampire," she murmured, then repeated it.

"Yes," Matt gently affirmed.

"I never thought…" Elana shook her head.

"Never thought what?" Matt prompted.

Elana inhaled sharply as though he'd prodded her in the ribs. She sat up straight, and her cheeks flushed a faint pink. "Sorry, I—I never thought…" The blush deepened. "Two days ago, I never thought I'd get into Haven. I've always wanted to. Now the first thing I learn when I get here is that I'm a vampire. It's just…a lot."

Matt chuckled. "Technically, I think the first thing you learned was that we were offering you forty thousand dollars to fix your truck."

Elana made a sound that could have been a laugh or a sob. "Right. Of course. Silly me, how could I forget?"

Matt did not reply to this, choosing instead to study Elana's nonverbal language. She had taken her hands off the arms of the chair and crossed them in her lap with her fingers loosely twined. Every few moments, she idly twisted a simple gold ring on the index finger of her right hand. It was wide enough that it looked like a man's ring. Her father's wedding ring, perhaps.

Her back was straight. The blush hadn't faded, but she wasn't hiding it. She wasn't stammering excuses or protesting. Her voice had been mildly breathy. Her eyes were alight with excitement in addition to the shock.

Matt casually faced the consort, who had not moved from behind the desk nor said anything during Elana's initial reaction.

Valeria met his gaze and raised one perfectly stenciled eyebrow. What was his opinion?

In response, he spoke to Elana while holding the arbiter's gaze. "This is all very new to you."

Elana was still staring at her knees. She again laughed breathlessly. "You're telling me. I drove in thinking I'd accidentally offended the arbiter and she had to kill me."

Matt bit his tongue hard enough to draw blood so he wouldn't laugh. That was *exactly* the kind of joke you would *not* make in front of Valeria Draven if you knew what was good for you. It proved beyond a shadow of a doubt that Elana Bishop was not a vampire who had been hiding for unknown decades on Haven's doorstep.

He nodded at Valeria and flashed her a very subtle thumbs-up. Elana was genuine.

The answering smile that bloomed on the consort's face made the growing excitement in Matt's stomach freeze.

Elana was not only genuine, she was a genuine *mystery*, and having the Arbiter of Shadows take a direct interest in you was not always the boon one might believe it to be.

Elana Bishop's life was about to get *very* interesting.

CHAPTER SEVEN

The initial shock passed like a semi barrelling by too close for comfort. It left Elana with a hollow sensation in her chest, as though someone on the semi had carved out her heart and lungs on the way by.

She gradually became aware of the soft leather under her hands, the muted hum of whatever high-tech climate control kept the room at the perfect temperature, and the faint taste of blood. She must have bitten her tongue or her cheek while silently freaking out.

Elana swallowed. She drew a deliberate breath, rolled her shoulders up and back, straightened, and slipped a hair closer to the edge of her chair. She would face this with the aplomb and sangfroid—no pun intended—she had learned from her years working as a woman in the blue-collar world. She would be fine. This was nothing she couldn't handle.

It was only her entire life turning upside down and inside out. No big deal. Right?

"Thank you for telling me," Elana hesitantly began. "I doubt I ever would have found out otherwise."

Matt shook his head and pursed his lips. "The human medical system isn't equipped to deal with vampires. More likely you would have been written off as a genetic anomaly and told to go on with your day."

"If I looked into it at all," Elana pointed out. "Not much reason to go to the doctor for being stronger than the average Jane."

"Fair point."

Elana shifted her gaze to the arbiter and fought the reflex to swallow again. The woman's eyes weren't daggers. They were *stilettos*. Her incessant scrutiny unnerved Elana. Was it a calculated choice of body language, or was Valeria Draven just *like* that? *Six of one, half a dozen of the other*, she supposed.

"Why tell me? Why go to the trouble?" Elana frowned. "Unless—am I required to move into Haven now?"

Valeria didn't bat an eye. "You are welcome here, should you choose to relocate, but you are not required to join those living under the grace of the SpiderKing."

"Why not? I thought all initiates were required to stay within Haven. Is that not what I am?"

The consort steepled her fingers and leaned on the desk. "You are a special case. Vampire society places extreme importance on lineage. You are unaware of yours. This must be rectified, if only for our records. Rogue vampires will not be tolerated. Your existence must be explained."

She cast her gaze up and down Elana. "It would be one thing if you had recently developed your abilities. Unexpected and nonconsensual transformations occur even in these enlightened times, thanks to chance and unfortunate encounters with the darker elements of the world. A disreputable medical professional or a drug dealer who thinks they're being funny—in any situation where blood is spilled, vampires can be created.

"But you have had these abilities as long as you can remember." Valeria's stare skewered Elana and pinned her to the chair. The butterflies, so recently calmed by the ebbing adrenaline of revelation, stirred anew. "Is that not correct?"

"No, that—I mean, yes, that's correct." Elana stumbled over the overly formal syntax and bit her tongue again. "I was always the fastest in gym class. As a kid, I rearranged my bedroom dozens of times while Dad was out on jobs because I was bored and didn't think anything of it. I'd carry in three bags of groceries on each arm before I was fifteen.

"I never *looked*...built, I guess...so like I said, I didn't think about it. It was normal. It didn't come up much until I started working for Dad, and the other guys would look at me funny. But since Dad would say, 'Oh, she's always been like that,' they let it go."

Elana's hands had found their way back to her lap while she wasn't paying attention. She twined her fingers and twisted them until they ached as her life crossed her mind's eye in a very different light—no longer the sepia tone of memory, but the overly vibrant surrealism of reframing.

Scrambling up trees. Biking faster than any kid her age, even the boys who did nothing but play sports. Never getting tired, not even when she'd been out on the soccer field all game without a break. Splitting and hauling firewood on camping trips. Scoring the divisional blue ribbon for track and field four years in a row.

She'd been the MVP of every athletic team she'd joined, not only because of her impressive physical prowess and capability but because her coaches never had to worry about her grades slipping. She'd maintained a perfect GPA through high school and community college without breaking a sweat—another thing she'd done her best to sweep under the rug because people got weird about stuff like that. They'd say, "Why'd you stay home and take over your father's company when you could've gone to an Ivy League school?"

Elana had been accepted at almost all the colleges and universities she'd applied for, although that hadn't been many. The truth was that she hadn't known what she wanted to do beyond working with her father and tinkering with the gadgets that came in. She'd been happy enough with her life that she hadn't seen the advantage of taking on hundreds of thousands of dollars in debt for a piece of paper.

She cleared her throat. "Are vampires smarter than humans, too?"

Matt answered her. "We tend to be natural critical thinkers and sponges for information, in a similar way that we're naturally gifted at physical skills. Vampire society's advanced nature lends itself to supporting higher education, and since basic needs are met, we're more able to focus on those pursuits...but biologically smarter? Hard to say."

"We're privileged," Valeria concluded. "The SpiderKing

believes it prudent to maintain the delicate balance of isolation and engagement with the human world for reasons related to that privilege. This is why rogue vampires are not tolerated and why we must determine your lineage.

"It will be up to you what to do with that knowledge, but it would behoove you to know that a life which has been entwined with the supernatural from the beginning will be of great interest to the SpiderKing. You will not escape his notice henceforth."

"That sounds ominous," Elana reflexively joked, then wished she could swallow her tongue. "Uh, sorry. I shouldn't be glib. It's just…"

Valeria waved it off. "You have experienced a great shock. We all cope in our own way. To be truthful, you are not incorrect. It *is* of significance that the SpiderKing should take an interest in you. You are a rogue vampire who, until a chance meeting, did not *know* she was a vampire. This implies a great many things, few of which are pleasant, and you will be the center of an investigation that will become very personal even if you do not elect to assist in it."

Ice trickled through Elana's veins as Valeria spoke. "What do you mean, if I don't 'elect to assist?'"

"We will investigate your heritage regardless," the arbiter stated. "We will advise you of the outcomes of that investigation as they pertain to you. They might not. We do not require your permission nor your approval to act in accordance with vampire law since you have not yet joined us, but our actions might affect you."

Elana blinked several times as she wrestled with that

sentence. "You're being awfully cagey," she finally told the consort. Her throat threatened to close on the borderline impertinent words, but she was done dancing around.

Before Valeria could answer, Matt's warm hand closed around Elana's. She jumped, but his grip was comforting, not restrictive, and he met her surprised look with a gentle smile.

"This is a lot. We know." His voice was soothing like chamomile tea. "It throws your entire life into question. Don't worry about the legalese for now. Go home and process. It's a hard truth. When you're ready, we'll be here to talk about it. No, it's not common for initiates *or* humans to leave Haven and return freely, but you're under the protection of the Arbiter of Shadows. You'll be fine."

Elana gripped his hand. It was soft and had no calluses, but it was strong nonetheless.

He had a point. She was not in the best frame of mind to contemplate a legal system she knew the bare minimum about. She had a hell of a lot of thinking to do.

"But…coffee," she protested.

Matt chuckled, but not unkindly. "Rain check. Cross my heart."

Elana grinned as the banter sprang to her lips. "Can vampires do that?"

"Haven't been smited yet." He rose from the chair and effortlessly brought her with him. "I'll see you to your truck, Miss Bishop."

Valeria remained seated as Richelieu escorted Elana out. He opened the door for her and glanced back at Valeria, meeting her gaze briefly.

"Help her," she mouthed and was pleased to see him nod. Richelieu was competent, observant, and compassionate, the ideal candidate for ensuring Miss Bishop didn't go too far astray. Valeria had no interest in allowing her new puzzle to slip through her fingers.

Elana mentioned many aspects of her childhood that fit perfectly with being an initiate but had *not* mentioned being photosensitive or burning easily in the sun. It was nearly unheard of that a vampire of such low level would not require extra protection from ultraviolet light. That meant Elana Bishop was already more powerful than she knew.

This was precisely the type of secret Valeria Draven excelled at solving and one of the reasons the SpiderKing had selected her as the Arbiter of Shadows. She would determine where Elana Bishop had come from and why she was the way she was. Then she would mold her into whatever the SpiderKing required.

CHAPTER EIGHT

For the first time in her life, Elana hesitated before climbing out of her truck when she arrived at work. She sat with her hand on the handle and idly brushed the lock with her thumb while staring out the windshield at the men in hard hats and high-vis vests with whom she'd spent her working life.

She'd always felt like one of them thanks to her natural strength. She'd *belonged* on job sites, hauling furniture and construction debris and tossing banter through the dusty air. Laughing raucously at terrible jokes. Choking back convenience store coffee.

Elana had been "one of the guys," only with great hair and a nice rack—though woe betide anyone who dared comment. None of the guys who worked with her would let Elana be objectified. A passerby had once wolf whistled at her, and the entire crew had booed them so loudly Elana had covered her ears.

Now...

She was a *vampire*. You couldn't *get* further from "one of the guys."

If she left Ashford, would she have to sell the business? If she did, she'd have to tell the guys. Hell, even if she *didn't* sell the business, if she moved, she'd have to tell them. There would be no getting around it.

Elana steeled herself and gripped the handle. Until she decided whether to move to Haven, she still had a life outside the wall, and she would not let her crew down.

She pasted on a smile, opened the door, and swung out of the cab, tossing her hair over her shoulder. "Jerry!" she hollered. "Save any work for me?"

Jerry tipped his hard hat to her. His megawatt grin was visible from here. "Always, boss! Left the hardest bits for you!"

She jogged over. "Aw, you shouldn't have," she teased. "I might make the new guys nervous."

The big, burly man chortled and gently shoved her upper arm. Even a gentle shove from Jerry was enough to make many stumble, but Elana's feet remained rooted to the gravel. Yesterday, the feeling would have made her smile. Today, it made her stomach turn.

"Good for you if you do, I always say. They gotta know who's boss!"

If she told them, she'd lose their respect.

Elana forced the corners of her lips up another degree. Be normal. Act normal. Normal job, normal life, normal everything.

If she didn't tell them, the rest of her life would be a lie.

Elana threw herself into the work.

Today was a brainless day. They were cleaning up a

construction site before the contractors moved on to the next phase. They'd be hauling scrap wood, drywall, rebar, et cetera. They'd separate the junk by type and toss it into their respective dumpsters, then haul those away.

The upside to the easy jobs was that you didn't have to think about them. The *downside* was that this freed you up to think about lots of other things. Usually on days like these, Elana would amuse herself by theorizing about the latest developments in Haven drama and occasionally daydreaming about what it would be like to be a vampire.

These mental distractions were *unwelcome* today, to say the least.

Instead, Elana focused all of her attention on her crew. Jerry had hired a couple of new hands last week, and this was the first time Elana had met them. Business was booming for Bishop's. They had contracts booked out for months and enough cash flow that they *could* hire more people to keep adding work.

How could she justify leaving?

Elana shook the thoughts away and refocused on the new hire nearest her. He was around six-foot-two, had thick brown hair with a nice wave, a bushy but well-kept beard, and dark brown eyes. About her age, if she had to guess. His name was Jesse, and he'd worked construction before joining the hauling crew, based on the lingo he was casually tossing around.

He was cute.

Oh, what the hell.

Elana caught Jesse's eye at coffee break and raised an eyebrow.

Jesse smiled and nodded, then lifted his cup in greeting. "Boss."

She shook her head. "Elana, please."

"You got it. What can I do for you?"

Elana sipped her coffee. "Just looking to get to know you. I like to know my people."

Jerry was a few feet away. He snorted. "She's flirtin' with you, son. Careful now."

Elana grinned, leaned over, and smacked Jerry on the forearm. "Fuck off, Jerry, at least let me get ten minutes into the small talk before you blow my cover."

"Gotta keep my boys safe."

"Oh, he's safe with me." She looked at Jesse and dialed her grin down to a friendly smile. "Before you freak out—Jerry knows me too well, so yes, I *did* intend to ask you out if you were interested, but I *also* intended to get to know you a little first. No pressure, though."

To her relief, Jesse's face betrayed no trepidation, only amusement. "Well. Can't say I expected to get talked up by the boss on my first day."

Elana shot Jerry a look. "This is his *first day?* I thought you said he did the Chalmers job last week!"

Jesse chuckled. "Not his fault. I had to call in for a family emergency that day. This would have been my third shift if I didn't have to handle my mom being in care. Jerry was great about it, by the way. I really appreciate you guys' flexibility. Most employers are real dicks about that kind of thing."

Jerry tipped his hat to Jesse. "Only continuing the proud tradition from old man Jeremiah. You treat your employees right, and they'll treat you the same."

Jesse nodded. "Amen to that. Jeremiah—that was your dad, right, Elana? I was sorry to hear he passed, and sorrier that I didn't get to meet him. He sounded like an awesome guy and an even better boss."

Elana's smile turned to a faint wince. "Yeah. He was. Thanks."

Jesse noticed her shift and delicately lightened up. "Enough about sad things. I hear there was some flirting going on?"

Elana snickered. "Buy me dinner first, then we'll talk."

Jesse laughed. "Wait a second. I thought *you* were asking *me* out! Why am I suddenly buying you dinner?"

Elana fluttered her eyelashes at him and ignored Jerry's guffaw. "Because I'm a pretty lady, that's why."

"A pretty lady who could throw me over the fence without blinking," Jesse retorted. "I'm pretty sure *I'd* be the lady in this relationship!"

The knot in Elana's stomach that had been growing all morning loosened a touch. Maybe this wasn't such a stupid idea after all. Perhaps she *could* be normal if she found the right people.

"How does pizza sound? The Italian place on Beauford is my favorite."

"Pizza's great. I'll pick you up at six?"

"Make it seven. I gotta get all this drywall dust out of my hair."

"See you then."

Jesse pulled up in a black Chevy Camaro. It was a newer model, maybe a few years old, and well-maintained. It didn't gleam like he'd just waxed it, and there was dust on the wheel wells from the job site, but it was clean and in great condition.

Elana respected people who could take care of their possessions. It was something her father had taught her from a very young age. You could always tell when people brought their electronics in for repair who had taken care of their things and who hadn't.

Usually, when someone cared about their possessions enough to maintain them, it meant they cared about the people in their lives even more. That wasn't *always* the case. Sometimes people cared *more* about stuff than relationships, which never ended well, but it was a decent marker.

Elana jogged down her front steps. She'd showered and put on fresh jeans and a clean T-shirt, but she and Jesse had agreed not to make this a big deal of a date. They'd have pizza and beer, chat and hang out, and see where the night took them.

Elana wasn't certain where she wanted that to be. She wasn't much for casual hookups, as a rule. She could see the appeal, but it wasn't her style. On the flip side, she wasn't opposed to hitting the bedroom on the first date if the chemistry was there.

The thought struck her as she stepped off the sidewalk that if being a vampire made her better at everything else, it might make her better at sex, too…whatever *that* meant.

Jesus Christ, woman! Get your head out of the gutter. She shook herself and opened the passenger's door.

Jesse was a great guy. Elana was thoroughly enjoying herself by the time they reached the restaurant, and that didn't stop all through dinner.

"What do you like about hauling?" he asked her as he attempted to pull a slice of pizza off the pan. The cheese stretched to eight inches before he gave up and grabbed a knife to sever the strings and wrap them around the end of the slice.

"You don't think I just took over my daddy's business?" Elana half-teased. She'd expected this question. Anyone she dated, as soon as they found out what she did for a living, asked her why she did it. Typically, they asked, "Why would you work a job like that?" with an air of disgust, as if someone "like her" deserved better, which was bullshit. There was nothing wrong with a good, solid, blue-collar job.

Jesse shook his head and swallowed his mouthful of cheese, sausage, and bell pepper. "Nah. You could've sold when he passed. Hell, you could pass it on to Jerry if you didn't want it. But from the stories the guys told me, the crew's basically been your family since day one.

"In my experience, folks who grow up in a family business either stay because of obligation and hate every second, or they love it because they saw the passion their parents had. I'm guessing you're the latter. So, what do you like about hauling?"

Elana leaned back against the smooth leather of the booth and contemplated her half-empty bottle of beer.

"That's very astute of you. I doubt most people give *anything* that much thought, let alone a hauling company."

"I'm not most people." He flashed her a cheeky grin and winked.

She fought the urge to squirm. *You're certainly not.* "It's satisfying. The parameters of the job are as clear as you can get. Show up, haul shit, leave. The to-do lists are easy to check off that way, and I've always liked a job well done.

"As much as I like hauling, my real love in the business is the electronics. Dad used to leave me gadgets and gizmos to play with when I was a kid, as soon as I was old enough to be left alone. I loved taking them apart, messing with the insides, and figuring out how to put them back together. Sometimes I could make them work again. Sometimes I just broke them, but I learned a lot along the way."

Elana looked up to find Jesse beaming at her. She blushed. "What?"

He shook his head. "Nothing. Just…imagining a mini version of you surrounded by bits of wire and circuit boards."

She chuckled. "A lot of magnetic tape was involved. I can't tell you how many cassette tapes I unspooled and tried to spool back together."

"VHS or audio?"

"Both. Any. All of the above. Pretty sure Dad once brought me a Betamax tape…or, no, was it an 8-track?" Elana took a swig from her bottle. "Ah, I don't remember. That was a long time ago. Did I answer your question?"

"Sure did." Jesse mopped stray pizza sauce off his plate with his crust. "I'm glad you've found something that suits you."

"Have you?"

He smirked. "It's probably not a good idea to tell my boss that I don't know whether I'm in the right job."

The base of Elana's bottle *clacked* against the table as she burst into laughter. "Fair point! Oh, man. I am curious, though, and I won't fire you if you say no. I know most guys do hauling as an interim job. It's tough work and it can be pretty boring—and it's not without its risks. This is not the kind of job that lends itself to five-year plans."

"Where do you see yourself five years from now? Not hauling mildewed furniture, lemme tell ya." Jesse snickered and finished his piece of pizza. "I dunno, to tell you the truth. I was doing construction before this. Industrial stuff, the big buildings, you know. Lots of concrete work, which meant late hours so we could get good conditions for setting."

He made a face, considered the remaining pizza, then opted to sip his beer instead. "I never had a life. Some of the guys didn't mind, but I wanted to hang out with friends, maybe date. And honestly, it was like watching paint dry."

"Or watching concrete dry?"

"Ha ha." He grinned. "I've thought about going back to trade school. Maybe for woodworking or electrical. I like making things with my hands rather than massive machines."

Elana nodded. "I can definitely understand that."

She let the conversation lull and ate most of another piece of pizza before venturing, "So…dating?"

The corner of his mouth turned up in a smile that

tickled her insides. "I haven't settled with anyone yet if that's what you're wondering."

Elana laughed. "You don't seem the type to two-time. I figured if you were taken, you would've told me."

"Hundred percent. I don't do secrets."

The feather duster tickle in her soul instantly soured, turning into an unpleasant mess of slimy tentacles. She kept the smile pasted on and hoped he wouldn't notice that it no longer reached her eyes.

"I don't like secrets either." The words were true, but they felt brittle. She *didn't* like secrets. Keeping this one was killing her. "I mean, within reason. Nobody needs to know about all the skeletons on date one."

Jesse's laugh eased the shame coiling in her gut. "Oh, definitely. That's a second-date activity at the earliest. You have to suss the person out first."

"Totally." Elana smiled. "And? How am I doing? Do I measure up?"

His answering smile felt like a warm blanket, and the quirk in his eyebrow sent a spark due south. "I've had a great time. I hope we can do this again. You?"

"Absolutely."

And next time, I'll get your opinion on vampires.

They exited the restaurant into a gorgeous summer evening. The sun was barely setting, casting a hazy orange hue over the city.

"There's a fantastic little ice cream shop near here,"

Jesse remarked. "Want to get a sundae and walk off the beer in the park before I drive you home?"

"I'd love that." Elana's sincerity surprised her.

They bought sundaes—hot fudge for Jesse, caramel for Elana—and strolled through the nearby park. It was nothing special, a green space with a few bike trails and the occasional bench, but the sunset turned the trees into fiery sentinels and cast long shadows across the ground.

Elana scraped caramel off the side of her cup and savored it. "I've really enjoyed tonight."

Jesse paused in digging out the last drops of ice cream from his cup to smile at her. "So have I. I'm glad you caught my eye on break. I think we really vibe."

"Agreed. It's nice to find someone you can talk to easily." She gestured for his empty cup, then tossed both into a trash can beside a bench. "Unfortunately, we should probably head back. I know for a fact we both have an early day tomorrow."

Jesse chuckled, but it was half a groan. "And here I hoped I might be able to bribe my boss to let me come in late...should have sprung for the extra caramel..."

Elana laughed. "I'd entertain the idea, but Jerry would *never* let us hear the end of it."

"Damn. Maybe I gotta buy *him* extra caramel."

"He's a strawberry man."

"Noted."

They walked back to the Camaro and drove off into the growing twilight. The entire way to her place, Elana debated asking him in. The chemistry was undeniable. She'd caught him looking at her with a smolder in his eyes as many times as she'd cleared her throat and pressed her legs together.

It didn't help that she was stressed out. A good roll in the hay would do wonders for her nerves, that was for damn sure.

However, Jesse didn't like secrets, and neither did she. Asking someone to be intimate with you *before* dropping the bombshell that you were a vampire and hadn't known it until the day before felt underhanded and downright nasty. If she wanted a chance with Jesse, that was not the way to go about it.

Her resolve was sorely tested when he pulled up to the curb outside her house because he turned and slid a hand onto her thigh. Not too far, certainly not inappropriately, but *definitely* suggestive—then he leaned in for the kiss and gave her the space to pull back.

She met him halfway.

The kiss was *good*. Not quite *electric*, but for a first kiss, it was one for the books. She got a hand up in his hair, his hand was creeping higher on her thigh, and her heart rate was rapidly climbing into "see you later, brain" territory.

Then her phone went off.

"Goddammit," she muttered as she pawed behind herself for her purse. "Shut up, I'm *busy*..."

Jesse chuckled against her cheek, and all she wanted was to drag him inside.

Elana's mood instantly died when she saw the icon on the notification. It was the Haven Security app, and the message started with, "Your presence is requested."

She heaved a sigh. "Fuck."

Jesse pulled back. He kept his hand on her leg, but his vibe shifted from sexy to concerned. "Everything okay?"

"Yeah, I just..." She waggled the phone. "This isn't a notification I can ignore, as much as I'd like to. Sorry."

He smiled sympathetically. "God, do I ever know that feeling. That's okay. I'll happily take a rain check, and I'll see you tomorrow."

"Thanks. I appreciate that."

Elana shoved her phone back in her purse and opened the door. She got one foot on the pavement when he called her name, and she turned back. "Yeah?"

Jesse's face was the picture of earnest honesty. "Whatever's up... Look, I know we basically just met, but I know what it's like to have shit go down and not have someone to talk to. If you ever need an ear or anything else, give me a call. I'll do what I can. Okay?"

Elana smiled, although her heart was as torn as it had been all evening. "Thanks, Jesse. Seriously. See you tomorrow."

He nodded. "Have a good night."

"You too."

She stepped back and closed the car door. He didn't drive away until she had her front door open.

Jesse was a good guy.

But it wasn't like vampires were *bad* guys...right?

CHAPTER NINE

The full text of the message read,

> **Your presence is requested in the consorts' training grounds tomorrow at 9:30 AM. A driver will meet you at your domicile at 8:00 AM.**

Elana sat on the edge of her bed and scratched her head. She could not fathom what this was about. A pickup time *an hour and a half earlier* than the appointment time? And what were the training grounds?

Still, for all it said "requested," the driver would be there. Didn't seem like she had much choice.

Elana sighed and texted Jerry.

> **Let the guys know I won't be on-site tomorrow, please and thanks. Being called in on more Haven business. Sorry Jer.**

She opened her browser and typed in her favorite gossip site for all things Haven, northcarolinavamps.com. It *sounded* kitschy, but the webmaster was serious about providing detailed and accurate information about the Haven community, and the forum moderation team was stellar.

Elana was midway through searching the attached Wiki for "training grounds" when Jerry's answering text scrolled in.

No problem, boss. We've got your back. Good luck in there.

She fired off a thank you, then went back to the website. Elana was puzzled that she hadn't heard of any training grounds in Haven before. Then again, she'd always been most interested in the lineage and politics of Haven, not so much its day-to-day workings.

The search produced a handful of results, the first of which was what she was looking for.

The consorts' training grounds was the umbrella term for the facilities the consorts and guardians used for training. Obvious in retrospect, although that confirmation did nothing to explain why Elana was being summoned *there.* The facilities included indoor and outdoor dojos, an Olympic-class swimming pool, a large green space, and an indoor firing range.

Maybe they wanted to test her latent vampiric abilities to see *how* strong and fast she was. Could that somehow be linked to their investigation into her lineage? Should she bring her vaccination records? Would they do a full physical?

Elana blew out a deep breath and consciously lowered her shoulders from around her ears. A new wave of nerves had replaced the warm and exciting feelings from her date with Jesse. She'd need to bring workout gear and a change of clothes—and a *nice* change of clothes, at that. There was no telling who she might meet at the training grounds.

The driver would pick her up in eleven hours. She was glad her date hadn't gone any later than it had and that she routinely got up before seven AM. Otherwise, she would have been scrambling to get ready.

Elana flopped back onto the bed and stared at the ceiling.

"Oh, ceiling fan, we're really in it now," she muttered.

Before she could entirely slip into rumination, her phone buzzed again. She groaned faintly and fumbled for it on the comforter. This would be about work or Haven, and she didn't want to deal with either topic.

It was neither. Instead, her heart leaped when she read the name "Vicky" on the notification.

HEY GIRL. I'm back in town! You up? Say you are! We HAVE to talk.

Elana giggled. She and Vicky had been best friends since high school, where Vicky had been the only girl in their grade who hadn't thought Elana was a freak for being good at everything. Vicky did great in English, contrary to her texting style, but she never got the hang of math. Elana had helped her study. In return, Vicky had single-handedly kept Elana in the social circles of Roanoke River High by sheer force of will.

After high school, Vicky went to UNC Chapel Hill for journalism and parlayed her charisma into a job as a travel blogger for Condé Nast. She'd been taking her afro and her insatiable appetite for kitschy accessories around the world since.

With Vicky jet-setting around the world and Elana quietly ensconced in Ashford, the two friends did more emailing and Skyping than they got to see each other in person. Vicky's family was still in Ashford, so every once in a while Elana got a text like this out of the blue.

She hadn't turned one down yet, and she wouldn't break that streak today.

It helped that she and Vicky had *both* been vampire-mad in high school. If she could tell anyone what was going on, it would be Vicky.

Elana texted back so fast her poor autocorrect struggled to keep up with her flying fingers.

Are you on the ground? Are you here? Tell me where. Late drinks? Coffee? Don't hold out on me!

Within seconds, the phone rang with a video call, and Vicky's round, mahogany face filled the screen. Today, a lemon yellow headband accented her chestnut brown afro, and matching shimmering eyeshadow made her deep brown eyes pop.

"*Elana!*" Vicky's grin nearly made Elana turn the brightness down on her phone. "Where are we going? What are we doing? I just touched down at the airport. Are you at home?"

"I don't know, I don't know that either. Did you call me before or after you got off the plane? And of course I am," Elana replied through laughter.

"Before, silly—as if I could wait!" Vicky's camera reversed to show the interior of an airplane. "I figured if I called you now, we could meet somewhere since you live in the ass-end of middle class white picket fence suburbia!"

Elana's face already hurt from smiling. "Meet at our usual place?"

"Sold. I'll taxi there. How are you, girl?"

"Oh, Vicky, have I got news for you..."

"*Spill*," Vicky insisted, complete with an emphatic palm on the table that made the patrons at the next table jump. "You're the *worst* for not telling me on the phone, I swear to God."

Elana nervously glanced around the bar. The Lilac and Juniper was on the higher end of the bars in Ashford, so it was considerably less raucous than most of the watering holes around town. While that meant Elana and Vicky rarely had to deal with obnoxiously drunk assholes hitting on them, which was why they'd made it their preferred hangout, it also meant less noise to disguise sensitive news.

Given that Vicky's entire outfit was the same lemon yellow as her headband and eyeshadow, she *kind of* stood out. Elana mildly regretted not asking Vicky to come over for coffee.

She sipped her drink. She'd gotten there a few minutes before Vicky, so she had ordered their usual—a gin and tonic for herself and a Manhattan for Vicky. As the tart bubbles of the tonic water burst over her tongue, she imagined the gin filling up an imaginary reserve of liquid courage.

"This is serious, Vick. Stays between us. Okay?"

Vicky's ebullient demeanor instantly sobered, and she wrapped a hand around her glass. "Understood, Lana. Sister code. No further than this table."

The use of their old high school nicknames sealed the figurative deal, and a tiny bit of the anxiety in Elana's gut released. She drew a deep breath and splayed her palms on the table to keep them from shaking.

"I'm a vampire." Elana pitched the words *just* loud enough for Vicky to hear.

Vicky blinked. She opened her mouth, then closed it. She narrowed her eyes at Elana, then looked her up and down. At length, she said, "You're serious."

"As the grave. And I figure I can make dumb jokes like that now, so."

Vicky took her Manhattan in both hands and sat back in her chair. "Ho-ly *fuck*," she murmured. "How the hell did that happen? I knew you were still into the scene, but I didn't know you were *that* far in. Don't you have to, like, bribe someone a bazillion dollars to get them to give you the Rights? Didn't think you could make that kind of money in hauling and electronics."

Her tone was light, but Elana knew Vicky wasn't mocking her. "You definitely can't," Elana teased. "Not unless you take the real sketchy contracts. No, I didn't pay someone. Actually…"

She traced the rim of her glass. "I've been a vampire since I was a kid."

Vicky's face slackened in shock, then hardened. "Wait a second. Is *that* why you were good at everything in school? You were a *vampire*?"

Elana awkwardly lifted one shoulder and glanced around the bar again. "Yes, but… I didn't know. I swear I wasn't keeping this from you. Honestly, Vicky, do you think I *could* have? Remember when we stayed up all night to see the bootleg footage of the Haven Gala in tenth grade? If I'd known I was a vampire, don't you think I would have *gotten us in?*"

The memory of the slumber party in question flickered over Vicky's countenance, and her frown eased to a nostalgic smile. "Oh, man. Those outfits were something *else*. Yeah, all right, fair point." She straightened and sipped her drink. "In that case, what the *actual* fuck?"

Elana groaned in recognition and sympathy and gave Vicky the rundown. When she'd finished, she clicked her glass on the tabletop and shook her head. "So that's where I'm at. I've been a vampire all my life and didn't know. As much as I miss my dad, I'm kind of glad he died before I found out. I think this would've killed him."

Vicky grimaced and put her hand on top of Elana's. "Probably. I'm sorry, hon. You've been on one hell of a rollercoaster the last few days."

"You're telling me." Elana looked up and met her friend's gaze. "You're not mad? Or scared?"

"Fuck, no." Vicky squeezed Elana's hand. "Are you

kidding? Yeah, okay, I'm a *little* freaked out that you didn't *know* because *what the hell*, but that's not your fault. Otherwise? I'm ecstatic! This is super cool! TBH, hon, I'm *jealous.*"

She winked, and Elana laughed. The tension dissipated, and Elana withdrew her hand to drink more of her gin and tonic.

"Thanks. I have to go back to Haven tomorrow morning to the consorts' training grounds. No idea why. They're not big on context."

Vicky chuckled. "We did always appreciate their carefully cultivated air of mystery."

"Well, now it's a pain in the ass." Elana drained her glass. "How long are you in town for?"

"Quick turnaround this time—helping my mom handle my aunt's estate—*but* I'll be back later this month for two weeks. Mama needs a vacation."

Elana snorted. "And you're taking it in *Ashford*? Not somewhere in the Caribbean? Are you secretly a masochist in addition to being a travel blogger?"

Vicky threw her head back and laughed. "God, no. I *was* going to vacation in Aruba, now you mention it, but I got word that my best friend in the entire fucking universe just found out she's a *vampire*. If there's one thing I know about vampires, that means she needs an entirely new wardrobe and then some…and what kind of best friend would I be if I didn't tag along?"

Tears prickled in Elana's eyes. Suddenly, she felt so much less alone. "Thanks, Vick."

"Any time, Lana. One thing, though."

"What?"

"You gotta get me into the next gala. Do you have any idea what Condé Nast would pay me for an exclusive travel digest on *Haven?*"

Elana chuckled. "I'll see what I can do. Let me tell you about Mr. Sexy Voice…"

Vicky's eyes lit up, and she flagged the waitress down for more drinks.

CHAPTER TEN

Elana was on the curb at 7:59 AM. She'd tied her hair back in a thick braid and wore a teal jumpsuit. The athleisure wear had been an impulse purchase the year before when she'd considered signing up for a gym membership. Not that she'd needed one to stay fit since the hauling job kept her in great shape, although in hindsight, it was more likely due to the vampire blood. Still, it had seemed like a good idea at the time.

Over her shoulder, she slung a gym bag with a more active outfit—shorts and an old T-shirt—and some hand and knee braces from her varsity days. She'd never gotten hurt on the field, but she played hard enough to make her coaches nervous. She'd bought the braces to pacify them.

Also in the duffel was a garment bag holding a tan pantsuit. That pantsuit had seen her through several job interviews and was the fanciest outfit she owned after the dress she'd bought from Zizi days before. It would have to do until she had an opportunity to update her wardrobe.

I'm moving to Haven, aren't I?

Elana twitched the thought away as a glossy black Lexus pulled up. The windows were tinted more heavily than Elana thought anyone but a vampire would get away with, and the engine purred.

The luxury SUV rolled to a stop beside Elana, and the doors unlocked with a quiet *clunk*. Elana opened the back door, swung her gym bag in, and sat beside it on the black leather seat.

Quiet classical music filtered through from the front seat, where a woman who looked approximately Elana's age sat in the driver's seat. Her hair was as black and glossy as the Lexus and was tucked into an elegant chignon below her chauffeur's cap. Her uniform was black too, with subtle charcoal gray piping along the seams. Her skin was a darker shade of tan, and her dark blue eyes met Elana's in the rearview mirror as Elana closed the door behind her.

"Good morning, Miss Bishop." Her accent was clear and crisp, and she spoke the king's English. "Are you prepared for your appointment?"

Elana patted her gym bag. "I think so, although I have no idea what I'm walking into. I did my research."

The woman accepted this answer with a nod, put the Lexus into gear, and drove away. Vampires weren't big on explaining things, it seemed.

The drive to Haven was uneventful. They sailed through the checkpoint without a hitch, this time entering through the Gate of Secrets instead of the King's Gate. This avenue straddled the divide between the Quarto and Senkyem districts, Senkyem being the neighborhood where the consorts' training grounds sat.

Elana admired the buildings on the Quarto side of the

street first. Quarto was the district dedicated to the written word. The King's Archives, a monolithic structure in the district's center that towered over the rest, dominated the cityscape. Every record of Haven's history rested within its vaulted halls. Apart from the archives, Quarto was full of libraries, bookstores, and schools. The University of Haven occupied nearly a quarter of the district. The neighborhood's architecture was distinctly Edwardian beneath Haven's traditional supernatural flair.

On Elana's left spread the classical Japanese-inspired vista of Senkyem. This district was dedicated to the outdoors and included ornamental gardens and parks in addition to the consorts' training grounds. When the chauffeur turned left and entered the district, Elana got a better look at the verdant flora that spilled from the planters along the sidewalks. Elana wouldn't have called herself a green thumb, but she was reasonably certain that some of the flowers in the arrangements were *unearthly*. No natural plant ought to *glitter.*

Their journey ended when they passed under the huge forest green arch that signified the entrance to the training grounds. All guardians wore the same forest green, apart from those under the Arbiter of Shadows' command, who wore black. This indicated the training grounds were not for public use…yet Elana was here.

The chauffeur stopped outside a low building with floor-to-ceiling glass walls. *What a pain to clean,* Elana briefly thought, before realizing vampire technology probably meant they never *had* to be cleaned.

"The receptionist will direct you," the chauffeur informed Elana. The locks *clicked* open.

"Thanks." Elana waited for any acknowledgment. When none came, she awkwardly opened the door, shouldered her gym bag, and left the car.

A few short steps took her to the sliding glass door. As she crossed the threshold, the sudden conviction seized Elana that she should have bought designer sneakers for the occasion. Surely, arriving at the consorts' training grounds in anything but Nikes or Air Jordans costing at *least* several hundred dollars would be grounds for ejection.

She forced herself to draw a deep breath and let it out before approaching the young man at the desk. Everyone she'd seen in Haven so far appeared idealistically youthful. Where were the old people? Or even middle-aged? Elana knew that seriously extended lifespans came with vampires' advanced technology. Still, she'd never considered how *eerie* it would be to exist in a world where everyone stayed young and beautiful forever.

The young man—smooth dark skin, shaved head, full lips—raised politely questioning eyebrows as she approached. They were perfectly plucked. "Welcome to the consorts' training grounds. My name is Abeo. May I help you?"

Elana smiled and hoped her nerves weren't visible. "Nice to meet you, Abeo. I'm Elana Bishop. I was told to be here for 9:30 AM, but I wasn't told more than that."

Abeo glanced down at a pane of glass on his desk. Elana had initially taken it to be a picture frame or document holder, but now that she was closer, she realized it was a *computer*. Through the glass, she saw a small analog clock in the corner and a scattering of application windows.

Everything inside the windows was blurred from her perspective. It looked like something straight out of a sci-fi movie.

"Ah, yes, here you are." Abeo's voice and accent reminded her of a Caribbean beach. "The consort will be with you shortly in Training Room A. You're welcome to warm up however you like. This is your first time at the grounds, yes?"

"Sure is." Elana barely managed to get the words out. *The* consort? Was Valeria coming back *again*? Why did she like Elana so much? Was this part of the investigation?

Abeo beamed at her with pride. "Then please avail yourself of everything we have to offer. We boast the *best* equipment and facilities in the world. Explore and enjoy, Miss Bishop."

"I will. Thank you. Which way…"

He laughed, although not unpleasantly, and indicated down the glass-windowed hall. "You will see the signs."

"Thanks again."

"My pleasure."

Excitement grew as Elana strolled down the corridor. Sure, she was nervous and had no idea what she was in for, but that didn't mean she couldn't enjoy the luxuries and opportunities while she had access to them. As long as they didn't spring a bill on her at the end, she might as well take advantage of what Haven offered.

Training Room A turned out to be more like Training *Building* A. The room was the size of at least two gymnasiums. Climbing ropes and cables attached to nets hung along every wall, attached to frameworks in the ceiling that Elana guessed could fold out into obstacle courses. The walls were otherwise devoid of equipment, but there were two sets of heavy double doors at the other end of the room, which she presumed led to storage rooms.

The floor was polished and stained hardwood. Elana made out several lines she recognized—including basketball, and the thought of vampires playing basketball amused her to no end—but more that she didn't. Perhaps they were games from other countries, or maybe vampires had their own team sports they didn't share with humans? Perhaps she was about to find out.

A single, normal-sized wooden door stood on either side of the large double doors. The honey-colored wood glowed in the light streaming down from the row of windows around the ceiling. Each pane would be made of UV-filtered glass to ensure the health of any low-level vampires training in this gym, although Elana doubted many vampires below guardian ever set foot here.

The first of the smaller doors was marked as a dressing and shower room, with no indication of gender. Elana tilted her head and crossed to the other door. Its placard was identical. Maybe vampires didn't care about seeing each other in the nude? Their technology was advanced, so maybe their sensibilities were too. She shrugged and pushed open the door.

The room beyond was closer in style to a spa than your standard high school locker room. Elana spied a sauna in the corner beside a curtain that led to shower stalls. The rest of the room was lined with wooden niches with hooks, obviously meant for leaving your belongings behind while you trained. The floor was smooth, pebbled stone.

Elana changed into her workout gear, left her bag in an

alcove, and returned to the gym. The digital clock on the wall read 9:15 AM, so instead of snooping through the equipment rooms, she opted to do a full physical stretch and warmup.

She had finished stretching and was running a loop around the gym when the entrance doors swung open, and Valeria Draven walked in at 9:30 on the nose.

Valeria wore white even in the gym. Today, she had on a tennis skirt and matching T-shirt, and her sneakers were equally snow-white. Her hair was snug underneath a white bandana. Somehow, Elana was certain that each item of clothing cost a week's wages for any of her crew…even the bandana.

Elana jogged to a stop and did a half-bow, unsure of the protocol when meeting an arbiter in a gym. "Arbiter Draven."

"Miss Bishop. I am glad you came prepared."

"Heh. I'm glad I thought to look up the training grounds, and I'm glad my guess was right. The message didn't say much. What are we doing?"

Valeria rolled her shoulders once and sank into a fighting stance. "You will train with me. We will spar. Do you know any martial arts?"

Elana started, then regrouped and mirrored Valeria's stance. "Uh—not really. I was more of a track and field girl. I tried tae kwon do one year when I was in middle school, but I didn't like the teacher much. Are we seriously going to—"

Valeria moved like water and lightning combined, and before Elana could say another word, she hit the floor with an *oof*.

"Up," Valeria ordered. "Try again."

Elana scrambled to her feet, backed up a step, and narrowed her eyes. "Oh, so we're doing this *Karate Kid* style, hey? Jesus, you could *warn* a girl before—"

Valeria darted forward again, but Elana caught the movement this time and pivoted. It wasn't a pretty dodge, but it meant she didn't have the wind knocked out of her by polished wood. She'd take it.

The arbiter's lips quirked in a tiny smile. "*Good.* You are already learning."

"Learning *what?*" Elana scowled. She immediately erased the expression, certain that showing displeasure with a consort was the kind of thing that would get you killed instead of thrown on your back, but Valeria chuckled.

"What it means to be a vampire," Valeria explained. "Whether you choose to join us or not, it would be irresponsible of us as a people not to train your abilities. You are more dangerous if you do *not* know yourself than if you do."

"I suppose it also means you know what I'm capable of if I go rogue."

Far from the suspicion she expected to see on the consort's face, Valeria smiled. "Precisely. Let us begin."

"You mean we hadn't already—*oof.*"

Hours passed, each flowing into the next. Valeria was a strict but efficient teacher, and Elana was a fast learner. The martial arts-based warmups introduced Elana to ways of movement she'd never tried. While she didn't manage to pin or flip the arbiter, she landed several touches.

After the hand-to-hand came tests of endurance and

strength. An attendant arrived to help arrange the structures hanging from the ceiling and walls, and soon Elana was climbing and swinging through ropes and nets like a monkey. These exercises were familiar enough, although Elana had to use muscles in mildly unfamiliar ways.

Between climbing the course like a jungle gym from hell and Valeria's insistence that she do the loop faster each time, Elana had no doubt she'd be sore as anything the day after. Hauling junk had nothing on vampire training.

By the time another attendant arrived and called Valeria aside, Elana had broken a sweat for the first time in as long as she could remember, and the exercise high had hit her full blast. She dropped to the planked floor at Valeria's beckoning and jogged over.

"I must attend to other business," the consort informed Elana. "I apologize that I must cut our session short."

Elana's gaze flicked to the wall clock. It was after 1:00 PM. This was *short*?

She only nodded. "Of course. The king's business can't wait. I understand that."

Valeria smiled again. Over the past few hours, she had warmed up considerably—although perhaps it would be more correct to say that her attitude toward Elana had shifted from reserved professionalism to impressed respect.

Elana had noticed when Valeria's demeanor changed from patient teacher to pleased mentor. It had been when Elana landed her first touch in the warmups, and from that point on, Elana's joy and excitement had rapidly eclipsed her wariness and fear.

Being a vampire was *fun*.

Valeria continued, "However, I will leave you in Gustav's capable hands." She indicated the man who had come to find her. He was about an inch taller than Elana, had muscles that strained the confines of his shirtsleeves, and a jawline that could cut bricks. "You will finish the training I had set out for today. Then you may return home. He will update me on your progress."

The bulky man regarded Elana with a curious eye. Elana got the feeling he wasn't sure what to make of Elana or why a consort was spending time with a nobody. Truth be told, she still didn't get it either, but she'd firmly decided she wasn't complaining anymore.

Elana smacked a fist into her palm. "Great. Let's do this, Gustav. I'm ready."

CHAPTER ELEVEN

Elana arrived home late in the afternoon, dropped off by a different chauffeur in a different luxury car. On one shoulder, she carried the gym bag. On the other was a slim messenger bag bearing the Haven crest—the wheel-and-spoke plan of the city with a simplified version of the SpiderKing's sigil in the center hub, marking the Citadel.

Within the bag was a manila envelope with the legal contract outlining the reparations she would receive...if she signed it.

The number had a couple more zeroes now.

Matt Richelieu had met her at the end of her training session with Gustav to give her the envelope and satchel. He'd apologized that he couldn't spare the time to walk her through it right then but offered to take her for brunch the day after as a business meeting and a rain check for their last planned brunch.

Elana had accepted. Having someone knowledgeable about Haven's intricacies from the other side of the wall could only be beneficial. Besides, she wasn't turning down an opportunity to listen to Mr. Sexy Voice over pancakes.

She'd opened the envelope on the ride home and clapped her hand over her mouth to avoid making terribly uncouth noises.

Four million dollars.

The SpiderKing was offering her four million dollars and a chance to take up residence in Haven. The four million was *not* contingent on her relocation. She'd get the money either way.

In exchange, Elana would agree to cooperate fully with Valeria Draven's investigation. This included regular training sessions until the investigation was complete and required Elana to make herself available for any other engagements as requested by the arbiter. Once the investigation was finished, Elana would be released from the obligation and could do as she pleased.

Elana would also receive the investigation's full results if she consented to sign a strict non-disclosure agreement, which could be amended at the close of the investigation at the SpiderKing's pleasure. If Elana did not sign the NDA, she would receive only what information the SpiderKing deemed permissible to make its way into the public sphere.

In other words, not much.

But also, *four million dollars.*

Elana sank onto her living room couch and let her gaze wander over the house. She'd lived in this bungalow with her dad her entire life. Jeremiah had moved here with his infant daughter after Elana's mother, his wife Tessa, had died when Elana was born.

Tessa Bishop had been diagnosed with pre-eclampsia at

thirty-two weeks. With Elana being their first and only child, Jeremiah and Tessa had sought the best care for Tessa they could, and they'd followed the treatment plan exactly. The doctors had said all would be well, and Tessa's and baby's chances were good.

Delivery had been long and strenuous but ultimately successful.

Then the eclampsia had set in. Seizure after seizure, and eventually the doctors could do no more. Tessa Bishop died with her husband at her side and her newborn daughter in the bassinet two feet away.

Jeremiah had sold their two-bedroom split level three weeks later. He hadn't been able to stomach the sight of the nursery Tessa had painted sky blue—her favorite color.

Then he'd built a life in the sleepy suburbs of Ashford... and three decades and change later, he'd joined his wife in whatever lay beyond.

Now Elana had the option of making more money with one signature than her father had in his life and leaving it all behind. The IRS couldn't touch it. Reparations from the SpiderKing's coffers could not be taxed as income.

With four million dollars, Elana could do whatever she wanted. She could sell the business to Jerry and travel the world or move into Haven and discover what it truly meant to be a vampire. If she signed the NDA, she would learn *how* she'd become a vampire, but she couldn't tell anyone else. It would mean if she didn't want to live a double life, she would *have* to sell the business. She respected Jerry and her crew too much to mislead them.

Her gaze caught on the old rabbit-ear antennae perched on the flatscreen TV. They were useless, a tchotchke, but an endearing and enduring example of her father's passions. Jeremiah Bishop had liked figuring things out and had wanted to remember and respect the past.

He had *not*, however, liked vampires.

Elana's father had never approved of her fascination with vampires and Haven. In his opinion, vampires were holding out on the rest of the world, keeping back technology that could make the world a better place. Technology that could save lives.

Technology that could have saved Tessa.

Elana had never argued the point. Vampires weren't *magic*, just…more evolved, maybe. Their advanced technology allowed them to do things regular humans couldn't, and if there was one thing Elana knew about regular humans, it was that power went to their heads. She didn't blame the vampires for not trusting the rest of the world.

She *did* wonder, once in a while, what might have happened if a vampire doctor had been present when her mother had been in labor, but it wasn't worth dwelling on.

Elana was roused from her rumination by her phone buzzing. It was a text from Jesse.

Got a hankering for Chinese. You in?

Elana tapped her phone on her thigh three times before typing.

Where and when?

A simple date was exactly what she needed right now.

It turned out that Jesse knew his Chinese restaurants as well as Elana knew her Italian ones. The *xiao long bao* were salty and savory, the *cong you bing* were crisp and chewy, and the chow mein complemented the entrées perfectly.

"What a great place," Elana commented between bites of scallion pancake. "It's so out of the way, though. Who put you onto it?"

Jesse chuckled. "I confess, I dated a girl who loved this place. We didn't click, but she told me the secret to finding great multicultural food is to find the places where immigrants eat. If a Chinese place is full of Chinese folks, chances are the food's good."

Elana raised an eyebrow and glanced around the modest restaurant. The smell of hot oil and garlic wafted in from the kitchen, and the sounds of Cantonese mixed with the grill's sizzle and the hiss of steam, but few of the tables were occupied. "It's *deserted* in here."

"Don't try to get a table at lunch."

"I'll take your word for it."

Jesse's amused smile turned to a light smirk. "Then there's the vampires."

Elana's other eyebrow joined her first. "What do you mean?"

He waved his chopsticks. "Oh, nothing really. I happen to know this restaurant gets *regular* orders from beyond the wall. Must be good if the vamps will spend money on it."

Elana slurped a mouthful of noodles to let the uncomfortable moment pass. It was a widely held stereotype that all vampires were stuck-up snobs with more money than sense—a society of "trust fund kids" who never had to work for anything and who only wanted the best. She supposed she could see the logic that if vampires ordered from a particular restaurant, the food must be high quality.

Still...Jesse's tone hadn't been particularly flattering. Had that truly been an offhand comment, or had it hinted at his real opinion on vampires?

Maybe it was a good thing she hadn't told him yet.

Elana firmly set the train of thought aside and picked up another dumpling.

Matt sent another car for her the next morning. This time, it was a sleek, navy Audi S3. A beautiful car and still well outside of Elana's pay grade, but not quite the giant waving red flag of wealth that the Lexus had been.

However, this cemented her suspicion that her F150 was not welcome beyond the wall. No one had explicitly *told* her this, but they hadn't offered any arrangements for parking nor a pass to hang off her rearview mirror, although vampires probably used something more high-tech than a slip of vinyl. While she *could* argue that they were being nice, it felt more like a tacit condemnation of her human ways than anything else.

Today's chauffeur brought her to a restaurant in Shestoi, the sixth district of Haven. Shestoi was the city's culinary heartbeat and food production district, a foodie's dream destination. Haven fed its population without outside assistance despite its meager size, again using technology unknown to the rest of humankind, thanks to the gardens of Senkyem and the greenhouses of Shestoi.

The brunch spot was Mediterranean-themed, vaguely Greek-slash-Italian. The waiter brought them tall glasses of water and menus and left them to it.

"I highly recommend the spinach crepes," Matt immediately offered. "If you like spinach at *all*, I cannot recommend them enough."

"I do like spinach." Elana cast an eye over the rest of the menu. It all looked good. The spinach crepes were as good a choice as any and would probably be a nice, light change from the oily Chinese of the night before.

"It's settled, then. When Steven comes back, we'll get two orders. Are you a coffee person?"

"Always and forever."

"Excellent. I had a feeling I'd picked the right spot."

Matt's smile was warm in a way Jesse's wasn't. Where Jesse was snarky, Matt was clever. Jesse was fun to joke with, whereas Matt was earnest. At another time in her life, when she wasn't struggling with existential angst, Elana might have gravitated to Jesse's combination of biting wit and honest compassion.

Right now, Matt's serenity and stability were much more enticing.

Also, she hadn't realized it until now, but they looked a *lot* alike. Maybe Elana had more of a type than she'd given herself credit.

Matt tapped the two menus into a neat pile and set them aside. "Did you have a chance to look over the contract?"

Elana's hand drifted to the messenger bag hanging off

her chair. "I did. It's... Well, *generous* is putting it extremely mildly."

Matt's beaming smile softened. "I know it's a lot."

"Can you tell me *why* it's so high?" She glanced around, then lowered her voice despite the fact that no one else was around. Vampires had enhanced hearing too. She'd always been able to hear conversations clearly from two rooms over. "Is this, like, hush money from the Runner's family?"

Matt chuckled. "Nothing like that. That chapter of the story is over and done. No, the four million is reparations for a life you ought to have had the chance to live. It's difficult to put a monetary value on years lived, but...well, I believe the going rate to raise a child to the age of eighteen is a quarter of a million dollars, and you're past that by several years."

"That still wouldn't put me at *four million*."

He acknowledged with a small gesture. "No. I'm afraid I can't disclose the specific reasons why the amount is so high, but I can assure you the document is legitimate. Did you have any questions about it?"

Elana rested her hand on the bag. "The money's mine whether or not I come live in Haven?"

"Yes."

"The IRS can't claw any of it back?"

"No. It's reparations, not income, and it comes from a monarch. We have special taxation treaties. If you were to invest any of it, you could be taxed on the interest but not the principal."

"All I have to do is cooperate?"

"Yes."

"Is there a backing-out clause? If Arbiter Draven asks me to do something I'm not comfortable with?"

Matt raised an eyebrow. "Is there anything you'd be so uncomfortable with that couldn't be mitigated by four million dollars?"

Elana blinked. "Well…there's probably *something*. I don't want to kill anyone."

"Okay. I'll make sure Arbiter Draven knows that."

"You're not serious."

"I am perfectly serious. Is there anything else?"

Elana felt like she was standing on the edge of a cliff rather than sitting at a patio table waiting for spinach crepes and coffee. She could turn back and walk away with her four million, keep her humanity as intact as possible, and try to live a normal life…

Or she could take the plunge.

She retrieved the manila envelope from the messenger bag, removed the contract, grabbed a pen from her purse, and signed on the dotted line.

Elana gawked at the ATM screen. She had never seen a seven-figure balance in her *life*, but there it was in black and white.

She withdrew five hundred dollars and decided to treat herself to the fanciest steakhouse in Ashford that accepted walk-ins. It had a rooftop patio, and the sunset was gorgeous, so she ordered her filet mignon and Malbec *en plein air* and sat on a dais that let her overlook the entirety of the city.

The monolith of Haven's wall loomed in the distance. Silhouetted by the dying light, Elana picked out the shapes of the Citadel and some of the better-known skyscrapers that jutted above the wall's expanse. She'd never been so naïve to think that she'd known everything about Haven. Still, she'd known enough to understand that the mysteries and power went far beyond what any tabloid forum or conspiracy site could fathom.

Now, she was a part of it. She'd been inside the city three times in as many days, and soon the number of visits would be too many to count. The beauty and possibility that lay inside those walls were hers for the taking if she was ready to accept the consequences of that choice—and it *was* a choice. The denizens of Haven were allowing her to feel her way through this previously unknown part of her life, and they were facilitating it for her, but it was ultimately her decision.

She'd taken the money. She'd consented to the investigation. She would dip her toes in the waters of vampirism.

The strains of the lounge pianist inside drifted through the open doorway. On the horizon, dark clouds billowed and Elana caught a flash of lightning. There would be a summer storm tonight, but Elana had time to eat her steak and drink her wine on this beautiful night.

CHAPTER TWELVE

The next summons to Haven came Saturday afternoon while Elana was folding laundry. The Arbiter of Shadows requested her presence at her offices in the Citadel of Accord the next morning at ten AM. A car would pick her up. No further information was provided.

Because that's not terrifying at all. At least the invitation to the training grounds came with a touch more data. What the hell do I wear?

She cast her gaze over the new clothing laid out on the couch beside her. She'd taken the day off Friday to go on a shopping spree after stopping by the salon to pick Molly's brain on her fashion recommendations. Elana now possessed a wardrobe much more appropriate to Haven's sensibilities, which made her feel as though she'd walked off a *Suits* set.

At least Havenites didn't dress like gothic vampires. Elana wasn't sure she could have bought neo-Victorian dresses—or whatever the appropriate aesthetic was called

—without resorting to the Internet, and the shipping would have been hell. Also, she didn't like lace.

She selected a black pencil skirt, a sky blue sleeveless blouse with a high collar, and a set of modest sterling silver chandelier earrings. Low black pumps completed the look.

Elana did a few rounds around the house in the pumps before bed. She was gaining confidence in heels but still needed practice.

She laid in bed and stared at the ceiling for a good long while before falling asleep. This summons unnerved her the most yet. It hadn't come from Matt but from the arbiter's office, and it made no mention of what the meeting was about. Was being cryptic a requirement for vampirism? Would Elana grow more enigmatic and hush-hush if she moved to Haven?

Elana determinedly rolled over and squished her head beneath her pillow. Dwelling on it did no good, but that didn't stop her brain from spinning around its hamster wheel.

The car that arrived to pick Elana up the next morning was the fanciest yet. The silver Mercedes bore the consort's emblem on the door—a solid black circle with the Spider-King's simplified sigil in the center in white. The door swung open at her approach, and she stepped into the black leather interior with the reverence of a young child entering a space that was Adults Only.

Today's driver was a man who looked considerably

older than most Havenites Elana had encountered. The hair peeking out from under his chauffeur's cap was silver, and he had crow's feet at the corners of his eyes, which were the pale blue of a hot, hazy summer day. When he greeted her, his voice had a subtle hint of Southern twang. Elana would have pegged him for a gentleman born a little farther south of Ashford and brought up in genteel company. The type of man who might have his daughters come out as debutantes.

He was no more forthcoming than any of the other drivers, unfortunately, and Elana arrived at the Citadel no wiser about the purpose of her visit than when she left home.

They took another route through the wall, entering through the Gate of Balance. This allowed Elana to see Haven's second and third districts for the first time. Thani, on her right, was one of two districts devoted entirely to residential buildings. Zevenda, the seventh district, was the other.

Thani's neighborhoods were arranged in small cul-de-sacs of townhouses and single-person dwellings. The architecture was eclectic in the extreme, unlike the carefully ordered themes of the other districts. Any vampire wealthy or powerful enough to own a house in Thani had free rein to build whatever they wanted, pending the SpiderKing's approval, but the rumor was that he had never refused a permit.

The result was not visual cacophony or chaos, as one might expect, but the strongest evidence Elana had yet seen of vampires' advanced sensibilities. Somehow, the chaos was enchantingly beautiful.

On the other side of the street, Etreta's high rises soared. The third district was the hub of business and industry in Haven and was organized with office buildings around the exterior of the wheel segment and factories hidden inside and underground. Haven did *not* stand for noise pollution.

Etreta had more pedestrian traffic than any district Elana had yet seen, with the possible exception of Senkyem. Etreta's passersby walked quickly and with purpose, unlike those in Senkyem, who strolled and stopped to enjoy the flowers.

The drive to the city's center passed more quickly than Elana would have liked. The wall of the Citadel loomed, and before she knew it, the taciturn driver had drifted to a stop outside one of the footpath entrances to the Neutral Zone.

"You know your way to the offices?" he asked.

"I do."

With a silent nod and the push of a button, he opened her door.

The Citadel was rarely deserted, and today was no exception. Elana spotted a dozen others scattered around the interior courtyard, all well-dressed and on their way to somewhere or other. One woman stood near the central memorial with her hands clasped behind her back. She wore a dark purple gown that swept the ground and trailed behind her by several inches, and her black hair was piled on top of her head in an artful disaster of a beehive.

Elana gave the woman a wide berth on her way to the consulate. She had no idea who this woman was but had no doubt she was a force to be reckoned with. She was quickly learning that her years of devouring forums and books had only scratched the surface of Haven's depths.

The consulate's doors were unlocked and swung open at her touch despite their towering size and impressive thickness. Elana's heels clacked on the marble floor, and she deliberately avoided stepping on the SpiderKing's sigil out of respect on her way to the staircase marked with the new moon. She was certain she was being superstitious but now did not seem like the time to unwittingly invite bad luck.

The trip up the long staircase felt less onerous than last time. Placebo effect, perhaps, or had she made progress in her day-long training with Valeria and Gustav? Regardless of the cause, Elana was relieved to reach the consort's door without being out of breath or having a stitch in her calf.

Her elation transmuted to anxiety when the door opened before she could knock and Valeria stepped out. Valeria wasn't wearing black—she had on a knee-length wrap dress in a white so blinding Elana could hardly look at it—but her eyes were dark.

Elana stepped back and bowed. "Arbiter Draven. I'm so sorry—am I late?"

"No. You are precisely on time. Come with me."

The terse sentence did little to soothe Elana's nerves, but she followed the silver-haired woman through the corridors in silence because the alternative was unthinkable.

Valeria unlocked a door into a sky bridge that led from the Citadel to the King's Archives in Quarto. They walked dozens of feet in the air with no architectural supports that

Elana could see, suspended in a transparent hallway that stretched across the open space with little care for the laws of physics.

The arbiter unlocked the door at the other end and led Elana into a small, circular room that appeared to serve as a portrait gallery and a museum showroom. The ceiling was far above them, and disk-shaped platforms hovered a couple of inches above the floor in a ring around the room. Elana assumed they would transport someone higher to view the paintings and artifacts collected in the niches that covered the walls.

The consort pointed at one of the disks. "Step on."

Elana obeyed. The platform rose smoothly when the consort joined her, confirming her suspicions. The disk did not wobble or shift under their weight. It felt like they were standing on a perfectly stable piece of the floor.

On the way up, Elana spotted artifacts from all over the world. The statues and frescoes depicting vampires in all their guises throughout history were easy to recognize. Many of the objects were foreign to her, and she had no idea what they did or how they were supposed to be used. Some looked futuristic, as though they were from eras beyond current history—which was nonsense, naturally.

The ascent came to a gradual stop two-thirds of the way up the room in front of a portrait. The woman in the picture had long, wavy brown hair and dark eyes. She wore a V-neck blouse in a deep red that highlighted her prominent collarbones, and her hands folded in her lap boasted many elegant rings.

Elana was uncertain why Valeria had brought her to

this portrait. The woman was beautiful, certainly, but what was she supposed to learn?

Her gaze caught on the plaque beneath the frame.

Tessa Hart. Consort of External Affairs and Diplomacy. 1967-2020.

Elana frowned. She looked between the plaque and the portrait several times. Finally, she had to ask.

"Is this a joke?"

The arbiter delicately raised an eyebrow. "Am I the joking sort, Miss Bishop?"

Elana had to admit that no, Valeria Draven was *not* the joking sort. Still...

"My mother didn't have a twin."

"That is correct."

"She died in 1992."

"She did not."

The matter-of-fact tone made Elana's knees threaten to buckle. She stayed upright through sheer force of will. She did not want to test whether the floating platform had invisible safety rails.

"My mother was a vampire."

"And a very powerful one, at that."

Elana swallowed hard. Her head felt like a helium balloon, and she could not look away from her mother's painted eyes.

"You bear a striking resemblance to her," Valeria stated.

"Dad always said I got her looks. I've seen pictures, but...nothing like this. This *is* a painting, right?"

The arbiter chuckled under her breath. "Even vampires cannot capture souls in images. Yes, it is a painting. A very good one, done by artists in the king's employ—artists who have studied portrait craft for generations."

Elana nodded. Her gaze drifted to the plaque below the painting, and she mouthed the words silently before saying, "She only died a couple of years ago."

"Yes."

Elana's throat caught the first time she tried to ask, but she managed it the second. "Can you tell me how?"

"An inter-House war."

The vitriol in Valeria's tone was strong and sudden. Elana quickly looked up and caught the tail end of a scowl marring the arbiter's porcelain face, so she tamped down her desperate want to know more about her mother's death. The morbid curiosity could wait. The rest of the curiosity could not.

Elana resisted the urge to scuff the toe of her black pump on the floating platform. "So...how did you find out? DNA test?"

"It was child's play to determine you were Tessa's daughter. That wasn't in question."

"Well, sure. Her name's on my birth certificate. But I didn't know she was a vampire when I was born. I don't know if my dad did, either."

"We did not know she had a daughter."

Elana's puzzled frown deepened. "Okay, I'm seriously confused now. Can we...can we walk back the timeline? I feel like I'm missing a *lot*." She met her mother's brush-stroked eyes again and added, "And could we do it on the ground? This is awkward."

"Very well."

Valeria clicked her heel on the platform, and it sank to

the floor. Elana examined several portraits in greater detail while they descended and some of the artifacts. When she'd first walked in, she'd longed to learn everything she could about everything in the room, but this new revelation…now, she *needed* to know.

By the time the platform reached the ground, Elana's shock had transformed into drive. The conviction she'd had all her life that she belonged in Haven was *true.* Her mother had *been* a vampire. *Elana* was a vampire.

Elana had been *right.*

She needed to know *everything.*

Valeria stepped off the platform and crossed to a low bench in an alcove. She sat, and Elana joined her.

"Your mother did not die after you were born." The arbiter opened the conversation with the same sensible, straightforward tone she'd used when she'd killed the Runner. The lack of distinction was not lost on Elana.

"She was very close to death. She received the Rights while in intensive care, and in the process of turning, was declared dead by the human medical authorities. She was brought to Haven, where she convalesced. Her turning was not easy."

"So she couldn't have come back." Elana had to force the words around the growing lump in her throat. "Dad thought she was dead. The entire human world thought she was dead."

"Quite so."

"Then how did I become a vampire if she became a vampire after I was born? Did the same vampire turn me?"

"No. You would not have survived. You bear her mark, not his. She turned you."

Elana's eyebrows drew together. "I never saw her."

"Our investigation is incomplete."

Elana sighed and cast her gaze up the wall toward where her mother's portrait hung far above. "She made an impressive life for herself here. I saw on the plaque that she was a consort. I didn't recognize her domain, though. Consorts' domains are usually a little less…verbose."

Valeria lifted a pale hand with perfect crescent-moon nails. "She was not one of the Eight to begin with. She was another type of consort—a concubine of the SpiderKing."

"A—A *concubine?*" Elana stuttered in surprise. *"What?"*

Valeria *tsked*. "Not as you think. Humans and your shallow sensibilities. We arbiters manage the king's affairs in large areas. My domain is Shadows, Arbiter Tarsin's is Knowledge, and so on. We wield great power at the cost of great responsibility. We may act without the king's immediate consent because he trusts our judgment."

Elana knew this but opted to keep quiet. Interrupting the Arbiter of Shadows was universally regarded as a bad idea, even among people who knew little about vampires. She was curious about concubines, however. How had she not heard about them before?

Valeria continued, "The king's concubines also manage the king's business in vital arenas, but under direct supervision—normally one of us, but occasionally His Majesty on matters of great importance."

"Who did my mother work for?"

"Your mother did a great deal of work for all of us. Her abilities and history meant she acted as an intermediary between humans and vampires in multiple fields."

Elana inhaled sharply. "External affairs… External

means *human*? I thought diplomacy would refer to politics between the Great Houses or the cities."

Valeria gestured assent. "She did that as well, but her true talent lay in human-vampire relations. Her skills made her a very powerful person in a very short time. She made many enemies, but she also accomplished a great deal for the SpiderKing. So much that, in time, she became the Arbiter of Sanctuary."

The Arbiter of Shadows shifted minutely on the bench and once again pinned Elana with her icy eyes. "In vampire politics, everything is power. It is our only currency of choice. When you live as long as we do, wealth is almost a given…unless you are stupid.

"Your mother was not stupid. She was *very* smart and extremely capable. She played the great game as though she had been on the board for centuries, not mere years. Her blood runs in your veins."

A shiver ran down Elana's back, and goosebumps rose on her arms. "Does that mean…"

"It means many things." Valeria's gaze flicked away, but she did not move. "Your mother opened the door for you, but it is your choice whether to step through. Should you choose to involve yourself, many possibilities await you… including the fate that befell your mother before her time. Vampires are at their worst in inter-House wars, yet it is the best system to keep the stupid—and *not* so stupid—vampires in line."

The goosebumps prickled. Elana wanted to smooth her hands over them but didn't dare. "How do you join a House?"

Valeria laid her hand on her knee. "You have much to

learn before that point. We will go to the training grounds now. I wish to have you measured for a sword."

The conversational whiplash was not enough to tamp down Elana's instant, giddy desire for a *sword*. "Like…a fencing épée?"

Valeria arched an eyebrow. "No, a *sword*. Are you a vampire, or are you an *aristocrat?*"

CHAPTER THIRTEEN

Elana left work on Monday with a spring in her step. She'd be back in Haven the following day to work on her sword technique and martial arts training with Valeria, which was exciting enough. In the meantime, she was meeting Jesse for dinner that night.

She stripped off her work clothes and tossed them into the hamper the minute she got home. Today had been a scorcher, and she and her crew had been out in the heat the whole time. She was covered in grime and sweat and fairly had to *scrape* it off in the shower.

Elana emerged from the bathroom refreshed and smelling of the spiced floral perfume she'd found on the weekend's shopping adventure. The subtle scent put her in mind of exotic locales with plush rugs, desert vistas, and flowers that bloomed once a year. It seemed fitting for her new life *and* for tonight's restaurant selection. She and Jesse were branching out and trying Moroccan on for size.

The restaurant was a few steps up the decorum ladder from their usual fare, so they'd opted to dress up a bit.

Elana felt mismatched in her huge truck, dressed in a cream-colored blouse, black slacks, and strappy black flats. Every day she considered buying a second car, something like a sedan or a coupe. Maybe that would be this weekend's purchase.

The only reason she hadn't bought one yet was her father's voice in the back of her head, warning her not to change for the rest of the world and to be true to herself. Elana had been proud of her tomboy qualities and her comfortable status as "one of the guys" who drove big pickup trucks and hoisted bundles of lumber like they were handbags.

Did buying a smaller car mean she was abandoning that, or was it a matter of convenience? The F150 *was* a gas guzzler, and it was a pain in the ass to park...

It was also distinctly *not* a vampire's vehicle of choice, and Elana *was* a vampire.

She shoved the gearshift into Park and huffed as she turned off the engine. Dwelling on this right before a date was not a good plan. She was here to have a good time with Jesse and take her mind off the constant tug-of-war her life had become.

Elana smiled politely at the *maître d'* and told him she was meeting Jesse. The slim, dark-skinned man smiled back and indicated a table in the back of the beautifully appointed dining room, framed by a gorgeous scrollwork arch.

She passed the kitchen doors on her way to the table, and the aroma of too many spices to distinguish made her mouth water. She waved at Jesse, who smiled, waved, and stood to pull her chair out.

"Why, thank you," Elana good-naturedly teased as she sat. "You clean up nice."

"So do you. You look great." He took his seat again and straightened the cuffs of his pale green button-down. "This place is ritzy. I'm glad we dressed up. I think the guy at the door would've tossed me out on my ass if I showed up in jeans."

Elana chuckled. "You and me both. He's wearing a *suit*."

Their waiter arrived moments later. At his recommendation, they ordered mint tea, a *taktouka* salad, and a lamb tajine. The service was quick, and the dishes arrived at their table in good time.

"God, this smells *amazing*," Elana murmured as she lifted the lid from the tajine to reveal the bed of couscous, vegetables, and lamb. "This beats the brunch place in Haven hands down."

Jesse looked up from spooning *taktouka* onto a piece of fresh bread. "Brunch place in Haven?"

The sudden suspicion in Jesse's tone gave Elana pause, and she remembered the offhand comment he'd made the other night. Was he bothered by her going to brunch with someone else—thinking she might be two-timing him?—or by going to brunch in *Haven*?

Elana half-shrugged and scooped food onto her plate. "I honestly don't remember what it was called. I did a business brunch there with the guy from the guardians who's been helping me go over the reparations contract."

"Huh." He bit off a mouthful of bread, peppers, and tomatoes and chewed it methodically before swallowing. "I heard Jerry mention that. You hit some poor idiot trying to escape, right?"

"Right," Elana hesitantly repeated. Jesse wasn't *incorrect*, but she couldn't tell where his sympathies lay.

Jesse shook his head. His focus was on his food, and he stabbed his salad with more force than was strictly necessary to subdue vegetables. "Man. You'd think, if you had so many people trying to escape your crazy prison, you might realize the problem was local."

Elana's heart sank.

"It's a little more complicated than that." Would this go like her conversations with her father, or was Jesse the type who'd get angry? Did he have a history with vampires? *So much for a nice dinner date.*

Jesse looked up and raised an eyebrow. His gaze was openly skeptical and only a shade shy of hostile. "Is it? Really? If someone wants out of something, they should be able to leave. What'd they do to the poor guy? Is he rotting away in vampire jail behind that huge wall?"

"No."

"Dead, then?"

"Yes."

Jesse scoffed and speared a piece of lamb with his fork. "Did he get a trial before they executed him for exercising his right to free choice?"

Elana fought the urge to scowl. "That's not how vampire law works. When you become a vampire, you sign contracts. You have responsibilities. Running away automatically means you're in breach of contract, so the guardians are allowed to deal with you as they see fit to keep everyone—human *and* vampire—safe."

"Oh, bullshit. They just don't want their secrets getting out, that's all."

Elana's grip on her fork tightened. She drew a slow breath and deliberately relaxed her hand so she didn't bend the handle. "Vampires are powerful, even newly turned ones. They mess with your head. That Runner tried to rape me even after I hit him with my *truck*. Who knows what he would have done if he'd gone free?"

Jesse started at Elana's stark confession, but the hardness in his eyes instantly returned. "So lock the asshole up. Extrajudicial killing is crap. You don't shoot someone on the street without due process. That's all I'm saying."

Elana hissed through her teeth. "I don't disagree, but you're being awfully harsh in the other direction. They're not human, Jesse. They're certainly not American. They don't follow the same laws or have the same culture. We can't judge them by the same standards."

"Then they shouldn't live here," he retorted. "If they're gonna live on American land, they should follow American laws."

"Haven's been here since the founding of the Colonies," she shot back. "If that's the argument you're going with, then we ought to follow Cherokee laws. The SpiderKing wanted a place to live away from the Old World's BS just as much as every other colonist did."

Jesse scowled. "You know a hell of a lot about vampires."

"You got a problem with that?"

"Maybe I do. What's it to you?"

Elana folded her napkin, slapped it on the table, and stood. "I have a problem with anyone who's too much of a coward to admit they're biased and making stupid assumptions. Enjoy dinner. It's on me, courtesy of the kind folks at

Haven who paid for the repairs to my truck. I'll see you at work tomorrow, bright and early."

She stalked away, ignoring his sputtering, and slapped two hundred dollar bills down on the *maître d*'s podium at the door. "For pain and suffering. Whatever he doesn't eat, let the staff have. I'll be back another day with better company."

The tall man didn't spare Jesse a glance. "Thank you, miss. Have a pleasant evening."

Elana felt no less frustrated the next morning at the training grounds. Today, Valeria had her in an outdoor dojo with Gustav and two other martial arts masters. Each trainer specialized in at least two types of martial arts. The slight woman with the bun tied so tight Elana didn't understand how it didn't hurt knew *five*.

During the first few days of hand-to-hand training, Elana was confident. While unfamiliar, the movements were logical and easy to learn. Her mind was catching up to her vampire physique now that she was learning how to use it properly. She'd been making great progress, or so she thought. Gustav had applauded her drills the day before.

This morning, Elana felt like she'd forgotten everything Valeria and Gustav had taught her. The other two instructors, Tamara and Hong, had put her on her ass every round without fail and far faster than she would have liked. The series of movements she was supposed to use didn't make sense. She couldn't think fast enough to string them together to fend off her attackers.

She was bruised, aching, grumpy as hell, and beginning to lose hope. She felt humiliated.

Valeria stood off to the side, arms crossed, watching Elana like a hawk. *Or a spider,* Elana thought uncharitably. *Lurking in its web and waiting for the poor, unsuspecting fly to fly to its sticky doom.* The arbiter had said approximately a dozen words to Elana since arriving that morning, in a stunning contrast to her demeanor of the day before in the archives, and with every *oof* and *thud* that signaled Elana's continued failure, her face became darker.

Elana wanted to cry. She wouldn't—she was keeping the angry, discouraged tears at bay by focusing on the pain of her battered body—but *God*, did she ever want to.

Tamara put her on the floor again, knocking the wind from her lungs. Elana gritted her teeth and forced herself up without pause. She didn't know how to win, but she would not lose.

Gustav fell in beside his boss with the silent footsteps he had used to great effect over his many centuries. "She is struggling."

Valeria's right index finger twitched, but her gaze did not stray from the brunette who was getting her ass handed to her over and over again. "Yes. Your assessment?"

"She is thinking too hard," the broad-shouldered man replied. "She absorbed the training well, but she did so intellectually. With time, she could learn to fight like this, and she would be a force to be reckoned with—as long as no one took her off-guard."

Valeria's lips drifted toward a scowl. "Unacceptable. How many forms have you tried?"

"Half a dozen, Arbiter. Tae kwon do, karate, jujutsu, kung fu, muay thai, and aikido. She adapts well, but again, her understanding is not intuitive."

Valeria tapped her fingers once on her forearm and narrowed her eyes. After a long moment of thought, she declared, "Attack her."

Gustav tilted his head. "I apologize, but I do not understand."

Valeria flicked an exasperated glance at him. "Attack her. You and the others. Overwhelm her. Force her not to think."

Gustav eyed the already-overwhelmed woman in the process of being thrown to the ground once more by his colleagues. "Are you certain, ma'am?" Her eyebrow was enough of an answer. "As you wish."

Gustav caught Tamara's and Hong's gazes and beckoned them over. He quickly relayed the arbiter's instructions in hushed tones. Hong was skeptical but knew better than to argue, and Tamara was unperturbed.

They turned to face the sweating, panting woman who had stubbornly hauled herself to her feet. Her gaze was flinty, but a spark of fear lit within it when she saw all three squaring off against her.

Gustav did not fail to catch the mouthed "Oh, fuck," that crossed Elana's lips, either.

This had to be a punishment for something. It had to be hell. There was no other word for it, no other possible explanation.

For some reason, Valeria had set *all three* of the instructors on her. It hadn't been enough that Elana was proving she was supremely incapable of learning martial arts. Valeria needed her ground into a fine paste on the mat. Maybe they would bury her in the nearby flowerbeds.

Elana grunted as Gustav drove a shoulder into her back, then coughed as Hong kneed her in the gut, and finally yelped as she went down and Tamara kicked her in the ribs.

This wasn't fair. This wasn't *training*. This was torture, pure and simple, and Elana couldn't see the *point* in it.

She glimpsed Valeria's stoic, icy face through Hong's feet. The arbiter wasn't even *looking*.

Ire ignited in Elana's chest, and the frustrated lump in her throat turned into a choked-off yell instead of a sob.

Goddamn you, bitch. What, did my mother piss in your cornflakes or something? Fuck this shit.

If Valeria wouldn't play fair, neither would Elana.

Elana grabbed Hong's ankle and yanked at the same time as she twisted her body up and drove a foot into Gustav's knee. She wasn't strong enough to bring Hong down because his stance was too wide, but she pushed off Gustav's leg and got her other foot underneath her to spin up and kick Hong in the jaw.

Both men staggered back, or tried to. Elana didn't let go of Hong's ankle, and the resulting imbalance brought him crashing to the mat. Elana used the momentum of her kick to fling herself over his supine form and roll in an ungainly somersault a few feet away from the knot of people.

She bounced to her feet. Gustav was still up, and Hong was already moving, but Tamara was advancing on Elana *fast* with no regard for her colleagues.

Elana knew she ought to pivot, dodge, or do *something* that would mean she was out of the way of the woman's charge. Instead, she ran to meet her and crouched at the last second to drive her shoulder into Tamara's solar plexus at full speed.

The smaller woman let out an *oof,* but Elana didn't give in. She wrapped her arms around Tamara, swung her to the ground, and followed her down in an awkward imitation of a body slam. Next, she landed a right hook on Tamara's jaw, which snapped the woman's head over so fast that had she been human, Elana might've been concerned for her life.

She had no time to worry. Hong was back up and incoming, and Gustav was on his heels. Elana grabbed Tamara under the arms and hurled her at the two men. She collided with Hong, and the two collapsed into a pile of limbs. Gustav leaped over his colleagues only to receive a spin kick to the sternum that stopped his inertia. He stumbled over Hong's hand and toppled into the pile.

Elana brought her fists up to her chin and spun, certain she would find Valeria on the warpath. Instead, the arbiter brought her up short by standing still and *clapping.*

"*That's* more like it," Valeria proclaimed. Her dour countenance had lightened to a mildly impressed smirk. "Gustav, teach her krav maga. No holds barred. I'd suggest an emphasis on improvised weaponry, too."

Elana frowned. Maybe it was the adrenaline crash, but she was baffled. "But—everything you said about hand-to-hand combat being refined and humane—now you want me to, what, learn to *brawl*?"

Valeria's gaze turned to steel. "I want you to learn to *survive*, Elana. Refinement can come later. You must first work with your strengths. For you, that means reacting, not thinking."

In the blink of an eye, Valeria crossed the space between them and swung at Elana. Rather than try to defend, Elana took the hit and delivered an uppercut to Valeria's jaw.

The consort's head snapped up, but she came back grinning. Elana grinned too. Maybe she could figure this shit out after all.

CHAPTER FOURTEEN

Elana kept her eyes locked on Gustav's as they parried and swung around the gym. Her arms ached with every clash of their swords, but she refused to give an inch. Her frustration from last night's dinner fueled her drive. She'd already won two practice bouts.

The grunts and *clangs* of training surrounded them. Today, she and Gustav were not the only combatants in Training Room A, but two of a dozen or more. They had joined the guardians from Valeria's corps in their weekly sparring practice.

The guardians paid Elana no mind, too professional to be openly curious, but Elana had initially been hard-pressed to keep her attention on her training. The elite corps, comprised of men and women in roughly equal measure as far as Elana could tell, were a sight to behold. Their movements were precise and fluid, efficient and graceful, beautiful and deadly.

Elana was deeply glad she was on *their* side.

"Feet firm!" Valeria barked, and Elana's focus flashed to

the soles of her feet in time for her to shift her weight and block Gustav's swing.

She drove the burly trainer back step by step until he pivoted and feinted before ducking left and spinning under her arm. Elana had expected a thrust or a frontal assault. She turned with him a second too late and only succeeded in meeting the flat of his blade with her back.

"Round to Gustav," Valeria announced. "Again!"

Elana rolled her shoulders and squared off. They would spar until Valeria said they were done, at which point she would probably tell them to continue with unarmed combat. The first thing Elana had learned about vampire training was that it was relentless. Breaks came every four or five hours, not one or two, and the trainers expected your entire attention at all times.

They also expected you to progress quickly, or expected *Elana* to. Valeria had fed her a steady stream of information since day one, covering multiple martial arts disciplines and now armed combat. Elana caught on fast, in part thanks to her enhanced physique and quick mind but also because she was beyond determined to prove herself worthy of the arbiter's time and attention.

A muscle in Gustav's neck twitched, and Elana's focus narrowed to the immediate present. She flexed her fingers around the hilt of her sword, bent her knees a touch, and flowed forward before the trainer could move.

He parried and shifted. She did not relent and pushed him onto his back foot. He pivoted and leaned to the side, forcing her to step away. She turned the movement into a twisting slash that she paired with a step behind his leg, and with a quick twist of her knee, she brought him crashing to the floor with the point of her sword at his sternum.

Valeria *clapped.* Only once, but it counted. "Match to Elana."

Maybe it was Elana's imagination—or wishful thinking—but she'd swear Valeria was *crowing.* The thought made her heart swell with pride, regardless of its veracity.

A familiar, sexy voice broke into her burgeoning self-congratulation. "That was *well* done. I haven't seen a takedown like that from an initiate in…a long time."

"Miss Bishop is performing admirably," Valeria agreed.

Elana thought she might float away on the consort's praise. She caught her breath and grinned at Matt, who stood a respectful—and *safe*—several paces away. "To what do we owe the pleasure, Mister Richelieu?"

"I heard you were training and thought you might like to join me for lunch if the arbiter didn't have other plans for you. Work needs to be balanced with downtime and fueled with good food, and word has it you're working hard enough for two initiates."

"Three," Gustav grunted as he got to his feet. "This *novaya krov* is your best find yet, *sudiya* Draven."

"Thank you, Gustav. She has much potential. I intend to see she makes the most of it." Valeria favored Elana with a rare, thin smile. "Go clean up, Miss Bishop, then eat with Mister Richelieu. I will be in meetings until four o'clock. I will find you then."

"I appreciate your time, Arbiter." Elana sheathed her sword and bowed deeply, then turned to Matt. "I won't be long."

Matt chuckled. "Take your time. It's only eleven-thirty. I know how hard Arbiter Draven works her initiates."

Elana wiped the sweat from her forehead with the back of her sleeve. He had a point.

She politely took her leave and disappeared into the locker room where she'd stored her stuff. She loved every minute of the training Valeria was putting her through, but she would have been lying if she said she didn't love the dressing room more. Every time she was in here, she felt like royalty.

Elana stripped off her sweat-soaked clothes and tossed them in one of the washers in the corner of the room. The ultra-fast, two-in-one appliances made quick work of your gym wear, washing and drying them before you were out of the shower. Also, the included detergent smelled like the faintest hint of gardenias on Tuesdays.

Elana had noticed the preponderance of subtle scents in Haven. Nothing was overpowering, except on rare occasions, the smells of certain restaurants in Shestoi. Vampires did not shy away from rich aromas and flavors. Still, Elana could not understand the overt and universal commitment to sensory moderation…until she realized that vampires' natural enhancements included their sense of smell.

No wonder the "stop smelling like BO" facilities were so extensive.

From the washers, she went straight to the sauna. While it seemed counterintuitive to her the first day to get *more* hot and sweaty after an intense workout, Gustav's recommendation had served Elana well. Ten minutes of steam, heat, and silence let the aches, stitches, and sore spots melt away.

Next on the docket was a dip in the ice bath. Elana had already heard of this practice, but while she respected its proven health benefits, she still didn't *enjoy* it. The blast of frigid water jolted her wide awake, and she booked it to the showers.

The shower room was a luxurious tiled pool room that made Elana think of Roman baths. The central pool was heated and deep enough to swim in, and one end had several smaller pools with ledges where one could sit and soak like a hot tub. The walls had spigots and showerheads spaced every few feet, each with different settings, and a huge basket of wrapped soaps and loofahs sat at the entrance.

Elana picked out her favorite soaps—one for her hair, one for the rest of her—and made for her preferred shower. The rainwater head had an attachment that came off for ease of rinsing. She scrubbed herself down, then took her time rinsing and contentedly watched the suds slide away into the drain channels between the showers and the pool.

When the water ran clear, she padded back to the main room, grabbing a fluffy towel on the way from the racks at the door to the baths. She toweled off as she walked, then wrapped her hair into a makeshift turban while she dressed.

Elana was rapidly becoming convinced she needed to buy one of the infinite purses she'd seen in Premier. Carrying garment bags around all the time was a serious pain in the ass—and that didn't even touch on the inconvenience of carting around multiple pairs of shoes—but if she needed workout clothes, human travel clothes, and vampire business clothes in a single day, she didn't have much choice.

Or you could move to Haven and be done with it.

She sighed and buttoned her blouse. Living a double life was not her style. Jesse's behavior the night before had nudged her closer to throwing in the towel and moving full-time to Haven, but Jerry had texted her that morning and restored her faith in humanity.

Elana had dreamed of living in Haven all her life, but she had never believed it possible. She *loved* her life. How could she give it up?

She fetched her clean clothes from the dryer, folded them, and tucked them in her duffel. Then, after a quick date with the super-powerful hair dryer that somehow didn't turn her walnut waves into a poofy fuzzball, she left the training grounds and found Matt relaxing on a bench outside.

"I remember the day I learned vampires aren't allergic to the sun," she told him as she walked up.

Matt laughed. "Did it blow your mind?"

She grinned. "No. Unfortunately, I'd just read *Twilight*, so I figured it meant the glitter thing was the truth."

He snorted hard enough that he coughed. When the coughing fit lightened into laughter, he shook his head. "Oh, God. That series did a *number* on our reputation, let me tell you. We *still* get people asking if we sparkle—especially anyone from that side of the country—or the Italians. Oh, *man*."

Matt wiped a tear from his eye. "Enough of us thought it was funny that it became a fad for a while to douse yourself in body glitter before seeing humans. Those were the days."

"Did you ever do it?"

"Hell, yes. I thought it was the funniest thing since the garlic craze. I still have some glitter back home."

Elana grinned. They'd started walking, so Matt missed the glimmer in her eye as she inquired, "Does the Citadel throw a Halloween gala?"

"It leans a bit more toward the Samhain end of things, but there's usually *something*," he replied. He glanced her way, caught her smirk, and narrowed his eyes. "Wait. Why?"

She whistled innocently. "No reason."

They ate lunch in a *trattoria* in Shestoi. Elana devoured an entire Margherita pizza and half of a second before slowing down. She downed most of a carafe of water, then enjoyed the rest of her second pizza with a glass of wine.

She mopped up marinara sauce with the crust of her pizza. "So...where does the myth of vampires drinking blood come from? Why is it so persistent when it's obvious you—*we*—still eat?"

Matt crunched through the end of his pizza and wiped his mouth before answering. "Like you said, it's a myth. Old legends die *hard*. A transfer of blood *is* necessary to perform the Rights. It hasn't been done by mouth in centuries since it's terribly unsanitary and dangerous for both parties, but it's the kind of rumor that takes root in the imagination."

"That makes sense." Elana sipped her wine. "I used to read everything I could get my hands on about vampires. I knew it couldn't all be true, but I had no way of verifying any of it. I don't know what to believe...and until a few days ago, it didn't matter. I could believe as much or as little of it as I wanted because it didn't affect me."

"Now it does. Arbiter Draven told me what she'd found."

"I figured she would have. Does everyone know?"

He shook his head. "Only a select few. Myself, as your main liaison here in Haven. Gustav, as your secondary trainer. And the king, of course." He said this last almost as an afterthought.

"Of course," Elana repeated in shock. It didn't surprise her that Valeria would share the results of her work with the king. The consort worked for him directly. It was her *job* to tell him these things.

Still, knowing that the SpiderKing knew anything about her was...unsettling.

"You have questions."

Elana's cheeks warmed. "I want to know everything. I know I should be patient. I know there's an order I'm supposed to follow, and I need to trust the arbiter..."

"But you want to know. That's natural. Like you said, when you read about us before, it didn't affect you. It might as well have been a story." His eyes twinkled, and Elana knew he was thinking about glitter as much as she was.

"Now it's my story too," she finished.

He nodded. "Let's go to the library after lunch. There's no better place to ask questions."

Elana stuffed the last of her pizza into her mouth. Decorum be damned.

CHAPTER FIFTEEN

They walked to the library. Elana expected to swelter in the full sun, but the air was pleasantly warm, and a light breeze played with her hair.

She motioned at the gossamer canopy stretching out from the nearest skyscraper in view, a towering spire in Quarto. "I know the canopy filters UV rays, but does it also provide climate control?"

Matt nodded. "Not a huge amount, but yes. We keep the city comfortable by moderating the temperature somewhat, and we protect the infrastructure from more violent weather events, like hail and very strong winds. It's more efficient to devote resources to prevention than to repair."

"Makes sense. That's impressive work."

"The engineers and architects in Etreta are well-practiced geniuses of their crafts. I've lived here most of my life, and I still discover things that astonish me regularly."

"Do I want to know how old you are?"

"With everything you're learning in such a short time...probably not yet." He winked.

"I figured as much."

They strolled through Shestoi to Senkyem and appreciated the walk through the gardens on the way to Quarto. The closer they got to their destination, the higher the building loomed.

Elana did her best to trace the route she'd taken with Valeria from the consulate to the archives but could not see the sky bridge. "Are the sky bridges hidden?"

Matt confirmed with a nod. "It would mar the view. Seeing people walk in midair is a bit silly, even for us."

"Fair enough."

The King's Archives occupied upward of four city blocks. Cream-colored stone trim and keystones on the arches above the windows highlighted its terracotta bricks. The windows featured wrought iron sills. Each wall had columns of large windows extending out a couple of feet every few yards.

The main entrance was a pair of oak double doors twice Elana's height, banded with more iron. The SpiderKing's sigil was burned into the center of each door, with the symbol of the domain of Knowledge—the waning crescent—burned in underneath. The doors slowly swung open at a touch.

Elana's jaw dropped.

No images of the King's Archives existed outside of Haven. Entry was strictly forbidden to any human not on official royal business, and no recording devices were permitted. This ensured the security of the files and manuscripts in the collection, some of which were many centuries old. Elana suspected the "wow" factor for anyone walking in for the first time counted too. Vampires liked a good show.

An atrium that occupied at least a quarter of the building dominated the interior. An arched series of connected skylights formed the ceiling, allowing filtered light to stream into the space below. Tables, planters, and a fountain dotted the area. Far from being stuffy, the air felt cool and fresh.

Balconies surrounded the atrium. Elana lost count of the number of stories at fifteen. Spiral staircases rose the entirety of the building, three to each wall, and allowed entry to each floor. Given the number of stories, Elana suspected the staircases functioned more like escalators—then again, the ones in the consulate didn't, so maybe not.

Matt nudged her elbow, and she started. "Sorry," she blurted, then repeated herself in a whisper. "It's just...*wow*."

He chuckled. "I know. The archives are beautiful. Come on, we want the fifth floor of the northeast wing."

He led her through the atrium to one of the far staircases. As they ascended, Elana kept looking around her in awe. People drifted along the balconies and wandered between the tables below with stacks of books. Their murmurs created a soft susurration in counterpoint to the wash of sound from the fountain.

When they stepped off the stairs onto the fifth floor, the change in atmosphere hit Elana immediately. The cool, fresh air of the atrium disappeared, replaced by dry, perfectly room-temperature air without a breath of movement.

Matt must have seen her pause because he smiled. "More climate control. The atrium is kept comfortable for us. The archives are kept comfortable for the books. There are manuscripts not even the king will take into the atrium."

Elana mentally marveled at the vampires' capabilities, then shook herself and returned to the task at hand. "What's in this wing?"

"Cultural essays, mainly. I thought you might like a primer."

He motioned at a table in front of a window. Elana realized as she sat that it was in one of the outjutting windows and overlooked the rest of Haven.

"I'd love a primer. Like I said, I read everything I could get my hands on outside, but in hindsight, the accuracy of the information I got was...questionable at best." Elana cocked her head. "*Do* vampires have primers on cultural history? Don't most vampires grow up in the culture? Why would primers be needed?"

Matt sat across from her and tapped the table. In response, the oaken tabletop lit up as though a tablet were embedded in it. He typed as he responded. "Most vampires are given the Rights as adults. It's rare for a vampire to *grow up* as a vampire."

Elana watched his fingers fly over the interface. "I thought the younger schools were farther into Quarto. What are you doing?"

"Getting us some books. You're right. There *are* a couple of schools for younger vampires, and they *are* in the heart of Quarto. They're just not heavily attended. Vampires rarely have children."

"Why's that?"

Matt dithered over something on the screen, then decisively tapped. "Think about it. What do you know about how vampires age?"

Elana tilted her head. "Well...you don't. Sorry, *we* don't."

"Almost true." He flashed her a smile. "The simplest way to explain it is that vampirism slows the aging process to a snail's pace. If you become a vampire before your body has finished developing—usually in your mid-twenties—you'll age normally to that point before the reduced aging kicks in. If you're already beyond that, it keeps you at whatever stage of life you were in when you were turned."

Elana parsed this, then frowned. "So kids grow until they're adults, then freeze in time like everyone else."

"Correct."

"Wouldn't you run into massive population problems? Is that why vampires don't have many children?"

Matt half-shrugged. "It's not a mandate, at least not here in Haven. But consider the most basic reason for procreation."

She arched an eyebrow. "Continuing our genetic line? Wouldn't the Houses be *all over* that?"

He laughed. "Apart from dynastic leanings. If *that* was all that mattered, you bet your ass there'd be more vampire kids."

Elana squinted in thought, then inhaled sharply as her eyebrows shot up. "Oh. Societies that need labor have more children. Like in the old days, when you needed to have lots of kids so they'd help with the chores on the farm, one would eventually take over, and they'd take care of you in your old age."

"Precisely. That's not an issue with vampires, and we *don't* want a population glut, *ergo*..." Matt gestured with one hand. "Very few children. Also, the fewer children we have, the easier it is to keep them out of the figurative line of fire for as long as we can."

Elana frowned. "What? What does *that* mean?"

Matt tapped with finality on the screen, and the luminous interface disappeared into the table. "It means that vampires can be nasty." He met her gaze with a mild grimace. "If you were half the amateur sleuth I think you were, you already know how...*delicate*...vampire politics can be."

She winced. "I might have read a thing or two on the subject, by which I mean I devoured the tabloids every night and kept a running commentary on what I thought would happen next."

He snorted. "You and everyone here. I'll have to read yours sometime. I'd be fascinated to know how accurate the rumors are outside the wall. I'd bet on them being, oh, *maybe* fifty percent true."

"From your tone, *I'd* bet you mean they're a lot worse than we measly humans could imagine."

"Pretty much." Matt let the "we measly humans" comment slide, although he held her gaze a moment longer than was strictly necessary. "In any case, vampire politics and power plays can come with intense fights—verbal *and* physical. We try to keep our kids out of the worst of it if we can."

"That's kind. A lot of humans would say you were coddling them."

He shrugged again. "We can't keep them out of all of it, and in my opinion, it wouldn't be wise to anyway. If we can keep them from ending up in a literal crossfire... Well, that seems like a good idea to me."

"I'd agree with that."

Their discussion of vampire childrearing was interrupted by the *whir* of a drone floating toward them. The automated library cart paused at their table and *beeped* pleasantly before lifting a stack of books from its tray and depositing them gently in front of Matt.

He tapped a green light on the drone, and it floated away. Then he sorted through the pile of books and handed one to Elana. *Rebellion and Revival: Haven Through the Centuries.* The cover showed a bird's-eye photograph of Haven taken within the last twenty years.

"This is a good place to start," he told her. "Melinda Basset writes very accessibly and always includes glossaries and family trees. You should be able to check the facts of what you already know about Haven with this book. Then I'd suggest this one."

Matt slid a second book across the table. This one was thicker, looked considerably older, and was titled *A Comparative Study of Humans and Vampires.*

"This one's a bit dry, but it's still the leading authority on the physical differences between humans and vampires. It includes information on all stages of vampirism up to guardian. You don't necessarily have to read that far unless you want to. The first chapter, regarding initiates, would give you a good understanding of your abilities."

Elana set her hand on the cloth-bound book and let out a slow, measured breath. "You mean the person I've been since I was a kid and didn't know about."

Matt gently laid his hand on top of hers. He said

nothing but lightly squeezed her hand, and when she met his gaze, the look in his eyes spoke volumes. *I've been where you've been, and it'll be okay. I'm here for you.*

The moment lingered for several breaths, then Matt removed his hand and smiled. "I would love to stay and answer all the questions I'm sure you'll have, but I need to get back to work. Have I given you my number yet?"

"Uh, no." Elana fumbled for her phone in her purse and almost dropped it on the table. "Dammit. I swear I'm not the biggest klutz on the planet."

Matt chuckled. "You're training your vampire abilities for the first time. I felt like a baby giraffe when I was doing the same. You're fine."

"Oh, this is *normal?* Geez, I wish somebody had *told* me..."

He tapped the book. "It's all in here. You'll get caught up in no time."

Elana put Matt's contact info into her phone, then returned it to her bag. "Thanks. Seriously. For everything."

Matt stood and leaned on the table. "My pleasure. I think Valeria said she would find you around four PM when she was done with her meetings before the car brings you home." Elana nodded. "Great. In that case, have fun, and don't get into trouble."

Elana waved after him and tried not to read too much into his parting words. He was teasing her, not warning her. Nothing ominous about that. Right?

Right. Definitely. Nothing to worry about.

She sighed and dove into the books.

CHAPTER SIXTEEN

The next time Elana looked at her phone, it was already past two o'clock. Two-thirty-two, to be precise.

She sat up straight and stretched. A couple of vertebrae popped, and the tendons creaked when she rolled her neck. She'd been buried in the books for almost two hours and didn't think she'd moved once.

The first book was informative but not surprising. It had mainly confirmed most of what Elana already knew about Haven. She'd whizzed through it in no time flat.

The second book, on the other hand…

Despite being drier than the Mojave, the medical treatises had caught Elana's attention and held it fast. The detailed explanations of the differences between vampires and humans were fascinating. She'd read the entire chapter on initiates and had started the chapter on adepts when she'd looked at her phone. She didn't want to stop reading, but her eyes were crossing, and her brain was teeming with information. She needed to process.

Elana brushed her hands over the tabletop in an attempt to mimic Matt's gestures. Her first try did nothing, but the interface lit up at her second touch. Text in a steady, clean, sans-serif font appeared in light blue as though inlaid in the wood.

Patron: Bishop, Elana

Level: Initiate

Below the text, a small horizontal line flashed, presumably indicating where she could input text. Elana scooted her books aside and laid her hands on the table like a keyboard. She was pleased to see the interface respond in kind.

She tried typing, **Can I borrow books?** and hit Enter.

Borrowing privileges available for Bishop, Elana: Five (5) non-classified manuscripts, ten (10) e-books

Borrowing period: Twenty-four days

A square appeared on the right side of the interface and flashed twice. Elana frowned thoughtfully, then turned *Rebellion and Revival* over. She found a square of similar size on the back cover.

She passed the square over the scanner, and the table *beeped*.

Basset, Melinda. *Rebellion and Revival: Haven Through the Centuries.* **Successfully checked out.**

Elana pumped her fist. She tried the medical textbook next and was displeased when the interface flashed red.

This book is classified and may not be removed from the premises. An e-book is available for download to approved Haven apps. Would you like to continue?

Elana indicated yes, then spent fifteen minutes fussing with her phone to download the app in question. At long last, she managed it and quickly maxed out her e-book capacity. She'd have to be careful not to stay up all night.

She logged out and stood, leaving the books on the table as the interface had instructed. A librarian would be along to collect and reshelve them.

Elana returned to the staircase and descended to the atrium with her bag over her shoulder and the history book tucked in an outer pocket. The cool air of the open space was refreshing after the still atmosphere of the stacks.

She also realized with a start that she could hear conversations again. She'd seen people pass her nook but heard nothing while she was in the archives proper. Another vampire trick, no doubt. Very handy.

Elana shifted the strap of her bag higher as she approached the front desk, which she and Matt had passed on the way in. The woman behind it was taller than Elana by a few inches, and her black hair was in a tight ponytail that highlighted the long white streaks and her tall forehead. She wore thin, brass-rimmed glasses over her hazel eyes and a beige and navy pantsuit with wide pockets. She would have looked like the epitome of a stern librarian were it not for the thumbnail-sized anarchy symbol pin on her left lapel.

Elana glanced at the nameplate on the desk. Natalie Lawson, Head Librarian.

Natalie broke the awkward silence. "May I help you?"

"Uh—no," Elana blurted, then tried again. "I mean—yes. I'm new, and I'd like to see more of Haven. Any suggestions?"

To Elana's surprise, a friendly smile bloomed on the head librarian's face. She'd expected sour grapes from the tightness around her eyes. "Certainly. The Great Hall in Octava is always my first recommendation. It's open to visitors year-round, and the art collection is unparalleled. Check out the paintings in particular. Many are originals dating from the last millennium…or two."

Elana's jaw dropped. "That sounds incredible. I'll go straight there."

Natalie eyed Elana's bag. "You might want to borrow a glider. It's a long walk."

Elana blushed. "I don't know what a glider is."

The librarian chuckled lightly. "Not to worry. Everyone's new at some point." She turned and pointed at the front doors. "There's a glider station across the street. They're free for anyone's use. You'll figure it out as long as you can ride a bike."

Elana grinned in relief. "I can definitely ride a bike. Thank you for your help."

"Any time."

It took Elana a few blocks to get used to the floating bike, which felt like something out of *Star Wars*, but she managed not to crash into anything or anyone. Half the problem was the duffel bag. It was *not* designed to be carried on her back.

She sighed as she turned right to circle the Citadel. Maybe she ought to hunt down an infinity bag in Premier before she left for the day.

A stately storefront caught her eye, featuring mannequins with gravity-defying outfits. Elana eased off the throttle, coasted to a stop, and admired the display. Had vampires made fabric that couldn't wrinkle? *Would she never have to iron again?*

Not that most of her work clothes needed ironing, but the thought of fancy clothes that were easy to care for was deeply tempting.

"Great work, isn't it?"

The new voice startled Elana. If she hadn't been firmly gripping the brake, she would have shot down the road. As it was, the engine revved loud enough to make her and her new friend wince.

Elana let go of the throttle and winced. "Sorry."

The woman standing a few feet away smiled. "First time in Haven?"

"Not quite, but it *is* my first time on one of these." Elana indicated the bike, then stuck out a hand to shake. She'd never been one to make an overly flowery introduction. Straightforward was her style. "I'm Elana Bishop."

"Cathy Smith." The woman shook. Her handshake was firm, but her hand was cold. She looked a little older than Elana, maybe in her early forties, with a couple of wrinkles around her eyes and laugh lines in her olive face. Her black hair hung to her shoulders in loose waves, although some was gathered up at the back, presumably in a clip.

Cathy's fashion sense struck Elana as a cross between 1970s psychedelia and a 1920s Sears and Roebuck catalog. She wore elegant beige pumps with a pointed toe, a flowing calf-length dress only given shape by the fabric belt around her waist and the deep V-neck, and a hat with enough rosettes on it to look like a wedding cake. The colors were muted, but if Elana looked long enough at the geometric patterns on the dress, she'd swear shapes would pop out like a Magic Eye puzzle.

Something about Cathy made Elana relax. The woman had to be eccentric, even by vampire standards. Who wore a neutral-tone kaleidoscope out in public? Only people who were incredibly rich and didn't give a damn what anyone else thought.

"Did you buy your dress here?" Elana motioned to Premier in general. "It doesn't look like anything I've seen, but I'll admit I haven't had much chance to explore. I'm... new."

Cathy chuckled. "Technically, yes, but Arturo works in a tiny little atelier in the interior and only takes commissions. I think he'd be bored out of his gourd if I stopped asking him for new outfits every few months. Why? Are you looking? I don't know if my style would suit you. It doesn't suit anyone, really. Some days I'm not sure it suits me. On those days I go goth."

Elana blinked. Before she could stop herself, she blurted, "Can we be friends?"

Cathy's chuckle became a full-blown laugh. "Well! Aren't *you* interesting!"

"I could say the same! Are you even real, or did Matt slip LSD into my lunch?"

This set Cathy off again, and Elana joined in the laughter. Cathy's sunny, *laissez-faire* personality was contagious and a welcome breath of fresh air from the staid, ultra-reserved, snooty atmosphere that lingered through Haven.

When the laughter died down, Elana explained. "The last few days have been batshit crazy for me. I'm a brand-new vampire and a brand-new millionaire, and I'm rubbing shoulders with the Arbiter of Shadows on a daily basis. I didn't realize how badly I needed a friend *here* until I ran into you. You're nothing like anyone else I've met here. What do you say? Would you be willing to take a fledgling vampire under your wing and keep her sane?"

Cathy's gaze had sobered as she listened to Elana's tale. "Palling around with Arbiter Draven, hm? Brave girl."

"I didn't get much choice in the matter."

"I see. I assume there's plenty you can't tell me?"

"Not without asking her first—I'd like to keep my head—but she didn't tell me I couldn't make friends, so…"

Cathy nodded. "It's wise to seek out countering opinions. I'm of House Lucciola, which is about as far unrelated to House Draven as you can get."

This gave Elana pause. "Does that mean you're…"

"At odds with the Consort of Shadows? Oh, no, not in the slightest. I've no problem with our current arbiter's methods or policies. She's doing a fine job." Cathy smiled. "I only mean to say that my lineage is completely unrelated to hers. I have ancestral scions in Zevenda and Octava, but my House is quartered in Premier. Does any of that mean anything to you?"

Elana's eyebrows rose. "Probably not with the nuance that it means to you, but it tells me you're about as well-connected as the SpiderKing, and you've been here almost as long."

"As long as, actually. Settled here when he did."

"*You* did?" Elana gaped. "That means you're—"

Cathy winked. "Hush now. A lady never tells."

Elana put her head in her hands. "Oh, God. This is like running into an old lady on the street with a corgi, and it turns out you're making friends with the Queen of England."

Cathy laughed. "Liz was a good sort. Here, my dear. Come off that bike and let's go shopping. You didn't stop in Premier for shits and giggles. What are you looking for?"

Elana let Cathy guide her off the bike. Now, more than ever, she felt like she was living in a dream world. "I want one of those bags that holds everything but somehow stays a decent size and almost weightless. I'm so tired of having to carry around this damn duffel with all my changes of clothes. Do those exist or are they a marketing ploy?"

Cathy put her arm around Elana's shoulders and led her down the street. "Ah, yes. A perennial favorite, the dimensional bag. They're not quite infinite, but they're as good as. I know where to get the best ones. I'll get you sorted. This way."

An hour later, Cathy bid Elana goodbye a few blocks from the Great Hall at another glider stand. She'd love to stay and chat, but her second blood-cousin twice transfused on her great-uncle's side was hosting a soirée that night. She'd promised to bring goodies for his cats.

Yes, she'd been entirely serious.

Shopping with Cathy was as fun as shopping with Vicky. Vicky haggled prices with charm and a wink. Cathy already had the discounts in every shop in town. Elana had a dimensional bag in a beautiful steel gray with polished brass clasps, three new outfits, and an umbrella. Why Cathy had insisted on the umbrella, Elana hadn't asked. She had no doubt it would come in handy someday.

The whirlwind spree had taken a little over an hour. Elana had just enough time to poke her head in the Great Hall before Valeria would send a car for her.

Even among Haven's many architectural marvels, the Great Hall stood out. It resembled a version of the Louvre's iconic pyramid that had been swooped into a wave that reached the sky. Its exterior was similarly covered in glass panes, and the light of the afternoon sun glinted and reflected off it in a myriad of colors.

Elana slowed her glider to a crawl to appreciate the view. Haven packed a great deal of beauty into its relatively small footprint, and if she decided not to relocate, she wanted to drink in as much of it as she could.

But you're coming, aren't you?

She stopped and put a foot down on the road to keep it steady. She watched the sunlight playing off the museum for several seconds more while her thoughts chased themselves around in her head like so many dogs chasing their tails. Then she picked up her foot again and hit the metaphorical gas.

Elana steered the machine into another station, where it sat beside a dozen identical gliders, and headed into the Great Hall by descending a wide staircase below ground level to a pair of stained glass double doors set into the glass shell.

The mosaic style of the stained glass reminded Elana of a kaleidoscope. If you looked closely, however, you could pick out the SpiderKing's sigil and the symbol of Octava—the waxing gibbous moon—within the tessellated slivers of glass.

The interior was as magnificent as the exterior. The wave of glass rose above Elana's head, triumphantly reaching for the clouds, and the light filtered through and covered the pure white marble floor in iridescent rainbows—except for the section in the center that was cut out, creating a balcony over the next level down.

Elana approached the railing and peered over. The light from the ceiling illuminated a sundial inset in the floor below, which was inlaid with the sigil of Haven. It was stunning. She wondered whether the sundial shifted somehow with the seasons so it was always correct. Did vampires observe Daylight Savings Time?

Looking up, she spied a kiosk near the entrance to the galleries and grabbed a brochure. It included a map, a guide to the galleries, and a list of the other major museums and cultural centers in Octava.

Elana was deciding between the gallery of consort portraits and the gallery of landscape paintings when a familiar voice caught her ear. Valeria was giving someone the gears on the level below.

She sidled closer to the balcony and listened in.

"As I told you in our last meeting, Demoissac, the matter is not as simple as you believe. One cannot simply *walk* into Otellier." The arbiter's tone was measured and even, but Elana had spent enough time with her in the last several days to detect the displeased edge.

"One most certainly can, Consort...*if* one is prepared to act with the full backing of His Royal Highness." The man replying had a thin, reedy tenor voice that made Elana want to cover her ears. Demoissac, presumably. Not a consort himself, based on his use of Valeria's title. Perhaps a concubine? Was that a gender-neutral term in Haven politics?

Valeria's clacking footsteps stopped, and the other shuffling footsteps stopped with her. The group was close enough that Elana could see most of them. Valeria was a foot from the inlaid sundial, and the others were farther off.

If the man behind her was Demoissac, Elana didn't like him. He looked snivelly and conniving. He wore a suit and tie and had slicked his hair back over his ears. However, he looked like he *should* have been wearing a black robe and rubbing his hands together all the time in anticipation of the dastardly deeds he'd be doing an hour from now.

Valeria turned on her heel and faced the man, whom Elana was now certain was Demoissac. Quietly enough that Elana didn't think she'd have been able to hear without enhanced vampire senses, the arbiter replied, "I must have misheard you, Demoissac. You could not possibly be insinuating that the Arbiter of Shadows is not prepared to act with the full backing of His Majesty. That would be foolish, and you are not a foolish man. Tell me I'm wrong."

Even from twenty feet up, Elana felt the rest of the group draw back and hold their breath. Demoissac was about to get his ass handed to him, she was sure.

To his credit, he didn't flinch—or maybe that was stupidity. Elana didn't *think* you could be an idiot and make it far enough in Haven politics to have walk-and-talk conversations with the Arbiter of Shadows, but maybe Demoissac was really well-connected or rich.

"I would never deign to imply that the Arbiter of Shadows is incapable of performing her duties," he smoothly replied—though not to the actual question, Elana noticed. "You are correct, Consort. I am not a foolish man."

"I am glad to hear it, *Raoul.*" Valeria painted the name with poison. This time, Demoissac *did* flinch. "We will continue this discussion tomorrow. I trust you will have another option for me…since you are not a foolish man."

He bowed low enough that Elana thought his forehead might scrape the ground. "Naturally, Consort. Naturally."

The group dispersed. Elana made to move away from the railing but froze when Valeria looked up and caught her eye. She swallowed hard, expecting a disapproving glare—she *had* been eavesdropping—and was surprised when Valeria raised her eyebrows and made a small gesture toward the departing vampires.

This is what you're in for, the look said. *You won't be able to avoid it.*

Elana held Valeria's gaze for a long moment, then

slowly nodded. Valeria nodded once in return, then walked away under the balcony.

Elana sagged against the railing.

The ride home was quiet, as was every other ride back from Haven. Elana mulled over the day's events, including the smatterings of small talk she'd made with the other patrons of the Great Hall before her phone had buzzed to let her know her ride was ready. Vampire small talk was much like human small talk, right down to the weather. Elana thought it was funny since Haven's weather was controlled, but some things were universal.

She felt better about life, although still overwhelmed by the gravity of the choice that loomed before her. With the multitude of books on her phone, Elana felt considerably more prepared to face that choice—or would be after she read them.

All of that certainty flew out the window of the luxury sedan as they pulled up to her house. Jesse was sitting on the front step, and his face was a thundercloud.

CHAPTER SEVENTEEN

The Haven car departed as smoothly and impersonally as it had arrived, leaving Elana on her front sidewalk facing Jesse on the step. He watched it until it was halfway down the street, then returned his gaze to Elana. "Hi."

Elana held her new dimensional handbag tight under her arm and started up the walk. "Hi. Did we have plans tonight? I didn't think we did, but maybe I got my dates wrong. Sorry if I stood you up. It was entirely unintentional."

Jesse shook his head. "We didn't. I wanted to talk to you and I was in the neighborhood, so I dropped by."

Elana resisted the temptation to say, "Yeah, right," because her house was *not* near anything she could fathom Jesse visiting after work and she knew today's job site was on the other side of town.

Instead, she told him, "Hope you haven't been waiting long. Did you text? I didn't get it if you did."

"Like I said, just dropped by. No, I haven't been waiting long. Maybe five minutes."

"Good timing, then."

They faced each other for a long moment with Jesse on the steps and Elana on the lawn. She hadn't retrieved her keys from her pocket yet. Jesse still looked ready to throw down, and Elana had no interest in inviting him in until she figured out what the hell was going on.

When he continued to say nothing, she pursed her lips and cracked her neck. "Did something happen at work?"

"Nothing happened at work."

"Then I'll be blunt. Who pissed in your Cheerios?"

Jesse's mouth, which had been scrunched in mild distaste, twisted into a scowl. "Was that a Haven car?"

Elana's heart sank. She had expected this fight for a while now, to tell the truth.

She fished her keys out of her pocket and walked past him to the door. "Let's have this conversation inside."

He followed her in and stayed quiet while she deposited her handbag in her bedroom. When she returned, she asked, "Can I get you anything? Water, coffee, a beer?"

"Water would be great."

Elana nodded. She filled two glasses, then motioned for Jesse to join her in the living room. After they sat on opposite ends of her couch, she finally replied to his question. "Yes, it was a Haven car. Is there a problem?"

"Why are you still going there?"

She raised an eyebrow. "I've been dealing with reparations meetings. I've been very open about that."

"Those are one and done. Most of the time, people do it over the app."

"There were extenuating circumstances."

His scowl rose into a faint sneer, then darkened into a frown. He sat up, put his glass on the coffee table, and crossed his arms. "I don't like you going there. I don't like you seeing them."

Elana deliberately kept her posture open and her expression neutral. "It's my business where I go and who I work with, but since we've had a couple of good dates, I'll do you the courtesy of asking why. What's your issue with vampires?"

"They think humans are garbage," Jesse spat. "They think they're *so* much better than us and they can treat us like shit. It's crap. So they have advanced tech—who cares? They're still bloodsucking maniacs who wouldn't exist without humans. They're monsters. They're no better than us."

Elana's jaw tightened. It didn't matter that Jesse didn't know he was talking about her. Whether he'd have changed his tune if he *did* know didn't matter either.

"Jesse, *that's* crap," she told him flatly. "The bloodsucking maniacs and 'they think humans are garbage' parts, to be specific. You're right that they're no better than us, and they wouldn't exist without humans. They're no more monsters than we are. Quit stereotyping. It makes you sound like an idiot."

That was the wrong thing to say.

Jesse shot to his feet. His fists clenched at his sides. "I am *not* an idiot," he fired back. "I have *never* met a vampire who wasn't a triple-A asshole and who didn't make it their personal goal to make me feel like a smear of shit on the sidewalk. They hurt and use us, and they think they can make it all better with a few stacks of cash and some glorified magic tricks."

Elana forced her jaw to relax—it was getting sore—but stayed put on the couch. "Sounds like you've had some seriously awful encounters with vampires. Sorry to hear it. I agree there are some real nasty specimens...but I hate to tell you, Jesse, I've had my share of run-ins with equally nasty humans. Vampires don't have the monopoly on shitty behavior."

Jesse's ire was not soothed. His face was turning red. The hair on the back of Elana's neck stood up, and her arms felt cold. Her breath sped up. The walls felt too close for comfort with an irate man in the middle of her living room.

She didn't feel safe. She couldn't tell him the truth.

Elana had never wanted to leave the house so badly... and this was *her house.*

Jesse ground out, "Maybe, but even the worst humans can't fuck you up six ways from Sunday the way a vampire can. I don't want that for you, and I don't want you getting caught up in it!"

If only you knew. "Humans can do some pretty fucked-up shit to people." Elana slowly got to her feet. "Jesse, I can see this has you really upset. I don't know what happened to you that made you so afraid of vampires, but—"

"I'm not afraid!" he interrupted.

She held up her hands. "Sorry, wrong word. Look—have a drink of water, take a breath, and let's talk about this, okay?" Elana bent enough to grab his glass of water and offered it to him. "If it's important enough to you to come to my place after work without letting me know first, it's really important. I can respect that. Let's talk."

Jesse took the glass, but he didn't drink from it, and he gripped it so hard his fingers turned white. "I don't want you going there. I don't trust them. Don't go back."

Elana grimaced. "I can't promise that."

His hand shook, and his face darkened. "Why not? They're evil, horrible creatures that manipulate people to get what they want. Do they have something on you? Is that it?"

"No." She fought the urge to back up and struggled to maintain her temper. She'd never taken kindly to people telling her what she could and couldn't do, and this, on top of her existential crisis, was pushing her to the breaking point.

"Then why?"

Elana gritted her teeth. "It's none of your business, Jesse. I'm sorry, but that's how it is. I respect that you're uncomfortable—"

"*Uncomfortable?*" Jesse cut in. His hand wobbled, and water spilled onto the carpet. "I'm not just *uncomfortable*, Elana. I'm *pissed*. I found out from the boys that you know all about vampire shit, have for years, and now you're going into that goddamn prison city more often than you're coming out on *jobs*. What am I supposed to think? Am I not supposed to be worried about you? I'm your boyfriend, for God's sake! Doesn't that count for something? Doesn't that count for any *respect?*"

Elana's eye twitched. She dragged in a breath and let it out in a slow hiss. "I think you should leave."

"No! Not until you tell me what's going on!"

She walked around the coffee table toward the front door. "I wasn't aware we'd decided to make things official, but even if we had—shouldn't that go both ways? Shouldn't you respect my choices? You have no right to tell me what I can and can't do, and I don't owe you shit. I have nothing to tell you. It's *none of your business.*"

"I just want to protect you!"

Elana didn't turn to face him. She laid her hand on the doorknob. "I don't need you to protect me. To tell you the truth, I feel a hell of a lot safer with the vampires than I do with you—"

"*Fuck* you!"

She flinched as the water glass flew past her and smashed against the wall. Water splashed her arm. The base of the glass left a dent in the drywall, and the shards fell to the floor with muffled tinkling.

Elana's gut clenched. Her breathing was shallow as she opened the door. "We're done. Get out."

Jesse stormed past her. She closed the door behind him, locked it, leaned her forehead on the door frame, and stared at a chip in the paint until she stopped shaking.

Elana took several minutes to breathe and calm down before doing anything after Jesse left. She stretched out on her bed, closed her eyes, and let her thoughts go.

Elana's ties to the human world were fading one by one—or snapping, in Jesse's case. He had a point that she'd been in Haven more often than at work over the past week.

She'd enjoyed herself on-site, but her unease about her secret grew with every day. She wasn't one of the guys anymore and never would be again.

Her father had prided himself on being straight with his crew. Elana had done the same. If she couldn't do that anymore...she probably needed to cut that tie, too.

Jesse would think she was running into the vampires' arms, whatever that meant. In some ways, he might have been right.

On the other hand, Elana's mother had been a vampire. Maybe Elana wasn't running into the vampires' arms as much as she was diving into what should have been hers to begin with.

She opened her eyes and traced patterns in the popcorn ceiling with her gaze. The conviction that she would move to Haven was solid at this moment—solid enough that she wanted to pick up the phone and call a moving company. Still, she knew she shouldn't make decisions after a big fight.

Elana rolled onto her side and grabbed her phone from the nightstand. She texted Matt.

Hey—got a minute for a call?

She dropped the phone beside her on the bed and continued outlining shapes in the ceiling until it buzzed a minute later.

Sure. Everything okay?

Elana contemplated how to tell him, "Fuck no, my life's a disaster," for long enough that he called her first.

She accepted the call, hit Speaker, and left the phone beside her on the bed. "Hi, Matt. Sorry for bothering you."

"No problem. Honestly, I'm surprised you haven't called me sooner. The first week of being an initiate is usually a roller coaster. I expected more panicked SOSes, not less."

Matt sounded like he was on speaker, too. He also sounded calm and reassuring, and the relieved warmth that flooded through Elana made tears spring to her eyes.

"This is normal?" she asked in a thick voice.

"*Oh*, yes. Even though the grand majority of new vampires *elect* to take the Rights, the process is a huge life change. You're discovering that it happened without your consent *years* ago. You don't even know how it happened, for Christ's sake! Of *course* it's going to be difficult."

Elana let out a shaky breath and focused her attention on a single misshapen blob of plaster above her head. "That is both reassuring and terrifying."

"Understandable." She could hear his smile over the phone. "Let's start again. What happened?"

Elana briefly considered only telling Matt the barebones, then decided it wasn't worth the hassle. The way her life was going, she wouldn't see Jesse again, and nothing she told Matt was likely to get back to him anyway. She recounted the fight and gave Matt the necessary context, including that she didn't know why Jesse was so deeply prejudiced against vampires.

"What an awful way to get home," Matt sympathized when she'd finished. "I'm sorry, Elana. Are you okay?"

"I'm not physically hurt. I don't know if he was *trying* to hit me with the glass, but he missed, and he didn't attack me."

"You showed great restraint."

This comment, delivered by a voice farther away from the phone, made Elana start so badly she was pretty sure her heart skipped a beat.

"You didn't tell me the arbiter was there," she exclaimed breathlessly. "Shit—Valeria, I'm so sorry, this is incredibly unprofessional of me. I shouldn't be whining to you—"

"Stop," the consort ordered. Elana snapped her mouth shut. "Mister Richelieu and I were discussing your case when you contacted him. I, too, am familiar with the difficulties of adjusting to vampire life. You handled yourself admirably. In your shoes, I would not have been so understanding."

"You probably would have knocked him out in the first two sentences," Matt remarked with mild amusement.

"On a good day," Valeria agreed.

Elana didn't want to consider what Valeria might have done on a bad day. It made her think too much about everything Jesse had spouted.

She sat up and hauled in a slow breath, then exhaled in a long sigh. "Sorry. Panicking."

"Deep breaths," Matt advised. "You're gonna be okay."

"Yeah." Elana didn't speak for several seconds, focusing instead on getting her heart rate back to normal. "Okay. Um… Shit, I don't remember why I called you."

"Probably because you're freaking out about whether to leave your human life behind or not," Matt gently teased her. "Am I close?"

She groaned. "Pretty much spot on. I don't know what to do, Matt."

"Well, I can't tell you what to do, but I *can* tell you that you're perfectly within your rights whatever you choose." His tone was steady and kind, and reminded Elana of her dad at his best. "We haven't known each other long, but I can tell you don't make decisions lightly. You're strong, Elana. Not just in body but in mind and heart. You'll figure out what's best for you."

"You are also strong in will," Valeria added. She was not comforting but practical and matter-of-fact. "You are aware of the weight of the choice you face, and you do not take it lightly. When you decide, you will fully commit and without hesitation."

Elana drew another breath. The colony of butterflies in her stomach had calmed down. Her fear and panic drifted away, replaced by a quiet sadness underneath which lay a certainty unfamiliar to her.

She glanced around her bedroom. She'd redecorated it in community college—tearing down the posters of boy bands that had papered the walls through high school—but it hadn't changed since. The navy walls and white trim now made her think of a girl trying too hard to be an adult, pretending to belong to a world that wasn't hers.

How much more was that true of her life now?

Matt's voice pulled her from her musing. "Elana? Are you still there?"

"I am. Just thinking."

"Go train," Valeria firmly told her. "Work out this anger and anxiety. Occupy your body, and your mind will deliver the answer."

Elana frowned. "I don't have the equipment here. Should I come to Haven?"

Valeria chuckled. "You don't need equipment to train. Do what comes naturally. You are sufficient unto yourself, Elana. You are enough."

Elana stared at her phone in surprise. That was quite possibly the deepest compliment anyone had ever paid her. "I'll do that." After a pause, she added, "Thank you both. I really appreciate this."

"Any time," Matt assured her. "We're on your side. Can I pick you up tomorrow at eleven? There are files in the archives I want you to see."

"I look forward to it."

As Elana hung up the phone, it struck her that she *was* very much looking forward to it.

Elana ended up running circuits in her backyard, hidden from prying eyes by the fence she'd helped her father install in tenth grade. Exercising in your backyard wasn't weird, but Elana suspected the neighbors might think it strange that she was hauling around cinder blocks like they were dumbbells.

She worked out for two hours. Each time she hurled one of the concrete blocks across the lawn, she felt like she had released more anxiety. Every lap around the yard felt like half a mile closer to Haven. Every drop of sweat she wiped from her brow was more of her humanity draining away.

When the sun had fully set, Elana climbed the side of

her house and perched on the roof's peak. Another summer storm was rolling in on the horizon. Its flashes of lightning illuminated the skyline of Haven and its wall.

The other night, Elana had considered the lightning beautiful but distant. Tonight, she felt as though it was a part of her. Those bright, searing forks were the power that coursed through her veins and a light that pointed to her destiny.

CHAPTER EIGHTEEN

Elana had figured Matt was speaking figuratively when he'd said he'd pick her up the next morning and he'd send a car for her as usual. To her surprise, the man himself rolled up in an understated black Audi at five to eleven.

"You're early," she teased him. "What are we doing today? How am I getting back?"

"Like I mentioned on the phone last night, I have some files I want to show you. That said, I did some thinking after your call yesterday, and I have a few suggestions for errands we could run first. Apart from that, you're free to do whatever you want in the city. You can always book a car back if I can't bring you home."

Elana buckled herself into the front passenger seat and closed the door. "Really? I thought that was something only, like, you or Valeria could do."

He chuckled and put the car in drive. "No, no—but this tells me we need to get you an updated phone. The cars that have picked you up are Haven's taxi service. Any of

Haven's citizens can book them...although I will say, if you book them yourself, you have to pay for them."

Elana snickered. "Unless they cost a few hundred thousand dollars a pop, I think I can afford that. What are these errands you're talking about?"

"There are a number of things that new vampires tend to have trouble with while transitioning into their new lives—legal and business questions in particular. Like I said, I have a couple of suggestions, but ultimately, it's up to you whether you take any of them."

"Let's hear them."

"You own a business, correct?

"I do. I inherited it from my father when he passed." She quickly corrected herself. "*Technically*, I was already a partner. We set it up that way when he got sick. We'd always meant to, just didn't think we'd have to do it so soon..."

Elana cleared her throat. "Anyway. I've been thinking about selling the business to the lead foreman. He's been with the company longer than I've been alive."

"Does he want it?"

Elana slipped her phone from her pocket and tapped it on her thigh. "I haven't had a chance to ask him yet. Until last night's explosion, I wasn't sure I wanted to sell."

"Does that mean you're sure of it now?" Matt glanced her way again. "I don't want you to feel like we're pressuring you. That's the last thing we want."

Elana looked out the window at the passing buildings and pedestrians and sighed. "Yes and no, to be honest. Last night convinced me that my place is in Haven, but I'm reluctant to cut all ties with Ashford. I grew up here. The guys on the crew are my family. Jerry basically helped raise me."

"Jerry. That's the foreman?"

"Yeah."

"Have you told him yet?"

"That I'm a vampire? No. I didn't think I was allowed to. Wasn't that what the NDA was all about?"

Matt shook his head. "The NDA refers specifically to the details of the investigation into your lineage—i.e., your mother's actions. It's all hush-hush because she was an arbiter *and* a member of the House of the SpiderKing. You're free to tell whomever you want that you're a vampire. You just can't talk about what happened with your mother."

"Then I suppose I'll have to unless I want to entirely ghost him." Elana scowled. "That's not my style. He deserves better than that."

"Is he likely to take it well?"

Elana heaved a sigh and rested her head against the window. Her gaze dragged on a cocker spaniel trotting beside its owner's heeled boots until they passed it. "I don't know. He loves me like a daughter, but then again, my dad hated vampires. The crew is just as likely to make stupid vampire jokes as stupid human jokes. It's hard to tell how seriously any of them take it or how they'd respond."

Matt hummed in understanding, then focused on changing lanes around a slow driver. When they'd settled back onto their route, he spoke up again. "I think I might be able to *partially* solve your problem. One of them, anyway."

"Oh?"

"Turn your business into an LLC. You can keep the name and a controlling share in the company for the time being but add Jerry as a partner. It'll allow you to put yourself at arm's length without relinquishing that part of your family legacy. *Also*...nobody looks too closely at who owns an LLC, so you can remain on the books as long as you please without it becoming *truly* public knowledge that you're a vampire. If you decide to keep it quiet, that is."

Elana mulled this over. "I suppose that would also give me a steady income stream. I'll admit I hadn't thought about how I'd support myself after moving to Haven. Four million won't last as long as you'd think it might, not if I'm expected to keep the Haven lifestyle."

Matt chuckled. "A very important consideration."

"Is that one of the errands you were referring to? Filing the paperwork to turn Bishop's Electronics and Hauling into an LLC?"

"Yes. I didn't want to assume how familiar you were with corporate paperwork and wanted to offer my help."

Elana eyed him. "The more I learn about you, the more I wonder why you work as a dispatcher for Haven Security."

Matt laughed. "What can I say? I like helping people. Many vampires discover that since we have ample time to learn multiple skills, we end up with multi-headed careers. I started as a lawyer, then branched out into social work. After that, I decided to train as a guardian.

"Guardians at Haven Security function as case managers more than dispatchers. We've learned over the years that people tend to appreciate working with the same person over the course of their case rather than being passed off from position to position. My background makes me particularly good at it, especially in fringe cases like yours."

Elana chortled. "*Fringe* cases? What does *that* mean?"

"New vampires are relatively rare. Usually, it's a long process culminating in the giving of the Rights, where the new blood learns how vampire society works before they're inducted. There are always a handful of traumatic cases, of course, although they're mercifully few and far between. I get almost all of those.

"You're unique, at least in my history. You were a vampire, and you didn't know it. You've lived your entire life believing you were an especially impressive specimen of humanity, and now you have to sort out your history in addition to deciding how to move forward. You need someone to walk with you through the process—someone who not only has the experience but also the skills to ensure you're prepared to make those difficult choices."

Elana hummed thoughtfully, then smiled warmly. "You're right. It's a lot, and it's overwhelming. I appreciate your help."

"Any time."

She drummed her fingers on her leg, then added, "I think you're probably also right that an LLC is the way to go. I took a couple of business courses in community college, but it's been a while, so I'd be grateful if you'd pitch in on the paperwork. Are you still a practicing lawyer?"

"I am, as a matter of fact. In several states."

"Well, aren't *you* fancy."

Matt grinned and pretended to polish his nails on the lapel of his suit.

The paperwork went as smoothly as corporate tax paperwork ever went. This meant Elana and Matt walked out of the office building mildly dehydrated, peckish, and in Elana's case, faintly irritable.

"I can't believe you *like* doing that work," Elana groused. "I'm all for small business, but geez. The more involved your paperwork gets, the less it feels like *business*. Sometimes I get where my dad came from with his occasional libertarian leanings. Let me move off-grid and do my own thing, god*damn*."

Matt chuckled. "In my experience, the longer a vampire lives, the more they fit into one of two categories. One is comprised of the people who view bureaucracy as an art form, an elegant labyrinth of red tape meant to be appreciated for the system it is."

"Ugh."

"The other is comprised of those who would like nothing more than to dissolve every governmental entity on the planet and reform them into the system of their choice, be that absolute monarchy or absolute anarchy. There's not usually much in between."

Elana snorted. "I can't say I'd be a big fan of either."

"I believe it was Churchill who said that 'democracy is the worst form of government, except for all the others.'"

"Sounds about right." She stretched and popped a vertebra. "I vote lunch. Do you like tacos?"

"I could eat queso all day."

"Good thing you're a vampire and don't have to worry about heart attacks."

"So are you."

Elana beamed. "Hey, that's true! Extra queso for me!"

They found a taqueria with an open-air patio and devoured half a dozen tacos apiece, washing the chorizo and shredded beef down with chilled horchata.

Midway through her third taco, Elana paused to rescue a stray piece of tomato. "What's on the agenda for this afternoon? You didn't mention any of your other suggestions."

Matt swallowed and wiped his mouth. "I wondered if you'd like to go shopping."

She tilted her head. "For anything in particular?"

"Well…a car, actually."

Elana narrowed her eyes. "Why the hesitation?"

Matt sighed and laid his hands palm up on the table. "I've been debating the best way to broach this subject with you since this morning. Plenty of vampires become *very* attached to their cars, especially those who decide to sink their wealth into car collections, so I would understand if you didn't want to give up your truck. But the truth is…"

Elana crossed her arms. "It's not very *vampiric*."

Matt lifted his hands in a slight gesture of agreement. "I will admit there *is* a certain aesthetic that most vampires adhere to. However, if that were the *only* consideration, I wouldn't push it. God knows there are just as many vampires who are eccentric enough that one Ford F150 wouldn't be *so* out of place. That's not the problem.

"The *actual* problem is that it's *big*." He gave her an apologetic half-smile. "I'm sure you've noticed that most of Haven's streets are narrower than your average American road."

Elana nodded and uncrossed her arms, satisfied that Matt wasn't judging her beloved behemoth. "The city's laid out in more of a European style. I know I'd have a hard time navigating Jessie through the streets, apart from the central avenues." She huffed. "I figured I'd have to sell her eventually. Does it have to be now?"

He shook his head. "Of course not. But for your ease and comfort, you might want to consider buying something smaller."

"And flashier?"

"Couldn't hurt. There's a good dealership on the south side of Ashford if you're into imports…"

Elana scowled. "As much as I *do* like fancy Italian cars, no thanks. I've heard horror stories about the way they treat women. I'm not interested in being treated like your arm candy when I'm the one buying the damn car."

To her surprise, Matt beamed. "I have just the thing to help with that."

They made a quick trip to Elana's, where she changed into an outfit she never would have dreamed of wearing while car shopping. The designer pantsuit would have been at home on a red carpet or in a penthouse boardroom where she was staging a hostile takeover. Then, to Elana's surprise, they headed for Haven instead of turning toward the south side of Ashford.

As they turned onto the ring road, Elana ventured, "I'm confused. I thought we were buying a car from the fancy-ass luxury dealership in the city."

"We will, but the thing I mentioned that will help with sexist assholes being sexist assholes requires a trip to Haven first."

"Okay..."

Matt entered Haven through the Gate of Innovation, which marked the border between Etreta and Quarto—Progress and Knowledge. The way Etreta's Brutalist skyscrapers contrasted with Quarto's Edwardian edifices made Elana think she was walking a tightrope between two eras of the world half a century apart.

They turned into Etreta's financial district, where the stark architecture added small flourishes and pillared façades to the abundance of right angles and monoliths of concrete. Elana was less familiar with this district. Any drama worth following from the world of industry inevitably spilled over into Premier's and Octava's social circles, and Elana had never been one to follow stock markets or business periodicals.

That didn't stop her from being wowed by the imposing Tyndall stone building they parked in front of. It was only four stories high, a far cry from most of its neighbors, but the thick round columns and carefully carved stonework of the arches between them more than made up for its lack of height. The words Bank of Haven were carved in sharp relief above the entrance.

"Am I about to discover the racist underbelly of vampire society in the process of also discovering that my mother left me a shit-ton of money?" she inquired, amused. "Will we ride minecarts in a massive underground cavern to find my vault?"

Matt snorted. "No. We'll walk in and speak to the

unionized vampire bank employees about getting you an account and a credit card. Dealing with your mother's estate will come later, although I *do* think you'll receive a significant chunk of change. No dragons, either."

"Damn. I like dragons."

"Sorry."

Elana exited the car, still chuckling. Matt caught up to her on the stone steps and waved behind himself to lock the Audi. It beeped at the same time as they reached the doors.

The Bank of Haven's inside was equally impressive as the outside. They entered a two-story atrium where elegant chandeliers hung over the polished stone floor in a million shades of brown and black. The walls were the same beige Tyndall stone as the exterior. Elana spied large and small fossils everywhere she looked.

Matt led her to a teller's booth tucked away under another smaller arch. The woman behind the plexiglass had a ruddy face, coarse brown hair, and glasses on a beaded cord. However, the multitude of diamond-encrusted rings covering her fingers thoroughly undermined her secretarial demeanor.

"Afternoon, Mister Richelieu." She greeted them with a bright smile and a strong Southern accent. "How can I help?"

"Hello, Hilda. You look lovely as always." Matt offered a half-bow, and Elana hurried to mirror him.

Hilda waved a glittering hand. "Oh, fiddlesticks. You just say that so I'll waive your withdrawal fees."

Matt grinned. "The Bank of Haven *has* no withdrawal fees."

Hilda fluttered her eyelashes. "Must be because everyone tells me I'm pretty." They laughed, and Hilda set her gaze on Elana. "Who might you be, miss?"

Elana did another half-bow and wished she'd taken out an e-book on vampire etiquette. Was there a vampire Emily Post? She'd have to find out. "Elana Bishop. Nice to meet you."

"And you. Are you new?"

"Um, yes. Is it that obvious?"

Hilda chuckled. "You're doing fine. It's not often that Mister Richelieu comes in with someone I don't recognize, and being in his line of work, well… I'm a bank teller, miss. I can add two plus two."

Elana relaxed. "Fair enough. Yes, I'm new."

"You'll be wanting a bank account, then. Am I far off?"

"Not at all."

"And a credit card," Matt put in. "I'll co-sign if needed, but I doubt I will be."

Hilda was already typing on the interface inlaid in her desk in a similar fashion to the tabletop at the library. "Elana…Bishop…" She glanced up. "Middle name?"

"Rosalie."

"Gorgeous." Hilda added this, plus Elana's birthdate and current address. As she typed in the latter, she looked over her glasses at Elana. "When that updates, you come and see me."

Elana swallowed. "Yes, ma'am."

"Very good. Parents' names and Houses?"

"Um…" Elana glanced at Matt.

"Her father was human," he provided. "Jeremiah Bishop.

Her mother was a vampire. Tessa Hart. She'll be in the system."

Hilda's eyebrows rose a fraction of an inch. "*There's* a name I haven't heard in some time." She hit Enter, then allowed the computer to think for several seconds. When it *beeped* at her quietly, she smiled. "There we have it. You're all set. The system will print your cards right away—debit and credit."

Elana blinked, then frowned. "What? Don't I have to give you my current employment, income level, stuff like that? No way you can just—"

Hilda interrupted her with a laugh. "Oh, honey. You really *are* new."

She leaned over and plucked two plastic cards from under her desk, then slid them across the counter to Elana. One was white and had Elana's name at the bottom and the sigil of Haven at the top-right in black.

The other...

"This has no limit and is fully insured against fraud by the royal treasury," Hilda informed her, tapping the credit card with one bejeweled finger. "It is good anywhere in the world. There are no daily or transaction limits, either."

Elana gaped. "How can I... How is this...*what?*"

Hilda smiled. "With connections like yours, the bank doesn't ask for insurance. They know you're good for it. Your line is your word, and your word is your bond."

"Connections? What connections?"

"Connections in high places," Matt explained.

Elana narrowed her eyes. "Quit being cryptic. How high is high?"

Matt raised his eyebrows and pointed at the spiderweb sigil etched on the plexiglass. "*High.*"

Elana swallowed hard and gingerly took the card. "Thank you, Hilda."

"'Course, darlin'. You need anything else today?"

Elana glanced at Matt, who shook his head. "I don't think so."

"Then you have a lovely day. Buy somethin' nice."

CHAPTER NINETEEN

Elana numbly nodded and followed Matt out of the bank. She expected he would head straight for Ashford after starting the car, but instead he only drove a few blocks before pulling onto a quiet side street and parking.

"What are we doing now?" she asked with trepidation.

He laid a reassuring hand on her forearm. "Taking five. See that bench over there? Go have a seat, and I'll be right back."

Elana crossed to the bench he'd indicated, which sat beside a planter filled with a perfectly geometric flower arrangement. She sat and stared at the sidewalk and jumped when Matt sat beside her.

"Sorry," she muttered. "I'm just…"

"Overwhelmed," he supplied and nudged her arm. "Here. Coffee."

Elana accepted the paper cup and sipped from it. The coffee was dark and rich. The flavor rolled over her tongue and the heat spread through her chest.

"This is good."

"My favorite in the city, honestly."

Matt and Elana quietly sat for a few minutes, drinking coffee and listening to the tranquil back streets of Etreta. Everyone was at work now, so there was little pedestrian traffic. Background noise amounted to birds and the occasional insect.

Eventually, Elana broke the silence. "Sorry again. I'm trying my best to handle everything, but it's a lot."

"It's okay. You're right that it's a lot, and there's no shame in being overwhelmed." Matt exhaled a soft laugh. "It doesn't help that you're dealing with even more than most new vampires."

"Just because I didn't know I was converted so long ago?"

"That's part of it. The other part is how high up the chain you're coming in. You're an initiate, but you're not exactly *entry level*."

Elana blew a breath out. "No shit. What's all that about? What House am I in? I asked Valeria about it the other day, and she did the cryptic thing. I didn't think I'd hear more about it until…well, I don't know. Until somebody decided I was allowed to know more."

Matt hummed under his breath. "Vampires *do* tend to love surprising people. When you're functionally immortal, you get harder to surprise, so we like doing it to others. But in that case, Valeria wasn't trying to keep you in the dark for fun.

"Until last night, we weren't a hundred percent sure where you'd end up. Obviously, you have to be attached to *a* House, and it's rare that a vampire starts out attached to any House but the one that gave them the Rights."

"My mother's House," Elana put forward.

Matt nodded. "Except your mother's line effectively ended on paper when she died since she had no known vampire descendants. As a legally 'sire-less' vampire, you would become a member of House Arachne. Arachne is a client house of the House of the SpiderKing, established to cover all the awkward possibilities that crop up without having to resort to mounds *more* paperwork."

"I know House Arachne. It's in the lowest tier of Houses. No way am I getting a black card from the Bank of Haven with Arachne as my House. Therefore, that is *not* what happened."

"No, it's not." Matt glanced at her, then shifted his cup in his hands and drew a deep breath. "The final ruling was that until you decided otherwise, your mother's line would be reestablished, and you would join it. Unorthodox, but that's par for the course when it comes to Tessa Hart."

Elana narrowed her eyes. A pit opened in her stomach. "What House did my mother belong to?"

"The House of the SpiderKing."

Elana barely kept hold of her half-full coffee cup. "*What?*"

Matt rescued the at-risk beverage and placed it on the bench beside him. "Yeah. You're a member of the royal House now. That comes with plenty of rights and benefits, but also responsibilities."

Elana's vision blurred and her eyes stung. "Holy shit. Holy *shit*."

Matt put a hand on her arm. "You okay with a hug?"

Elana responded by leaning to the side until her shoulder thumped against his sternum. He chuckled under his breath, wrapped his arms around her, and held on tight. When she sniffled and a couple of tears slipped across her cheek, he gently turned her and let her bury her face in his shoulder.

Elana heaved a shaky breath and spoke into his collar. "This is like a gothic, Wall Street version of *The Princess Diaries* on steroids. Where's Julie Andrews? I demand Julie Andrews."

Matt held back a grin. "I'll get right on that."

"This is terrifying. I have *responsibilities* to a *royal House*? I only found out I was a vampire this week!" She coughed out a sob.

Matt rubbed her back. "I hear you. I'll help you navigate it, and so will Valeria. There are good things about Houses too. Good Houses take care of their people. What you do speaks to the prestige of the House, and the prestige of your House opens doors for those who don't know you yet."

"I haven't *done* anything," she murmured into his suit jacket. It came out muffled. "Nothing other than probably wreck a bazillion-dollar suit."

"That's what dry cleaning is for. It's fine." He smiled into her hair. "Vampires are strong believers in inherited traits, so—like mother, like daughter. Your mother already showed all of Haven—all of Haven that *matters*—the quality of your heart. By approving this House transfer, the SpiderKing is letting everyone know he believes in you.

"Trust the vampires, Elana. We're very good judges of character."

Elana sniffled again, then let out a long sigh and sat up. When she met Matt's eyes, a glint of humor shimmered in hers. "Okay. Existential crisis averted…for now, at least." She glanced around. "Mostly because out in the open isn't a good place to talk about all of this.

"But I want to talk about it more," she told him seriously. "I need to understand how much the man at the top is paying attention to me."

Matt's lips quirked up in a half-smile. "Let's just say he probably knows your sock size."

"Fantastic, because that's not scary or anything. How the hell did my mother become a member of the House of the SpiderKing, anyway? Can you tell me that much?"

He winced. "Actually, no. I have no idea how your mother joined the royal House. All records having to do with the royal House are strictly classified. Whatever the SpiderKing says, goes. Nobody argues."

Elana pressed her hands to her temples. "*Of course.*"

Elana didn't find her voice again until she and Matt arrived on the south side of Ashford, and the sprawling commercial parks and wide expanses of concrete covered in shining cars.

Matt pulled the Audi into a spot next to the door. Rows of beautifully engineered luxury cars stretched out in every direction. Elana recognized most of them—Porsche, Maserati, Ferrari, among others—but there were a few she did not. The chrome emblems gleamed on the polished hoods in red, black, and white, promising effortless speed and prestige.

Nerves struck the moment her foot touched the pavement. "I'm not sure about this," she murmured in Matt's direction.

A human wouldn't have been able to hear her, but Matt had no problem. He smiled, came around the car, and took her arm reassuringly. "You've got this," he muttered, then squeezed her arm again before letting go. "Just walk in like you own the place."

Elana drew a deep breath. She could do this. *Shoulders down, neck long, think* murder, *and walk.*

She scanned the show floor as she strode through the glass doors into the dealership. She spied a woman with long blonde hair behind a desk that said Sales. *Bingo.*

Elana took half a dozen steps toward her target before she was intercepted.

"Welcome, sir, ma'am! My name is Edward. How may I assist you today?"

Edward's voice was as slick as his short black hair, which was combed back over his ears. He was shorter than Elana by an inch—thank you, heels—and sported a tiny, perfectly groomed thatch of a goatee along with equally thin mustachios. He wore a black suit with a black tie, and while Elana now had enough experience to know it was an expensive label and had been tailored to fit, the cut was not as flattering as the man undoubtedly thought it was. Too blocky. It made him look short.

Elana's gaze instinctively flicked to Matt. He gave her an encouraging smile and nodded toward Edward as if repeating, *You've got this.*

Right. She'd be fine. Just had to take the bull by the horns.

She faced the salesman dead-on and put on her most winning smile. "I'm looking to buy a car."

Edward grinned back with a row of perfect teeth, which looked more like pearls than real teeth. His gaze shifted from Elana to Matt as soon as she finished talking. "I hoped so! What are we looking for today?"

Matt's answering smile was genuine, warm, and supremely indulgent. "Oh, it's not for me. It's for her."

Edward didn't miss a beat. "Of course, sir, of course." He turned his ingratiating smile on Elana, who fought back bile as he asked, "And what would the lovely lady's heart desire?"

Elana stomped on the urge to tell him to go fuck himself and kept her smile pasted on. "I want something small and simple. Nothing overly ostentatious. I want it to run without a hiccup for at least ten years."

Edward's eyes took on a hint of hardness, and he let out a brittle, false peal of laughter. "We might be hard-pressed to find you something that isn't ostentatious here, madam! We *do* pride ourselves on our ultra-high-class vehicles."

Elana gritted her teeth. "Could I speak with a female associate, please?"

The smarm came back in full force. "If that would make you more *comfortable*, I'm sure that could be arranged," Edward drawled. "I can set you up with Ashley right away and start the paperwork with finance to get you on your way that much faster. May I ask how you intend to make your down payment? It'll save me a few steps in the system."

"I'll be paying in full," she calmly informed him.

His eyebrows rose. "Will that be in cash, then, ma'am?"

His eyes flicked toward the back of the show floor, no doubt wondering whether Elana was legitimate and whether he would need to check for counterfeit bills.

Elana didn't bother to answer him. Instead, she allowed her smile to transform into a sneer worthy of the Arbiter of Shadows herself as she slipped her Versace wallet out of her Hermès Lindy handbag. She watched Edward's eyes light up with the confirmation that he was about to make a handsome commission because she had no doubt he would take the credit for the sale and leave Ashley in the dust. Then she delighted in the picturesque way his blood drained from his face when she held up her credit card.

The Bank of Haven's customers were *exclusively* vampires. The spoke-and-wheel sigil was enough to make most retailers treat you with more deference—or more attitude if the salesperson happened not to like vampirekind.

Most Bank of Haven cards were white and featured the Haven sigil in black in the top left corner. The symbol of the district where the cardholder's House was quartered appeared on the right side of the card, also in black.

Elana's card was the inverse and had no district symbol—only the SpiderKing's sigil in stark white on the jet-black background.

Edward gaped at the black card for several seconds before regaining his voice. "*Please* take whatever time you'd like to browse. We have a stunning Quattroporte just in that would suit your tastes admirably, I think—or if you prefer a German make, I would highly recommend the AMG EQE sedan…"

Elana let her smile get even harder. "I'd like to speak with Ashley, if you'd be *so* kind."

"O-Of course. Right away."

He nearly tripped over himself in his hurry, and Elana was hard-pressed not to snicker.

"Well done," Matt murmured. "He'll have fun explaining to his boss why he offended a top-level vampire."

Elana allowed herself to cackle under her breath.

The blonde saleswoman, Ashley, joined her once Edward had scurried into the back to grovel to his boss and get the paperwork started. The two women strolled the show floor with Matt a few paces behind.

Ashley looked Elana up and down and lightly narrowed her almond eyes. "I'm guessing…low-profile, stylish but not ostentatious. You prefer reliability over show and want something that will last and still impress several years down the line."

Elana raised her eyebrows. "Nail on the head. You're good."

Ashley winked. "The only way Edward gets sales is if he talks to the customers before I do. Are you looking to start or build a collection, or is this a day-to-day car?"

"Day-to-day," Elana confirmed. "I might start a collection down the line, but not yet."

"Do you drive manual?"

"I do. Better on mileage and less likely to be stolen. That said, it's not a dealbreaker."

"Understood. In that case…" Ashley tapped one dark green manicured nail on her chin. "Follow me. I think I have a few options you'll like."

Ashley led Elana past the gleaming Porsches and

Lamborghinis on display to another section. The BMW mark was easy to spot, but Elana didn't recognize the winged emblem or the flower emblem on the two lower-profile cars.

"Aston Martin and Lotus," Ashley offered. "We see less call for British imports—most people want the excitement that comes with an Italian model—but on occasion, we have people come in who are looking for something a little more dignified."

Elana hummed. "That sounds like me. What am I looking at?"

Ashley motioned at the cars nearest them. "Three BMWs, the M2, M3, and M4. Two Aston Martins, the DB12 and the Vantage. Two Lotuses, the Emira and the Emeya. See anything that catches your eye?"

Elana walked among the models, pondering, then pointed at a sleek sedan in a silvery gray with a diamond-shaped grille and thin headlights. "I like this one."

"The Emeya. She's fully electric and can hit sixty in less than three seconds on the 905-horsepower model. All the standard tech. Regular maintenance will be a little pricier than your average combustion vehicle, but somehow I doubt that will be an issue for your pocketbook. Want to take her for a spin?"

Elana's face split into a grin. "Oh, *do* I."

Ashley smirked. "Have fun. The paperwork will be ready to sign when you come back."

Elana's eyebrows rose. "You seem awfully certain I'll pick this one."

Ashley tapped her temple. "I have a feeling, and my feelings aren't usually wrong."

Elana drifted back into the parking lot and let out an elated whoop. Her heart raced with adrenaline and her cheeks hurt from smiling.

Matt gingerly released the grab handle and forcefully exhaled as he relaxed into the passenger's seat. "Did you learn stunt driving?"

She laughed. "I took a summer course a couple of years ago. Most fun I've ever had, and now I can do it in my own damn car. There are electric vehicle chargers in Haven, right? I'm sure I've seen them."

He nodded. "Full infrastructure, yes. Our fire department is also capable of putting out fires in electric vehicles."

"Really? Any plans to share that with the general public? I've heard electric vehicle fires are next to impossible to put out."

"It's on the docket. The king wants to share, but we have to be careful how we do it. Can't let too much advanced technology out into the wild."

Elana's breathing and heart rate were gradually slowing. She let go of the steering wheel and caught sight of Ashley through the dealership's glass wall. The saleswoman was smiling like the cat that got the cream.

Elana patted the center console. "Do we know how much this baby costs?"

Matt chuckled. "You have a Bank of Haven black card. Does it matter?"

"I guess not." She giggled.

He grinned. "I *do* have to tease you for picking a car that doesn't match *any* of your criteria. Didn't you tell that smarmy asshole you wanted something reliable and not flashy? EVs aren't terribly reliable yet, and Lotuses aren't known for *blending in.*"

Elana blushed and stroked the Emeya's steering wheel. "Yeah, well. Sometimes you just gotta live a little, especially when you suddenly become a millionaire. She's pretty, and she makes me *feel* like a million dollars. I'll get a boring Chevy something-or-other next time. Also, I *will* enjoy rubbing it in the smarmy asshole's face that he wanted to sell me something fancy and now he's not getting a cent of commission. Take *that.*"

Matt snorted. "Fair enough."

As Elana exited the vehicle, Ashley opened the dealership's front door and waved. "Everything you hoped for?"

"And more!" Elana replied gleefully. "Where's the line for me to sign?"

"Right this way." Ashley ushered them back into the building and past Edward sulking at his desk. Elana made sure to smile ever so politely at him as she walked by.

CHAPTER TWENTY

Elana beat Matt back to Haven by a full two minutes. She came to a smooth stop at the King's Gate entrance and grinned at the attendant in the booth. "Elana Bishop, coming home."

The young man cast his gaze over the gorgeous sedan and grinned. "I see plenty of fantastic cars in this job, but this one has them all beat."

Elana flipped her hair over her shoulder. "Why, thank you."

He chuckled and tapped the button that opened the gate. "Have a good night, Miss Bishop."

"You too."

It wasn't until Elana drove into the city proper that she realized what she'd said. *Elana Bishop, coming home.*

Haven felt like home. Haven *was* home.

This hit her like a cannonball to the gut, but combined with the high she was riding from her new car, Elana felt giddy with excitement instead of heavy with regret.

She drove more sedately to Quarto, where she pulled

into a parking space beside the King's Archives and waited for Matt to do the same. When he joined her on the sidewalk, she announced, "I'm ready."

He lifted an eyebrow. "Ready for what?"

"To move in. To buy a house, rent an apartment, whatever. I'm ready to come home."

Matt's other eyebrow joined his first, and he tilted his head. Then his lips curved in a slow and genuine smile, and he opened his arms to Elana. "Then let me be the first to welcome you home…initiate."

Elana embraced him and exhaled a relieved breath. After a long moment, she let go and stepped back. "Thanks."

"Welcome. What made up your mind, if I can ask?"

She looked around the skyline of the city around them and half-shrugged. "Just realized it already felt like home. Don't get me wrong, there are still loose ends I'll need to tie up that won't be easy, but…this is where I need to be. This is my place."

Matt's smile warmed further. "I'm thrilled to hear that. I don't think there's a better frame of mind for you to start looking into your mother's legacy." He motioned at the archives' front doors. "Ready to dive in?"

Elana rubbed her hands together. "I can't wait."

This time, Matt escorted Elana to the northwest wing, and instead of ascending the spiral staircase, he led her into the stacks on the main floor.

The books on the shelves were a uniform cloth-bound burgundy, each a hand's-width tall and three fingers wide. No text showed on the spines, and Elana saw no labels on any shelves or aisles.

Matt turned down one aisle that looked like all the others, and Elana frowned. "Where are we going? What are these books?"

Matt spared the multitude of mysterious annals a bare glance. "Old recopied records from centuries ago. Not what we're here for. We're headed to the arbiters' archive."

His tone made Elana think he was about to tilt a book and reveal a secret passage. As it turned out, she was almost correct. They came to the end of the aisle and hung a left, and a few more steps took them to what looked like an emergency exit fire door.

Matt rested a palm on the thick push bar of the door and beckoned Elana to do the same. When she did, the metal warmed at her touch.

Something pricked her palm, and she flinched. She shook her hand and muttered, "Ow," although it was more from surprise than any real injury.

Elana glanced at Matt, unimpressed. "Blood test? Really? No more advanced way of telling who's allowed in here?"

Matt shrugged. "Can't beat the classics."

Elana peered at her palm but could detect no puncture. She grumbled faintly, then followed Matt through the door and down a staircase to a corridor.

The staircase and corridor beyond put her in mind of an *X-Files* episode. It was perfectly square, lit by long tube lights with a faint green tinge, and looked more like the route to a bunker than a wing of a library. The walls and floor were poured concrete with no visible seams. Thin pipes and conduits ran along the crease between the drop ceiling and the walls, and while there were doors every few yards, none were marked.

"This place is *creepy*," she muttered. "Cold War era? Are we about to find the arbiters' stash of canned goods for the apocalypse?"

Matt snorted, then pointed at the lights. "You're not far off. Those emit a specific frequency of ultraviolet light that serves as a decontamination measure. This level would withstand a minor nuclear blast. We're going down two more levels. The records archived in subbasement two would survive Armageddon."

"That's where my mother's files are kept?"

"That's where your mother's files are kept."

The corridor's temperature was perfectly even, but Elana shivered. "Are all arbiters' records kept under that level of security, or are my mother's special?"

Matt paused before replying, "Yes."

She shivered again. "Oh."

Elana followed Matt in silence down the corridor to an elevator. He entered a code on a glowing keypad set in the wall, then leaned in and allowed a hidden device to scan his retina. When he motioned her forward, she went up on tiptoe to do the same.

He smiled and tapped her shoulder. "It'll adjust to your height. Stand normally."

She dropped to the soles of her feet and peered at the wall. "Fancy." She flinched as the bright green light flickered out of the concrete wall and flashed over her eye, then stepped back beside Matt. "Am I already in the system?"

"Yes and no. Your information is, but your permissions might not have updated everywhere yet. We're entering on my say-so this time, but you still need to be logged as a visitor."

The elevator doors slid open, and they stepped in. The car's descent was so quiet and smooth that Elana could barely tell they were moving. Otherwise, it looked like any other office building elevator. The only other difference was that the inspection certificate mounted above the floor selection buttons showed the SpiderKing's sigil and the signature of the Arbiter of Progress instead of the Ashford Department of Safety.

Subbasement two looked exactly like the floor they'd left, right down to the distance between the doors. Elana set aside the déjà vu that washed over her and focused on steeling herself for what was to come.

Matt stopped in front of a door that looked like all the others. He gestured at it and glanced at her. "You try first. In theory, this system should have been updated the soonest, so you should be able to access it."

Elana approached the door. "Does it have a code like the elevator? I don't know it."

"No code. All biometrics like the first door we came in. Hand on the push bar."

Elana swallowed and laid her hand on the metal bar. It warmed under her palm and pricked her skin. A breath passed without any change. She was about to tell Matt it hadn't worked when the doorframe flashed blue, and the lock *clicked*.

Elana hesitated.

"Whenever you're ready," Matt quietly encouraged her. "There's no rush."

She drew a deep breath and pushed the door open.

Beyond the thick metal door stood an unassuming office. A pale gray desk that could have been salvaged from any of her hauling jobs sat in the corner opposite the door, across the room on Elana's right. A chair stood behind it. Black shelving units packed with books, binders, and bankers' boxes covered the other walls.

Elana frowned as she came to the center of the room and did a slow turn. "This is underwhelming."

Matt snorted. "Not everything is a *great, magical mystery*," he intoned in a faux-dramatic voice. "Were you expecting a basin full of the silvery residue of collected thoughts?"

"Not gonna lie. Yeah, pretty much."

He chuckled. "That's subbasement five."

She narrowed her eyes. "I can't tell if you're joking." He winked, and she shoved his upper arm. "You're the worst."

"Broke the tension," he retorted and smiled when she sighed and did the same. "Did you figure out how to use the interface at the library, by chance? Or do you need me to show you how to use them?"

Elana sat behind the desk and waved both hands over the blank face. "I got it to work, but I wouldn't say I know all the tricks."

Matt came to stand behind her and gently paused her movement with a touch. "I see that. First lesson. Just hover to start. It'll pick you up faster that way."

After a quick tutorial, Elana had the hang of the interface. She found a file marked Inventory, opened it, and scanned the lengthy list. "These aren't only my mother's files, are they? The dates go back too far."

"You're right. This office has access to all the archived

files of all the Arbiters of Sanctuary dating back to the founding of Haven. Some files are line-locked—the personal files of the arbiters. Direct descendants and certain blood relatives can access those files, and some clearance levels can as well, or can request access."

Elana was contemplating what to read first when a question struck her. "How do you *stop* being an arbiter?"

Matt laughed, caught off-guard. "What? Why?"

She waved at the room. "Vampires are functionally immortal. You could have the same arbiter forever, or if they left the job, they might still be alive and on the outside. Are they allowed in to look at all the old files and possibly get in the way of the new arbiter's work?"

Matt leaned on the desk and hummed knowledgeably. "I see what you're getting at. You have a good intuition for this. I'm told your mother did, too.

"The simple answer is that an arbiter serves at the king's pleasure. Most of the time, what ends up happening is that they serve until they die or until the SpiderKing decides he wants someone new. Occasionally, those might coincide depending on how the arbiter in question has comported themselves through the job. Sometimes the parting is on good terms. When it comes to who has continued access to the archives, that's entirely dependent on His Majesty."

Elana rested her hands on the desktop. "He really is the definition of an absolute monarch, isn't he?"

Matt shrugged. "In some ways, yes. He maintains a tight hold on the things it is important for him to keep hold of and exercises his authority in such a way that it's always clear he *can* take control whenever he wants. Some might find his rulings unfair, but I don't. I've never seen him act in poor judgment. It's important to keep in mind that he works from a depth of life experience the rest of us can barely dream of."

"How old *is* he?"

Matt laughed. "I've never asked, and I don't know anyone who has. *Old.*"

Elana hummed thoughtfully. Then she returned her attention to the list of files. "How long can I be in here? What am I supposed to be doing?"

"As long as you have time for, and whatever you want. I can stay and help you with the filing system, or I can leave you to it. Read anything, but keep in mind none of it can leave this room except in your head, and if you act on anything you've learned in here without running it by me or Valeria first…"

"He'll know."

"Without a doubt."

"Not interested in pissing him off, I'll tell you that much."

"Wise."

Elana bit her lip. "I'd like to know how my mother became an arbiter. How she became part of the king's House. Hell, how she got involved in the king's business at *all.*"

Matt nodded. "Then you'll probably want to start with the procedural records from the years after she received the Rights in the early nineties. Those should be digitized."

Navigating the archives was not difficult. Elana soon found the report from the Arbiter of Legacy, Amelian Darcy, regarding the administration of the Rights to one

Tessa Marceline Bishop, née Hart, on the seventeenth of September, 1992.

"It doesn't say who gave her the Rights," Elana remarked. "Only that it was an 'unpremeditated administration.' That sounds like someone got in trouble."

"I wouldn't know," Matt admitted. "I agree it does sound like that."

"It *does* say her House is the royal house already, and this is only from October 1992. That didn't take long."

Matt pursed his lips. "I wouldn't want to speculate, to tell you the truth. There's enough royal business in here that putting a toe out of line could result in some nasty sanctions."

"Sheesh. Guess I'll wait until I've built up some more goodwill before I start digging into *that*." Elana backed out of the file and scrolled forward a few years, then scowled. "Is there a way to limit my search to files about her? She wasn't the Arbiter of Sanctuary yet, so most of these are records from whoever came before her, and while I'm definitely interested in the changeover, I don't want to confuse myself further by not going in chronological order."

Matt nodded and leaned in, stretching a hand toward the interface. "May I?"

She pushed a couple of inches back from the desk. "Be my guest."

He thanked her, then skated his hands over the input controls. A few seconds later, a new list popped up, and he moved back. "That should do it."

Elana pulled her chair back in and peered at the list. She moved to select the first file, then paused.

Matt frowned. "Something wrong?"

She shook her head. "Not exactly. It's just that…"

Elana pushed back from the desk, leaned her elbows on her knees, and stared at the interface. "I know next to nothing about my mother. Dad almost never talked about her. Her death—or, I guess, her *believed* death—was unexpected. It wasn't like she was sick for long… She didn't have time to record any messages for me or write any letters.

"I grew up with a few pictures. No recordings of her voice. It was the early nineties, and my parents were lower middle class at best—no fancy camcorders. Just a handful of pictures in a scrapbook she'd put together for their wedding."

She motioned at the desk. "Now I'm about to read her diary, for lack of a better word. I have no idea what I'm getting into. No concept of the woman I'm about to meet. All I know is that she was my mother, and I thought she died but she didn't. Instead, she disappeared into a city that stands *directly beside* the place I've lived my whole life, where she lived secretly as a *terrifically powerful* vampire until only a few years ago.

"I'm terrified." Elana hung her head when Matt put a hand on her shoulder. "I'm terrified that I won't like what I discover. That somehow, even though I have only the faintest sketch of who my mother was, this will destroy everything I knew about her."

Matt gripped her shoulder and gave her a moment before gently saying, "You don't have to read them. We can walk out right now if that's what you want. We can come back later, or you can come back on your own, or you can never come back at all."

Elana closed her eyes and considered this carefully. At length, she shook her head again and sat up. Her eyes were steely, and her jaw was set.

"No. I want to know who my mother was and what she did. I want to understand the legacy she left me. Otherwise, I wouldn't only be walking away from her, I'd be walking away from all of it. I couldn't live with that knowledge hanging over my head, whether I stayed in Haven or went back to Ashford. I have to know."

Matt nodded. "Do you want me to stay?"

"For now, if you wouldn't mind and if you have time, yes." She flashed him an apologetic smile. "I have a feeling there will be plenty of stuff in here I'll need context for."

He smiled. "I don't mind at all. That's what I'm here for."

"Translation?"

"Support."

Elana drew a deep breath, let it out in a *whoosh*, and squared off with the desk. "Okay, *Mom*. Let's see what you've got for me."

CHAPTER TWENTY-ONE

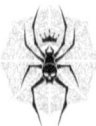

The first file was a formal letter, Tessa's official acceptance of the position of Arbiter of Sanctuary. Elana picked through the flowery prose and legalese until she reached the bottom, which was stamped with the king's sigil and signed *Tessa Hart*.

"I wonder if she changed her name for any reason other than the fact that Tessa Bishop was supposed to be dead," Elana muttered. "Why didn't she choose an entirely new name if she was trying to hide?"

Matt shrugged. "I suspect your mother avoided opportunities to cross paths with anyone who would have known her in Ashford. To be honest, those opportunities were likely few and far between anyway. Even in her previous position of Concubine of External Affairs and Diplomacy, I doubt those social circles overlapped much."

"Fair point." Elana chuckled as she imagined a high-society Havenite bumping elbows with the blue-collar workers of Bishop's Electronics and Hauling. The amusement soured when her brain superimposed her face over her mother's.

Her frown deepened as a thought struck her. "Hang on. My mother *died*."

Matt raised an eyebrow. "No, she didn't."

Elana scowled. "No, I *know* that—I mean, as far as everyone outside Haven was concerned, *yes, she did*. There was a funeral. *With an urn*. I've seen *pictures*."

"Ah." Matt exhaled a long breath. "I see what you're getting at." He tapped his fingers together in thought for several seconds, then grimaced. "Valeria is looking into your history and your mother's. I haven't had much opportunity to pick her brain on what she's found, and she's been tight-lipped so far when I *have* inquired, so I can't tell you anything certain. How much do you know about the process of giving someone the Rights?"

"Enough to know it can go *really* poorly, and even when it goes well, it's not fun. Beyond that, it's a closely kept secret."

Matt nodded. "Depending on the fortitude of the person undergoing the Rights, the process can take quite some time. If a person was, say, close to death, they might well appear to be comatose for a significant period… comatose on a level that human medical instruments might not register any signs of life."

Elana gaped. "Are you saying the hospital declared my mother dead when she *wasn't*?"

"That seems most likely to me."

"And then…the urn…"

"Was someone else's remains," Matt completed. "And

Tessa Bishop was whisked away to Haven to complete her transformation."

Elana slowly shook her head. "She must have been horrified."

Matt hummed in quiet agreement, then leaned in and tapped a few keys. The interface processed for a moment before producing a single result. "Try that."

"What is it?"

"Your mother's personal log."

Elana stared at the file for a long time before turning her chair to face Matt.

He raised an eyebrow and made a small gesture toward the door. "Are we done for the day?"

"No." She scrubbed her hands over her face and grimaced. "You've lived in Haven long enough that you were here when my mother was a concubine and an arbiter, right?"

"That's correct."

"Tell me what you know about her." She motioned at the desk. "Pull up whatever you want to illustrate, but I'm not the kind of girl who reads depositions and legislation in her spare time. I need some guidelines if I'm gonna hack through all of these."

Matt shifted his chair and leaned forward with his elbows on his knees. "Sure," he started, then let his gaze wander to the corner as he reflected. "Tessa Hart. What to tell you about Tessa Hart…"

He chuckled. "Well, the first thing anyone will tell you about Tessa Hart is that even though she was the Arbiter of Sanctuary, her nickname was the Battleaxe."

"What?"

"Mm-hmm. Don't get me wrong. She wasn't a war hawk. Her policy recommendations were peaceable by and large, and most factions of Haven politics—and global vampire politics—appreciated that. The moniker was popularized by someone who *didn't*. Arbiter Zilmann."

Tessa's eyebrows drew together. "Arbiter Zilmann as in the current Arbiter of Legacy?"

"The very one. Carlysle Zilmann hated your mother. Her House is quartered in Premier, and is descended from Old World blood. She had a bug up her ass from day one about your mother's rapid ascent to power, and she let that bias color every interaction with Tessa and every opinion she had on her actions. She was notoriously vocal in her implications that she'd conned her way into the royal House."

"Basically saying she was, what, not pure enough?"

Matt made a face and waggled a hand back and forth. "Sort of. The stereotypes about pure blood and stuff like that don't hold as much weight as a lot of human myth says they do. There's value in having a *long* line because vampires respect the maintenance of history and tradition. Still, anyone added to a House by Rights or marriage is considered to have that status unless they prove themselves unworthy of it by their actions. You're not less of a vampire if you're not born one, in other words, and that applies to Houses as well.

"Old World Houses are constantly vying for more power and prestige, so there's a lot of jockeying for position in Europe—particularly Eastern and mainland Europe. These days, that looks like Houses trying to woo powerful vampires from other Houses, or trying to sabotage other Houses. Once upon a time, it was more like outright kidnapping people—sometimes humans, not vampires—in this endless quest to make a 'supreme' House."

Elana's upper lip curled. "I don't like the sound of that."

"Neither did the SpiderKing. That's said to be among the reasons he decided to found Haven on this side of the Atlantic."

"Were there no vampires here before Haven?"

Matt started to shake his head, then stopped and half-shrugged. "I'm actually not sure. That is an area of vampiric history I am not familiar with. I know there were no established Old World-style vampire settlements in North America before Haven. I'd have to do some research."

Elana nodded. "Might be interesting. Never know what you'd find. So then…was Zilmann accusing the king of being hypocritical in 'recruiting' my mom?"

Matt chuckled. "Doubtful. Zilmann's House—that's House Vulicia, by the way, in case you don't know—has a long history of doing exactly that. It would have been terrifically hypocritical of *her* to accuse the king of doing exactly what House Vulicia was famous for."

"Never stopped a hypocrite before," Elana remarked.

"Point," Matt admitted. "It's certainly possible that played into Zilmann's dislike of your mother. Personally, I always thought the reason was a hell of a lot simpler."

"Oh?"

"She was jealous. Like I said, House Vulicia has a centuries-long history of doing whatever they could dream of to get to the top. I wouldn't be surprised if Zilmann had been grooming someone in a House related to Vulicia for the position of Arbiter of Sanctuary, with the goal of increasing her alliances on the consulate. She was probably pissed that the SpiderKing had plucked this nobody out of nowhere to fill the position.

"Plus, she *is* a war hawk. That was always the *overt* reason she didn't like your mother."

Elana crossed her arms and tapped her fingers on her elbow. "Who do vampires go to war with?"

"Other Houses, mainly, although Houses have been known to throw their weight behind nation-states in human wars just like any other faction in the world. Carlysle Zilmann, as the head of House Vulicia and the Arbiter of Legacy, is also a voracious landowner and resource mogul and has been for a couple of centuries. She didn't appreciate the Battleaxe swinging in and cutting off her profits."

"I wondered when the nickname would show up."

Matt smirked. "It started in a consulate meeting where Tessa attended as the Concubine of External Affairs and Diplomacy. She was pushing *hard* for a new subdivision in Zevenda where humans and vampires could live completely side by side. Zilmann wasn't a fan, but Tessa refused to budge."

Elana frowned. "I thought vampires and humans already lived side by side in Zevenda. Isn't that the whole point of the domain of Sanctuary? That humans and vampires can live together in peace? Hell, isn't that the whole point of *Haven?*"

Matt scrunched up his nose. "Again, sort of. Yes, the SpiderKing is friendly toward humanity. His primary goal in founding Haven was to live without Old World politics, similar to the reasons held by many immigrants to North America. Again, yes, Haven is supposed to be a city where humans and vampires can coexist, and some humans *do* live in Zevenda. Functionally, they end up sequestered and living separately from vampires.

"Your mother wanted to go further, to build shared apartment buildings and a shared community center. She wished to include humans in day-to-day Haven life, not only as contractors or guests.

"That was where she'd started. Tessa had a knack for getting people to listen to one another—or to make them *feel* like they were being heard. She came on the scene in 1993 and quickly made a name for herself in Etreta and Zevenda by brokering deals between human contractors and vampire businesses.

"Suddenly, humans felt as though they had an advocate and ally who was one of their own. On the other side, progressive vampires gained an effective liaison to the human world, someone who could make connections without the difficulty faced by so many vampires trying to 'make it' in the human world. She flourished."

Elana raised an eyebrow. "What difficulty are you talking about?"

Matt snorted. "Believe it or not, the biggest obstacle to human-vampire relations is *culture*." He motioned at his suit. "If you can't 'dress down' your speech, and you're not willing to physically dress down, a lot of humans—even executives!—will assume you've got a stick up your ass and won't give you the time of day.

"To be fair, there are *plenty* of vampires who believe

vampires are better than humans. Very few of them know how to hide it. It's another reason most vampire communities end up insular."

Elana narrowed her eyes. "So, my mother got one of the highest jobs in Haven because she *wasn't racist?*"

Matt burst out laughing. "In a way, I suppose! Her strength lay in helping someone see how the other person could meet their needs. Cutting through the bullshit to get to the heart of the problem and solving it by knowing the right people."

"I see. Where does the Battleaxe bit come in?"

Matt smiled with fond memory. "Tessa told Zilmann that she'd build the damn houses in the new subdivision herself if she blocked her subcontractors' access. Zilmann sputtered at her, said she had no respect for tradition and history, and all but threatened to run her out of the city. Tessa informed her that she'd use the battleaxe on the wall behind her to cut wood *and* keep her lackeys out of her way. Little did she know that battleaxe was older than the hills."

Elana snorted, then subsided into a wistful smile. "She sounds like a firebrand. I wish I could have met her."

Matt motioned at the desk. "If there aren't any recordings in the databases here, there will certainly be archived broadcasts elsewhere."

Elana blinked as tears sprang to her eyes. "Right. Of course, there would be. Wow. I... I could see my mom."

"And hear her voice." Matt cocked his head with a sudden thought. "As a matter of fact, I bet there's a recording of that meeting. It would have been broadcast on C-PAN."

"Haven broadcasts on C-SPAN?"

"No, C-*PAN*. The Consulate Public Affairs Network. Just let me…"

He reached over the desk and tapped a new search into the interface. When a selection of files appeared, he scrolled through them until he stopped halfway down the list and grinned. "There it is."

Elana stared at the filename. "That's a recording of my mother."

"It's a recording of your mother giving Arbiter Zilmann what for."

Elana reached around Matt's arm and double-tapped to open the file.

The interface disappeared, and the entire surface of the desktop became an HD video screen showing the interior of a room in the consulate—recognizable thanks to the marble walls and floor. It was a generic meeting room, round with the arbiters' sigils inlaid in the walls and eight small tables in a circle. The video had been filmed from a wall-mounted camera near the ceiling in the Premier section. Valeria Draven sat below the new moon symbol across the room in the Senkyem section.

In the bottom left of the frame stood Carlysle Zilmann, a tall and gaunt woman with a sharp jaw, black hair, and pale skin. Everything about her was *long*—long nose, long fingers, long legs. Elana wouldn't have been surprised to see her in long black robes, but she wore a severe black suit that gave her the air of a banker. Her gold-rimmed rectangular glasses sat on the tip of her nose as she looked down at the woman in the center of the circle.

Elana's mother.

Tessa Hart looked an awful lot like Elana. Her hair was a touch curlier than Elana's but fell to the same place on her shoulders and had the same warm dark brown hue. Her nose was different. Tessa's was rounder and shorter, whereas Elana's was slightly pointed. Her eyes flashed the same way Elana's did when she was mad, however, and *boy*, was she mad now.

Elana watched in silence as her mother delivered a flawless presentation on the merits of building the new subdivision in Zevenda. She argued that the benefits would by far outweigh the costs, and the long-term progress it would enable in *rapprochement* between Haven and Ashford was priceless. She had the contacts ready. There was no time like the present. All the consulate had to do was give the green light.

It was evident that Zilmann wasn't the only one unsure of the project, based on the skeptical looks on Arbiter Tarsin's face. But while Knowledge was perhaps cynical, Progress and Creation were on board, as Arbiters Amindóttir and Kyoi silently nodded with Tessa's presentation. Arbiter Mélissand appeared interested but unconvinced, sitting with her fingers steepled in her chair under Octava's waxing gibbous moon. Valeria was perfectly neutral, Elana couldn't see the Arbiter of Light from this vantage point, and the Arbiter of Sanctuary looked…

Elana frowned. The Arbiter of Sanctuary, to put it lightly, looked *murderous*.

She paused the video with a tap. "When did my mother become the Arbiter of Sanctuary?"

"2002," Matt replied.

"When was this meeting?"

"Early 1996. Your mother became a concubine in 1995 and hit the ground running."

"Who was the previous Arbiter of Sanctuary?" Elana pointed at the figure in the video. "She looks like she wants to flay my mom alive."

Matt lifted an eyebrow and leaned in for a closer look. "Huh. So she does. That's Arbiter Gow. She was a quiet, backbencher sort who held the position for a *long* time before the SpiderKing requested she step aside for your mother to take over. She accepted retirement without a fuss…at least, as far as I know."

"Was she allied with Zilmann?"

Matt slowly exhaled through his nose. "Gow was unassuming. She wasn't overtly opposed to anyone and mostly went along with whatever was suggested. Sanctuary was not the most prestigious position, as you might imagine, since it's the domain most associated with human affairs. A lot of Houses prefer to keep their hands clean, you might say. She took the post back when your mother died."

Elana narrowed her eyes. "Did she, now…"

Matt frowned. "Are you suggesting something was suspicious about your mother's death? And that Arbiter Gow might have had something to do with it?"

Elana shrugged as she stared at the short, stout woman in the brown suit. "Valeria told me she died in an inter-House war. I assume she knows everything about how it went down as the Arbiter of Shadows. If Gow had something to do with it, I imagine she knows, and it doesn't matter for whatever reason."

She shifted her focus to her mother, frozen in time as she told Zilmann about concrete pouring conditions and ideal work schedules. She stared at Tessa for several moments, then glanced at Matt. "Any chance I can order delivery in here?"

Matt snorted. "No way. But I *can* have food delivered to the main atrium for whatever time you like. Why? Planning a long stay?"

Elana straightened, then cracked her neck. "Suddenly I am *much* more invested in understanding everything my mother worked on. Also, Haven has hotels, right?"

"Oh, yes."

"Cool." She retrieved her phone from her bag and set it on the desk. "I'm gonna dive in and take notes. Does the embargo on information leaving this room mean I can't grill you with questions over supper?"

"Not if I find a sufficiently private place to eat. You're not allowed to take any materials out that are stored here, and if you leave your notebook anywhere that *anyone else* can find it, there'll be hell to pay, but…you're essentially Havenite royalty. As long as you don't fuck it up, no one will argue with you."

"Key words being 'as long as I don't fuck it up.'"

"Exactly."

CHAPTER TWENTY-TWO

After Matt left, Elana got up and stretched, then examined the contents of the shelves. Seeing her mother in action had rekindled her desire to pick apart every aspect of Haven's enigmatic systems until she understood them inside and out. To do that, she needed to be methodical. The time for emotional exploration was over for now. She needed to start at the beginning.

Her first stop was the original Haven charter. Its folio was among the first documents on the shelves. It was a facsimile—undoubtedly the original was kept securely elsewhere, and this copy was for reference—but the reproduction was beautiful.

The section regarding the domain of Sanctuary included illuminations featuring a duck with a line of ducklings following and a mother bear protecting her cub with an imposing roar. The drop cap S included a waxing quarter moon in the upper curve of the S, with incredibly detailed craters on the moon's sunlit face and tiny twinkling stars outside the curve of the letter, which was illuminated with gold leaf.

> Sanctuary. The Arbiter of Sanctuary pledges to welcome all those who seek refuge inside Haven's walls, pausing to observe neither primacy of House nor possibility of profit, but instead prioritizing the good of all beings. Those Vampyres claiming allegiance to the SpiderKing choose to share the bounty granted by Vampyr among those less privileged without adhering to unjust criteria determined by outdated thought and philosophy.

Based on Matt's description of Arbiter Gow's attitude in contrast to Tessa Hart's, Elana's mother's actions had far more closely aligned with the position's original goal of protecting and supporting anyone who lived in Haven, regardless of their history.

Elana smiled softly. Instead of discovering her mother had been a cold, heartless woman who'd abandoned her family to play politics with high-society vampires, she was learning that Tessa Hart had made the best of a situation she couldn't have foreseen. She'd fought for those who needed fighting for. That was good. Elana could be proud of that, and was.

Armed with this admirable foundation, Elana dug into the documents with vigor. She skimmed centuries of public records and read until her eyes hurt. The first

Arbiter of Sanctuary had followed the spirit of the charter closely, welcoming considerable numbers of humans into Zevenda. There had been pressure to select "adequate" humans, which Elana assumed meant humans with the potential to be given the Rights. Arbiter Andros had refused to bow to the lobbying and welcomed almost anyone.

Andros had died unexpectedly in the mid-1800s and had not selected or groomed a concubine as her successor. Nothing was written in the official records about her death, but Elana noticed an annotation marked with a new moon symbol. Following the footnote, she found a report from the Arbiter of Shadows of the time. It decreed that Andros' death had been suspicious, but investigation had revealed nothing.

Elana grumbled under her breath and wondered whether the nineteenth-century Arbiter of Shadows had been in cahoots with whoever had done Andros in. Even in these old records, it was obvious that the SpiderKing stayed at arm's length from the day-to-day running of Haven and did not interfere with his arbiters' decisions even when it seemed self-evident that something was going on.

"For someone who claimed he didn't want Old World politics following him to the New World, you didn't do a whole lot to stop it," she muttered.

The Arbiter of Sanctuary between Andros and Gow, Meskinaw, had largely been unenthusiastic about doing anything more than keeping the status quo. Elana supposed that when it wasn't abnormal for one person to hold the same job for upward of a century, and you expected to live for centuries more, a certain "long view" tended to take over.

Gow had taken over from Meskinaw in 1934, on the eve of World War Two. Much to Elana's frustration, Gow had kept her head down and offered nothing in the way of help for the war effort. Her notes were infuriatingly light on information. Her documentation was so stingy that for all Elana could tell, the woman might have been pro-Axis.

"Would certainly explain why she didn't want anyone new coming in thanks to Mom, and why she hasn't followed up on any of her projects since her death." Elana made a face and stabbed at the interface to close her latest document, then brought up the search query that contained her mother's records. These, unlike Gow's, were almost entirely digital, and the first file available to Elana was Tessa's log.

She stared at the line of text for a full minute before opening it.

The first entry was dated August 17, 1995. Three years after Elana was born and Tessa became a vampire.

> **I hate journaling. I hate it with a passion. But Valeria says I will regret my life choices if I don't keep a journal as a concubine, and I have to admit I see her point. If I don't keep track of my thoughts and decisions between all the meetings in my first official week in the position, I will end up making stupid mistakes.**

Elana sat back and blinked tears away. For the first time in the hours she'd been buried in the books, she wished

Matt were here. She could have used another person around to help ground her in reality.

She shook herself and returned to reading, where she quickly lost herself in her mother's nerves about her upcoming induction as a concubine—her fear that she would prove inadequate to the position, that the Spider-King would dismiss her, that she would fail...

> I don't remember receiving the Rights. I passed out in the hospital in Ashford and when I next opened my eyes I was in Haven. I woke up not knowing where I was or what had happened. My last memory was of Elana's scrunched-up newborn face.

"What?" Elana whispered.

She read the sentence again as her heart rate climbed. Then she grabbed her phone and whipped off a text to Matt.

> **She mentions me.**

Elana's gaze was irrevocably drawn back to the text on the desktop interface. She got several paragraphs in before her phone buzzed and scared her half to death.

> **Who mentions you?**

> **My mother. My mother mentions me in her journal.**

This time, his reply was almost instantaneous.

What? That's not possible. She had no contact with you.

Elana scanned the journal entry she'd been reading to ensure she was reading it correctly. Satisfied that she was, she copied a few lines of text into a message and sent the excerpt to Matt.

Tell me I'm reading this wrong, then.

Seconds passed, turning to minutes. Elana barely noticed, engrossed as she was in reading, and was startled when Matt texted her back.

You're reading it right. Your mother left Haven to see you without anyone knowing. What's the misspelled word supposed to be?

Elana chuckled.

Just a typo. There are a couple on every page. I would have thought Haven's autocorrect would work better, lol. I copied it word for word.

His response was quick.

It does. Those aren't typos. They're deliberate. I think there's an encrypted message in there.

Elana's eyes widened. That possibility hadn't crossed her mind.

I'm writing them down. Hurry up, I'm starving.

Elana grabbed a pen and paper from her bag and started jotting down the mysterious "typos," along with the date and topic of the journal entry, and the page the typo was on. She was squinting at her list when the smell of pizza brought her head up from the desk and lifted her eyebrows sharply. "I thought we weren't allowed to have food in here."

Matt grinned at her from the door with two pizza boxes balanced on one hand. "Turns out it's handy to have the Arbiter of Shadows on your side. Valeria *did* tell me that if we touch *any* of the manuscripts with greasy fingers, she'll personally shoot us both."

"Reasonable."

"I thought so. Hang on, I'll be right back." He placed their dinner on the desk, then disappeared out the door again. A minute later, he returned with a folding chair, which he set on the other side of the desk. "So, first things first. Your mother mentioned you?"

Elana was rummaging through her bag for the spare napkins she always kept with her and nodded absently. "Yeah. Which is weird. Valeria said *she* didn't know Tessa had a daughter, so I kind of assumed Mom had…well, not *forgotten* about me. I don't imagine you can go through labor and forget you had it."

"Stranger things have happened. Also, I don't know if Valeria told you, but your mother's Turning was not pleasant."

Elana retrieved the brown paper napkins and spread them over the desk, then flipped open a pizza box and selected a mouthwatering slice. "Ooh, deluxe... Yes, she did. I honestly figured the trauma of the Rights on top of what must have been a horrific hospital stay either closed off those memories or..."

She drew a deep breath and let it out in a *whoosh*. "Or she thought I hadn't survived and didn't have the heart to find out."

"Either would have made sense."

"Yeah." Elana motioned at the desk with the slice of pizza. "Except she found out at some point because she mentioned visiting me."

Matt swallowed his mouthful and nodded. "She would have had to, to turn you. After I replied to your text, I thought about it more and realized that was the simplest explanation. I'd been considering any number of outlandish theories, right up to someone stealing your mother's blood and giving it to you without you knowing. When I thought about asking you whether you'd had any hospital trips you didn't remember, it hit me that I was being ridiculous."

Elana snorted. "Raise your hand if you're not here," she teased, and Matt chuckled. "If you'd asked, I would have had to say yes because I've *never* been to the hospital that I remember. I've always been healthy as a horse."

"Another ridiculous statement."

"What, horses aren't healthy?"

"They're remarkably fragile. Unlike humans, who are resilient as hell, and vampires, who are even more so." He polished off his pizza crust. "But we're getting off-topic. Your mother mentions visiting you. When?"

Elana checked her notes. "The first mention is in the fall of 1993. I would have been a year old."

She drummed her fingers on the edge of the pizza box as she selected another piece. "Dad had a nanny come in and watch me while he was working. A family friend who passed away before I really remember her, in '97... Mrs. Gilda. She would have known Mom. I wonder if Mom snuck in or what."

"She doesn't say?"

"No. She barely mentions anything about the visits, only that they happened. Compared to how much detail she puts in about everything else, it feels weird. I wonder if she was afraid someone might read it."

Matt thought about this while chewing, then shook his head. "If she was worried about someone reading the entries, she wouldn't have mentioned you."

"Fair enough." Elana bit her lower lip. "I think she gave me the Rights in August of 1994. The entry that mentions me only reads, 'It's done,' and the ones after that always mention how I'm healthy and growing well."

Matt pointed at her with his half-eaten slice of pizza, then quickly brought it to his mouth to rescue a precarious bit of bell pepper. "Mothers care whether their kids are healthy."

"Sure, but with the 'It's done?' Also, it had to have happened pretty early on, or else I wouldn't remember *always* being stronger and smarter than every other kid my age."

He acquiesced with another wave of the pizza. Elana wiped her hands on a napkin and folded her hands in her lap. "What would have happened if she'd told someone?"

Matt sobered. "The punishment for giving the Rights to an individual incapable of consent without consulting the Concubine of Nurture beforehand is death. There are *extreme* cases where the vampire responsible has been pardoned, but it's rare. Turning someone is not supposed to be undertaken without significant discussion, and that becomes exponentially more important if the person in question can't make the decision themselves."

"The Concubine of Nurture. That must be someone who works for the Arbiters of Creation and Sanctuary, right?"

"Correct. The domain of Creation covers the Rights in general, but the domain of Sanctuary becomes involved when there's any question of extraordinary circumstances —when giving someone the Rights would save their life."

"I was a healthy kid even before the Rights, by all accounts. Turning me was definitely not a necessity."

Matt nodded. "My point exactly. Unless your mother knew something no one else did, including your father, giving you the Rights was a serious breach of vampire law. Your mother would have known that by then."

Elana frowned and pulled her notebook closer, then scanned the lines of scrawled text. "Everything I read and watched about her this afternoon tells me she didn't do anything without a reason. I suppose it's *possible* that turning me was an impulsive move, but if that was true, I would have expected her to do it as soon as she could. Waiting almost two years suggests plenty of foresight."

"I agree with your assessment. She deliberately gave you the Rights. We just have to figure out why." Matt sat back in the folding chair. It creaked. "Vampires at the initiate level are typically encouraged to stay within Haven as much as possible at first. Adepts have more freedom. We'd have to request records from Quarto to determine when she advanced unless she mentions it in her journal."

"If she does, I haven't gotten that far. Does that mean she was sneaking out?"

Matt lifted one shoulder. "Not necessarily. No one's *barred* from leaving, as a rule. She might have been concealing her reasons for visiting Ashford, but it might not have been a secret that she was going beyond the Wall. If you have dates, we could check them against the guardians' records."

Elana ran her tongue over her teeth thoughtfully, then hummed in disagreement. "Let's not. Not yet. We haven't talked about the encrypted messages yet. I went back and found the first 'typo,' and it's three months before she turned me."

Matt scooted his chair closer to the desk and motioned at the open pizza box. "Done for now?" At her nod, he closed the box and shoved it to the side. "Is that a list of the typos?"

"Mm-hmm." She pushed the pad of paper toward him and watched his face as he scanned her notes. "Any ideas?"

He frowned and shook his head. "I don't see a pattern in the incorrect letters, but then, I'm no detective. I'm a lawyer and a social worker. This makes me want to get a cryptographer from Senkyem."

Elana grimaced. "That feels like tipping our hand. What if Mom was hiding something serious? We have no idea who might be on our side. Or my side, I suppose I should say. You have no stake in this."

Matt chuckled. "You're my case. Even if you weren't, I like you. I'm on your side."

Surprising warmth bloomed in Elana's chest and made her smile. She hadn't realized how tense she'd been until the warmth eased her shoulders down from her ears. "Thanks. I appreciate that."

"Most welcome. Now..." He tapped the notebook. "You might have a point. We're better than Europe, but God knows Haven's politics are still a maelstrom at the best of times."

"Or maybe a spiderweb?" Elana winked.

Matt snorted. "Probably more accurate. I think we should take this to Valeria. If anyone can help us, she can, and she and your mother were close."

"Mom didn't tell her she'd turned me, though. Are we sure they were close?"

Matt drew a slow breath and exhaled it through his nose. "I have a theory. It's harebrained, but it's a theory nonetheless."

"Let's hear it."

"Your mom found something out. Something that would have put Valeria in danger if she knew. You know your mother died in an inter-House war. When I say that Haven's politics are a maelstrom at the best of times..."

"Those were *not* the best of times, I take it."

"Very much the opposite." Matt tapped the notebook again. "If that's the case, maybe your mother started leaving clues. The Arbiter of Shadows can access any arbiter's personal files if they petition the king with cause. Maybe your mother intended for Valeria to hear about this at some point. Regardless...it will be *very* difficult for you, for *us*, to investigate this without Valeria finding out. It would be best if we told her now."

Elana worried the tip of her tongue between her teeth and searched Matt's face. She saw no hint of guile or dishonesty, only the genuine desire to find the truth. Then she looked at the desktop, where her mother's face peeked out between napkins in an image from one of the many meetings Elana had watched.

Elana was beginning to get the feeling her mother had left *her* something, not Valeria. Maybe for Valeria too, but definitely for Elana. She had no proof yet, but the conviction was strong. She wouldn't find out unless she decrypted these messages—if there was anything to be decrypted—and right now, the safest way to pursue that was through Valeria Draven. Any other path would have put her on the *opposite* side of the Arbiter of Shadows, and that was not a wise place to be.

She nodded. "Okay. We'll talk to Valeria."

Matt laid his hand on the notebook. "*I'll* talk to Valeria," he corrected. "I promise I'll tell you how it goes, but I think for propriety's sake it would be best if I do this one myself. Do you trust me?"

Elana's stomach rolled, but she let the discomfort pass. "I trust you." Matt had given her no reason not to. She hoped this wouldn't be the first time he did.

"Then I'll do that now or as close to now as possible." He slipped the notebook into an inner pocket of his suit jacket and stood. "Have you found a place to stay yet?"

"Not yet, but I will." She tidied the napkins and paused as her mother's face caught her eye again. "Do I have to be out of here by a certain time?"

"Stay as long as you like, but keep in mind that you still need sleep." Matt smiled and put a hand on her shoulder. "Let me know where you end up crashing for the night. I'll tell you as soon as I have anything definitive from Valeria, and we can talk at breakfast tomorrow?"

"Sure." Elana checked her phone and uttered a short laugh as she saw the time on the screen. "Jesus, it's already after seven? I've been here longer than I thought."

"History has a way of sucking us in…especially when it's your own."

"No kidding." She stretched and popped a couple of vertebrae. "I won't stay much longer. Good luck with Valeria."

"Thanks. Good luck with your mom."

He left her the rest of the pizza.

CHAPTER TWENTY-THREE

Matt parked his Audi under a copse of trees in a quiet area of Senkyem, near the Wall. Out here was the closest any part of Haven got to rural with its open fields and tall trees, although the roads were paved and one only had to turn to see the dense cityscape.

He crossed the road from the trees, hopped a low wire fence, and strode through the field of golden wheat until the sole of his shoe tapped on a metal hatch. Then he knelt amid the stalks and flattened his hand on the metal plate. One pinprick later, the hatch irised open and allowed him entry to a long tunnel with a ladder lit by small disc-shaped light fixtures inset in the walls.

Matt descended the ladder, and once he was fully inside the tunnel, the hatch closed above him. Thirty rungs brought him to a landing, where he stood patiently until the floor detached from the walls and sank farther underground.

The floating platform deposited him in a spacious, well-lit chamber that resembled a war room because it was one. The wall of screens opposite the entry point was dark, as were the numerous consoles that dotted the semicircular control bank beneath them, and the room was empty apart from himself and the Arbiter of Shadows.

Valeria sat at the head of the elongated oval table that commanded the center of the room. The middle of the table was cut out, so projectors set into the floor inside the ring of the table could display any information needed for discussion.

The arbiter did not look up from the papers in the file folder open in front of her. She wore a simple white turtleneck and slacks, and the arms of her shirt were pushed up past her wrists. Hints of line tattoos glimmered in the light, but the ink was too pale to be seen properly against her skin.

Her inquiry was curt but not cruel. "How is she doing?"

"She's wrestling." Matt pulled out a chair a few places down from Valeria, far enough away that he could not easily read the documents on the table, and sat. "She's determined."

"You wouldn't be here if you only had good news."

"She found something."

"Undoubtedly."

"Tessa knew about her, but I'm sure you already knew that."

"I had surmised as much but had no proof yet."

"Really? I thought you would have already scoured Tessa's files for anything useful."

When Valeria looked up, Matt caught the flash of pain in the pale woman's face before the professional mask settled back into place. This surprised him more than Valeria's admission that she had not read Tessa's files.

"I have not had time," Valeria replied smoothly. "Nor an urgent need to do so. She's only been dead four years."

Matt knew better than to call attention to the lapse in the façade. He nodded, put his elbows on the table, and leaned forward. "Fair. Well, I can confirm what we'd theorized. Tessa left Haven and gave the Rights to Elana when she was about two years old."

Valeria hummed a quiet acknowledgment and motioned for him to continue.

"Based on her journals, it looks like Tessa visited Elana multiple times within a few years. Elana hasn't read them all yet, so it's not clear when the visits stopped precisely, but I would guess before the age of three."

"Avoiding memories that would be hard to explain."

"Yes." Matt folded his hands. "There's more. Elana believes she's found evidence that her mother left encrypted messages in her journal."

Valeria arched an eyebrow. "What sort of messages? Ciphered text?"

"It might turn out to be in code, but currently the only clues are typos." He retrieved Elana's notebook from the inside pocket of his jacket and slid it across the table to Valeria. "A list of everything we've found so far."

She snagged the coil-bound notebook, flipped it open, and scanned the columns of text. "I see no immediate pattern, which is intriguing in its own right. I've seen plenty of coded messages in my time, so I recognize many of them on sight. Plus, Tessa would have had to deliberately disable several aspects of the secure logging program to do this. She was smart, but that wasn't her area of expertise."

Valeria closed the book and slid it back to Matt. "Excellent work. You two have been using the Sanctuary room in the lower archives, correct?"

"That's correct."

She hovered her hands over the table and initiated one of the ubiquitous inlaid interfaces. Her long white fingers flew over the keys, tapping out commands too quickly for Matt to catch. "I will arrange assistance. Tell no one what you're doing, and tell no one what she's found."

"I assumed as much."

Valeria favored him with a rare, short smile. "I knew there was a reason I kept you around."

Matt chuckled under his breath. "I'd hope there's a few. I'm going to make sure our newest citizen sleeps. Is there anything I need to keep her away from?"

Valeria dismissed the table interface and briefly considered Matt's question before shaking her head. "Not beyond the usual. Don't let her stick her head out too far yet. She's not ready, and unfortunately, the mess your sister is dealing with has to be my top priority right now."

"That bad, eh?"

"I had to take the White Fang into Ashford."

Matt hissed through his teeth. "Fuck. Okay. I'll let you work, then, and I'll only call if we absolutely need something. Good night, Valeria."

"Good night, Mister Richelieu."

Elana's phone rang and jolted her out of her careful note-taking. She put a hand over her heart and exhaled deeply to calm her jangled nerves before picking it up. Matt was calling.

"Hi. How did it go?" she asked him. "Or did you not get to see her yet?"

"I saw her. We're good to go. She'll get us something to help with the encrypted messages by tomorrow morning."

"That's great." Elana yawned and pulled the phone away from her ear to look at the time. "Oh, Christ, it's after nine. I should wrap it up."

"Probably." Matt's amused voice crackled through her speaker. "If you let me know where you're staying tonight, I can show up to take you to breakfast tomorrow morning."

She wedged the phone between her ear and shoulder and started tidying the books spread out on the desk. "Sure, I can do that. Um… Do I have to clean everything up in here? Or can I leave things out overnight?"

"The only other people who can access that room are Arbiter Gow and Valeria, short of someone directly petitioning the king or obtaining a warrant…which would also go through Valeria. Up to you."

Elana pursed her lips. "I'll clean up. I don't trust Gow."

"Valeria would be proud."

"She doesn't trust Gow either?"

"Valeria doesn't trust *anyone*. I'm reasonably certain her motto is literally, 'Trust no one.'"

"Wonder if she's an *X-Files* fan…" Elana muttered while gathering papers into a loose pile. "Damn. I need both hands to do this. I'll let you know where I end up tonight. Talk soon?"

"Talk soon."

Matt hung up. Elana pocketed her phone, then tapped the papers into a neat stack and slid them into her new dimensional handbag. She quickly replaced the books on the shelves and tried various keywords in the desktop interface until she figured out how to wipe the search history.

"Won't stop Valeria, I'm sure, but it might make following my footsteps harder for anyone else," she murmured. "And…done. Okay. Hotel time."

Elana sat back in the chair and stretched her legs out in front of her while she scrolled through hotel listings on her phone. A ritzy place in Premier that reminded her of the Hollywood Roosevelt caught her eye with high ceilings, chandeliers, and a pristine outdoor pool. She was about to scroll by with her standard dismissal of "Too expensive" when she remembered it was *not* too expensive.

Feeling like a preteen allowed into the high school girls' clique—overly excited to the point of giddiness with an undercurrent of "someone will discover I don't belong and kick me out"—she booked the king suite before she could second-guess herself, and skipped out of the bunker-like archive while humming *Singin' in the Rain* for no other reason than it felt appropriately fancy.

Elana hesitated the tiniest of moments before handing her Emeya's key fob to the valet driver. They knew who she was thanks to her reservation, and no establishment in Premier would dare fuck with a member of the royal House lest their reputation go underground faster than you could say "SpiderKing."

She was glad she only had her dimensional handbag and could politely decline the bellboy's assistance when he asked if she had luggage. No way in *hell* would she hand over a bag full of notes about encrypted messages hidden in the former Arbiter of Sanctuary's files to just anyone.

All thoughts of conspiracies and cold cases were shoved to the back of Elana's mind when she walked in the door.

The lobby of the Haven Arms reminded Elana of the consulate's atrium but hue-shifted to a dusty rose. The pink marble floor gleamed under the warm light of the crystal chandeliers, three of which hung a story above from a high, arched ceiling covered in gorgeous Art Nouveau floral illustrations. The smooth, natural swirls were echoed in the molding that lined the ceiling like piped icing on a wedding cake. The ironwork railings circling the second-floor balcony walkway and every standing lamp and mounted sconce on the main floor repeated the motif.

Marble pedestals with graceful vases full of fresh flowers sat beside overstuffed armchairs and divans in alcoves along the lobby's walls. The interior of each alcove featured more Art Nouveau artwork, this time in the form of stained glass windows depicting different flowers. Elana's favorite was a purple and yellow iris, closely followed by a white orchid.

The receptionist at the front desk had smooth, dark brown skin, a round nose, and warm eyes. Her hair was nearly the same color as her skin, tightly curled, and pulled into a high bun. She wore burgundy lipstick that made her lips look like a deep red rosebud. The navy hotel uniform was well-tailored and accentuated her curves perfectly. Her nametag read Sophia.

Elana approached with a smile, and Sophia smiled too. "Checking in?"

"I am," Elana confirmed. "Elana Bishop."

Sophia's hands drifted over the interface behind the desk. It emitted a slight *beep*, then Sophia looked up to meet Elana's gaze again. "You're in room 502, Miss Bishop. A wonderful choice. Will you need anything sent up now?"

Elana's stomach growled. She'd eaten a significant amount of pizza, but she'd also done a *huge* amount of research. "Is there a room service menu?"

Sophia beamed. "Naturally. Did you want to order immediately?"

Elana considered, then shook her head. "I'll call from upstairs. Thanks."

"Of course. Enjoy your stay."

"I'm sure I will." Elana grinned and headed for the elevators tucked into another set of alcoves at the back of the spacious lobby. The car's interior was mirrored, but the mirrors had a neat etched pattern that made you look as though you were inside one of the Art Nouveau paintings from the lobby's ceiling. Elana admired the effect until the elevator *dinged* and opened onto her floor. Room 502 was at the end of the hall.

Elana opened the olive green door with brass filigree trim into a hotel suite that wouldn't have been out of place in a palace. The walls were painted the same olive green as the door, and the crown molding matched the door frame's intricate brass metalwork. Plush espresso-colored carpet squished under her heels, promising to cushion her toes as soon as she removed her pumps.

All of the furniture was overstuffed like the divans in the lobby. From the door, Elana could survey the entire suite, which was laid out in an open-concept floor plan. It allowed the guest to go from the king-size four-poster canopy bed to the expansive sofa in front of the full wall of windows overlooking the lush central courtyard to the Jacuzzi tucked in the corner. The latter bubbled and glowed from within.

A bookcase stuffed with novels and other light reading material was immediately to Elana's left, inside the door, and on her right was a well-appointed kitchenette with a fully stocked minibar.

Elana kicked off her heels and let her toes sink into the deep carpet as she sighed happily. "Score one for ridiculous impulse purchases."

She hung her purse on the coatrack—also of Art Nouveau-style brass that matched the tree-like designs on the foot- and headboard of the bed—and padded to the kitchen. Her bare feet appreciated the switch from warm carpet to cool porcelain tile, the color of which matched the rug.

The room service menu was perfectly aligned with the cappuccino-colored granite counter. Its script flowed over stiff cardstock and described the main kitchen's French-inspired offerings in mouthwatering detail. *Moules et frites,* beef bourguignon, Alsatian tart, *quenelles,* coq au vin…

Elana leaned on the counter and contemplated the rest

of her evening. She was hungry but not starving and still had half a pizza left in her bag if she wanted something substantial. So, not an entrée. She wanted something to snack on, preferably while soaking in the hot tub. *Aha*—she knew just what to order.

She turned and hovered her hand over the counter as the menu instructed, and the ordering interface appeared in bright blue inside the brown granite. A few taps, and she'd ordered a delectable charcuterie board and a bottle of wine. *Parfait.*

The charcuterie board arrived fifteen minutes later, heralded by a polite knock. Elana answered the door clad in the complimentary dressing gown she'd discovered in the bathroom. That room was big enough to hold a Jacuzzi and a queen-sized bed. Her hair was piled on her head, held by a pair of pencils she'd shoved in as makeshift hair sticks because she'd forgotten to put a new elastic in her bag after hers snapped in the last training session.

The staff member who greeted her at the door was a perfect gentleman and made no comment about Elana's disheveled appearance. Elana was pleased by his professionalism, especially since she'd all but forgotten how *not* put-together she was until she opened the door and a stray lock of hair fell over her eye. Not the best look for a member of the royal House...but maybe she'd be passed off as eccentric.

Nobody's bothered when eccentrics disappear, her mind warned her. *Be careful.*

Elana put her paranoia aside and accepted the small rolling cart from the young man, whose nametag read Sutton. When she bid him goodnight, he tapped his polished black heels together, bowed, and left. His coattails fluttered slightly in his wake.

Elana rolled the cart over to the Jacuzzi with only minor difficulty. There, she removed the dome from the brass serving platter and tucked it on a lower shelf, and her mouth promptly watered at the sight and smell of the array of delicacies she'd revealed. A small loaf of *pâté de campagne* sat beside a dish of duck rillettes, followed by a mound of delicate slices of cured ham and a perfect semi-circle of *saucisson* rounds.

The other half of the board included three cheeses—Brie, herbed goat cheese, and slices of Gruyère—and half a baguette each of sourdough and rye. Tucked among the meat, cheese, and bread were bunches of red grapes, tiny bowls of olive oil, Dijon mustard, fig jam, honey, cornichons, and olives, and a scattering of blueberries.

She popped an olive into her mouth and enjoyed its refreshing, tangy brine while she dithered over selecting her next morsel. She decided to smear some rillettes over a round of sourdough, which she topped with a dollop of fig jam before taking a bite and involuntarily moaning with delight.

"*Christ*, that's good," she muttered. She closed her eyes and finished it off.

Next, she uncorked the bottle of red wine she'd selected at random and let it aerate. She had no idea if this Pinot Noir paired well with anything on the platter, but she didn't care. Then she shed the dressing gown and hung it on the spindly yet sturdy wooden chair beside the hot tub, presumably for exactly this reason.

Elana hadn't packed a bathing suit or bothered to buy

one on the way. Most of the shops were closed this late in the evening anyway. Therefore, she was skinny-dipping in the hot tub, completing her evening of indulgence with everything short of an escort, and she was utterly unapologetic about it. The stress was melting away, and she hadn't climbed into the Jacuzzi yet.

Slipping into the hot, bubbling water made her sigh in relief. Before sitting on the underwater ledge, she poured herself a glass of wine, which she set on the tub's edge. Then she sank up to her chin and spent several long moments letting the jets massage her.

Elana let her eyes drift half-shut and gazed at the baskets of soaps, oils, and loofahs artfully arranged on the shelves on the other side of the tub. Most hotels would never allow you to use products in a Jacuzzi since cleaning the things was a royal pain in the ass. Vampire hotels must have solved those problems.

She floated across the tub—it could fit six easily—and surfaced with only a light splashing of the tiles. After pondering, she selected an oil infused with jasmine and poured a little into the bubbling waters.

Then her phone rang.

Elana grumbled. It was all the way over on the bed, and she did not want to get out of the tub. But it might be Matt —or *Valeria*—so…

Wait. Her new phone had a functional voice assistant.

"Hey, Spider," she called and waited until she heard the answering *bleep*. "Answer call."

"*Elana!*" Vicky's excitement crackled over the line.

Elana grinned. A catch-up chat with Vicky was *precisely*

how she wanted to spend the next little while. "Hang on, Vicky—do you have time for a video call?"

"Depends. How scandalous are you?"

"Well, I'm currently going commando in a hot tub in the ritziest hotel I've ever seen while eating a charcuterie board and drinking wine that probably costs a month's rent in some cities…"

"*Shut. Up.* Get your ass on video call right now, and yes, I *do* know what I just implied."

Elana cackled as she hauled herself out of the hot tub and over to the phone. "You're *awful.*"

"And you love me!"

Elana sank into the king bed with a relaxed sigh and dropped her phone on the feather duvet. Chatting with Vicky, even though they hadn't dug into anything deep, or God forbid, *classified*, had lifted Elana's spirits considerably. Sometimes you needed to gossip about dumb shit like wine, cheese, and sexist assholes at car dealerships.

She wanted to tell Vicky the whole story. She'd held back because while *Elana* trusted Vicky, she knew that wouldn't pass for secure in Valeria's estimation in a million years. Therefore, Elana still had plenty on her mind about her parents, especially her mom, and the relief from the phone call was ebbing already.

Elana opened the drawer of the nightstand in an attempt to distract herself. It was late. She needed to sleep. Maybe the Haven Arms provided complimentary vibrators…

Nope. Only a remote control. There was a television hidden somewhere.

Elana pressed the power button on the remote and a holographic display shimmered into existence a couple feet past the end of the bed. It sank in midair until it was at perfect eye height for Elana in the position she was currently in.

The default channel, as with most hotel TVs, was the news. Haven News Network was a twenty-four-hour news channel with twelve two-hour segments, each with a pair of hosts. It wasn't broadcast outside the Wall, but it maintained a public YouTube channel with highlight clips of daily headlines that might be of import to the human world. Elana had subscribed the day it had gone live.

The late-night anchors were Amadon Thierry and Olivia Nonsuch. Elana was reasonably familiar with the pair, although her favorite hosts were Kelly Pier and Reggie Philson, who did the morning show.

Tonight, Amadon and Olivia were recapping the latest developments in a trade deal Haven was hashing out with DC. Arbiter Amindóttir was pushing for a decrease in the visa requirements for vampires wanting to work in executive positions. Secretary Daughtry was holding out for increased fees on goods imported through the US to Haven.

Amadon subtly implied that the American government—meaning the humans—was being greedy and trying to carve money out of a trade that wasn't rightfully theirs. Elana remembered plenty of newscasts on Ashford's local station that all but accused the vampires of sitting on piles of cash like Scrooge McDuck. *Everything changes, and everything stays the same.*

Elana stretched and sighed. Her eyelids were drooping. The economic details were over Elana's head and beyond her desire to care, but the regular mention of arbiters and the consulate reminded her again of her mother.

As Olivia introduced a short clip of Amindóttir speaking to reporters at the consulate's press conference earlier that day, Elana wondered how often vampires showed up on the Ashford news—or national news—when talking to human politicians. Had her mother ever spoken in public? If she had, had Jeremiah seen her?

She fell asleep unsure whether she wanted to know the answer.

CHAPTER TWENTY-FOUR

Elana woke to sunlight streaming through the wall of windows. She blearily rubbed the sleep from her eyes and regretted not finding the curtains before turning in the night before.

She slid out of bed and stretched. Several vertebrae popped in quick succession, and her arms and legs ached pleasantly. She'd worked hard over the last couple of weeks and last night's intense relaxation had done her a world of good. It wasn't even eight o'clock yet, but Elana felt like she'd slept twelve hours. Maybe she'd have to buy a house with a hot tub...

Her phone buzzed. She glanced over to see Matt's name on the screen along with a one-word text.

Breakfast?

Elana yawned and grabbed her phone to text him back as she headed for the bathroom.

This place has a kick-ass breakfast menu. Want to join me here?

She brushed and braided her hair while waiting for him to text back. She tied off the braid as his message scrolled in.

Sounds great. What time, and what's your room number?

The idea of Mr. Sexy Voice in the hot tub ran through Elana's mind—or maybe *streaked* would be a better word. She blushed.

502. Text when you're here. Any time after 8:30 is fine.

He texted back a thumbs-up, and Elana went to pick her clothes for the day. She opted for a pair of wide-leg beige slacks, strappy sandals, and a navy blue ruffled short-sleeved shirt that in her humble opinion, made her boobs look *killer*.

She might have still been thinking about Mr. Sexy Voice in the hot tub. She'd never tell.

Matt texted at 8:35 and arrived on the fifth floor at 8:40. "Do you know, I've never stayed here," he commented as he walked into Elana's suite. "Thought about it a few times but never took the plunge. Is it worth it?"

"*Oh*, yes," Elana assured him from her spot at the kitchenette island, where she was examining the room service menu anew. "Any requests for breakfast? It's all French."

"Surprise me."

"Cool." She brought up the interface embedded in the kitchen island and tapped in her order. "It says food will arrive within twenty minutes."

"Excellent. This suite is gorgeous." Matt was touring the room, checking out the paintings on the walls, the Jacuzzi, and the view from the windows. "Great view, too. It's a lovely courtyard."

Elana chuckled. "I appreciate it much more this morning than I did last night. Got here with no sunlight left."

Matt sat in a puffy armchair and settled in comfortably. "Yeah, it was late by the time you texted me you were headed here. Did you find anything else interesting?"

She went to join him in the sitting area, opting for the couch. "Oh, plenty interesting. Nothing definitive, but lots more of the 'typos.' I also learned more than I ever thought I would about Haven's refugee and immigration policies. My mom was *hardline*."

"That she was. I wasn't close enough with her to tell you *why*, if you're wondering, but I can absolutely confirm that she was a staunch proponent of more open borders and more lenient requirements for asylum seekers."

"Did she have many friends?"

Matt leaned back in the armchair and crossed one leg over the other. "I don't know. She was as social as was expected of an arbiter and a concubine before that, and she was always friendly whenever I saw her, but I didn't run in the same circles as she did. You'd have to ask Valeria."

Elana gave a theatrical shudder. "Ask the Arbiter of Shadows about her dead friend's other friends? That sounds like a surefire way to get glared out of the room and maybe off this mortal coil."

Matt laughed. "She's not as bad as all that... Okay, maybe she *can* be, but she's not *always* like that. Some of the façade is just that—a façade."

Elana raised an eyebrow. "I'll believe it when I see it."

"When you practice a specific way of acting around people for decades..."

"How old *is* she?"

"That is a carefully guarded secret."

"You don't know."

"I do not."

Elana shook her head and whistled through her teeth. "Damn. She could be as old as Cathy or as young as you. Unless you're as old as Cathy, in which case that's a stupid comparison."

"Who's Cathy?"

"Did I not tell you about Cathy? Cathy Smith, House Lucciola. We ran into each other the other day in Premier and hit it off."

Matt's eyebrows gradually rose. "Cathy *Smith* of House Lucciola. *Wow.*"

"Is she a big deal? I got the impression she was a big deal."

"She's not a *small* deal, that's for sure. House Lucciola has never shown itself to be particularly ambitious in the political arena, but they've quietly built a small empire in the fashion and textiles industries over the centuries. Originally Italian, as I'm sure you guessed."

"I had. Is there still an Italian branch?"

Matt cast his gaze to the ceiling in thought. "I believe so? Genealogy isn't my thing, and Lucciola keeps itself out of trouble. Cathy is the head of the American branch of House Lucciola. You said you and she hit it off?"

"We spent a couple of hours shopping. She asked me over for tea next week."

"Will you go?"

"Planning to. She and I had a lot of fun shopping. I also asked her to help me learn the finer points of vampire etiquette and social graces, and she accepted. Valeria's teaching me tons, but I need a...a vampire Jane Austen. Someone to help me navigate the complexities of the *ton*, as it were."

Matt tilted his head. "I'm not entirely certain Austen would help you in a Regency romance. She wasn't exactly a fan of the social norms of the time."

Elana rolled her eyes. "Oh, you know what I mean."

A knock at the door brought Elana to her feet. Her stomach growled in anticipation as the scent of fresh bread wafted through the door.

This morning's staff member was a petite woman with a short brown bob who beamed at Elana when she opened the door. "Your breakfast, ma'am!"

Elana glanced at her nametag. "Thank you *very* much, Nicole. Do you want last night's cart, or will housekeeping take it later?"

"I can take it now, ma'am. It's no trouble."

Matt overheard and wheeled the cart in question over to the door, where Nicole took it and bid them a good morning with a polite bow. Elana brought the breakfast cart into the kitchenette and pulled plates from the cupboards.

"We've got *oeufs cocotte*, a few types of bread—baguettes, gibassiers, croissants, pain au chocolat—and coffee." She licked her lips. "I could get used to eating like this."

Matt grinned, accepted a plate, and filled it with food. "You might have to hire a chef unless you plan to take cooking courses."

Elana tore off a mouthful of pain au chocolat and spoke through it. "Either or. Don't care. *Damn*, this is good."

"Manners!" Matt scolded her through laughter. "Don't let Valeria catch you like that!"

Elana swallowed and wiped her mouth with a napkin, then perched at the kitchen island again and took her next bite more sedately. "Never in a million years. What's the news from our illustrious leader, anyway? Or…what's the opposite of *illustrious*? *De*-lustrious?"

"I think *tenebrous* would be closest," Matt mused.

"Perfect. What's the news from our tenebrous leader?"

"First, I don't think she wants to be your leader, but that's a whole other kettle of fish." Matt broke the yolk of his egg and scooped a spoonful of white and yellow goodness onto a piece of baguette. "She's having top-of-the-line cryptography software licensed to your fingerprint on the citywide systems."

"That's it?"

"That's the best she can give us right this minute. Another big, *flashy* issue went down last night, and it's taking up most of her bandwidth."

Elana grimaced. "Ah. Understood. Don't get me wrong,

I'm grateful, but I'm not a cryptographer. I kind of hoped she'd, you know, *assign us* someone to help."

Matt shook his head. "The fewer people who know what's going on with this, the better. She assured me that neither of us needed any prerequisite knowledge to run the software. Basically, it sounds like we plug in whatever data we have and let it do its thing."

"Oh, it's like a decryption algorithm."

"Something like that." He stirred his coffee meditatively, then tapped the drips off the spoon and laid it in the saucer. "I meant to ask you yesterday, but the opportunity never came up. Do you have a plan for talking to Jerry about Bishop's Electronics becoming an LLC?"

Elana broke a gibassier in half, inhaled the aroma of orange and anise, then set one half down on her plate and nibbled on the other. "Not yet," she admitted. "I hadn't thought about it since we went over the paperwork. It's probably not a good idea to leave it too long with everything happening."

"I would agree with that. Do you need any help?"

"No, I'll be fine. Just have to make it happen. Thanks for reminding me."

Matt hummed in acknowledgment and returned to his eggs. Elana took another bite of the sweet, buttery, spiced bread, but it was less enjoyable than the last. Between the expensive luxuries and the dangerous conspiracies, she was getting caught up in the vampire world and leaving "real life" behind…only this *was* her life now.

She bit her lip and frowned at the pastries on the tray. She'd arrange something with Jerry soon. Very soon.

"Are we using the same room as before?" Elana inquired as she and Matt walked into the archives. The fresh scent of the plants and the fountain was refreshing. Even with the climate control from the canopy, it was a hot and muggy day in Haven.

Matt nodded, and the two proceeded to the underground office. It surprised Elana how quickly she'd gotten used to the multiple levels of security between the day-to-day workings of Haven and the areas she was working with. It felt natural to her, which she hadn't expected.

While she appreciated a mental puzzle—taking a break from hauling to fix someone's broken gadget was always a welcome change of pace—these days she felt like she was exercising a whole new set of skills. She had spent little time untangling word puzzles over the years and even less time paying attention to *social* puzzles.

She set the thoughts aside as she slid into the chair behind the desk and smoothly brought up the interface. She started when Matt chuckled. "You look like an old pro already."

Elana tossed him a cheeky grin. "I'm not *that* old." She poked around the interface and frowned. "Okay, maybe I *am* that old. Where's this software you said she was installing?"

"Oh, no, that's not quite how it works." He pulled the spare chair to the other side of the desk and sat across from her. "It's cloud software, essentially. She gave me a command to activate it. Hang on."

Matt slipped his phone out of the inside pocket of his

suit jacket—dark brown pinstripe today—and scrolled through several things before exclaiming, "Got it!"

He turned the phone around and showed it to Elana, who peered at the screen. "Make sense? I can call if we need more instructions."

Elana's gaze flicked back and forth over the text, and she shook her head. "No, this seems pretty good. If I fail miserably, then sure, but let's give it a go first."

With her gaze still on Matt's phone, she typed in the command shown on the screen. "Thanks. It says I need to point it to the data… Do I give it the raw data from my mother's journal? Or do I give it my notes?"

"You might need both," Matt remarked. "Raw data for crunching and your notes to narrow it down."

"Good point." Elana stuck her tongue out a touch as she continued to type. "Adding to the list of things I am not—a programmer. This stuff is insanely complex."

Matt chuckled. "Let it never be said that vampires are late adopters. Just because a bunch of us wear old, frilly clothing doesn't mean our minds aren't sharp as razors."

"I believe it. Okay, I think I have it right. Now I press Enter…" Her hand hovered over the key. "I'm nervous. What if it doesn't find anything?"

"Then we keep looking somewhere else."

Elana exhaled forcefully. "Yeah. We keep looking."

She pressed Enter. The text on the interface disappeared, replaced by a small spinning circle. "It's thinking. I suppose that's a good thing."

"Definitely. If it didn't spend time thinking about it, that would mean it's an idiot, or we did something wrong."

"Or there's nothing to find."

"Point."

They waited in silence for five minutes before Elana got impatient. "I'm gonna keep reading." She grabbed one of the books she'd begun the day before. No sooner had she opened it than the interface *dinged* and spat out a line of text.

"Of course," she grumbled. "I start doing something *useful*, and you engage."

"What does it say?"

"Veridian," Elana read. "House Veridian, then a pile of numbers. All eight-digit strings. What comes in eight-digit strings?"

"Dates," Matt suggested.

"That would make sense." Elana copied the text into a new document, then stared at it. "Do you know House Veridian? I was waiting for it to ring a bell, but I can't think of anything. I don't know them."

Matt pursed his lips. "They're an old House, but they're small. I didn't think they had any foothold in Haven. Strange. I'll follow up on this in my channels as well, but maybe for now you should try to find any mentions of House Veridian in your mother's files."

"Sounds wise."

"I have my moments."

Matt started making calls, and Elana started digging. A simple search for the keyword "Veridian" found nothing in Tessa's journal. After a quick online search gave her several related terms to try in case her mother had subtly encoded the references, Elana found multiple instances where her mother mentioned salads for no particular reason. She marked these passages for deeper investigation, then dug into House Veridian's history.

Unfortunately, as Matt had alluded, there was little to find. House Veridian had begun as a cadet branch of House Vireo, which traced its lineage back to Roman times. It had broken off from the main family in the thirteenth century in Italy and made a small but reputable name for itself in ceramics and architecture. A respectable family, if not a flashy one.

Matt was also correct that House Veridian did not have an official scion in Haven. However, they had a representative in Anna Bonetti, who was born to Marsilia Scovo of House Veridian in 1884 and married Giacomo Bianchi of House Sotalia in 1957. Giacomo's father, the head of House Sotalia, had been granted quarter in Haven in 1912, and Giacomo had moved into the walled city with his new bride.

House Sotalia wasn't terribly interesting, either. They specialized in luxury paper products and investments and were quartered in Etreta. Nothing to see there.

Except Tessa had gone out of her way to leave a message for *someone* that involved House Veridian. There *had* to be something to see here. Elana hadn't found it yet, but she would.

Elana went back to the list of dates and looked them up one by one. Maybe she would get lucky and discover something that would blow the story wide open, but even if she didn't, she could gather information on each date, and they could look for patterns.

She stretched and yawned. When she'd dreamed of

being a vampire in high school, endless research was not how she imagined spending her time.

CHAPTER TWENTY-FIVE

When Elana unlocked her door and crossed the threshold, heaviness hit her like a Mack truck. She'd expected the frivolity of her hotel stay to pass, but she *hadn't* expected to feel so discouraged coming *home*.

"This isn't home anymore," she murmured as she let her gaze wander over the living room. "This is just where I used to live."

She hauled in a deep, shaky breath and let it out. Vicky wasn't back in town yet, or she'd have called her to help ease the transition. Elana had come home with the intent of staying the night so going to see the guys in the morning wasn't so much of a commute. Now she questioned the wisdom of that decision. If returning to Ashford made her this miserable, maybe she'd be better company on the job site if she returned to Haven tonight.

Elana shook herself. She was being ridiculous. This was *her house*, dammit. She had made it her own in so many little ways growing up, and she wasn't about to throw the baby out with the bathwater even if she *was* leaving. She wouldn't do that if she were moving house in the human world, so she wouldn't do it when she left for Haven.

Her gaze fell on the shelf of photo albums next to the decorative fireplace. Maybe a trip down memory lane was in order to help her remember the good so she could bring it with her.

Elana sat cross-legged beside the shelves and slid the first album out. It creaked as she opened it, then crackled lightly as the plastic pages rustled and bent for the first time in years. She couldn't remember the last time she'd opened this. It might have been third grade.

Her father had rarely looked through the photo albums. Not while Elana was around, anyway. Elana didn't blame him. It was hard enough for her to look at the old pictures of Tessa and Jeremiah. She couldn't imagine how hard it had been for him.

Elana slowly turned the pages. This album was full of Elana's school photos and candid shots her father had taken at sports games and Christmas concerts. Elana remembered most of the events pictured with nostalgia but no deep sentimentality. Until she'd met Vicky, school had been where everybody thought she was weird and Elana didn't know why.

She quickly finished that album and returned it to its place. She drifted her fingers along the spines of the remaining handful until she reached the last. The white spine had yellowed with regular use, although her father had never taken it off the shelf as far as Elana could remember. No, all of the oil and dirt that had turned the rounded white album cover to a creamy beige had come from Elana's fingers.

This was her parents' wedding album.

It was thin—less than half the size of the albums from Elana's school years—and held only a few dozen pictures. Tessa and Jeremiah hadn't been able to afford much in the way of wedding photography. They'd bought disposable cameras as wedding favors, so they had a riot of candid shots taken by their overly emotional friends.

Elana loved looking through this album, although it made her heart ache. Her parents' joy and excitement bled through the paper and the years. She'd never seen her father as happy in life as in these photos. Not that he'd never been *happy*, but...never *that* happy.

Jeremiah's dusty brown hair stuck up like a broom head in the pictures. That had been the style, or so her father claimed. Elana suspected he hadn't cared, and neither had her mother. They'd been together for years before getting married—the wedding was more or less an afterthought, something thrown together to make legalities easier since Elana was coming along.

Most of the pictures were from the reception—lots of dancing, lots of food, the classic picture of Tessa and Jeremiah feeding each other cake. Tessa was resplendent in her tea-length white gown, all lace with a simple silhouette. She looked young and happy, and her baby bump was *just* beginning to show. Jeremiah wore a black tux that was a little too small for him, short in the arms and legs, and unbuttoned because he likely couldn't close it.

The Bishops might not have been stylish, but they had been *very* much in love.

Elana flipped through the album even more slowly than she had the first. She lingered on each page and gazed at her parents' joyful faces. What would they want her to do? Would they understand why she was making Jerry the active partner in the business and why she was leaving Ashford? Would they support her?

What would they have thought *before* Tessa was turned? What had their dreams been? A simple life, to hear Jeremiah tell it. Tessa had wanted to raise Elana, then return to being a grade-school teacher as she'd been on the road to becoming before she got pregnant. Jeremiah had been happy with the business.

But after Tessa's "death" had turned it all upside down...

Had Tessa's messages been meant for Elana? Elana had to believe so. Why else would Tessa have turned her toddler daughter? If Tessa hadn't wanted Elana to follow in her footsteps, she surely would have left Elana and Jeremiah alone.

Elana touched the last picture in the album, a candid shot of the newlyweds dancing. Tessa had her head on Jeremiah's chest, and Jeremiah held one of Tessa's hands. Both were resting their free hands on the slight curve of Tessa's belly. Tessa's eyes were closed, and she smiled softly. Jeremiah was kissing the top of Tessa's head.

She shifted the album, and something rustled behind the last photo page. She frowned, flipped it, and to her surprise, discovered a small bundle of envelopes bound with an elastic band. The top one read "To my Tess" in her father's handwriting.

Elana removed the rubber band and flicked through the

letters. Half were from her father, and half from her mother. Love letters, evidently. Should she read them?

Elana's chest and throat already burned with suppressed tears, but she could stand a little more heartbreak. She sighed and opened the first. It was dated six months before Elana was born and was short. Her father was a man of few words.

> Tess,
>
> I know you're only in Washington state, but it feels like a million miles away. I'm terrible at writing letters, so I'll just say I love you more than… I don't know… More than the sky is blue and the grass is green. Don't think about it too hard because the grass will NOT be green when you get home thanks to this drought.
>
> Take care of baby Lana and come home soon.
>
> J

The corner of Elana's mouth quirked up in a sad smile. Her father had always told her that Tessa had picked Elana's name early, but he never mentioned that they initially nicknamed her Lana. Another thing lost to Tessa's death, she imagined. Jeremiah had lost so much to Tessa's death.

The next letter was her mother's.

> Jer,
>
> The conference is going swimmingly. No, I'm not swimming in the Pacific, no matter how much I want to. Morning sickness is horrible and every time I get a whiff of the ocean air I want to barf again, but I'll do anything for our little Lana girl.
>
> I'll be home soon. Promise. Don't water the yard. The grass is plenty green enough here for both our love. You wouldn't believe how green it is here. It's beautiful.
>
> See you soon.
> T

Elana exhaled slowly and paged through the remaining letters one by one. They spanned a month. Tessa had gone to a conference in Seattle, but she'd taken sick in the last days and canceled her flight rather than fly pregnant and ill. She'd begged a favor of someone she'd met at the conference to get her into care, and she'd ended up staying the month in Seattle.

Tessa wasn't clear in the letters about the details of her illness, although there were references to phone calls. Maybe she and Jeremiah had discussed those details on the phone. The letters focused on how much they loved and missed each other and how much it tore at them both to be so far apart.

Five months later, they'd be apart forever. No wonder

her father had hidden these letters away. Elana wondered when he'd tucked them into the wedding album. She'd never seen them before.

It was clear that when Tessa died, Jeremiah lost his soulmate. Elana couldn't imagine her mother feeling any differently when she woke up after recovering from the Rights and realizing Jeremiah believed she was dead.

Jeremiah had wanted a quiet, steady life. Instead, he'd lost his wife and been thrown into single-parenthood on top of owning a small business.

What had made her decide not to contact him, and why had she surreptitiously visited Elana anyway? Had she already known something that would have endangered Jeremiah and Elana? Or had she been too afraid that Jeremiah's prejudice against vampires—which Elana still didn't fully understand—would have overridden his love for her?

Surely not. *Surely* not.

Tessa had given up that love. *Why?*

Elana sniffled and brought a hand to her cheek, which came away wet. She hadn't realized she was crying.

Her phone buzzed, and she absentmindedly pulled it out of her pocket while wiping tears from her eyes.

You around? Want to apologize for the other night.

She blinked. What had Matt done that he needed to apologize for?

Elana glanced at the sender, and her heart sank. It wasn't from Matt, it was from Jesse.

Her gaze fell on the letters again, and the phrase "call

whenever you need me, I love you even in the middle of the night" popped out from her father's writing.

Elana's dread transmuted to anger. Jesse hadn't bothered to contact her once since storming out after *throwing a glass at her.* Fuck that noise. He wasn't worth it.

Appreciated but not interested, thanks. Please don't contact me again except for work purposes.

She sent the text and turned off her phone.

CHAPTER TWENTY-SIX

Eight-thirty AM saw bright sun already beating down on the Bishop's Hauling crew. Jerry was pleased to see his boys carting two twenty-four-bottle flats of water into the shade of their break area as he pulled into the parking lot of the construction site in his truck.

Some crews didn't take hydration and breaks seriously to maximize work time, but he and Jeremiah Bishop had never worked that way. As a result, Bishop's turnover rate was low, morale was constantly high, and word of mouth got around that they did good and efficient work.

He parked, killed the engine, and downed the dregs of his black coffee before unbuckling his seatbelt and opening his door. He swung his legs out of the driver's seat and landed on the gravel with a *thud*. He leaned over and tightened the laces on his steel-toe boots, then slammed the heavy truck door shut and locked it.

Jerry strode to the other guys and waved at those who noticed him. This was a big, multi-day job requiring over a dozen workers present, especially in this heat. They all wore breathable clothes, but you still needed high-vis vests, hard hats, and work boots. Everybody needed their turn in the shade faster than official breaks would roll around, so you brought extra folks and spelled them off. Sure, it cost the company more up front, but that investment paid off in loyalty tenfold.

He crunched into the shade under the break tent and grabbed a bottle of water. "Mornin', boys. Everyone in who's supposed to be?"

"Yessir," Nate replied. Nate was a good guy. Young and green but determined and hardworking. Jerry had nicked him at a job fair last year and hoped he'd be around for a good while yet. Might even be able to nudge him into a foreman position if he wanted to stick around.

"Is the big boss comin' in today?" Zac asked. Zac had been with Bishop's for years and showed no sign of flagging interest. Zac loved being the guy who carried the biggest, heaviest loads. Jerry was reasonably certain he benched five or six hundred pounds on the regular...and also suspected Zac had a quiet crush on Elana Bishop. To his credit, he'd never breathed a word of it anywhere Jerry could hear.

Jerry shook his head. "Not today, s'far as I know. But who knows, she could always surprise us."

Jesse, the new guy, scoffed.

Jerry lifted an eyebrow. "Somethin' you wanna share with the rest of us, Aulback?"

The dark-haired young man rolled his eyes. His stubbled jaw was set in a way that gave Jerry pause. While you didn't have to be *happy* to do good work on a construction site, if you were pissed off, you were more likely to miss important shit and possibly get someone hurt.

"She'll surprise you, all right," Jesse grumbled.

The half-dozen other guys in the tent, all in various states of job readiness as they tied boots or donned their high-vis vests, universally turned to subtly look away from Jesse. Jerry internally grimaced. That told him Jesse had been badmouthing Elana where Jerry couldn't hear and nobody had brought it up. Maybe it had only started this morning, maybe not, but it heartened him to see that nobody else seemed to *agree* with Jesse's complaints. Either way, he couldn't let it stand.

Jerry had worried when Elana took Jesse on a date. She was her own woman, and it wouldn't have been the first time she'd dated a guy from the crew, but it *was* the first time she'd done so after Jeremiah had passed. There was a difference between dating the boss' daughter and dating the boss. He'd kept his fingers crossed that things would go well, but evidently, they hadn't.

Jerry cleared his throat. "Mind if I ask you to say a little more on that subject, son?"

Jesse flashed a glare at him. "She's a bitch." He turned the glare on the other men as they bristled. "Yeah, I said it. Your precious boss is a cold-hearted, fang-fucking bitch."

Jerry straightened and frowned. "You're out of line, Aulback," he warned.

"I don't give a fuck," Jesse shot back. "Ever since she ran into that poor asshole who just wanted to live his own damn life and the bloodsuckers gave her an obscene amount of cash to keep her mouth shut, she's been putting on airs."

He made a mincing, impotent, flapping motion with his hand and his upper lip curled. "You all fucking worship her like she's some kind of goddess. She's not fucking worth it. She dropped all of us *real* men the moment one of those pointy-toothed snobs gave her the light of day. She's nothing but a perverted *whore*."

Utter silence fell in the break tent. Only the hot wind rattling the cable that tightened the canvas roof made a sound in the shocked, angry aftermath of Jesse's outburst.

Jerry stared at Jesse for a long moment while he schooled his instinct to lay into the young man for all he was worth. Based on the twitching jaw muscles and flashing eyes of the other men in the tent, he wasn't the only one who wanted to defend the honor of the woman they'd all worked with and respected.

But Jerry had watched Elana grow up as Jeremiah's best friend and the best man at his wedding. If anyone was punching Jesse Aulback's lights out, it would be him. Unfortunately, that was not the standard of management his late friend had insisted upon, so Jerry would have to remain disappointed.

"You done?" he asked Jesse through gritted teeth. "Said your piece?"

"Sure have, grandpa." Jesse spat on the gravel.

"Good. Your employment with Bishop's Electronics and Hauling is terminated, effective immediately. You'll receive your final pay in the mail. Get the fuck off my job site and don't let me see tail nor hair of you again."

For a second, Jesse looked like Jerry had slapped him. Then the flinty anger surged back into his eyes, and Jerry thought he might have to lay the young man flat after all to keep the job site from turning into an all-out brawl.

Luckily for Jerry—and the administrative division of the Ashford City Police—Jesse's brain appeared to re-engage. He grabbed his hard hat from the table, shoved it on his head, and stalked out of the tent.

Right up to Elana Bishop, who stood three yards past the break tent in a bright orange vest, yellow hard hat, and well-worn steel-toed boots.

Jesse stopped cold outside the tent. Jerry didn't move. Elana could more than handle whatever this idiot threw at her.

The muscles of Jesse's neck worked as he swallowed. Elana watched him levelly, arms at her sides. Jerry noticed she held herself differently, almost like how MMA fighters stood before a bout started.

In the second smart decision Jesse had made that morning, gravel scraped under his boot as he pivoted and walked around her. He passed too close to her for comfort, but she refused to move, and he stumbled as he knocked into her shoulder and she didn't budge.

The quiet lasted until his scuffing footsteps led to the creak and slam of a truck door, followed by the rumbling of a diesel engine and a heavily pressed accelerator pedal.

When the sound of his muffler faded, Jerry tipped his hard hat to Elana. "Sorry you had to hear that."

Elana shrugged. "Good call firing him. If he was willing to shit-talk me, he's certainly willing to do the same or worse to his colleagues. That's not the attitude of a Bishop's employee. You all deserve better."

"So do you, boss," Zac piped up. His arms were crossed,

and a thundercloud had settled in on his brow. "We know better."

Elana smiled. "Thanks, Zac. I know." She pulled a pair of work gloves from her back pocket and slid them on. "Let's leave him where he belongs—in the dust—and get to work."

Valeria Draven was used to being avoided. She managed those in her employ fairly and well but wasn't what you'd call a people person. She understood that the persona she cultivated was hardly welcoming. This was deliberate on her part, given that her area of expertise and business was espionage, counterespionage, and what most would term extrajudicial activities.

She had ceased being surprised when people crossed the street rather than walk by her. She cut an imposing figure in day-to-day life and used it to her advantage. She preferred people to approach her on her terms, not theirs. It meant she could easily sort those who *did* into two categories—those who were stupid, arrogant, or both, and those who were already intimidated. Valeria was more than capable of reading both and dealing with them accordingly.

All of this meant she *was* surprised when someone not only did *not* deliberately avoid her on the sidewalk as she strode along Willow Avenue in Senkyem, but they made directly *for* her.

The Arbiter of Shadows did not let her surprise show on her face. She merely raised her eyebrows a degree as the man approached. He was taller than she by a couple of inches, wore his black hair in a long, thin ponytail, and sported a simple but stylish light gray suit with a small pin on the right lapel. When he came close enough, she saw that it was an enamel lily. Not an insignia she immediately recognized, but distinct enough that she committed it to memory.

"Arbiter Draven. Christopher Donovan." The man's voice was a light, smooth baritone. He had a hint of a North Carolina accent. Not a native, then, but someone who had lived in these parts long enough to adopt the dialect. "Pardon me for interrupting. I'm sure you're extremely busy."

"I am. I assume you wish to speak with me."

He half-bowed, extremely politely, and nodded. "Yes. I'm a staff reporter with the *Haven Chronicle*. I simply wanted to inquire after your new protégé. Her name is Elana Bishop, is that correct?"

Alarm bells rang loudly in Valeria's head. "No comment."

"Is it true she's Tessa Hart's daughter?"

Klaxons joined the bells. "No comment. If you'll excuse me, I have a meeting. Good day." She strode past him without another word, fast enough that no argument could be made.

She did not *hurry* to her next appointment, which was indeed a meeting, but she walked faster than she needed to. When she arrived at the building in question, she ducked into a private office first—after courteously but *firmly* insisting that its occupant take a ten-minute break.

As soon as she was alone, she dialed Matt's number and

did not hang up until he answered. "Mister Richelieu. Thank you for taking my call."

"Of course, Arbiter." Matt was utterly professional as always, although an unexpected call from Valeria never meant anything good. "What can I do for you?"

"Elana is raising eyebrows." She laid out her encounter with Christopher Donovan. "Verify that this man is who he says he is, then *be careful.*"

Matt was silent for a moment. "Yes, ma'am. Right away. I'll have that information to you within the hour."

"See that you do."

Valeria hung up without further chitchat—she was even less of a chitchat person than she was a people person—and set the matter aside. She had important business to attend to, and it did not do to be distracted.

Unfortunately, the curl of disquiet in her gut refused to leave.

CHAPTER TWENTY-SEVEN

"Thanks for letting me treat you," Elana told Jerry as they waited to be seated at the bar. McCoy's Bar and Grill was the best joint in town for cheap beer and greasy nachos, and Elana had spent more than a few evenings in here watching football with the guys and knocking back drinks and chips.

Jerry chuckled. "When your boss offers to take you for dinner, one-on-one, it means one of two things. You're fired, or she's closing up shop. Either way, you don't say no to free food."

"Smart man."

The waitress—Natalie, a cute twenty-something with bleached-blond pigtails that made her simultaneously look five years younger and ten years older—ushered them to an open spot at the bar. "Anything I can get you right away?" she bubbled. "Or do you need a minute to look at the menu?"

"Two pints of whatever's on tap and a platter of loaded nachos," Elana requested.

"You got it!"

She bustled away, and Elana elbowed Jerry as they watched her go. "Hey now, old man, get your mind out of the gutter."

Jerry snorted. "She's young enough to be my daughter. I wasn't lookin'. So, which is it?"

"Huh?"

"Are you lettin' me go, or are you closing the business?"

Elana shook her head. "Geez. I know small talk isn't your thing, but come *on*, Jer."

"I just wanna know what mindset I gotta enjoy this beer in. Cheers, darlin'." This last was to Natalie, who pushed two brimming pint glasses of yellow beer across the counter.

"Thanks," Elana added. She sipped her beer, then set it down. "Neither, actually. The day I fire you is the day hell freezes over, and I'd never sell Dad's business…except to you, if you wanted it."

Jerry swallowed a long draught of beer, then licked his lips and set the glass down. "You askin' me if I do?"

"Yup. Well, sort of. I'm turning Bishop's into an LLC, which means I can add partners more easily. You're the only one I want in right now. I trust you to keep your hand on the tiller and to keep the boys in line."

He contemplated the condensation on his glass. "I'm not much with numbers."

Elana scoffed. "That's bullshit and we both know it, but honestly I was gonna hire an accountant anyway and save us both the trouble. Not much would change, Jer, except that you'd get to make the decisions on paper as well as on-site. *Well…*" She rolled her eyes and corrected herself.

"Tax shit would change. But that's what the accountant's for."

Jerry was quiet for a long moment, thinking and drumming his fingers on the cool countertop. Finally, he asked, "Why? Is this something to do with your dad passin', or is it because of the whole Haven thing?"

Elana's heart quavered, and her gut rolled over with enough vehemence that she wasn't sure she'd be able to eat the nachos when they arrived. Still, Jerry had been there through the ups and downs of her entire life, so if she couldn't trust him, she was out of luck no matter what.

"Bit of both. Can I be straight with you?"

"Wouldn't want it any other way."

Elana drew a deep breath and let it out slowly—and she was glad she'd taken the time to do so because Natalie returned at that precise moment with a huge, steaming platter of corn chips covered in jalapeños, green onions, and liquid cheese.

"You two have yourselves a good time," the waitress said cheerfully. "Flag me down if you need anythin'."

"Will do. Thanks." Elana pulled a chip out of the mound and toasted Jerry with it.

They both ate a couple of hot, spicy mouthfuls and grumbled about burning the roofs of their mouths. Then Elana took a drink, swallowed, and decided there was no time like the present to watch her entire world crumble apart for good. It would make moving to Haven that much easier.

She pitched her voice just loud enough for Jerry to hear as she declared, "I'm a vampire."

Jerry's salt-and-pepper beard stopped moving as he

crunched through the nacho in his hand and paused. His silvery-blue eyes locked onto hers, and the crow's feet at their corners tightened.

He put the half-eaten nacho on his plate, chewed, swallowed, and ran a calloused, suntanned hand through his messy, sweaty hair. Elana wasn't much better. Nobody looked runway-ready after a full day cleaning a construction site.

Say something, Elana silently urged him. *Please, for the love of God, say something.*

"That explains a lot," her pseudo-second father replied at last.

Elana blinked. He wasn't throwing the nachos in her face and storming out. He didn't seem angry, hurt, or betrayed. Surprised, maybe, but not shocked. She seemed more surprised than he was, to tell the truth.

"It does?"

Jerry nodded. He picked up the abandoned nacho and finished it, then chased it with another long pull of beer that nearly emptied his pint glass. He caught Natalie's eye, motioned at the glass, and smiled when she gave him a thumbs-up.

Elana waited until she couldn't anymore. "You're not mad?"

He exhaled through his nose and his lips twitched toward a smile. "God, no, I ain't mad. Why the hell would I be mad?"

"Because...because..." She waved ineffectually. "Because everyone thinks vampires are horrible creatures who suck blood from virgins and enslave entire countries, and, and... y'know..."

Her voice trailed off as she caught the fond amusement on Jerry's face. "Why are you looking at me like that?"

Jerry held up a finger. Natalie was coming. When she left after delivering Jerry's second pint, he replied. "Because you're the same little girl I remember hauling two-by-fours from her daddy's truck bed. Hell, Elana, part of me always wondered.

"Never gave the thought much credence because it would have been weird as hell, but there's strong, and there's *strong*. To hear Jeremiah tell it, you were no slouch in any other arena, and that wasn't just a proud father talking. I saw all that too. Like I said, it explains a lot."

Elana felt like her entire lower body had…disappeared. Her head was floating above the barstool in McCoy's. She had become disembodied due to her world turning inside out.

"I thought for sure you'd be mad. Dad…" She swallowed hard as tears welled up in her eyes. She angrily ate three mouthfuls of nachos and washed them with beer before regaining her composure. Jerry let her do so without comment.

Elana set her glass down with slightly more force than was necessary and winced. "Dad *hated* vampires, and you two were best friends. I don't understand."

Jerry's face creased in a bittersweet smile. "He never wanted to talk about it. Well, I figure there's no harm now. Before I do, though…"

He poked a jalapeño off his nacho, then held it in one hand and kept her gaze. "I don't need the details, all right? Not unless you wanna tell me. I respect you same as anyone else. Always have, always will. You earned that respect more than anyone I've ever worked with. Don't care what you are, and that goes for anything."

He paused, considered, then winked and added, "Except maybe Mormons, but that's just 'cause they creep me out." He smiled warmly once again. "Okay? That understood?"

Elana gave him a lopsided but genuine smile in return. "Yeah. I hear you, Jer. Thanks."

"Anytime." Jerry crunched the nacho into oblivion, then folded his hands on the bar counter. "Your dad hated vampires because of what happened to your mother."

All of Elana's warm and fuzzy feelings turned to ice in her veins. Had her father *known* that Tessa had become a vampire? Had Elana been barking up the wrong tree this entire time?

"You know she died soon after you were born," Jerry continued, eyebrows raised in a request for confirmation, and when Elana nodded, he went on. "It was horrible. Seizures and shit. Jeremiah saw some of it before the docs whisked her off to the ICU. Stuck with him for the rest of his life.

"He stayed with you. They wouldn't let him into the ICU anyway, but he didn't want to leave you alone. Tessa would've wanted him with you, I think. She and I went way back too, don't know if I ever told you that. God, I miss that woman. She had a smile like the sun coming out on a cloudy day. Made you feel like a million bucks any time she laid eyes on you."

He sighed and returned to the story, his gaze drifting aside as he recalled the details. "There was a fancy-ass vampire doctor visitin' the hospital that day. Don't remember his name or…House, or whatever. It's Houses, right? They have Houses?" He met Elana's gaze briefly, and a touch of color came into his cheeks. "You have Houses?"

"We do," Elana numbly replied. That *had* to be the vampire who turned her mother. Her mother's words from her journal floated through her head: *I woke up not knowing where I was or what had happened. My last memory was of Elana's scrunched-up newborn face.*

Jerry nodded. "Right. Okay. Anyway, like I said, I don't remember who he was, only that he was some big shot specialist who'd *deigned* to come *bestow his knowledge* on the idiot humans." He rolled his eyes. "Or that's how the rumor had it. I know how to run a crew. I don't know medicine, and I sure as hell don't know vampires. Maybe he was nothin' special.

"Jeremiah got it in his head that this guy coulda done something to save Tessa. Vampires have all these fancy gadgets, like they come from sci-fi, and all this science we don't understand. So the way Jeremiah looked at it, this doctor should've helped. 'Had a *moral obligation* to help,' was the way he put it. He didn't, and Tessa died."

Elana's head reeled. *Except he* did *help, and she* didn't *die.*

Jerry drank more beer and sighed. "Way I figure it, the guy probably didn't know Tessa was there, much less that she was dyin'. If he did, what's it to him? Maybe he couldn't have saved her anyway. I don't know. I wasn't there. That's what I've told myself for thirty years so it didn't eat me from the inside out like it did your father."

In an uncharacteristic display of emotion, Jerry reached across the table and put his hand beside Elana's. Not *on* her hand—that would be far too much physical affection for a reserved man of Jerry's caliber—but next to it. Elana caught his drift.

"I'll love you no matter what, Elana. You're like a daughter to me, and you always will be. Bein' a vampire doesn't change that one whit. But promise me one thing."

"Anything I can." Her throat caught on the words. She felt gummed up with emotions she could barely stop to name, let alone process.

"Don't be like that, okay? I dunno what's gonna happen now that you're a vampire, how you're gonna change or what you're gonna learn. But if the time comes that you can help someone because you're a vampire—if you can use those gizmos and big brains to help us little folks—do it. Do the right thing. Please."

Elana put her hand on top of Jerry's. "I'll do my best. I promise."

He flipped his hand around and gripped hers hard, like the way he'd grip a sledgehammer. Unyielding, powerful, and brave. "That's my girl. That would make both your parents proud."

She had to tell Matt.

Elana white-knuckled her way through the rest of dinner. Jerry agreed to become a partner, no surprise there. She'd bring the paperwork, and they'd get it done that week. She didn't taste any of her food and felt sick all the way home.

The moment she locked the door, she pulled her phone from her handbag and called Matt. He answered on the second ring.

"Good evening, Elana."

"There was a vampire doctor at the hospital in Ashford the day my mother died," Elana blurted.

Several seconds of silence later, Matt replied, "I'm calling Valeria. Please hold."

Elana wedged the phone between her shoulder and ear as she hopped out of her shoes and changed into comfier clothes. She had one arm through a sweatshirt when Valeria's voice came over the line.

"Miss Bishop?"

Elana grabbed the phone with one hand and hauled the sweatshirt on the rest of the way. "Arbiter Draven. I'm so sorry to interrupt."

"It's fine. This is a top priority case. Repeat what you said to Mister Richelieu."

Elana drew a deep breath and repeated it word for word.

"I see." As ever, the arbiter's tone was calm and level. "Very interesting. This detail did not come up in my investigation."

Elana's eyebrows creased. "You're the *Arbiter of Shadows*. Don't you have access to *everything* that has *anything* to do with Haven vampires?"

The depth of solemnity in Valeria's voice chilled Elana to the bone. "With very, *very* few exceptions, yes."

"What exceptions are those?"

"I believe you can extrapolate. I will not speak further on this on an unsecured line. When I have more information, Miss Bishop, I will contact you."

Elana sat on the edge of her bed and stared at her reflection in the vanity mirror across from it. She still felt like her head was entirely disconnected from her body. "Thanks."

"Thank *you* for bringing this to my attention. I trust the source is reputable?"

"Yes," Elana immediately responded. "It's second-hand through Jerry from my father, but they were best friends and my father would have no reason to lie about this. It's *possible* that he was wrong, but…I doubt it."

"Understood. I will return you to Mister Richelieu."

Elana mutely nodded before realizing that Valeria couldn't see her, but before she could say anything, she heard Matt's voice in her ear again.

"You okay?"

"Not in the slightest. I feel like I've been socked in the gut with a wrecking ball."

"I can only imagine," he sympathized. "You see Gustav in the morning, right?"

She groaned. "Yeah."

"Then I'd recommend getting some sleep if you can and working out all these emotions in the gym tomorrow."

Elana reflected that this would likely be easier said than done.

CHAPTER TWENTY-EIGHT

Thwack.
Thud.
"Ow..."
"*Vstavat'!* Again!"

Elana groaned and forced herself to her feet. After the resounding and surprising success of her conversation with Jerry the night before, she'd expected to sleep well and wake the next morning raring to go. She knew she'd need to be because she was scheduled to be back at the consorts' training grounds first thing.

The universe had not gotten the message.

She squared up with Gustav and raised her fists. The burly Russian vampire reminded her of a sideshow strongman when he wore the blue singlet he had on today with short black curls peeking out from his chest and bulging muscles on full display. He was only missing the thin, waxed mustache.

If he was a strongman, she was the slapstick clown. He'd put her on her ass more times than she could count.

They circled each other with slow sidesteps, never breaking eye contact. Elana stepped in, and he stepped back like a dance. She pressed forward, and Gustav pivoted. Elana threw a jab at his face. He batted it away, then came in with a right hook to her solar plexus that she had to spin to avoid. Gustav met her spin with a swift kick to the ribs, and she yelped.

She skipped away and resisted the urge to press a hand against her ribs. Her sole saving grace at this point was that Valeria wasn't in the gym today. Elana was making an ass of herself all on her lonesome.

Thank God for small mercies.

Elana faced Gustav. She crossed the four yards between them at a jog, then hopped up on one foot and twisted into a spinning kick. Gustav caught her ankle with his and brought her crashing down to the mats once again.

She landed on her back, hitting with a *whumph* as the impact pushed the breath from her lungs. Elana barely managed to roll aside in time to miss Gustav's follow-up attack, an elbow-forward body slam that would have broken a human's sternum.

Elana flipped to her feet. She still hadn't taken a breath and her chest was beginning to ache from the negative pressure. She tripped, rolled into a forward somersault out of necessity, then stumbled into the wall. The shock of the cool brick against her sweaty skin kicked her brain and body back into alignment, and she gasped.

The break was short-lived. Gustav rammed into her from behind and knocked her head into the wall. Pain lanced through her forehead, and she cried out.

"*Uncle!*" she yelled on her next breath.

Gustav didn't relent. Oh well. Worth a shot.

Elana awkwardly twisted her lower half until she could bring her knee up, and *hard*. She was supposed to fight dirty, so dirty she would fight.

Gustav grunted and his hold on her shoulders lessened. Elana took the opportunity to shove backward. When he staggered one foot back, she dropped and drove her shoulder into his chest, anchored her foot on the wall, and pushed him with a full-throated shout.

He tumbled but kept hold of her shoulders and brought her with him. When he hit the floor, he used Elana's momentum to roll them over and pinned her to the mat.

Elana met his gaze when her spine hit the mat once more. Fury curdled in her gut when she saw that he'd barely broken a sweat. He looked as neutral, unbothered, and professional as ever. *Goddamned ice-cold Russian son-of-a-bitch bastard,* she fumed. *Fuck you and the horse you rode in on, I swear to* God.

She bucked. He held firm. She yanked at her arms and wriggled. He moved with her and used her squirming to adjust his grip even tighter. She snarled and brought her head up to attempt a nose-crushing headbutt, but he backed off.

No matter how Elana strained and struggled, Gustav was immovable. Finally, unable to move or gain any leverage, she let her head fall with a *thump* and tapped the mat twice.

"Checkmate," she rasped. Her last yell had come entirely from her throat, not her core—and they'd started this spar a solid twenty minutes ago.

Gustav, apparently satisfied that she had recognized the

futility of the situation, immediately released her and stood. He eyed her, likely weighing whether to offer her a hand, but she scowled and dropped her gaze to the floor as she struggled to her feet.

"You are better than this." He wasn't asking her a question, not even in the stilted way Elana suspected was left over from speaking Russian for much longer than he'd spoken English. That was a statement and a disappointed one at that.

Elana still didn't meet his eyes. She brushed herself off and carefully stretched. She winced at an unpleasant pull in her ribs, and flinched when she turned her head and something twinged in her neck.

"Are you ill? Is it your time of the month?"

She crossed her arms, looked at his feet, and did her best to keep the petulance and irrational rage she felt out of her reply. "No." *Even if I was on the rag, it wouldn't matter, you sexist asshole.*

"Then why do you suck *so bad* today?"

The incongruity of the utterly professional Gustav asking her why she *fucking sucked*, plus the mild note of exasperation in his tone, took Elana off-guard and made her look up. Gustav never got snippy. He was always the infuriatingly level-headed Zen master.

He caught her gaze and stared her down. He had also crossed his arms, and the look on his face was somewhere between curiosity and frustration.

Elana deflated with a sigh, but her jaw remained clenched. "I just have a lot on my mind," she grumpily informed him.

Gustav barked a single laugh. "*Voz'mi sebya v ruki.* Too

bad, so sad. Nobody who is trying to kill you will give a good goddamn what you are thinking about."

A muscle in Elana's cheek twitched and her fingers flexed on her forearms. "Are people trying to kill me? I don't think so!" she shot back.

Gustav shrugged. "That is not the opinion of Madam Arbiter. I answer to her, not you." He let his arms fall to his sides, then brought them back up in a defensive stance. "Get out of your head, *gore lukovoye*. When someone is punching your lights out is not the time to consider all of life's mysteries."

Elana huffed. "I'm not considering *all of life's mysteries*, Jesus. I'm *going through some shit*. It's perfectly normal to be a little preoccupied when you're navigating multiple massive life decisions in the span of a few weeks."

Gustav made a talking motion with one of his hands. "Blah, blah, blah. All *I* hear is the whining of a little girl who just had her ass handed to her. I do not *care*, Bishop, nor do your enemies. The fastest way to die in the world of *vampiry* is by believing you are *special*.

"You are not special. You are a baby vampire, and if this is how you wish to present yourself to the big bad wolves in the Houses and the consulate, I will wash my hands of you this instant. Then I will report to Valeria that you are a sniveling child who could not tie her shoes without crying for her mommy."

As Gustav spoke, Elana's ire rose. By the time he finished, she was seeing red. *"Don't you dare talk about my mother that way,"* she ground out through her teeth, then flew across the room and laid into him.

She came out swinging with an uppercut, followed by

an elbow to the temple. He flowed with the blows, then pivoted with her and aimed a haymaker at her jaw. She ducked, spun, and delivered a heel kick to his kidney.

Gustav staggered, then skipped backward into a falling reverse somersault to dodge Elana's follow-up kick. Back on his feet, he met her flurry of jabs with his forearms, parrying each and forcing her back across the mats to the middle of the room.

She dug her heel in and blocked his raised arms with hers. She panted and held his gaze for two heartbeats, then dropped like a rock into a squat and whipped around in a low flying kick to the side of his knee.

Gustav jumped, but a hair too slowly, and her leg caught his rising ankle and sent him spinning sideways. Elana drove a fist into his falling face—a bulls-eye on the nose—and he tumbled backward, spinning from the force of the hit.

She dashed forward and leaped on top of him. He latched onto her upper arms with both hands and forced them to continue rolling. Instead of allowing him to pin her, Elana kept them going by kicking out hard with one foot, then slammed the other down to stop the roll when she was on top. The *thud* of her sole on the mat echoed through the gym.

Elana didn't bother trying to pin the big Russian. She was strong, but he was a higher-level vampire than she was, and was therefore stronger by definition. Instead, she straddled his waist and proceeded to deliver as many rapid-fire punches to his jaw and head as she could in the few seconds she would have before he threw her off.

She managed five before Gustav hurled her aside. She

hit the floor with a shoulder and kept rolling, coming up in a three-point stance as the burly trainer charged her.

Elana stayed down until the last possible second, when she saw his footing change. He was coming in for a spin kick to her head.

She let him get both feet off the ground, then sprang forward, snagged his ankle, and threw him across the room like a discus. She sprinted after him and tackled him while still in midair. Where he had weight, she had speed.

The two slammed into the mat with Elana's knee driving into Gustav's solar plexus and her forearm across his throat. She hiked her knee up a few inches until she knelt on his sternum and shifted her forearm aside in favor of getting both hands around his throat and pressing firmly on the pressure points on either side.

Elana held on for dear life while Gustav rained blows onto her arms and side as his face reddened and his eyes bulged. She refused to tap out again. It was *not* happening.

At long last, Gustav's arms flopped out in a T and he slapped the mat twice. Elana jumped off him and caught her breath from a few feet away while he gasped and coughed.

When he finally spoke, his voice was raspy but deeply pleased. *"That's more like it,"* he growled, then grinned. *"That's* how you show those *ublyudki* you're not to be trifled with!"

Gustav's praise devolved into another coughing fit, but he waved Elana off when she approached in concern. He pushed himself to his feet, hacked one more time into his elbow, then turned bloodshot, shining eyes on her. "I'm fine, Bishop. All the better since you proved I haven't wasted my goddamn time training you."

Elana blushed and tried to scowl again. The truth was she was too relieved she'd finally bested Gustav properly—not to mention he wasn't pissed off that she'd almost killed him *and* he was *proud* of her—to manage any surliness.

"I still don't think anyone's going to try to kill me," she teased.

His answering laugh turned into another cough. "I wouldn't be so sure, my girl. I wouldn't be so sure."

CHAPTER TWENTY-NINE

After a long, hot shower and a date with the fancy hair dryer, Elana left her Emeya in the private parking at the training grounds and took a glider to the archives. The climate control canopy made the weather tolerable, and she spared a thought for the Bishop's crew toiling away at the construction site in the oppressive heat beyond the Wall.

She parked the glider at the station near the archives' entrance and dismounted. It truly *was* similar to riding a bike, once you got the hang of having no wheels, and it was much easier to ride with the dimensional bag rather than her duffel.

She spotted Matt approaching on the sidewalk, waved, and waited for him to join her at the doors. "You look like someone pissed in your Cheerios," she informed him when he was close enough to hear. "What happened?"

"Do I?" Matt shook himself and wiped the displeased expression from his face. "Nothing I can talk about, unfortunately."

"More of the unpleasantness Valeria was dealing with the other day?"

"Yeah. Did I mention she had to take *her* helicopter out into Ashford?"

Elana's eyebrows rose sharply. "Oh, shit. That's not good."

"It most certainly is not. In comparison, what we're dealing with is…well, it's not *less* dire, but it's less *immediately* dire." He opened the door and gestured for her to go in. "As long as we keep it quiet, anyway. So, *shh*."

Elana snickered and refrained from saying anything more until they reached the office in subbasement two. As soon as the door was shut, she asked, "Found anything interesting yet?"

Matt scowled. "Interesting? Sure. *Useful?* Not yet, unfortunately. I'm still at the bits-and-pieces stage and about ready to tear my hair out."

"Oh, no, not your beautiful wavy hair," Elana teased.

Matt snorted and ran his hand through his thick, dark hair. "Don't worry, I know it's my moneymaker. I'd never dare do it any harm."

"Are you kidding? You could make bank on your voice alone." Elana blushed. "Uh, I mean…never mind."

Matt raised an eyebrow. "*Oh?*"

In for a penny, in for a pound. "No one's ever told you that you have a nice voice?"

"*Nice* voice, sure, although I can't say it comes up in conversation much."

"Probably because anyone thinking about it is too busy swooning."

He chuckled. "That's a bit more than *nice*."

"You *might* be listed as Mr. Sexy Voice on my phone," Elana confessed, reasoning that her cheeks couldn't burn any more than they already were.

Matt's chuckling turned into full-blown laughter. "I *see*…" He grinned and dropped his voice another third into late-night radio DJ land. "So, *Miss Bishop*, shall we get on with the investigation?"

She smacked his upper arm and sat in her chair with finality. "Yes, let's, and quit being a dork."

"*I'm* being a dork?"

"You're being a dork," Elana informed him with impressive neutrality. "I am being perfectly reasonable, sensible, and not at all silly."

Still snickering, Matt slipped several volumes off the shelves and stacked them on the desk. "God forbid you be *silly*."

"Quite so." She pulled up the desktop interface and exclaimed with satisfaction. "The cryptography program finished its search and analysis. Come see."

Matt joined her and peered at the program's output. "Wow. That is a *lot* of results."

Elana cracked her knuckles and rolled her neck. "Sure is. We have our work cut out for us. I'll start digging into this. What are you working on today?"

"I'll start by tracing House Veridian's connections to every House quartered here in Haven. If I don't find any beyond what we already know, I'll look into their connections with Houses *not* represented in Haven."

Elana gave him a thumbs-up, then focused on the file in front of her. They'd run the cryptography program overnight on the entirety of Tessa Hart's journal. It found, notated, and cross-referenced every instance of the hidden messaging, then compiled the data into a single file that included links to every other file referenced.

The result was an extensive and *expansive* list of everything Elana's mother *might* have attempted to leave behind for her daughter to dig up. The number of entries in the list easily ranged in the hundreds. It was certainly possible the cryptography program had found false positives, but Elana and Matt had decided to chance more false positives than risk missing important information on false negatives.

Elana scrolled back to the top of the list and opened the first file. The quarterly report from the consort's Office of Sustainable Agriculture discussed the latest harvest of enriched, cross-bred vegetables. The terminology was deeply unfamiliar, so she skimmed it for anything obvious, then frowned and backed out into the main list.

The second file was a news article detailing a draft agreement between an Etretan firm and a manufacturing plant in Michigan. While this was written in layman's terms and Elana had no trouble reading it, she again did not see any obvious connection to House Veridian. Maybe the cryptography program had come up with more false positives than she'd hoped.

On to the third file, which was a purchase order from an apartment complex in Tessa's district of Zevenda. The superintendent of the complex at 780 Nightingale Avenue had ordered cleaning supplies and a dozen boxes of laminate flooring. Apart from seeing her mother's signature on the scanned page, which made Elana's heart flip-flop, she was at a loss for how this could connect to any conspiracy. Maybe the super had been cleaning up after a Veridian-related incident and had to redo the floor?

Elana sighed, sat back in her chair, and took a moment to think. She had to be missing something.

The program had helped them find the connection to House Veridian in the first place by decoding Tessa's typos into ciphered keywords, which led them to the encrypted references to the obscure House. They had told it to base the new search on the information it decrypted, so…

Elana minimized the list of files and opened the program's command log. The overnight output showed the program had gleaned the new references from recurring text fragment patterns that coincided with the stray letters.

Elana rubbed her temples. The layers of encryption made her head hurt. Had her mother been a natural cryptographer, or had she used a similar program to encode all of this? That would remain a mystery unless Tessa had left a note explaining her process—and there was no way she would have.

Everything Elana had found so far pointed to her mother being conscientious, exacting, and comprehensive in her precautions. Leaving the equivalent of a treasure map was not her style. For the same reason, Elana doubted her mother had hired help. If anyone would have known, it would have been Valeria.

That meant there had to be a reason Tessa had hidden references to these files. Something connected the quarterly report to the news article and the purchase order, or at *least* something connected each item to the larger plot.

Elana opened the three files again and spread them out on the desk. They were all early in the chronology of the list, each having occurred in 2000, but they didn't share a date or a month. None of the major players in any incident showed up in any of the others.

She huffed, and Matt looked up. "Something wrong?"

"I haul heavy things and get paid for it," she grumbled. "I don't solve crimes."

He raised an eyebrow. "You also fix electronics, don't you?"

"Yes, but that isn't solving crimes either."

Matt chuckled. "Maybe not, but it *is* solving puzzles. I thought you liked figuring out why something didn't work, and *making* it work. This isn't much different."

Elana drummed her fingers on the desktop. "You have a point."

She returned to the files and squinted at the text. Fixing a broken gadget required finding the bit that was broken. Sometimes that was obvious, and sometimes it was *not*. When faced with the latter case, your best bet was to take the whole damn thing apart, piece by piece, and put everything in careful order so you could put it back together.

The biggest question in Elana's mind was *what this puzzle was about*. Was it solely a people puzzle, or was House Veridian plotting about a specific place or object? Maybe they were building up to a plan on a certain date?

Elana grabbed her notebook and jotted down the dates, names, and locations mentioned in each file, as well as a couple of keywords to indicate the topic. They'd found patterns once. They could do it again.

Two hours later, she sat back in her chair and cracked

her neck. "If I stare at this any longer, I'm gonna throw something against a wall."

Matt stood and stretched. "Sounds like time for a break. Find anything?"

She tapped the notebook, which was again covered in lines of inky text. "Lots, but no idea if any of it means anything. You?"

"Ditto. Trade you?"

"Sure, what the hell." Elana reached across the desk and snagged Matt's legal pad, then held her spiral-bound notebook out to him.

After several moments of reading, she mumbled, "These names seem familiar."

"They should since half of them show up on your list."

Elana snapped her head up. "Seriously?"

He laid her notebook on the desk, and she put his legal pad beside it. As she scanned the lists, her jaw slowly dropped.

"Holy shit. You weren't kidding."

"I was not." Matt leaned over and pointed at names on both pads. "These show up several times. Irina Rivera, John Maclean, Jasmine Brooks. There are bound to be more."

He marked each repeated name as they flipped the pages. Elana quickly lost count. Dozens of names showed up on both lists, most of them half a dozen times or more.

When they reached the end of the lists, she crossed her arms and leaned on the desk. "I think I know what's going on here."

"Oh?"

"Yeah." Elana tapped the last column in her notebook,

where she'd written the keywords pertaining to each file. "There's no rhyme or reason to these. The names show up linked to everything from crop rotation in the Senkyem greenhouses to junior paralegals in Etreta and exhibitions in Octava. I was trying to find a pattern *there*, but I think the point is that there *isn't* one. All these people connected to House Veridian…they have their fingers in *everything*."

Matt scanned the keywords column, his lips moving soundlessly as he read them. He flicked back a page, then another, and on the third, he abruptly stopped and hissed in the back of his throat.

Elana sat up straight. "What did you find?"

He pointed to an entry. "Smithen Industries."

"They're an avionics company. What about them?"

Matt grimaced. "Before they pivoted to avionics, they made weapons. They still do, in all likelihood, just in a subsidiary and not as their main production line."

"Okay…" Elana narrowed her eyes. "I can't say I'm a huge fan of weapons manufacturers in general because they're usually involved in shady business somewhere, but that's true of just about any company. Surely that's the same in Haven."

"Oh, it is, but that's not my point. My point is the House that runs Smithen, House Ateles, was one of the primary aggressors in the inter-House war that killed your mother. It was never proven beyond a reasonable doubt, but it was most likely an Ateles who was responsible for your mother's death."

Elana's arms felt hot and her legs felt like lead. Her head spun and her throat was so dry she couldn't swallow.

Matt was still staring at the name on the paper. "If House Ateles is linked to House Veridian, and your mother was investigating House Veridian…"

"Then House Veridian killed my mother," Elana finished.

CHAPTER THIRTY

Elana went home in a daze. Circumstantial evidence wasn't proof, but it sure felt damning from where she sat. Tessa Hart had been investigating why House Veridian had connections to almost everything that happened in Haven, and in retaliation, they'd had her killed.

It was *possible* that House Veridian hadn't known about her mother's investigation, but it seemed unlikely. She'd spent some time that afternoon researching the inter-House war that had led to her mother's death, and the motivations for it struck her as flimsy. Sure, everyone in the world had been going stir-crazy at the time, but Haven had been shielded from most of the upheaval. Vampires lived almost forever, so a year of lockdown was a drop in the bucket for people who routinely had millions of dollars set aside for a rainy decade.

Far more likely, then, that House Veridian had found out about Tessa's prying, and lest their grand plans become public, they'd orchestrated the assassination of one of the SpiderKing's arbiters. A ballsy move, to be sure.

Unfortunately, Elana still didn't know what those grand plans *were*. Every discovery in this conspiracy felt huge in the moment, but their importance rapidly diminished with the smallest amount of perspective.

She unlocked her front door, went straight to the couch, and collapsed onto it. She rolled onto her back, drew a deep breath, and sighed. The house didn't *smell* like home to her anymore. It smelled of cleaning products, dust, and her father. Her childhood. It smelled old beyond its time.

Elana frowned at the ceiling. It was time to do something about that.

"Thank you for agreeing to come," Elana told Cathy as the flamboyant vampire climbed into her passenger's seat. Today, the eccentric matriarch wore a jumpsuit that looked as though it had been wrapped on like an Ace bandage if it came in teal houndstooth.

"Wouldn't miss it for the world!" Cathy grinned and slipped her big brown sunglasses with rhinestone horns down her nose to meet Elana's gaze. "I love house hunting. I've lived in the same townhouse for centuries—I'm a bit of a homebody, all things told—but window shopping is among my dearest pastimes. Not to mention door shopping, wall shopping, light fixture shopping…"

Elana laughed and put the car in Drive. The electric motor was silent as they glided forward. "Is it just that you've never found anything more to your liking than where you are now?"

"Partially, yes. The other part is that I like playing pretend. It keeps me young and spry." Cathy flashed Elana a grin. "Where are we headed?"

Elana drummed her fingers on the steering wheel. "I haven't decided. I know the primary residential districts are Thani and Zevenda, but I'm not sure which I'd prefer. I'm concerned that if I apply for residence in Thani, I'll be perceived as overeager and punching above my station. Haven politics are stormy. I don't want that."

Cathy nodded. "You're smart, just like your mother. You have the right of it. You have the pedigree to live in Thani, certainly. No one would dare *openly* argue with someone in the House of the SpiderKing choosing to live in Thani, even if they are a renewed cadet line."

"Renewed cadet line—oh, you mean my mother's line." A thought struck Elana, and she narrowed her eyes. "I hadn't told you who my mother was."

Cathy chuckled. "My dear, I've lived in Haven since its inception, and you are the spitting image of your mother. It was *not* hard to work out."

Elana blushed. "Fair enough."

"Anyway, yes, that's what I mean by a renewed cadet line. Arbiter Hart's line ended with her death and has since been reopened by order of the king. Officially, it would look bad to snub *anyone* in the royal line, even an off-shoot, but…"

"Behind closed doors, people talk."

"Exactly. There will be those who will consider you no better than an Arachne—not that there's anything wrong with being in Arachne. People *will* catch on the stupidest things because people are stupid. It's how we are."

Elana cocked her head and glanced sideways at Cathy. "Most vampires I've talked to *somewhat* adhere to the belief that they're better than humans. You don't seem to."

Cathy chuckled. "We have some natural advantages, I suppose, but we all come from the same stock. Vampires can make the same idiotic mistakes that any human can… and in my experience, our mistakes typically come with greater consequences thanks to those natural advantages. I'm under no illusions when it comes to my kin."

Elana smoothly turned onto the road circling the Citadel and curved toward Zevenda. It would only take them a few minutes to reach the seventh district. "Do you have children, or is that a general statement?"

"Both, although I'd like to think I taught my kids better." Cathy stretched and fiddled with a chunky ring on her right pinky finger adorned with a ruby the size of her thumbnail. "I had Horace before I moved to Haven. He's still back in England. Patricia's in her traveling stage, but I wouldn't be surprised if she settles in Haven after she's shaken out the wanderlust. She likes it here."

"Would you like to have her closer to home?"

Cathy shrugged. "I love my kids. I wouldn't complain."

The gleaming peak of the Great Hall caught Elana's eye as they drove past Octava, and she recalled the dressing-down Valeria had given to Demoissac, whoever he was. *I wonder if he's connected to House Veridian.* The budding conspiracy was constantly on Elana's mind. She'd dreamed about spiderwebs stretching across the city last night, and didn't feel as though she'd gotten any restful sleep.

"Don't you ever get tired of the drama?" Elana inquired. "All the mudslinging and subterfuge?"

Cathy cackled. "You think it's bad here? Try doing a semester abroad. When you get back, Haven will seem like a quaint, *quiet* hamlet."

Elana debated telling Cathy what she and Matt had found about House Veridian and her mother's death, but they hadn't verified that Cathy wasn't connected yet. Better safe than sorry. Nothing prevented her from asking about history, however.

"Even when inter-House wars break out, like the one a few years ago?"

Cathy hummed sympathetically. "That *was* a nasty business. Came out of nowhere, like a gangsters' spat over a city block. Granted, most inter-House wars simmer for a good long while before they bubble up and spill over, so that might not have been a surprise. Still…"

She shook her head. "I keep my finger on the pulse, and I didn't see it coming. Truly a shame your mother got caught in the crossfire. I'm sorry, my dear."

Curiouser and curiouser. "Thank you."

Elana turned into the arch that marked the entrance to Zevenda's calm, winding residential streets. While there was no strict architectural code for Zevenda, most buildings adhered to modern American suburban style—bungalows, modest apartment and condo complexes, and the occasional McMansion. Not quite white picket fence Stepford suburbia, but definitely in the post-war population expansion vein.

A small frown curved her lips as her gaze flicked over the houses. "I'm not sure this is my jam either," she admitted. "Living here would feel like putting a sign out on the lawn that said, 'Hey, I'm as good as human, come and get me!'"

Cathy laughed. "It's true that many of the Houses quartered in Zevenda are younger, mostly Houses started by older vampires who chose to break away from their natal or sired Houses for one reason or another. While that *can* result in the older, established Houses looking down on them for the *truly* unforgivable crime of *breaking with tradition*, it also means the Houses quartered here ally with one another far more easily."

Elana signaled, rolled to a stop at the floating stop sign, and turned right. "Oh? That's interesting. I would have thought there would be *more* suspicion among new Houses, trying to grab whatever scraps of power they could from the older Houses."

"In other vampire strongholds than Haven, that's certainly common. I suspect the difference here is thanks to the larger proportion of immigrants—American colonists or more recent, doesn't matter. The underlying drive in so many new Havenite vampires is independence from old systems and disappointment in tradition."

She chuckled suddenly. "That said, I can already see the signs of Havenite Houses becoming gentrified. Everything happens faster in America."

"Tell me more," Elana urged. She was admiring the houses on this street, but she'd drive around for hours if it meant Cathy kept talking about Haven's interior political structure. Maybe she could ask *her* about House Veridian.

No, don't. They're not officially here, she reminded herself. *That would play your hand, and you don't know if Cathy's connected to them yet.*

"About the new Houses, or the Houses becoming gentrified?" Cathy clarified.

"Both," Elana blurted, and smiled when Cathy laughed.

"Aren't you eager? Very well then." The fantastically attired woman settled into her seat and folded her hands in her lap. "Let's see. It started in earnest around the turn of the millennium with House Verocia and House Athetrix. Both had been started only a handful of years after Haven's founding—Verocia was a branch from the Italian Venusia family, and Athetrix a cadet branch of Jaculus. Old Romanian family. Very strong blood.

"The founders of Verocia and Athetrix would never have attained status in the Old World. Too many branches with more seniority, no room to grow. The SpiderKing likes families that don't let their histories define them too strictly, so he let them in.

"I didn't think too much of them myself, beyond appreciating their tenacity. It takes guts to forsake the protection and prosperity of an old, established House like Venusia or Jaculus, even when you're in no danger of ending up on the street.

"When the brand-new Houses started popping up—Chelem in the thirties, Tanyuro in the seventies, and Sylvila in the nineties in particular, riding the dot-com wave—Verocia and Athetrix got snooty." Cathy chuckled fondly, and Elana wondered again how old the eccentric vampire was.

"They'd host soirées and only invite Houses with Old World roots, for example," Cathy continued. "Never overtly, because that would be *tacky*, but they'd throw a party for their closest friends, and it would *happen* that no one from the new Houses was on the list. They'd put out requests for bids on new contracts, and the winning bid would always be a House with at least two centuries of experience. Things like that."

Elana arched an eyebrow. "Two centuries? That's awfully hypocritical. Didn't you say they were only founded when Haven was? *They* don't even have two centuries under their belts."

"In that line, yes, you're correct. They were trading on their ancestral lines' prestige, although they'd come to Haven to get away from all of that."

"It's all about fear, isn't it?" Elana mused as she turned into a series of duplexes with vaguely Frank Lloyd Wright-esque architecture. "These are pretty."

"And a pain in the ass to secure. Get yourself something with defensible terrain and windows you can lock, girl."

Elana blinked. "You're kidding me. Don't houses in Haven come equipped with, like, bulletproof glass and shit? And what am I defending *against*, anyway?"

Cathy turned a steely gaze on her. "Trust me. When life in any vampire community is good, it's sunshine, rainbows, and little bunny rabbits. When something goes sour, you want triple-thick steel bars on your windows and through all your walls."

Elana returned to the artery road with a shiver running down her spine. Cathy looked out the window again, and for a time the two drove through Zevenda's quiet, picturesque streets in tense silence.

Cathy broke it. "Because you're right, Elana. It *is* all about fear. Fear of secrets, fear of lies. Fear of power, and what happens when power gets into the wrong hands…

Except there are far too many people who think their hands are the only ones safe enough to wield that power and don't truly consider what it means to be powerful."

She glanced to her left, and when Elana caught her eye, the older vampire's disgusted look took her by surprise.

"I was wrong earlier when I said I don't think we're better than humans."

"Oh?"

"In some ways, we're a hell of a lot worse."

CHAPTER THIRTY-ONE

The rest of the drive passed in amiable conversation about Zevenda's various neighborhoods as Cathy tried to lighten the mood, and Elana didn't argue. The more she learned about Haven's inner workings, the more it reminded her of a cross between *The Sopranos* and *The Tudors* on steroids. At this rate, she'd unearth the conspiracy her mother had discovered only to find it was connected to a dozen other conspiracies crisscrossing the globe.

In the end, Elana decided she'd prefer to live in one of three neighborhoods—Willow Creek, Gloriana, or Anne's Rest. Willow Creek was her favorite. It included a nice mix of standalone houses, walk-up apartments, and a couple of condo complexes. It was only a ten-minute drive from Lomida Avenue, the main Zevendan artery.

Gloriana was a bit too posh for her taste—mostly mansions bigger than she preferred to live in—but the vaguely Victorian aesthetic did something for her. On the other hand, Anne's Rest was comprised of adjoining townhouses in an English style. While Elana in theory appreciated being close enough to your neighbors to ask for a cup of sugar from the front step, she didn't know whether she'd be welcomed yet.

Elana thanked Cathy for her company and dropped her off at her townhouse in Premier, which backed onto a jeweler's. When Cathy caught her eyeing the necklaces on display in the front window, she chuckled and lightly elbowed her.

"You should buy one," Cathy suggested.

Elana scoffed. "I have no need for a chandelier necklace with that many precious stones. It would clear out my bank account."

Cathy tapped her nose with a finger. "Many young people don't realize the investment potential of precious stones. Don't get diamonds—they aren't worth the sparkle—but other precious gems and metals appreciate significantly with time and are easily resold. Much better than keeping all your financial eggs in one metaphorical basket."

Elana raised an eyebrow. "Even if that basket is the Bank of Haven?"

"*Especially* then." Cathy leaned over and kissed Elana's cheeks. "Ta, my dear. I'll keep an eye out for houses for you. Tea soon?"

"Tea soon," Elana promised, then waved. When her friend was in the door, she put the car back in Drive and headed for the Citadel. Her second-last appointment of the day was with Valeria, and it did *not* do to be late for appointments with the Arbiter of Shadows.

Elana parked in a lot on the edge of the Citadel and headed in. The dip in temperature that occurred when you went through one of the eight shallow tunnels surrounding the Citadel always made her shiver. She knew the wall's thermal mass contributed to the lowered air temperature in the arches, as did the shadows cast. Still, she'd always wondered whether there was a scanning device embedded in the bricks that ensured no one was smuggling contraband into the Neutral Zone. Maybe she would find the answer to that mystery later.

Even fewer people than normal occupied the courtyard today. Elana spied a woman in a long gown with artfully braided hair at the central memorial but could not tell whether it was the same woman she'd noticed on a previous visit.

I'd say hello if she weren't so clearly paying tribute, but I don't know whether that would be rude. I seriously need to check out a book on vampire etiquette...or have tea with Cathy.

She entered the consulate and went straight to the staircase with the new moon. Today, she felt less superstitious about walking over the king's sigil in the floor, but she *did* feel like he was watching her. She'd felt that way since Matt had joked the king probably knew her sock size, but the gut feeling of being watched intensified in this room.

Just nerves.

Elana shook them off and ascended the stairs. They were easier each time she visited. Even years of working with a hauling crew hadn't resulted in as much strength and endurance training as a couple of weeks of working with Gustav and the others.

She found the door Valeria had indicated, marked with a plaque that read Mirabilis. A memorial plaque? Something marking a donation? A House? A person's name?

Elana opened the door and stepped into a room that reminded her of a war room from medieval times. A huge oval walnut table dominated the room, taking up over half its square footage. Matching high-backed chairs sat at evenly spaced intervals around the table, each cushioned with dark green velvet. The table gleamed with light thrown from the iron chandelier overhead, which could have held torches as easily as LED tubes.

The walls were blank and of a black so deep Elana honestly could not tell if they had any structure or were truly flat. There could have been small alcoves or doors around the room's circumference, and you'd never know. They absorbed the light so all that existed in the room were the table and chairs.

Valeria sat at the head of the table, an incongruous point of white in the darkness. She gestured at the seat next to her but said nothing. After Elana sat, the arbiter folded her hands on the table and held Elana's gaze.

"Tell me all the Houses you know that are represented in Haven."

Elana blinked. "Um...SpiderKing, Arachne, Lucciola, Richelieu...Verocia, Athetrix, Sylvila, Chelem, Tanyuro..."

She closed her eyes and rattled off every name she could remember from the lists she and Matt had compiled earlier, as well as the Houses each of the current arbiters belonged to and any others she could come up with... including House Veridian.

When she opened her eyes, Valeria hadn't moved. Her eerie stare made Elana want to squirm in her chair, but she kept very still.

"Which of those Houses have Old World roots?"

Elana blew a breath out and thought for a moment. "SpiderKing, obviously. Lucciola, Richelieu. Verocia and Athetrix do, but not in their main lines. Veridian does. The Arbiters of Legacy, Light, Sanctuary, and Vision are Old World, but Progress, Knowledge, Creation, and yourself are New World."

"Are there any other distinguishing features between Houses?"

"Definitely. There's a difference between Houses that are represented in Haven but have solid roots in other countries and Houses with Old World roots, but the branch represented in Haven isn't the main line. I don't know of any Houses off the top of my head that started in Haven and have planted scions elsewhere, but there might be some. Those would have different intentions than Houses that maintain their entire representation here."

"Good." Valeria's face did not match her verbal praise. Elana had rarely seen the arbiter look so pinched. Valeria seemed downright *concerned.*

"How would you determine a vampire's House allegiance in situations where they are linked to multiple Houses?"

Elana bit her lip. "That's a hard one. Most people think that whatever House you belong to on paper is the one you're most loyal to. That's true in most cases, but it's less of a majority than you'd assume. You have to consider how tight their individual alliances are—marriage, fostering, siring, birth, et cetera—and that doesn't account for political alliances either.

"For politically active vampires, your best bet is to analyze which House their personal political leanings align with. Next, you'd look at business alliances and finally personal alliances. Whoever their actions most openly agree with, that's where their allegiance will lie when push comes to shove—*if* it's not a situation where openly allying themselves with that House would cause them social hardship. If it would, chances are good they'll officially toe the line of whatever House they belong to in name but will use whatever resources and opportunities they can to support the House they truly align with."

Valeria nodded curtly. "You have learned well."

Elana frowned and leaned in. "If it's not too forward, can I ask what the deal is with the third degree? When you messaged about this new 'class,' I expected whiteboards and memory cards, not an interrogation."

The corner of Valeria's mouth twitched down. "I don't waste time with small talk. You know that."

"Absolutely, I just—" Elana's phone went off mid-sentence, and she winced. "Sorry. Forgot to put it on silent."

She retrieved it from her pocket, and her frown deepened when she saw Matt was calling. He usually texted first, which probably meant this was urgent. She held it up to show Valeria. "It's Matt. I think I should take this."

Valeria nodded, and Elana accepted the call.

"Hey, Matt. Everything okay?"

The guardian sounded tense. "Whatever you're doing, you need to stop and meet me *now*."

Elana blinked, then pulled the phone away from her ear and switched it to speaker. "I'm with Valeria. You're on speaker."

Matt didn't miss a beat. "Hello, Arbiter. I'm so sorry to

interrupt, but I've lucked into a time-sensitive lead. I need Miss Bishop. It's imperative."

Elana's eyebrows were rapidly approaching her hairline. She'd never heard anyone speak to Valeria that way, and she half expected the arbiter to Force-choke Matt over the phone or something equally terrifying. When Valeria's expression didn't change, the odds of Matt living through the next thirty seconds seemed to drop even further.

All the white-suited angel of death said was, "Go."

Elana wasn't about to argue. She shot from her seat and was halfway down the stairs before remembering she was supposed to meet Jerry to sign the LLC papers that evening.

"Matt, how long will this take?" she asked while hurrying down the stairs.

"I have no idea."

"Damn. Okay."

"Problem?"

"Nothing I can't reschedule. Where am I meeting you?"

"I'll send you an address. See you soon?"

"See you soon."

The line went dead. As Elana sprinted across the floor of the consulate's atrium, she hurriedly tapped in an apologetic text to Jerry.

Have to cancel. So sorry. I'll be in touch.

Something tugged in her gut when she pressed Send. It felt more like she was burning bridges than rescheduling. Her connections to the human world were snapping, one by one.

CHAPTER THIRTY-TWO

Elana didn't know the address Matt texted her, but it was in Thani, so chances were good it was someone's house. She floored the accelerator on her Emeya until one tight corner convinced her she needed to take a refresher stunt driving course or back off. Since professional driving instructors were in short supply at this specific moment, she backed off.

She followed the built-in GPS to a neighborhood of Thani she'd never visited, marked by an intimidating arch that resembled the Gothic façade of Notre Dame Cathedral. She swallowed hard and looked for security guards or anything to deny her entry but saw nothing.

Cautiously, Elana drove under the arch. Rays of light sprang from the underside and bathed her car in a grid. While the sight startled her, it put her mind at ease because it was now clear that she was going somewhere terrifically important.

She was glad she'd opted for one of her most stylish outfits before coming into Haven this morning. The loose beige blouse, mocha trousers, and strappy heels weren't flashy, but paired with the topaz bracelets and matching hairpin, anyone with a good eye would recognize the price tag.

Elana reduced her speed to a respectable slow cruise. The architecture in this neighborhood had more in common with castles than houses, or manor houses at the very least. Each had sprawling gardens that stretched to fill the block, and Elana couldn't tell how far back from the road the lots went. This neighborhood did not skimp on luxury and made no attempt to hide its wealth. Who on Earth were they meeting here?

The GPS brought her to a winding cobbled drive that pierced a thick hedge of foliage under yet another arch, this one of spiraling iron. The twisted iron above the entrance spelled Richelieu.

Oh.

Nerves seized Elana. Her arms went cold, then hot, then cold again. Matt had sent her to the seat of House Richelieu. This neighborhood had to be L'Arrondissement, where the Houses belonging to the House of Cardinals were quartered.

The House of Cardinals was a House of Houses, *per se*, a collection of Houses with Old World roots that had chosen to support the SpiderKing in his establishment of Haven, each for their own reasons. Most came from mainland Europe, although a couple hailed from farther afield. The House of Cardinals included at least one West African House, a Thai House, and a couple of Baltic and Eastern European Houses. The only thing the component Houses of the House of Cardinals had in common was that each had over a millennium of history, and more child branches than anyone could count.

Well, that and being richer and more powerful than ninety-nine-point-nine percent of the global population could dream of.

Elana's heart pounded as she rolled up the drive. When Richelieu Manor came into view, she'd swear her heart briefly stopped.

The three-story château could have been plucked from the French countryside. It wouldn't have surprised her if the plans had been based on the original Château de Richelieu, although the extent of the relation between the vampiric House and the French duchy was a closely guarded secret.

She coasted to a stop outside the imposing mansion and gazed at its pointed black roofs and elegant white marble statues in alcoves. Suddenly, the topaz hairpin felt like cheap glass, and the expensive clothing felt like a costume. She couldn't go in there. Elana felt like she belonged wholly to the human world for the first time in days.

The huge dark oak front doors opened, spilling golden light onto the front steps. She imagined a late-night garden party with the attendees in Baroque fancy dress, women in bustles and domino masks and white curled wigs descending the steps, and a frisson went down her spine.

It was only Matt leaning out the door, beckoning to her. "Elana!"

Elana parked and turned off the Emeya, then took her heart in her hands and jogged up to meet him. "Are you sure it's okay for me to be here?" she asked *sotto voce* as she followed him into the manor. Then she caught her breath and whispered, "Holy shit."

The interior was even more palatial than the exterior. Paintings stretched from floor to ceiling in ornately molded and gilded frames. Every surface gleamed, either polished marble or metal, and any scrap of fabric was a sumptuous brocade or velvet.

She instinctively pulled back and paused one step into the foyer. "Holy *shit*, Matt, I cannot be here," she repeated. "I need to change into something worth five figures and advance at least two levels of vampirism before I can set foot in this place."

Matt grabbed her forearm and encouraged her forward as gently as he could without outright tugging her. "Yes, yes, my family is obscenely rich, and we show it off. Now is not the *time*."

Elana would not be budged. He huffed and got right into her personal space. For a split second, Elana thought he would haul her over his shoulder and *carry* her down the hall, but he leaned in and whispered, "I've set up a video call with a friend of your mother's. A friend *in House Veridian*."

The floor dropped from under Elana's feet. A heartbeat later, adrenaline surged through her veins and her surroundings sharpened into surreal clarity. *"In House—"*

Matt shushed her through his teeth. *"Yes.* Let's *go."*

They speed-walked the decadent halls until Matt ushered Elana through a thick, iron-banded door into a cozy study. Full bookshelves lined the walls, and a monumental mahogany desk sat across from a mantelpiece covered in antique animal figurines. Two overstuffed green armchairs and a coffee table matching the desk occupied the middle of the room. The only thing in the room that didn't fit the décor was the sleek silver MacBook sitting open on the desk.

Matt gestured for Elana to take the seat behind the desk. "They'll call any minute."

Elana sat and stared wide-eyed at the white cord of the headphones snaking across the desk. "Who's *they*? How did you set this up?"

Matt grimaced. "They've agreed to talk about why House Veridian went after Tessa, but beyond that, it's better you know as little as possible."

Elana wasn't impressed. "Plausible deniability only goes so far."

"I had to swear on my House's honor that I'd keep their identity secret. We have to take what we can get, Elana."

"Oh, because *that* won't come back and bite us in the ass." The black screen of the computer lit up with a window filled with gray static. "Is that the call?"

"Yes. You take the earbud with the mic." He grabbed the other.

Elana did so, then frowned. "Wait. Why are we using a MacBook? Does this desk not have the—"

Matt cut her off with a hissed, "*Security,*" and tapped the Enter key.

A faint silhouette of a head and shoulders appeared in the static. The effect made Elana's eyes want to cross.

"Hello?" she ventured.

"I don't have much time," the silhouette replied. The voice was heavily filtered, rendering it impossible to discern any identifying characteristics. They could have been an old man, a teenage girl, or anything in between. "I agreed to this call as a favor to your friend."

"Who, Ma—" Matt elbowed her *hard* in the ribs, and she redirected. "My mother?"

"Your friend," they repeated.

The sensation that she was in a spy movie got stronger with every moment. "Understood. What can you tell me?"

"Her actions threatened to undo centuries of work. She was seen as a meddling nobody who put her nose where it wasn't welcome."

Elana's eyebrows drew together. "I thought you were her friend. You're not talking like you were friends."

"Personal feelings don't come into it. They can't. Emotions are a liability, one that *will* be exploited. She played the game well, but she cared too much. She got in the way. Be careful you don't get in the way, too. I can already tell you're like her."

Elana glanced at Matt, then looked back at the screen. "Is that a threat?"

"It's the truth. Sometimes the truth is threatening, but it's still the truth."

Elana made a face. "You're very good at saying things that don't mean much."

"You haven't learned the language. I'm sure your friend can translate."

"How did my mother die?"

"She got in the way," the anonymous source repeated. "She noticed one too many things she wasn't supposed to see, and someone noticed her. It didn't take long for them to realize how much she knew and how dangerous she could be. My House doesn't make or *take* threats lightly, and it knows how to operate in the shadows.

"So, in short, they pulled some strings. Making a death look like collateral damage is a walk in the park for them. You call in a few favors, grease a few palms, and the deed's done without anyone being the wiser for it."

"Even under the SpiderKing's nose?"

The staticky figure chuckled. "They've got you believing that too, have they?"

Elana turned to stare at Matt in utter confusion, but he motioned her back to the screen and tapped his watch.

"There's no proof that House Veridian was involved at all in the inter-House war that killed my mother," Elana stated. "None of the aggressor Houses had any connection to Veridian. Are you saying that's not true?"

"You already know it's not true, or your friend wouldn't be calling me," they replied. "Like I said, my House knows how to operate in the shadows. We've been doing so for a very long time."

Elana opened her mouth to ask another question, but the figure held up a hand and turned its head to the side. After two full seconds of silence, the figure disappeared, and Matt and Elana were left with pure static. They waited several more seconds to see if the figure would return, then took out their earbuds and laid them on the desk.

"I have to say, that wasn't as enlightening as I'd hoped it would be," Elana lamented. "We have word of mouth 'evidence' from someone in House Veridian—someone you claim is in House Veridian, anyway. While I believe you, I didn't personally see any proof of that, and they claim they had my mother killed through clandestine, untraceable means."

"Not untraceable," Matt corrected. "We found the connection to Smithen Industries."

Elana scoffed. "Sure, but that's flimsy as hell." She sighed. "What are we doing with this, Matt? Can we use everything we've found in the archives and take House Veridian to court for my mother's unlawful death?"

"Doubtful, at this point. If we took this to the arbiters, we'd be laughed out of court. It's all circumstantial and piecemeal, and while my word as a Richelieu carries significant weight, you're right that this won't hold water." He gestured at the MacBook. "Honestly, we'd have an easier time bringing them to justice if they came after you first."

Elana stared at him. *"What?"*

"We could prove they have a vendetta against your family. A vendetta without cause, unless they were willing to chance exposing whatever web of intrigue they've been building for centuries."

Elana shook her head. "What the hell am I doing?" she muttered. Then, louder, she added, "Why am I getting myself into the messy, bullshit politics that got my mother *killed*? What is *wrong* with me?"

Matt was unfazed. "You want the truth. That's the highest calling there is, if you ask me."

Elana let out a single, mirthless laugh. "The *truth*? Can I even *find* the truth here? The more I see of Haven, the less I believe it's any better than what the SpiderKing allegedly ran from. How is this any different? *Is* it different? Tell me, Matt. You're old enough. You have to be—or you must know what it's like in other vampire strongholds. Is this better? Is it *really* better?"

Matt perched on the edge of the desk and gazed at her seriously. "Yes. It's much better. It might seem like the SpiderKing has no impact in the day-to-day lives of Havenites, but that's not the case.

"He built Haven on principles that might as well not exist in most other vampire strongholds—the rule of law being one of them. Sure, it's *his* law, and it's harsh at times, but it's a *fair* law, and he makes a point of listening to his advisors…even the dissenting ones. Usually, if a vampire ruler is batshit crazy, you're out of luck. Kill them if you can and move on. The SpiderKing's not like that."

Elana crossed her arms. "It sounded like your source didn't believe he exists."

Matt rolled his eyes. "There *are* people who don't believe he exists because he's so rarely seen."

"Have you met him?"

"I have not had the privilege, but I understand Valeria has spoken to him."

"You've never even *talked* to him?"

"He's an incredibly private person."

Elana let her head fall back against the chair's headrest. "From where I'm sitting, it looks like Haven is exactly like every other vampire city-state, but with a thick coat of paint to make it look pretty. It has all the same bullshit drama under the surface, and everyone pretends everything's fine until someone chips the paint. Hell, how do we know the *king* didn't have my mother killed?"

Matt's eyebrows shot up. "Because if he had, the person who would've done it would be Valeria. Do you think she'd allow you to entertain this line of investigation if that were the case?"

"Maybe. To keep me where she wanted me. To see how much more I could discover that my mother hadn't. Like big tech companies hiring hackers to find their vulnerabilities—only I'll be quietly disappeared afterward. Actually, the big tech companies probably do that too, let's be real."

Matt took a slow breath. "I think you need to see more of what Haven is *really* like. So far, you've seen a whole lot of the old-style politics that, yes, creeps in on the edges. Let's call it a day, get a good sleep, and tomorrow I'll show you how Haven is different. Deal?"

"Deal," Elana grumbled.

CHAPTER THIRTY-THREE

The next day was mercifully cooler than the last several had been. The air no longer bathed her skin in humidity even under Haven's canopy, and Elana felt no temptation to shave off her hair because it was sticking to her neck. The change in the weather was an even more welcome relief when Matt pulled into a solar panel-covered parking garage outside one of Senkyem's many outdoor gardens.

Elana arranged the loose cowl collar of her blouse as she exited the car. She'd picked light colors and flowing fabrics today in case the weather turned hotter again. "Thank God we didn't try to do this yesterday. It's almost *nice* out."

Matt closed his door and locked the Audi behind him. He also wore light colors today, a beige morning suit with leaf-shaped cufflinks that gleamed gold and green in the sun. "I wouldn't complain if the wind picked up a bit, but beggars can't be choosers."

Elana chuckled. "You mean you can't pull up the Haven weather app on your phone and order a nice breeze?"

Matt snorted. "That's above my pay grade."

She blinked. "But not impossible?"

"Well..." He winked and gestured at the entrance to the gardens. "I promised to show you what Haven is really like. This ticks as many boxes in one go as I can think of."

They walked under the decorative wicker arch woven through with vines. They could have walked between any of the saplings planted along the sidewalk's edge, but Elana had noticed that courtesy was *highly* considered in Haven.

Being gauche wasn't simply a faux pas. It could mean your House took a serious social hit. Since Elana was a member of the royal House, she hardly wanted to chance pissing off her patron. It would be her luck that her uneducated blunder would result in the first public appearance of the SpiderKing in living memory. Now *that* would be awkward.

The garden Matt had brought her to visit appeared to be an orchard, or perhaps a tree nursery. Neat rows of saplings, much like those surrounding the garden, stretched out ahead of them and formed a loose arrangement of lanes. The trees matured as they walked forward, and soon the lanes were walkways shaded by cool, leafy branches.

Elana appreciated the lush foliage and the occasional rustle of wind, but she couldn't figure out what Matt was trying to show her. This was a beautiful orchard, but how did it make up for the backstabbing and manipulation that happened in the halls of power?

They paused at an intersection, where Matt directed Elana to turn right. This aisle had different trees—still deciduous, but the leaves were differently shaped—and the ground was rocky. Small creeks flowed between the tree trunks and across the path, which was dotted with small bridges.

At the next crossroads, they turned left. This third section was grassy underfoot, and a strong tang of overripe fruit pierced the air. Elana peered up into the trees and spied large orange fruits hanging in bunches from the top branches. A couple of yards farther down the lane, a long ladder disappeared into a tree's foliage, and if she squinted, she could make out someone harvesting the fruit high above.

Another left turn took them suddenly into a winter wonderland, except while several inches of snow covered the ground on either side, the path remained summery and warm. The conifers that stretched over their heads bristled with cones so black they might've been blue.

No. Not cones. Massive *blackberries*.

Elana was thoroughly puzzled. Was this one of Senkyem's culinary gardens and not a decorative garden as she'd assumed? Or a research garden, perhaps?

The latter hypothesis gained significant weight when they turned the next corner and walked back into summer...and a landfill. All down this lane, trees sprouted from piles of trash. Elana's stomach automatically flipped, and her nose twitched in anticipation of the reek of cooking garbage. Much like the wintery section they'd come from, they smelled nothing.

One more turn brought them to a much more pleasant area, filled with wide, flowering trees with light pink and blue blossoms. Elana expected an overpowering perfume, but everything smelled of clean laundry—unlike the landfill area, which had smelled of nothing.

Matt beckoned her off the path toward a particularly thick-trunked tree. They sat beneath the span of its gnarled, twisting branches and watched the gossamer petals float in twos and threes to the grass below for a short time.

He picked up a blue petal and rolled it between his fingers. "What do you think?"

Elana caught a pink petal and let it rest in her palm. It was velvety soft and lighter than a feather. "This place is seriously weird."

Matt laughed. "I've never had *that* reaction before to the conservatory gardens, but I suppose you're not wrong. Why do you think they're weird?"

She raised an eyebrow. "We walked through three seasons in fifteen minutes, and that doesn't count the *literal piles of garbage*. This is a *conservatory?* I thought conservatories were supposed to be uber-posh places with fancy greenhouses and perfectly trimmed plants."

"Only in books." Matt was still chuckling. "Arbiter Draven and Arbiter Kyoi share a strong interest in the root word of the term conservation, as well as a deep drive to make the world a better place. The conservatory gardens are among Haven's most impressive projects if you ask me, and I know about *most* of Haven's projects."

He motioned back along the path they'd come from. "Every section is dedicated to researching and creating plants—most obviously trees, but innumerable smaller plants and micro-organisms as well—that address specific goals. Some projects work on sustainable agriculture in extreme conditions. Some work to address global cleanup initiatives.

"The trees we're sitting under now? Their petals can be turned into fabric with minimal environmental impact, and they scrub half again as much carbon dioxide from the air as the average tree."

Elana leaned back on the tree in question and gazed up at its cotton-candy blossoms. "That's great and all, but it doesn't do the world a lick of good penned up behind the Wall."

"Ah, and *there's* where Haven is different from the Old World." Matt grinned. "It's *not* penned up behind the Wall. Old World Houses and city-states create stuff like this all the time, but they charge an arm and a leg to use any of it. An arm, a leg, and your firstborn kid, really."

Elana wasn't convinced. "So the SpiderKing charges less? Whoop-dee-doo."

Matt shook his head. "No. He doesn't charge *anything*. No purchase fees, licensing fees, or punitive fees if stray seeds get blown into somebody else's field. Nothing."

Now Elana was suspicious in addition to being unconvinced. "What's the catch?"

"Haven-trained vampires have to come in and teach proper care and maintenance every fifteen years. *That* we charge for, but it's a pittance compared to what you'd pay most seed companies over the same time, and the return on investment is almost incalculable."

She narrowed her eyes. "*Teach* care and maintenance? Not *do* care and maintenance?"

"You heard me right. Haven sends people in to train whoever will be doing the day-to-day care for the trees or ecosystem in question, and they come back and train the next batch fifteen years later. There's still turnover in that fifteen years, and sometimes the ecosystems suffer for it, but they're all engineered to last centuries. A few years of imperfect care is highly unlikely to kill off an entire crop."

Elana's frown shifted from disbelief to puzzlement. "I don't understand. Why? That's not profitable. How can Haven stay afloat with projects like this? And how can you be sure someone isn't charging people on the side?"

Matt smiled. "Profit isn't the SpiderKing's priority. He lives on the planet and is likely to continue living on it for a very long time, so he has a vested interest in keeping it habitable.

"Since he can't run an entire planet by himself, he needs to keep the rest of the population going. He has the resources—financial and brain trust—to make projects like this happen, so he does. Also, if anyone tried to cheat his customers, he'd know. You don't want to make him unhappy."

"You make him sound like a god lurking in the shadows, stretching out a hand every so often to save our poor souls…or to smite anyone who's pissed him off."

Matt chuckled and shrugged. "Demigod, maybe. He is an *incredibly* powerful vampire. Honestly, I think it's a damn good thing he chooses to be as kind as he does, even if the goals are partially self-motivated. Can you imagine the damage he could do otherwise?"

Elana opened her mouth to agree but gasped when a throwing knife hit and stuck in the bark of the tree immediately beside her head. The *twang* of the vibrating metal rang in her ear.

On instinct, she grabbed the leather-wrapped end of the knife and wrenched it out of the tree, then rolled aside. A second knife embedded itself in the tree where her head would have been had she not moved.

Matt had leaped to his feet and darted behind the trunk. He hauled Elana to her feet, and the pair pressed against the rough bark.

"What the fuck?" Elana hissed. "Who the fuck would—"

"That's a stupid question," Matt hissed. "Run!"

Elana sprinted away without bothering to ask where. While the knives had come from one direction, there was no guarantee other assailants weren't lurking elsewhere. Back to the car was their best bet, but there was a good chance their attackers had followed them. Could she remember the number of turns they'd taken and find her way back along a different route? Each of the sections had been roughly the same length...

Rapid footsteps swishing in the thick carpet of flower petals approached from behind. Elana took a running leap and scrambled up the nearest trunk. The soles of her shoes were *not* built for climbing trees, so her feet kept slipping on the bark, but she swung herself up successive branches and made it a few dozen feet off the ground by sheer stubbornness.

Elana hugged a limb and peered through the nebula of pink and blue. The blossoms were so thick she could see little of what was occurring below her, but she could *hear* the rustling and scraping of her pursuer. Maybe the lack of breeze was a blessing after all.

She held as still as possible and waited until her assailant was directly below her. Then she whipped the throwing knife down in a straight line and dropped from her branch to follow it. The shriek of the blade's bull's-eye was cut off by Elana knocking the wind out of her opponent as she collided with them and the pair plummeted to the ground.

Elana landed on top. Her attacker was a slight but wiry woman wearing all black, including a face mask with a sheer panel over the eyes. Elana's knife had scored a hit on the woman's shoulder.

Elana yanked the knife out and stabbed at the woman's neck, but the woman was faster. She threw Elana to the side, bounced to her feet, and sprinted away.

Elana brought her arm back to throw the knife, then thought better of it. She'd barely started training with ranged weapons and didn't want to lose this knife.

Unfortunately, her hesitation meant two things. One, the woman disappeared into the pink and blue forest. Two, a man the size of Gustav but a foot taller slammed into her from behind.

Elana blindly stabbed behind her with the throwing knife, stomped on the man's instep, then tried to twist around. He held on tight despite Elana hitting flesh with every flailing strike. He grunted and groaned but got his hands up to her throat and squeezed.

Spots bloomed in her vision as she struggled for air. Whoever this guy was, he was *strong*. Her knees went weak, and she gave in, trying for a deadweight drop, but the man gave her no quarter.

Elana was mentally cursing herself for barely managing *three weeks* as a vampire before House Veridian did her in when an angry yell swam through her wavering consciousness. She squinted through the blurry pink and blue. Someone in beige with a *sword* was coming toward her.

The person with the sword was still yelling as they swung the blade and sliced the forearm of the big man choking her. He didn't let go, but his grip faltered enough for Elana to gasp in a breath and stab him in roughly the same place he'd been slashed.

He let go. Elana dropped to her knees, coughing and hacking. The person with the sword ran past her, following the man and shouting, but came back a couple of seconds later and yanked her to her feet.

"Can you run?" It was Matt.

Elana tried to say yes, but speaking felt like razor blades were tearing her throat, so she nodded. Her head swam, and she stumbled against Matt.

"Okay. Come on. Deep breaths. Keep hold of that knife. Follow me."

Elana's first few steps were closer to a stagger than a sprint, but as she gulped the clean air, her vision cleared, and she stopped feeling like a disembodied head. Her throat burned, but she could see and breathe, and now that the rest of her body was getting oxygen again, she could run in a straight line.

They ran headlong through the conservatory gardens' groves, Matt with his sword raised, Elana still clutching the throwing knife. When they came to the saplings, Matt slowed down a touch and directed Elana off the path.

"We'll leave through the back," he told her in a low voice. "Have to assume they're watching my car. They might have booby-trapped it depending on how confident they were they could take us out. Either way, I'm not chancing it."

Elana couldn't argue. She followed Matt through the young trees to an exit similar to the main entrance that opened onto a less-trafficked street. They crossed the street and went half a block into a low complex of buildings that reminded Elana of a strip mall with more refrigeration units attached to the roofs than any restaurant could ever use. These had to be connected to the gardens' research somehow.

Matt ducked behind a building and nudged Elana to put her back against the wall. He did the same, then shifted his grip on the sword to one hand and fished his phone out of his pocket. "Call Valeria," he brusquely ordered and pushed the phone into her hands.

"I can't—" Elana began, and as though to illustrate the point, her voice broke and she wheezed.

"I know. Just call her, and I'll talk." Matt put both hands on the sword's hilt again and stood in front of Elana in a perfect defensive stance. Elana hadn't known Matt could fight with a sword. She had to assume he'd stolen it from one of their attackers unless his suit jacket's pockets were dimensional and he kept a sword in them for fun.

She pressed the Wake button on Matt's phone. The fingerprint sensor shifted from red to light green under her finger, and the screen lit up. She would have to ask him why her fingerprint opened his phone later.

Elana located the voice call app and found Valeria's contact at the top of the list, to no surprise. She tapped it, hit Call followed by Speaker, then turned the phone to point at Matt.

The arbiter's terse voice sounded through the speaker a moment later. "Go."

"We were attacked in the conservatory," Matt informed her. "Minimum of three."

"Any dead?" Valeria sounded calm as ever. If she was surprised, she hid it well.

"No. When they couldn't immediately overpower us, they ran."

"Injuries?"

"We did some damage to two of them. We have blood samples, although they might have altered their genomes if they suspected they were likely to be attacked. Elana's hurt, but she'll heal. One of them got a good chokehold on her."

"Are you safe?"

"Not currently being attacked. My guess is they ran after delivering their warning."

"The blood samples—they're on weapons?"

"A sword and a throwing knife."

"Very well. Enact Protocol Omicron Twelve."

"Aye, ma'am."

The line *clicked*, then buzzed with a dial tone. Elana ended the call and raised an eyebrow.

Matt gestured with the sword back the way they'd come. "We're going to take a shortcut to somewhere we can stash these weapons. Then we'll get somewhere safe."

Elana nodded. Breathing already felt less like swallowing glass. Vampires really *did* heal fast.

She followed a pace behind him out of the alley, farther down the street, and behind the "strip mall" of laboratories and offices. He stepped up to a door and laid his palm against it, similar to how they'd opened the doors in the archives, so she turned to guard him with the stolen throwing knife while the locking mechanism verified his identity. When he tapped her on the shoulder, she backed through the door, and only turned when it had firmly closed and she was satisfied it was locked.

"A subway?" The question bubbled up before she could stop it, and she winced at the ache in her raw throat.

"More or less. Not for public use. This is how we guardians get around the city without interrupting the flow of traffic—and how we sneak up behind people. Everyone knows this system exists, but only guardians can access the tramways. You can only get around that restriction if you're maintenance, and even then, any extra access has to be okayed by Arbiter Draven."

Elana descended the double-wide staircase at a light jog. She was mildly stunned at how quickly she was feeling better. She'd thought her rapid recovery after the intense training bouts had been thanks to the excellent recuperation facilities at the training grounds. She hadn't been lucky enough to get a hot shower after going toe-to-toe with the two goons, but she'd be back to normal in a few minutes.

The tramway system was not as overtly decorated as the upper city, but it was still plenty elegant and sophisticated. The patterns in the brickwork walls reminded her of Byzantine architecture, although with spiderwebs and the phases of the moon rather than ornate Arabic calligraphy.

Elana zoned out on the tram ride, gingerly cradling the throwing knife in her hands while leaning on a wall and dozing. Matt sat across from her in the car with the sword across both knees. They were both splattered with blood from their attackers, Elana more so than Matt.

This will be a bitch to get out of these clothes, Elana absent-mindedly thought.

They made a short stop at a guardian office, where Matt bagged the sword and throwing knife and put them into cold storage. He also asked if Elana had a spare shirt in her bag because the blood on her blouse might be traceable. Elana was too tired to protest. She turned her back, stripped off the blood-speckled blouse, then pulled a button-down from her bag and donned it.

Back on the tram, Elana quietly stated, "I don't feel safe going home."

Matt hummed. "No?"

She shook her head. "My house is not exactly a panic room, and the police in Ashford are a bit of a joke. If House Veridian already wants me dead badly enough that they're willing to come after me in broad daylight in a public place, breaking and entering will be no object."

"You can stay with me tonight if you want. I have a spare room. My sister uses it most of the time, but she's away at the moment."

Elana's eyebrows shot up. "In the manor? *What?* You're not serious."

He chuckled. "I don't live at Richelieu Manor. None of us do, actually. Mostly it gets used for hosting fundraisers. I have a condo in L'Arrondissement. Top-of-the-line security, of course. Nothing but the best for the House of Cardinals."

She stared at him for a long moment, then finally nodded. "Okay. Seems like my best bet. Thanks, Matt."

"Any time. Although the offer is partially out of self-interest since I'm pretty sure Valeria would have my head on a silver platter if you died *now*."

Elana snorted. "Gee, thanks. Your care and concern are noted. Also, you have a sister, and she's a vampire too? I thought vampire kids were extremely rare."

Matt chuckled. "My immediate family tree is…interesting. I'd be happy to tell you the whole sordid tale another time, but long story short, my parents were Richelieus but not vampires. My parents had Claudia some time after we three were given the Rights."

"How long afterward?"

"You're still not getting it out of me. A man has to have *some* secrets."

"We have more than enough secrets to go around. Spill," she cajoled.

"Nope."

CHAPTER THIRTY-FOUR

The guardian tramway deposited them at an underground station below Thani, near to but not within L'Arrondissement. Elana thought she spied fleurs-de-lis in the mosaic patterns on the walls, but they were subtle enough that she couldn't be sure.

They emerged into bright sunlight filtered through foliage. Large, well-established trees arched over the street from both sides and the boulevard down the center. They'd come up out of a tunnel that resembled a Metro station entrance. A non-guardian could go down the stairs from outside, but the guardians-only door at the bottom would stymie them.

Matt led her down the tree-lined street, and they walked for ten minutes before turning the corner and arriving at the entrance she'd driven through the day before to reach Richelieu Manor. Twenty minutes later, they arrived at a tan and cream mid-century modern two-story condo building. It featured flat roofs, large rectangular floor-to-ceiling windows on the upper floor balconies, and simple geometric railings.

The three-building complex nestled among carefully tended and landscaped yards with low hedges, water features, and tidy flowering bushes. A few trees peeked above the roof, but only by a few feet, unlike the soaring canopy over the street a few yards away.

"I was expecting something a little more Baroque," Elana remarked as they walked up the front path. "No moat and drawbridge?"

"That's medieval." Matt chuckled. "I've never been a big fan of the overly elaborate architecture of my ancestors. I like a simpler touch. I promise it's just as secure."

Elana learned how secure that was when entering Matt's condo. His door required handprint and retina scans as well as a physical key and a code on his part, and it wouldn't open until Elana had scanned her hand and retina as well. The pad also pricked her palm for a blood sample like the door at the archives.

Inside, Matt pointed out the varying security features. They included reinforced walls and windows, multiple security cameras with wide-spectrum video and audio recording, and radar.

Elana frowned. "I thought no one flew over Haven?"

"That's exactly why you check anyway."

Elana couldn't argue with that. "Do all Houses have security like this?"

"The major ones. Have a seat. Want a beer?"

"*God*, yes." She plopped onto a curvy, sunset-orange couch and kicked her heels off.

Matt appeared a few moments later with two cold

bottles. After handing one to Elana, he sat at the other end of the couch. "Yeah, the major Houses all have high-level security like this. Most of the time it's a pain, but..."

"When the annoying humans come knocking, you can shoot lasers at them from the hedges?"

He snorted. "No. Well, we *could*, but most of the security isn't for humans. If a human with malintent got this far into Haven, we'd have *way* bigger problems."

"Then it's all to guard against vampire attackers?" Cathy's words floated through Elana's head. *In a lot of ways, we're worse.*

"Pretty much." He sipped his beer. "Open conflict in inter-House wars doesn't happen often in Haven, but vampires have universally long memories and *selectively* short fuses. You don't want to be caught off-guard."

Elana hummed in acknowledgment and worked on her beer in silence for a while as everything bounced around in her head. "Why are they doing this?" she finally asked.

Matt looked up from his nearly empty bottle. "Wish I knew. Obviously, your mother got too close to something, and they assume you'll do the same. I don't think they could have figured out that you already know. We've been *extremely* careful."

This wasn't reassuring. Elana finished her beer and eyed the hall. "Spare room back there?"

"Yep. Third door on the right. Has its own bathroom with a shower. I'll order...Chinese? How does Chinese sound?"

"Like salty heaven."

Elana left her empty bottle in the kitchen, then headed down the hall. Matt's taste in décor matched his taste in clothing—a touch retro, leaning to classy vintage. The paintings hanging in the hall were mainly abstracts with an Atomic Age flavor. She could see any of them as trade paperback covers for mid-century sci-fi novels.

The spare room was tidy and simple with Scandinavian-inspired furniture similar to the set in the living room. It boasted curved silhouettes, smooth fabrics, and solid colors. She spotted a few signs that his sister stayed there with some regularity—jewelry hung on the vanity mirror across from the bed, the closet door left partially open to reveal clothing hanging inside, and a spare pair of lovely patent leather pumps inside the door.

Elana found more signs of life in the bathroom, which reminded her of the sea with its blue-green glass accents and beige walls. The tub-shower was a cool sky blue porcelain, and the white shower curtain featured the faint translucent silhouette of seashells. Several small bottles of makeup and cleanser sat in a neat row on the sea glass countertop, and a purple toothbrush sat in the holder.

All in all, Matt's place displayed his wealth in unobtrusive ways to the general observer. Elana felt more comfortable here than she had in any other building in Haven so far. It felt like a *home*, albeit one that had security tighter than the Hague.

She had a quick shower and changed into a spare set of clothing in her bag. She was increasingly grateful that she kept multiple outfits in there—*and* that they stayed wrinkle-free. Cathy had insisted she spend the extra money for that particular perk, and she had been *so* very right to do so.

Elana emerged from the bedroom to the tantalizing

smell of fried noodles and salty beef. Sitting at Matt's kitchen island and watching the most ridiculous soap opera she'd ever seen, she felt almost normal. Matt told her the show had been rebooted several times over the past two *centuries*, first as a stage play, then a serialized novel, then to modern television.

When she turned in for the night, she was pleasantly full of food and had no lingering ill effects from the attack in the gardens, apart from a serious uptick in her paranoia levels. Even knowing that Matt's condo was locked tight, she caught herself jumping at every sound. Falling asleep was difficult. She'd start drifting off only to remember the sensation of being choked out, and she'd jump and wake herself up again.

Elana's eyes fluttered open to the sound of her phone buzzing on the nightstand. She reached over without looking and fumbled it from there to the bed, where she accidentally dropped it on her face.

"Ow."

She retrieved the phone from where it had slid under the covers, rubbed her eyes with her other hand, and peered at the screen. Cathy had sent her a message.

Found a great house for you. Open house at 9:00. Meet you there?

Elana glanced at the time. Five after eight. After all that trouble falling asleep, she'd slept in. She texted Cathy back.

Just woke up. Where is it?

Cathy's reply was quick.

Zevenda. Willow Creek, actually. Are you in Ashford or Haven?

Elana sat up and cracked her neck.

Haven. I'll meet you there.

Cathy texted back a confirmation while Elana was pulling her shirt over her head. By the time she was properly attired and had brushed her hair and done her makeup, it was already eight-thirty.

She entered the kitchen to see Matt sitting at the island with a cup of coffee in one hand and a plate of Danishes in front of him.

"Morning," he greeted her. "Since you didn't mention you needed to be anywhere, I didn't wake you up. I hope that's okay. I know I always need a bit of extra sleep after a day like yesterday. Coffee?"

"Please." Elana slid onto the other stool and grabbed a Danish. Red jelly peeked out between its latticed puff pastry, and the top glistened with icing and sparkled with crystal sugar. She bit off a chunk and relished the explosion of raspberry in her mouth.

Matt poured her a cup and slid it across the island with a spoon, then indicated the small pitcher and pot at her elbow. "Cream and sugar."

"Thanks." She took another bite of the Danish, then doctored her coffee. "Cathy thinks she's found me a house."

"Oh?"

"Mm-hmm. In Willow Creek, which is where I wanted to live if I could. There's an open house in half an hour. I'm meeting her there."

Matt beamed. "That's great! Want me to drop you off, or are you planning to take a glider?"

Elana grimaced. "Right. I forgot my car's still in the training grounds parking lot. If you wouldn't mind giving me a ride, I'd appreciate it. I'm meeting Valeria at the training grounds later, so I can glider there after the open house."

"Sounds like a plan."

They left the condo through a basement entrance. It led into an underground parking garage with half a dozen vehicles, including a glider that looked *far* more impressive than those in the public transit stations. Elana admired its gleaming, bright blue hull on the way by as Matt led her toward an Audi that could have been a twin to the one he usually drove, except it was red.

"Is that the vampire equivalent of a motorcycle?" she asked as they got in the car.

Matt chuckled. "Sort of. Plenty of vampires invest in classic motorcycles too, but I prefer the hovering kind. They're a bit more forgiving when it comes to road conditions."

"Fair enough."

The exit ramp from the underground garage opened onto a concrete pad behind the condo, where a retractable panel in the ground slid back to allow them egress, then slid shut behind them. Elana's stomach tightened when they drove into the sunlight, and she reflexively withdrew into the seat and glanced around.

Matt noticed and put a hand on her knee. "If it wasn't safe, the perimeter sensors would have warned me. I can't guarantee your safety once we're off Richelieu land, but no one will sneak up on us here."

Elana made a face. "God, I'm so *nervous* now. I don't want to spend my life looking over my shoulder and waiting for someone to shank me. Can I get perimeter sensors installed in my brain? I'm only half joking."

"Heh. You probably could, but I know for a *fact* that Valeria would scoff. She's been training your awareness as much as your physical prowess, you know. You're not defenseless in a fight, and it'll take a lot to get the jump on you."

"That doesn't help me with ranged weapons."

Matt shook his head. "Vampires are only allowed to use short-range weapons to settle disputes in Haven without going through the arbiters. There are systems in place to detect and stop unauthorized long-range weapon use."

"Systems can be tricked."

"Then why rely on the sensors?" She had to admit he had a point. "Elana, I know you're shaken, but you have two choices here. Either you live in terror, or you trust what you've learned. Which is it going to be?"

She pursed her lips. Surely, there had to be a third option that combined a sensible level of fear with a reasonable amount of confidence in her abilities and allies.

A short time later, they pulled up in front of an understated bungalow that would have fit in on any street in

Ashford. Three long, narrow windows were spaced evenly to the left of the front door, which stood at the top of a simple set of concrete steps, and two smaller windows were set higher on the right side. The front lawn was neatly kept with simple flowerbeds brimming with pink and purple flowers on both sides of the door. An elm tree grew in the front-right corner of the lawn and shaded the area beneath its large canopy.

Cathy stood on the front steps and waved when she saw Elana through the windshield. "Did she fly here?" Elana wondered under her breath and couldn't tell if Matt's smile was a confirmation or appreciation of the joke. She wouldn't put it past Cathy to know how to fly.

"Let me know if anything happens," he told her. "And *trust yourself.* You'll be fine."

Elana thanked him and left the car. She waved at Cathy, then stepped around Matt's Audi and crossed the lawn to the door. "I hope you haven't been waiting long."

"Not at all," Cathy assured her. "I hope *I* wasn't interrupting anything."

Elana was at a loss as to what Cathy was implying until the older woman glanced in the direction of Matt's receding car, at which point she laughed and shook her head. "Just ended up crashing at his place last night rather than going back to Ashford," she explained. "Long story. So, how'd you find this place? I like it so far."

"I thought you might." Cathy's eyes twinkled, and she laid a finger beside her nose. "I have my ear to the ground at all times. You know that. I heard about this place going up for sale not long before I messaged you. Let's take a look, shall we?"

She opened the door and ushered Elana in. The front door opened onto the living room, which was furnished sparsely in the style of a show home. A spotless couch held perfectly placed throw pillows, meaningless art hung on the walls, and the books on the shelves could have been pulled from a thrift store bulk sale. No one lived in this house or hadn't in a while—or maybe it had been rented prior to being sold, and the tenants' possessions were gone.

Regardless, the staging had the desired effect. Elana walked in, her heeled footsteps echoing lightly off the hardwood floor, and could easily see herself putting her stamp on the place. She'd hang red curtains to catch the sun coming in the south-facing windows and make the main floor seem warm and inviting, and she'd put a TV on the west wall with a couch opposite...

Cathy wore a subtle, self-satisfied smile as she walked Elana through the house.

A pass-through wall showed the kitchen, which was modest but well-appointed. It had been updated with new stainless steel appliances and a black and white tile backsplash over butcher-block counters. It had no island nor a separate dining room, but the kitchen was large enough to accommodate seating for six and had a patio door opening onto a spacious deck and backyard. Elana could see herself hosting barbecues if she didn't get sucked into the vampire *haute société* of garden parties.

An open staircase led to the basement from the back door, which was in the kitchen and directly across from the front door. They ducked down to take a quick look, and found a mainly open basement with a den, a full bathroom—black tile with a shower stall—and a rec space big enough for a pool table. "You could put a bar *there*," Cathy suggested. "And there's a corner in the utility room that would make an *excellent* wine cellar."

Back on the main floor, they took the hall that led to the other half of the house. Four doors led off the hall to one bathroom and three bedrooms. The upstairs bathroom was done up in yellows and whites, which Elana immediately decided she would change to green. The two spare bedrooms were nothing special, but the master bedroom had a gorgeous bay window with a window seat overlooking the lush backyard.

"I *thought* you'd like that," Cathy commented when Elana paused to gaze out the window and trail her fingers over the cushioned window seat. "You struck me as a girl who likes a connection to nature. The ensuite's lovely, too."

Elana tore herself away from the view of lilac bushes and the raised beds of the vegetable garden to peek into the tiny ensuite. It made her think more of a dressing room with a toilet and a sink than a full bathroom, but it was cozy. She appreciated the idea of not having to leave her bedroom to get ready in the morning, especially since she regularly had to look a lot nicer than she would when showing up on a job site.

"The closet's dimensional," Cathy confided on their way back to the main area. "All of the storage is. No trouble with space here."

They exited through the back door and meandered around the backyard. Elana inhaled the scent of the lilacs and let out a long sigh before pinning Cathy with a raised eyebrow. "You know a *lot* about this house."

Cathy grinned. "I know a lot about a lot of things."

Elana wagged her finger. "Don't try to deny it. There's no realtor here. We didn't have to get a key from anyone—or if you did, you didn't mention it. Do you own this house?"

Cathy chuckled. "Guilty as charged. I own a few dozen properties around the city. I run them at arm's length. Goodness knows I can't be bothered to deal with the minutiae. I've been renting this one out for a good long while. I couldn't remember if it was still on the market after the last tenant moved on. When I confirmed this morning that it was, I figured you had to see it. I think it's just your style."

"It *is* beautiful, and it seems super comfortable. I assume that since you own it, it's safe? Like you warned me about before?"

Cathy nodded. "I wouldn't show it to you otherwise. If you like it and want to put in a bid, I'll have the specifications forwarded to you. You're more than welcome to have an independent appraisal done to ensure I'm telling the truth about what's included."

She raised a hand to stall Elana's protest. "Before you make noise about trusting me, I appreciate the thought, but it's unwise. You wanted to be my friend so I'd give you advice on how to survive being a vampire. Here it is. Trust no one, check everything, and cover your ass." She winked. "*Especially* when it comes to your friends."

Elana chuckled and shook her head. "Cathy, you are a piece of work in the *best* way."

A self-satisfied smirk covered Cathy's face. "You *flatter* me."

CHAPTER THIRTY-FIVE

Elana arrived at the consorts' training grounds decently early for her appointment with Valeria. She'd ended up going with Cathy to put in a bid for the house. That involved calling Matt to help with paperwork and booking an independent appraiser to verify the documents Cathy provided. After a quick lunch, she'd taken a glider to Senkyem, where she patted her Emeya's hood on the way through the parking lot.

When she checked in at the front desk, the mousy receptionist who worked Tuesdays directed Elana to a room she hadn't been in yet, Training Room D. She found it easily, ducked into the locker room to change into her workout gear, then came out and warmed up while waiting for Valeria to arrive.

Training Room D was much smaller than the gymnasium that was Training Room A. It was maybe the size of the main floor of the bungalow she'd visited that morning, and its walls were windowless expanses of gray metal panels. The floor was the same. She tapped on it with her knuckles, and it rang quietly and was unyielding. It would *not* be pleasant to fall on, and Elana didn't doubt she'd be doing plenty of falling.

These rare one-on-one training sessions with Valeria happened every so often as a way for the arbiter to gauge Elana's progress. From the looks of it, today's session would be something special.

Valeria strode in at the stroke of one, wearing a sleek white tracksuit. As a greeting, she stomped, and a volley of arrows made of light shot from the walls toward Elana.

Elana dropped like a rock. The arrows passed over her harmlessly, clattered to the floor, and disappeared, but Elana couldn't stop and count herself lucky because Valeria was already running at her and aiming a kick at her ribs.

Elana rolled to the side and sprang to her feet. She met Valeria's flying fists with a flurry of parries and blocks, only to trip over a line of light that had stretched out across the room. It *definitely* hadn't been there ten seconds ago.

She twisted as she toppled and managed to get a hand underneath her, which she used to redirect her momentum into a messy somersault. Coming out of the roll, she gasped and threw herself to the side to avoid a fireball launched from the opposite wall.

Elana scrambled backward in an awkward crab walk and pushed herself upright as quickly as possible. The arbiter advanced on her slowly and inexorably, now holding a sword—again made of light—in a perfect fighting stance.

"Which domains are most closely aligned with Light?"

Valeria demanded before darting forward a step and aiming an elegant but deadly slash at her forearm.

Elana skipped backward and flailed her arm out of the way. "Progress, Nurture, and Vision! *What is going on—*"

Valeria interrupted her. "Which Houses quartered in Haven trace their roots back the furthest?"

"SpiderKing, Lucciola, and—*fuck!*" Elana yelped as Valeria sliced across her upper arm. "Jesus! Did I miss the weapons rack coming in?"

She glanced around and spotted several glowing vertical lines beside the entrance. They were either a trap or weapons hanging on the walls. Either way, putting some distance between herself and Valeria seemed like a *very good idea*, so Elana booked it.

On the way there, she had to leap several boulders that erupted from the floor, duck another volley of arrows, and dodge a lethal ice spike. When she got within a few strides, the lines of light resolved into a selection of weapons, and relief flooded her for the briefest moment.

Elana grabbed the first one she could reach, which turned out to be a spear. She hadn't done any spear training yet, but if she wasn't mistaken, the point of today's lesson was "survive at all costs with whatever you've got handy," so she wasn't about to dither over her choice.

She spun in time to catch Valeria's sword with the spear's shaft like a quarterstaff. Elana's arms trembled with the force of holding the wiry woman back. Valeria was much stronger than she looked, which came as a significant surprise. You could *see* Elana's biceps when she flexed.

With an almighty shove, Elana forced Valeria back a step. In that breath of reprieve, Elana dropped into a squat and twirled the spear above her head to ward off an immediate counterattack, then attempted an awkward roll to the side with the spear held at arm's length.

She managed it with only a slight tap of the spear on the floor and came up into a three-point stance a couple of yards away from Valeria.

Then the lights went out.

Elana's breath caught in her throat. For a split second, she thought they'd lost power, then realized the likelihood of that was nil. This was another tactic, and she'd already run out of time to adapt.

She whipped the spear in a wide arc in front of her and let its momentum carry her around in a full circle. Something *thudded* against the shaft, and Valeria's quiet grunt gave Elana a jolt of satisfaction.

Elana ran. For all she knew, Valeria could see in the dark. Elana had no idea *how* powerful a vampire Valeria was, but at minimum, arbiters were required to be level five sentinels. As the Arbiter of Shadows, in charge of espionage, counterintelligence, and defense of an entire city-state, Valeria could easily be level six or seven, emissary or archon. The medical textbook Matt had recommended only went up to level four, guardian. Although she'd read it back to front, she didn't have the first clue what Valeria was capable of other than "a lot more than Elana was."

Elana tripped on a rock, invisible in the pitch-black, and sprawled across the floor. She hit several more rocks on the way down with her arms and face and groaned. She instantly realized this was a mistake because she heard the scuff of pivoting shoes on the floor and rapid footsteps.

Elana scrambled to her feet and sprinted away with the

spear tucked beside her like a football. This was undoubtedly the wrong way to hold a spear, but she preferred looking like an idiot in the dark to being skewered by the Arbiter of Shadows.

She stumbled on more rocks but managed to keep her balance until she ran into the wall with her arm outstretched. Valeria's footsteps continued to follow.

She can't see me, but she can hear me.

Elana put her back against the wall, crouched, and listened. When she thought Valeria was within a few yards, she braced the spear with both hands and swung it in front of her as hard as she could about a foot off the floor. She was rewarded with impact, the sound of skidding, and the solid *thump* of a body hitting the floor.

This time, Elana dashed forward two strides and jabbed blindly where she believed Valeria's body was based on the sound of impact. She scored twice, then tipped over in surprise when Valeria yanked on the spear.

Abruptly, Elana was on the floor grappling with the Arbiter of Shadows, completely blind. Valeria tossed the spear aside, and it landed with a clatter some feet away. Elana was too preoccupied with her attempt to get hold of any part of Valeria to go after it.

Valeria had one hand on the front of Elana's shirt. With the other, she grabbed Elana's hair and pulled. At the same time, she spoke into Elana's ear. "Explain Senkyem."

Elana yelped and instinctively grabbed the wrist over her head. Valeria was attempting to use the hair pull to force Elana up and back, but Elana growled and brought her right fist around to connect with Valeria's jaw. The blow was hard enough that her knuckles ached, but Valeria did not relent.

Elana didn't understand the question. *Explain Senkyem?* It was a district, its domain was Shadows, its arbiter was the woman who was currently trying to kill her, and it was full of gardens, which confused everyone because why would…

Oh. That was what Valeria meant.

Valeria redoubled her murderous efforts by wrapping Elana's ponytail around her fist and pulling even harder. She followed the yank with a knee to the solar plexus. "I asked you a question."

The constant hair-pulling was bringing tears to Elana's eyes. Fighting dirty was one thing when your opponents were well-trained martial artists. As much as Gustav and the others were brutal in the ring, their styles were still built on their specialties.

Valeria could all-out *brawl*.

Elana dug her nails into Valeria's wrist and clawed the other hand down her face. She kicked out with one foot and found a rock sprouting from the floor. She levered off it to force Valeria to the ground with Elana on top of her.

"Senkyem represents the duality of life and death in the opposite way as Premier," she ground out between her teeth. She grabbed Valeria's ear and pulled it, then slapped it as hard as she could before yelling the rest of her response in the boxed ear.

"The gardens are to remind you of the value of life so you don't lose sight of your moral code while destroying the king's enemies. Premier's focus on luxury is supposed to remind the Arbiter of Light of the folly of greed and the danger of reaching beyond one's means."

Her last word was cut off by a *crunch* and a screech as Valeria drove her forehead into Elana's nose. Blinded by pain, Elana flailed while Valeria flipped them over. Her head hit another rock. A heartbeat later, Valeria boxed both her ears.

Before Elana could take a breath, the arbiter flipped her over a second time, bent her arms up behind her back, and knelt painfully on her forearms with one knee. Valeria's hands came to either side of Elana's head and oh-so-gently twisted it to the side.

"Why should I not kill you?"

If Elana hadn't been able to hear Valeria's breathing, she would have thought the arbiter hadn't broken a sweat. Her voice was calm and cool as it had been every time she spoke. Elana, on the other hand, was cycling between furious and terrified. Had Valeria invited her here *to kill her?* If anyone could make a death look like an accident, it would be her—but she wouldn't *need* to. No one would argue if the Arbiter of Shadows decided someone needed to die.

If Valeria Draven decided Elana Bishop needed to die, she wouldn't ask. Elana would already be dead. Therefore, this was another test of Elana's political prowess.

Elana screwed her eyes shut and breathed through the pain of what *had* to be a broken nose. "Because I'm useful. Because my mother found something out and it's a hell of a lot easier to use me to get to the bottom of it than it would be for you to do it yourself.

"Arbiters are spiders, like the king. You work from the

center of your web. You never know what that web will catch. It caught my mother. It caught me. It *will* catch House Veridian."

Valeria didn't move for several long, agonizing seconds. Elana thought she'd gotten the wrong answer.

"Can you win?" the arbiter finally asked.

"Against you? Not a hope in hell," Elana immediately replied. "Against House Veridian? Yes. Not on my own—I'm not that arrogant—but yes."

Valeria lifted her knee from Elana's arms, and Elana gasped at the renewed blood flow. The lights snapped on, and she flinched, first at the brightness and second at the pool of red on the floor beneath her face.

The floor relaxed back to its smooth, gray, featureless state. Valeria gently rolled Elana onto her back and touched a fingertip to either side of her nose. A burning, itching sensation filled Elana's sinuses, making her want to sneeze uncontrollably and scream. The feeling ceased before it became unbearable, and while her ears still rang and she was dizzy, she could tell her nose was no longer broken.

Valeria looked her over and nodded once. "Good." She stood and left the room.

As she walked away, Elana noticed a few spots of blood on her white tracksuit in places that couldn't have been from Elana's crushed nose. She *had* scored a few hits. She was reasonably satisfied with that.

She slowly got to her feet. Whatever high-level vampiric shit Valeria had done to her nose hadn't done anything to soothe the other minor injuries she'd incurred. Elana expected they'd heal quickly after what had happened in the gardens yesterday.

A quick look around the room told her the weapons had disappeared like the environmental hazards had. High-level vampire shit, indeed. Time for a fucking *shower.*

Elana jumped when she discovered Gustav outside the door. "Hi."

"Good fight," Gustav informed her.

Elana half-heartedly snorted. "Saw that, did you? Is there an observation room?"

Gustav shrugged. "A window. And yes. Madam Draven requested I observe your progress."

"That counted as good, did it?"

He nodded. "You handled the unexpected admirably. You landed hits on the arbiter even at a severe disadvantage. It took over five minutes for Madam Draven to subdue you, and you did not allow her to inflict many injuries. You also maintained your composure and rationality even when badly hurt. You did *very* well."

Elana took a couple of breaths as she processed this. Gustav seemed happy to wait. At length, she shook her head. "I don't understand why she doesn't explain anything. Am I a *bug* to her?"

The corner of Gustav's mouth turned up in a tiny smile. "No. You are clay that she is shaping. Many would kill for the privilege of training with her, even if it meant being pounded to a pulp every day."

Elana rubbed her eyes, then regretted it when her fingers came away bloody and her eyes stung. She blinked furiously. "I get that. I really do. I just wish I knew what she was training me *for.*"

Gustav clapped her on the shoulder and ignored Elana's wince. "She will explain when you are ready. Go clean up."

Elana gratefully stumbled for the showers, where she lost herself in hot water and soap that made the smell of iron wash away.

Twenty minutes later, her phone buzzed in her bag as she gingerly toweled off. She wasn't bleeding anymore, but her brain hadn't quite accepted that her nose wasn't broken, and she still felt tender everywhere. She wanted a beer and the biggest tureen of fettuccine alfredo she could buy.

By the time she fished her phone out, the caller had given up and left a message. It was Cathy, she saw. *News about the house,* Elana imagined.

She keyed in the code for her voicemail and let the message play while she dressed.

"Elana, my dear!" Cathy sounded cheery, but then, she almost always did. That didn't tell her one way or the other. "Your bid's been accepted! Congratulations!"

Of course, it's been accepted, Elana thought. *I'm pretty sure I could have lowballed you several hundred thousand dollars, and you'd have sold me the house because you liked me.*

Elana's train of thought died as her stomach dropped through the floor.

She owned a house in Haven.

She, Elana Bishop, *owned a house in Haven.*

Elana hit End. Her fingers trembled so badly that she missed the Call button on Vicky's contact card the first time she tried to press it. Then she held the phone in one shaking hand and prayed she wouldn't catch her friend in transit or a meeting. *Please, Vicky, please...*

"Lana!"

Elana's knees turned to jelly, and she sank onto the locker room bench. "*Vicky.* I'm so glad I—is this a bad time? Please say it's not a bad time."

"Not at all! What's going on? You sound *spent.*"

Elana chuckled under her breath. "In more ways than one. Vicky, I just bought a house."

"Ooooh, congrats! Housewarming party?"

"I don't think you get it, Vick. I just bought a house...*in Haven.*"

Silence lingered on the other end of the line for several long moments—long enough that Elana wondered if she'd lost service. Then Vicky came back with a hushed, "*Oh my God.*"

"Yeah."

Suddenly, Vicky was all business. "My plane leaves in two hours," she informed Elana. "I land in Ashford at seven PM, and I will be on your doorstep at seven-thirty with a mountain of cardboard boxes, seventeen rolls of packing tape, and a truly irresponsible amount of booze."

Elana slumped against the cold wall and laughed breathlessly with relief. "You're a saint."

"I don't think saints drink, doll."

A few more promises of "be there soon" and "keep breathing, you'll be fine," and Vicky hung up to catch her flight. Elana stared at the opposite wall and reflected that her life had gone from zero to a hundred in a few weeks and showed no sign of slowing down.

She needed to call Jerry to finish the LLC paperwork.

She needed to sign house paperwork and pick up the keys. She needed to *pack*. She was reasonably certain she had an appointment with Valeria again tomorrow—or was it the day after—and those were only the items on her to-do list that she remembered offhand.

What did you get me into, Mom?

Elana drew a deep breath, steeled herself, and stood. She tossed everything into her bag, checked her hair in the mirror, and left the locker room with her head held high.

Elana Bishop, initiate of the House of the SpiderKing and daughter of the late Arbiter of Sanctuary, had bought a house in Haven. She would continue her mother's work and unearth the truth about House Veridian. She would do her mentor proud. She would do her *mother* proud.

First, she would murder the biggest bowl of pasta she could find because being a vampire required way more carb-loading than you'd ever think. After that, everything would be okay.

Right?

THE STORY CONTINUES

The Story continues with book two *Danger is in the Unweaving,* coming soon at Amazon

Claim Your Copy Here

A vampire's destiny unfolds in a city of secrets and shadows.

Elana thought she was just a normal human until she hit a vampire with her car. Now she's thrust into a world of ancient Houses, deadly conspiracies, and vampire politics.

Sinister force lurks in the shadows. House Veridian has been plotting for centuries, and her very existence threatens their plans.

Elana and her allies race against time to expose the conspiracy before it's too late. She must master vampire politics, forge alliances, and stay alive long enough to uncover the truth.

The stakes? The future of Haven itself.

Will Elana rise to become the leader Haven needs and avenge her mother's death? Or will House Veridian's web of lies and betrayal prove too intricate to unravel?

MICHAEL'S NOTES

SEPTEMBER 18, 2023

First, thank you for not only reading this story, but also for flipping all the way back here to see what I have to ramble about!

Vampires: Old Flames and New Shadows

There's something about vampires that just gets my creative mind firing it's synapses.

Maybe it's the sharp teeth, or perhaps it's the way they can make a bad hair day look mysterious and alluring.

My own downfall - my hair is not well behaved.

My love affair with these nocturnal neck-biters started a long time ago, and it's no secret that the Kurtherian Gambit series was born out of that fascination.

It's wild to think that Bethany Anne and her crew have been causing mayhem and saving the universe in multiple languages now—German, French, Spanish, Italian, Danish, and soon, fingers crossed, Japanese! (Kon'nichiwa, vampire readers!)

MICHAEL'S NOTES

About six or seven months ago, I found myself staring out the window, wondering, "What's next?" I'd sent vampires into space, had them mingling with aliens, and let's be honest, they probably have more frequent flyer miles than I do at this point. But I could not shake the itch to return to those fanged fiends.

The question was, how could I revisit vampires without retracing old steps?

Enter the idea that's been tickling my brain for a few years: Earth's hidden epochs of civilizations. We've all heard the theories—Atlantis, Lemuria, Mu—the possibilities are endless. What if, nestled between those ancient epochs, there was a vampire civilization?

One so powerful it nearly wiped itself out, leaving only a sole survivor.

Imagine that survivor watching as the new vampires he created began embodying the very flaws that doomed his own people. Humans, for their part, are aware of the vampires skulking in the shadows. So, when America was still a fresh canvas, our lonely vampire saw an opportunity. He crossed the ocean to establish a city—a sanctuary—for vampires. He called it Haven.

He left behind the tangled web of European politics (though, let's face it, some political BS is like glitter—it gets everywhere and never truly disappears). In Haven, the vampires thrived, developing technology that outpaced even the most cutting-edge human inventions. All because this ancient vampire guarded the true origins of their kind, a secret he wasn't keen to share.

Now, here's where it gets interesting. Unlike many of my other stories, this character remains a phantom. *No grand entrances, no flashy battles.* He's the unseen puppeteer, the SpiderKing at the center of the web, pulling strings that might take years—or decades—to unravel. The vampires of Haven, the ones you meet and (hopefully) love or loathe, are all dancing to the subtle tunes he plays.

Creating this new series has been a thrilling challenge*. It's a dance of shadows and whispers, a maze where the walls are constantly shifting. And I will admit, it's been fun watching the pieces come together, even if sometimes they surprise me as much as they might surprise you.

So, will you catch a glimpse of the SpiderKing? Will his machinations tilt the balance in favor of Haven or lead it toward ruin? Only time—and a few more chapters—will tell.

Here's to old flames rekindled and new shadows explored. I hope you've enjoyed stepping into this world as much as I've enjoyed crafting it for you.

Until the next adventure,
 Ad Aeternitatem,
 Michael Anderle

* We have another series Chimera coming at you, and another about a Vampire Bounty Hunter for 2025 in the SpiderKing Universe.

P.S. If you've got thoughts, theories, or just want to chat about all things vampire (or why glitter is the herpes of the craft world), drop me a line!

P.S.S. For more musings, sneak peeks, and possibly questionable life advice, don't forget to subscribe to the MORE STORIES with Michael newsletter HERE: https://michael.beehiiv.com/

BOOKS BY MICHAEL ANDERLE

Sign up for the LMBPN email list to be notified of new releases and special deals!

https://lmbpn.com/email/

For a complete list of books by Michael Anderle, please visit:

www.lmbpn.com/ma-books/

CONNECT WITH THE AUTHOR

Connect with Michael Anderle

Website: http://lmbpn.com

Email List: https://michael.beehiiv.com/

https://www.facebook.com/LMBPNPublishing

https://twitter.com/MichaelAnderle

https://www.instagram.com/lmbpn_publishing/

https://www.bookbub.com/authors/michael-anderle

www.ingramcontent.com/pod-product-compliance
Lightning Source LLC
LaVergne TN
LVHW091700070526
838199LV00050B/2223